Search for the Bark Warwick

A Novel

by

Sherry Ann Miller

Published and Distributed by:

Granite Publishing and Distribution, L.L.C.
868 North 1430 West
Orem, Utah 84057
(801) 229-9023 • Toll Free (800) 574-5779
Fax (801) 229-1924

Page Layout & Design by Myrna Varga • The Office Connection, Inc.
Cover Design by Tammie Ingram

ISBN: 1-932280-33-2
Library of Congress Control Number: 2004101865

First Printing, March 2004

10 9 8 7 6 5 4 3 2 1

Printed in the United States of America

Search for the Bark Warwick

is dedicated to:

Dad, who never gave up his dream of circumnavigating the globe. May the Lord allow you to sail that vessel on the other side.

And to Dad's sons:

Lee, who became the patriarch of Dad's family before he wanted the job, yet fulfills his role with honor.

Frank, who just might be the first to live Dad's dream.

Burke, from whom I finally learned to fish.

Roarke, whose dreams are grander than them all, and whose resilience has no end.

Dave, who is generous of heart and home.

Al, whose example guides me toward a more righteous goal.

Kip, who proved that God is found where we least expect Him.

May you each find your guiding star and follow it steadily to home port, where Dad will draw you to him, for he is the wind behind your sails.

With all my love,

Shoosey-Q

Chapter One

Escape from Blackwell Tower

*"She was a pretty ship of about eighty
tons and ten pieces of ordnance."*
John Winthrop, April 10, 1630

1635—Chatham, England

*T*he cold March fog penetrated Rebecca's hooded cloak, making the thick, green velvet damp and heavy. Her back ached fiercely, as though she'd been splayed with a hot iron straight from the fire, and her hands ached from carrying two heavy satchels at her sides, but the pain could not match the determination that coursed through her. Refusing to acknowledge her own agony, she continued the journey, her feet throbbing from the distance she'd walked, which she judged roughly at over eight miles. If the fog didn't impede her progress, the blackness of night could.

Rebecca had not been drawn to the Chatham dockyards for commerce or trade, for she had nothing to sell and no money with which to purchase. Her only purpose was to escape. She had no plan; only the hope stirring within her heart and the prayers whispered in

her hours of desperation. Over and over again, she begged the Lord God to help her find safety from her persecutor.

In her search for the bark *Warwick*, would she find a haven of security, or just another spider's den of torture and deceit? Now that night had fallen, wrapping the sleeping city in a blanket of darkness, she prayed that she would be able to find her way to the square-rigged sailing vessel without being discovered.

Her blonde hair, once neatly coiled at the nape of her neck, came loose in tendril curls that dangled out from beneath the hood, framing her face and wisping across her eyes as she hurried down the alleyways and dark streets of Chatham, hiding in doorframes whenever she heard any sounds nearby. She pulled the locks of hair away from her face. In doing so, she felt the flush of fever upon her forehead, but even this she disregarded.

Suddenly, Rebecca heard footsteps quickly drumming toward her on the cobblestone street. She nearly panicked. Stepping into the shadow of an alley, she breathed silently, praying for God's mercy. She would never go back to Blackwell Tower now. Never!

Even a watery grave seemed more welcome than facing what lay in store for her if she remained in Chatham . . . especially now that her father was dead. He'd turned forty-seven years old last week, yet Jeremiah Webster should have lived to see sixty. Easily! He'd been in perfect health until his imprisonment. Rebecca shuddered and forced back the tears. Her father was dead . . . dead at the whim of Edward Blackwell, one of the wickedest men she had ever met. Sir Edward Blackwell III . . . the man to whom she was betrothed.

The sound of footsteps came ever closer to her and she held her breath. Ten seconds, twenty, thirty. Then the sound diminished in the

impenetrable fog, leaving Rebecca alone once again. She sighed in relief and waited a few more minutes in the black, misty silence.

Hefting the awkward satchels in both hands, she resumed her journey, making slow, but soundless progress. Inhaling deeply, her nostrils caught the strong smell of tar and timber mixed with the savory scent of the sea. She knew that she didn't have much farther to go before she reached the wharf.

Just a few more steps and she would arrive at the Chatham dock-yards, where the Royal Navy's chief arsenal was stored in buildings so massive they made Blackwell Tower seem minuscule by comparison.

Chatham housed one of the largest dockyards in all of England, with sailing vessels the size of tall buildings resting in its harbor. The Royal Navy's considerable fleet lay at anchor, secured for King Charles and the defense of England. This was a place where merchants, with their various wares and goods shipped between Chatham and other ports around the globe, became rich and powerful.

Lord Blackwell had a number of sailing vessels under his command. He traded wool and linen from Scotland for tobacco and corn from Virginia, tea and pewter from England for salt cod and otter fur from Massachusetts.

Again Rebecca heard footsteps behind her and she crouched down near a street vendor's empty wagon. This time there were several people coming toward the quay, military men, judging by the sound of their boots against the cobblestone.

"Search all of them!" A familiar man's voice shrieked hoarsely. The sound sent shivers up her spine.

Edward Blackwell, the Third, had evidently discovered that she was missing. Rebecca expected this, though it did not make her any

less fearful. Edward would stop at nothing until she acquiesced to his wishes. With her father's cold body not yet in his grave, Edward had nothing left with which to coerce her. Yet, if he hadn't arranged for her father's imprisonment to begin with, her father would still be alive. Had Edward made any effort to spare her father's life, she would have married him come Monday next, fulfilling the agreement she'd made with him. But Edward did nothing to keep his end of the arrangement. Now her father was dead, which nullified the betrothal, and she did not feel obligated to continue the charade any longer.

As flames from several torches swept toward the docks, Rebecca shrank deeper into the shadows beneath the old, empty wagon, hiding behind one of the solid, wooden wheels. While waiting for what seemed like hours, she heard the shrill barking of dogs as they were disturbed by Edward's guards. All the ships, shallops and caravels along the docks were searched from top to bottom, but she was not found in any of them.

Then she heard another familiar man's voice, calling: "Master Blackwell! Master Blackwell!"

Rebecca smiled to herself. It was Barnaby Wilson, Edward's personal butler. Praise be to God that she had found friendship in Blackwell Tower.

Edward came forward quickly. "Wilson? Where is she?"

"Right after you left, sire, one of your carriages was seen heading easterly, toward London. Perhaps she is trying to escape in that direction." Wilson's heavy breathing, apparently from running to catch up with Edward, echoed nearby.

Edward seemed to contemplate this information. Then, "She's not on board any of the ships here. Perhaps you're right. Guards!" he

bellowed, dismissing Wilson without another word. "Guards! Quickly!"

The pounding of a dozen men's footsteps, including Edward's, echoed up the quay, diminishing in sound until nothing more could be heard. When the quiet of the darkness comforted her once again, she heard Wilson whisper. "Go with God, my Lady."

Creeping out from beneath the wagon, she whispered back, "I shall, dear Wilson. I shall."

Wilson gasped and turned away, muttering something beneath his breath that sounded very much like a prayer in her behalf.

Cautiously, Rebecca stole into the night fog, hoping to find the *Warwick* quickly, praying that the ship would be exactly as Wilson had told her earlier that day. She had to wait a little longer than she wanted, what with the seamen aboard the docked vessels having just been awakened by Edward and his loyal guards. With visibility less than ten feet, the bark could be anywhere and she might not see it, yet she dared not wait until daylight. The only thing she knew for certain was that the bark was at anchor near the southwest quarter of Chatham Bay, and her master planned to sail at first light, if the weather proved suitable.

After a short time, the quay became quiet and still once again. Stepping out to the very edge of the wharf, Rebecca listened carefully for any sounds that might resemble the lapping of water against a wooden hull. Far away in the distance, and to the southwest of the bay, she could faintly make out the melody of a seaman's song. It was a strange chanty and reminded her of tales she'd heard as a child regarding haunted ships at sea. Some large ship was anchored several hundred feet from the dock in Chatham Bay. If Wilson's directions were correct, it could well be the *Warwick*.

Since she had no ability to swim out to it, Rebecca located an old shallop, a small boat about fifteen feet long, with a short mast and pointed ends that curved upward. Rebecca dropped her two heavy bags down into the boat, then untied its lashing and climbed hastily aboard. Immediately she learned the wobbly nature of seafaring vessels, for the unwieldy beast wanted to rock side to side, as though it had a mind of its own. Fear thickened in her throat and she found it difficult to swallow. But Rebecca was determined. Without looking back, she pushed the shallop away from the dock with all her strength. Since there was no wind, she decided not to pull out the sail lashed to the stocky mast. Besides, she wasn't sure she would know what to do with a sail if there was any wind.

What little Rebecca knew about boats could be measured in a thimble. Terminology was one thing, but actually getting into and maneuvering one of the precarious water-lappers was quite another.

Groping around, Rebecca found an oar in the bottom of the shallop and picked it up, hoping to row out into the bay toward the sea songs she heard. It was the first time she'd ever been in a boat and she found the art of rowing to be much like a magician's trick. Too many strokes to her left and the shallop turned to the right, while too many strokes to her right and the shallop turned left. To make rowing more difficult, her left strokes could not match the strength of the right, for the pain in her left shoulder blade restricted her movement. Determined, she continued trying. After several lame attempts at heading the unwieldy boat away from the dock and toward the middle of the bay, she finally concluded that two weak strokes to the left, then one strong stroke to the right kept her on a somewhat steady course.

The sound of the oar slurping through the water alarmed her and she made several attempts at keeping the noise to a minimum. She

could taste the salt air heavy on her lips, as the smell of fresh fish lingered around her, making her eyes water from the overpowering aroma. A small splash to her right startled her and she shuddered, wondering what creatures might be lurking below awaiting a tasty meal.

When she finally reached the point where she could make out the lines of a large ship, the singing stopped. Rebecca lifted her oar from the water and coasted silently forward, the shallop slicing through the glassy surface, almost without effort.

Forcing the pain away, she concentrated on the *Warwick*, if indeed this was the *Warwick*. Wilson had told her it would be the largest vessel, and the first one she would come to in the southwest end of the bay.

She chose to believe that the ship in front of her was the *Warwick*, until proven otherwise. It was a fairly large ship capable of carrying at least eighty tons burthen. The bark had five cannons to port and five to starboard, three masts, a tall, beam-wide aftercastle, and a much smaller forecastle. It carried four square sails, two for each of the front two masts. The mizzenmast, the third and final mast back from the bow, was set up with a spar for a triangular sail with the flag of England at its head. Because the bark was at anchor, all the sails were gathered up to their respective, wooden yard spars and lashed securely with robands. The boat, itself, was constructed of thick wood beams and planks, with some sort of rope, like hemp, coated with black tar, wedged between the planks, making the ship sturdy and water-tight.

Rebecca judged the *Warwick* to be about sixty feet long and eighteen feet wide at its beam. Surprised, Rebecca felt amazed at how much she had learned of a vessel's terminology since living at Blackwell Tower the past few months. Already she knew left as port and right as starboard. The beam was the widest point from port to starboard, nearly the center point between the stern and the bow. The immense

size of the *Warwick* dwarfed the shallop.

Since she could still hear voices aboard, Rebecca remained completely silent. Some men were talking near the bow, though she couldn't see them through the dense fog. She hoped this meant that they could not see her, either.

"Master Dunton says if the wind picks up, we'll weigh anchor tomorrow."

"I heard he's bringing Lord Blackwell aboard at six of the morning."

"Why?" the first man grunted in disgust. "His Lordship isn't bringing that rogue son of his, is he?"

"I hear that young Edward is busy these days. They say he's having difficulty keeping his new wench in line."

There was a gruff laugh from the other man. "The woman must have nerves of steel, agreeing to marry Lord Blackwell's son. He was different before . . . but now—"

Interrupting, the first man defended Edward. "The poor man went daft when his first betrothed died."

"The second won't last no longer if he doesn't return to his senses," said a third voice.

Rumors," said the first, "and we're worse than a gaggle of geese, squawking about the gander behind his back."

"You didn't say why Lord Blackwell's coming with Master Dunton?"

"Something about the stores. Said he was shorted five cases of hardtack and the supplier won't cover it."

"Lord Blackwell will make him. He won't take no guff."

Relieved that it would be Lord Blackwell, and not Edward, who

would come aboard the *Warwick* in the morning, Rebecca slid the oar through the water with as much stealth as possible, and maneuvered the small boat aft. Squinting, she could just make out some writing engraved into the stern. Then she smiled. To her good fortune, the *Warwick's* name was clearly legible. She sighed in relief and thanked the Lord God for His miraculous guidance. Tears filled her eyes, but she held them back. There would be time for tears when she was safe.

Although she looked around both sides of the bark, she didn't see a ladder or a rope anywhere that would assist her in climbing aboard.

The waters of Chatham harbor were flat and smooth, almost like glass. She hoped that the tide wouldn't move her too far away from the bark before she had to abandon the little shallop. For the moment, she was filled with gratitude at her good fortune of having found the *Warwick* at all.

After another hour or more, the men finally went below and Rebecca could no longer hear any sounds from them. She continued to wait another lengthy hour, hoping that all the men would be sound asleep before she attempted to climb aboard. While waiting, she rowed soundlessly toward the bow and noticed that there was a thick rope-like net lashed between the forecastle and the tip of the bowsprit, apparently to protect the crew from drowning should they fall overboard near the bow. Into this net, she tossed her two heavy satchels. Removing her green velvet cloak, she tossed it into the net as well, and heard something strike the shallop in the process. Her emerald broach, which once belonged to her mother, must have fallen off the cloak. She searched for it carefully for several minutes, but could not find it inside the shallop. It had probably glanced off the shallop and into the water. Rebecca could waste no more time on regrets. *What's one more lost treasure after losing my father?*

After untying the ribbons at the back of her dress, she retied them in front, at her waist. Bending over, Rebecca grasped the back hem of her long dress and pulled the hem between her legs and up to her waist, where she tucked it into the ribbons, then tied the ribbons once more, this time over the cumbersome fabric to hold it in place. This would prevent the skirts of her dress and petticoats from impeding her attempt to climb aboard.

Timing would have to be everything if she was to make it onto the bark before daylight. Since it was still pitch black out, she judged that it couldn't be much later than four of the morning. By five the sky would begin to lighten, and she saw no sign of that yet.

Assessing the size of the shallop, Rebecca knew she couldn't stand on the gunwales or the boat would overturn. The shallop was pointed at both ends, with the bow end curved upward and forward in a lazy arch at least three feet taller than the gunwales. Crawling carefully, Rebecca managed to get closer to the bow of the shallop. Then, grabbing the tall, curved bow with her hands for stability, she pulled herself up onto her feet where she rocked precariously, praying the boat would steady itself. With her right arm stretched as high as she could reach and her left arm floundering slightly, she found herself about two feet too short to reach the net above her. Stepping upon the gunwales, Rebecca panicked when this action made the shallop roll from side to side in a threatening manner. Dismayed, she tried several times to jump from the bottom of the boat high enough to reach the net. After the fifth failure, she almost overturned the small shallop.

When the boat finally stopped rocking, she sank into the bottom of it and pulled her knees up to her chest. Wrapping her arms around her legs and placing her forehead against her knees, she forced herself to calm down, which was no small feat. She was shaking so badly that

she wasn't certain she could make another attempt. Placing a hand against her forehead, she wiped away great droplets of perspiration and realized that she was burning up with fever.

Wearily, Rebecca looked up at the bow of the shallop and pondered the situation once again. Both pointed ends were no more than four feet below the edge of the net. If she positioned the shallop so that the bow was directly under that edge, then ran full speed up the curve of the bow, she could use it as a jumping-off point and make a giant leap into the net. The only problem that she could discern was that if she failed, she would land in the water, which might awaken the men on the ship. More likely, she would drown because she didn't know how to swim.

Rebecca considered all the alternatives. If she remained in Chatham, she would eventually be found by Edward Blackwell and whipped into submission. If she tried to flee into another part of the country, he would hunt her down as though she was a guarded piece of chattel. If she failed to reach the net, death would be almost welcome. Her fate seemed perilous, at best.

On the other hand, if she reached the net and found a place to stow away on board until the bark reached the Americas, she would find freedom. She could hire out as a seamstress or a school teacher and make her own way in the new world.

But if she was caught as a stowaway, she could be thrown overboard, where she would drown anyway. What other options did she have? Despair would bring her no solutions.

The only particle of hope in her life right now was that which swelled within her heart and soul, telling her she *had* to reach the net.

If she made the jump safely and was discovered, she would beg

Master Dunton not to cast her overboard. A few weeks ago at a dinner party, she had heard Lord Blackwell telling Edward about Master John Dunton, saying that the only reason Dunton had never been made captain was because of his gentle regard for the other seaman and those less fortunate. This attitude was inappropriate. A captain must take a firm hand, mete out punishment according to the standards set down by royal decree and win the respect of his crew out of their fear for what he would do to them if they failed him. When Master Dunton could do that, then he would be given a ship to captain. Rebecca prayed that Master Dunton's tender heart would be kindled with mercy toward her.

With that prayer in her heart and with no regard for the outcome, since she considered her life lost almost entirely, Rebecca maneuvered the shallop into position. She stood up near the stern, and with the swiftness of a gazelle, ran the shallop's length, then up the bow's curve to the most forward point, from which she took a mighty leap into the air. Fortunately, she landed on the net at her waist, then tumbled head first down the inside of and into a curled-up position.

Thanking the Lord God with all her heart, it took her almost a quarter hour to calm herself afterward, but she'd made it. After she reposed herself, she gathered her cloak and satchels and climbed over the net to the foredeck. Finally, she was aboard the *Warwick*, and with no one the wiser. Stealthily, she stepped around the starboard side of the forecastle, then slipped into a narrow hall with two doors, one to her left and one to her right.

Inhaling soundlessly, Rebecca placed a hand on the door to her right and pushed gently against it. Inside, she saw a set of built-in beds, one above the other. An older man was sleeping upon the larger, lower bed. Gasping in surprise, Rebecca pulled the door closed, praying the

man had not heard her. Then she turned to face the second door. Pushing it open, she saw a much larger room, with a square dining table ample enough to seat four people on wooden chairs that were pushed up against it. Another set of beds, wider than those in the first cabin, was built in the outside corner of the room, one above the other. A small lantern, with the wick turned to its lowest position, dangled from a hook in the ceiling above the table, illuminating the room dimly.

A boy of perhaps seven or eight slept in the lower bed. Rebecca slipped into the room, closed the door behind her and looked at the boy with great tenderness. He wore a cotton nightshirt, though he'd apparently kicked the blanket off his small body sometime earlier. He was probably the cabin boy, a glorified title for a young man whose main task was to fetch things for the officers aboard ship. His dark hair seemed nearly black against the pillow, and he had a faint sprinkling of freckles across the bridge of his nose. The lad was quite handsome for a child and she found herself drawn to him in a way she'd never felt before. Something warm and maternal sang inside her, and she wanted to lie down beside him and snuggle him close in her arms. Instead, she pulled the blanket up over his slim body and tucked it gently around him.

The need to hold another human being close to her, to comfort her as her father had done many times in her life, overwhelmed her. Wearily, she sank to the floor, her back against the door, her knees drawn up against her chest.

Rebecca's father was gone; he could never hug her again, nor cradle her in the circle of his strong arms. When her mother died several years past, her father had comforted Rebecca. He had the inherent ability to recognize the sadness in her eyes and knew when she needed his strength. At such times he would sit beside her and rest her head upon

his shoulder, rubbing her arm comfortingly, listening while she poured out her fears and anxieties. Now she had no one. She was completely alone in the world.

The pressure of the door against Rebecca's left shoulder blade felt like a knife slicing her open. She eased forward a few inches to relieve the excruciating pain.

Tears of grief and anguish for her father, yet relief and thanksgiving for herself, finally overcame her. Silently, she wept away the past several hours of fear and desperation, until the tears ceased.

Rebecca pulled her satchels with her and slid beneath the lower bed, wrapping up inside the damp velvet cloak while using the bags to hide her body. She prayed someone would not bend down and look under the bed. Shaking with fever, she forced herself to close her eyes and remain still. With the strength of her iron will, she made her body relax into a calm state she had not felt in months.

Quite amazingly, Rebecca slept.

Chapter Two

The Motherless Boy

". . . and a little child shall lead them."
Isaiah 11:6

*T*homas Dunton, a precocious eight-year-old, awakened with a start. The lantern above the table had burned out, but a gray sunrise illuminated the ship's cabin through the single window, making it light enough to see. A strange noise was coming from somewhere in the room and he would not be able to go back to sleep until he found its source. Perhaps the ship's cat had crawled in through one of the windows and was purring softly, but it didn't sound quite like a cat to Thomas.

He sat up and listened, but the noise stopped immediately. Thinking he'd only been dreaming, young Thomas collapsed back on the bed and tried to resume his sleep.

Once again the strange noise disturbed him. This time he did not move. He lay in a fetal position, thinking to himself. *What could it be?* Listening intently, he finally decided the sound was coming from beneath his bed.

He was certain that if he moved the noise would stop again, so he stayed motionless and listened for a long time. As soon as he heard the sound again, he knew it wasn't the purring of a sleeping cat. It was more of a soft hiss-poo, like a child sleeping . . . beneath his bed.

Unable to stand the suspense any longer, Thomas rolled over and put the top half of his body over the edge of the bed, his hands cushioning his head on the floor. The sound stopped.

Thomas latched onto a strange-looking bag beneath his bed and pulled it out. What he saw startled him. He jerked up quickly and banged his head on the top bed. "Ow!" he exclaimed, rubbing the spot with his hand. But the damage to his head wasn't bad enough to deter him from looking under the bed a second time.

A pretty woman with long, curly blonde hair looked out at him from beneath the bed. "Who are you?" asked Thomas.

She put a finger over her lips and whispered, "Please, tell no one that I am here."

"Tell me who you are and I'll think about it," Thomas bargained.

"My name is Rebecca," the woman said. "Rebecca Webster."

"Did you run away from home?"

"I have no home."

"Are you a stowaway? Because if you are, they toss stowaways overboard on this ship."

"Only if they find me." Rebecca slid out from beneath the bed and straightened her dress.

"I won't tell," said Thomas, considering that it might be fun to have a secret all to himself. "How come you're running away? Looks to me like you're rich enough to have your own home."

"How would you know that?" She opened one of the satchels and pulled out a hair brush.

Thomas took the fabric of her green cloak into his small hand and placed it near his nose, then he inhaled deeply. "Father says that women who smell sweet, like you do, have lots of money to spend on perfume. He says perfume is real expensive. So if you'd spent your money on a home, instead of on perfume, you wouldn't have to run away."

"It's not my home from which I'm running," she sniffed, brushing at the tangles in her long, golden hair.

Thomas noticed her eyes getting moist, and realized she was about to cry. He stepped to a shelf where he removed a clean handkerchief. "You can use this, if you want."

"Thank you," she said as she dabbed at her eyes. "You're very kind."

Thomas let out a big sigh. This was going to be a tough assignment, keeping a secret as big as Rebecca from his father and the other men aboard ship. She wouldn't exactly fit into his pocket like some of his other treasures. Then he struck upon an idea.

"Hiding you won't be easy, but I think I know how to do it," he declared. "I'll make a privacy curtain around my bed. If I tell Father that I'm a man now and need my privacy, he'll respect that. You can sleep in my bed at night. Then I'll make a nice soft spot for me, underneath my bed, and I'll climb in there after Father goes to sleep. That'll work."

"For perhaps ten minutes," Rebecca said. "Your father surely isn't that gullible. If I were your parent, I'd want to know what you're hiding and I'd check up on you while you were sleeping."

"That's because you're a girl. Men give one another space when

they ask for it, especially aboard ship."

"Do you have a name?" she asked, surprising him.

"Oh!" He grinned. "Thomas Dunton, cabin boy and son of John Dunton, Master mariner aboard Lord Blackwell's ship."

"How old are you?"

"Nine in June!" Thomas squared his shoulders and tilted his head, jutting out his chin proudly.

"Nine in June? Why, you're nearly a man!" She gave him a tender smile.

"This will be my fourth year aboard! By the time I'm twenty, I'll be master of my own ship. By twenty-five, captain! I have plans for my life!" Thomas sucked in his stomach while expanding his chest.

Rebecca chuckled. "I see."

Suddenly they heard movement out on deck.

"It's Father!" Thomas declared.

Fear settled upon Rebecca's face and her eyes widened.

"I'll keep you safe. I promise!" Thomas insisted.

Rebecca slid back under the bed as far as she could until her back was against the wall.

Thomas stuffed her garment bag underneath the bed and pushed it up against her. Then he quickly made his bed and let the blanket hang over the side to protect Rebecca further. Satisfied that he'd done his best to hide her, Thomas removed his nightshirt and put on a tunic, then slipped into his breeches and long stockings. He was just putting on his shoes when he heard his father's voice in the hall.

Chapter Three

The Master Who Would Not Be Captain

*"Bear ye one another's burdens, and so
fulfill the law of Christ."*

Galatians 6:2

John Dunton lowered his head to avoid hitting the top of the door frame as he stepped into the small cabin where Thomas was supposed to be sleeping. His height always caused a problem in the forecastle. Ducking had become an automatic response to the situation. To his surprise, his son was nearly dressed on his arrival.

"Good morning, Son." He smiled, and his brown eyes smiled with him. He ran a hand through his sandy brown hair and watched with amusement as Thomas finished buckling his shoes, a feat that took him many months to learn, as John recalled.

Thomas gave him a mischievous grin and threw himself against John in a generous embrace. "Father!"

Hugging him for a few minutes, John stroked the boy's ebony hair and wondered for a moment at how attached the two had become since bringing Thomas aboard three years ago. "Don't tell me you missed

me," John teased. "I told you I'd be back by daybreak."

"I couldn't hear you snoring," bantered Thomas. "It's difficult to sleep without that, Father."

Smiling, John lifted Thomas up into his arms and pressed his nose against the lad's cheek. "It couldn't be that bad!"

"How would you know?" quipped the boy. "You're always asleep when it happens."

John laughed aloud, kissed Thomas on the forehead and put him down again. "I'm glad you've made your bed early. Lord Blackwell will be here in a moment. He's cajoling the vendors into compliance for me."

"Why don't you do that, Father?"

"I may look big and mean, Son, but I believe kindness is a better way than using force."

"But the men look down on you for it," said Thomas earnestly.

"Some do, I suppose. But I don't have any enemies and I go to sleep at night with a clear conscience. That's better than some, I'd wager."

"Father," Thomas hedged, his face contorted into a look of sheer agony.

"Yes, Thomas."

"Father, have you ever made anyone walk the plank?"

John looked away for a moment. It was, perhaps, the most serious question his son had ever asked him. Finally he answered, "That's the captain's job."

"Would Captain Dawson make anyone walk the plank?"

"I'm sure he has," John replied, though it left a bitter taste in his mouth to admit it.

"How bad does a person have to be?"

Smiling warmly, John said, "I suppose if he murders someone, or if he puts another at risk to save himself."

"What if he stows away?" Thomas' eyes gleamed with earnest and John could tell his son was very serious in his regard for this question.

"Of course, that is the punishment decreed for anyone who stows away."

"But what if it was a child who did it?"

"You're not thinking of stowing away on some other ship, are you Son?" John asked.

"No. Of course not. I'm not that brave." He gave a timid smile.

"Well, I suppose that if it were a child—"

"—or a woman?" interrupted Thomas.

"Or a woman," John agreed, "then I suppose the captain may want to take into consideration the circumstances that drove them to it."

"Would Captain Dawson do that?"

John shrugged. "I don't know, Son. Captain Dawson is hard and exacting when it comes to breaking the law."

"Then what happens to someone who finds a stowaway, but doesn't report it to the captain?"

"I suppose they'd be just as guilty as if they'd stowed away themselves."

Thomas visibly gulped with this information and John felt a chill run up and down his spine. Surely his son wasn't saying—

A knock came at the door. John sighed and considered for a moment the predicament his son might be in until a second knock interrupted him. "Yes, come in."

The door was pushed open and Lord Blackwell, a tall, wispy man with silver hair, pale blue eyes and a pointy nose shaped like a rose thorn, entered the cabin. Lord Blackwell could also be compassionate and genuine with his employees, as John well knew, but he was exacting when warranted. His only failing, as near as John could tell, was his blind spot for his only son, Edward, the third.

"Come in, Lord Blackwell. Sit. Cook is preparing our breakfast. Thomas, dash down to the galley and bring it back with you. Will you do that?"

"Yes, Father." Thomas left the room quickly, not looking back to smile at John as he normally did. Something had upset the child. These troubling thoughts were interrupted by Lord Blackwell.

"The correct number of boxes have been put aboard, John. I expect it won't happen again. Though why you couldn't handle this matter yourself. . . ." He left the sentence open, as though expecting an explanation.

"I could have and usually do. But this particular vendor has been shorting me every trip of the last three. I felt that a word from you, at last, might hold more sway with him."

"Cut him off, John. Get your supplies from somewhere else next time."

"With your permission, sir. I would have done earlier, but I did not want to offend him, since his daughter is betrothed to your son."

"You speak of Sarah Jenkins. Did you not hear that she died eight

months past? No, you'd have been in America at the time. Quite unexpected, it was."

"I'm sorry to hear that."

"Edward has rebounded by now and is engaged to another woman."

"Rebecca Webster?" questioned John, hoping to pry a little more information from his Lordship. "The dockyards this morning were filled with gossip of Edward's searching every ship at the quay for her. I have been wondering why Edward would go to such lengths to find her."

Lord Blackwell gave him a look of bewilderment. "Rebecca is betrothed to Edward. She's been living with us at Blackwell Tower since her father's imprisonment last December. Apparently a neighbor caught him pilfering. We received word yesterday that her father died in prison. Rebecca must be out of her mind with anguish. I expect that she's wandered off somewhere in a daze and will soon be returned to us."

"Then she didn't run away, as the rumors suggest?"

"I can't imagine why she would. She has everything she could ever want at Blackwell Tower, and from all appearances, she seems a perfect match for Edward. Dedicated to him, she is. Of course, we know that love usually comes after the marriage union, but I dare say that she's shown all the signs of loving him already. Ever attentive to his needs, smiling, laughing at his tales and fussing over him."

Having heard enough in regards to Rebecca Webster, John changed the subject. "At any rate, now that I have your permission, sire, I will look for another vendor."

"With my blessing, John."

The cabin door opened and Thomas entered, carrying a tray full

of pewter dishes. The cook, James Taylor, followed behind him. A swarthy man with bald head and long mustache, James set a tray on the table that held a pot of porridge, pitchers of milk and honey, and a kettle of steaming, black tea. While Thomas placed bowls, spoons and cups at the table for both his father and Lord Blackwell, James poured the tea.

"Will Captain Dawson be joining you, Father?"

"No, Son. He's not back yet, though I expect him to arrive shortly."

"Very well. May I sit with you?"

"Be a good lad," pressed John, "and help Cook with the other men's breakfast."

"Yes, Father." Reluctantly, Thomas left the room, carrying the empty tray with him.

John spooned hot porridge into both bowls and passed one to Lord Blackwell, along with the honey and milk.

"Are you comfortable with the *Warwick* now, John?" Lord Blackwell drizzled honey over his bowl of porridge.

"Yes, sir. She takes to the wind on all points of sail and handles both a coming and following sea with the grace of a spirited woman."

"I have taken the liberty of asking both Captains Dawson and Walket to give me a full report on your influence with the men on this trip. I'm thinking that you may be ready to captain your own ship, perhaps the *Warwick*, since you seem to manage her so well."

"What makes you think I would want to be captain?"

"Come, John. Every master wants to be a captain someday."

"I'm not sure that I can be lumped into that category, your Lordship."

"Yes, I've heard that the men don't fear you, that you're their friend and confidante. This is your only character flaw, John. It has troubled me over the past few years."

"And it seems that I've heard this speech more than once," said John, stirring milk and honey into his porridge. "To tell you the truth, sir, if I have to act as executioner or whip master over one of the men under me, then I would prefer not to have the title of captain added to my name." He took a spoonful of porridge and swallowed it.

"John, you're the master of the ship. Anything that happens aboard is directly linked to your willingness to make the men obey you."

"Forgive me, your Lordship, but the master of the ship, by definition, is responsible for the stores aboard, the safety of the ship in general and the navigation. If she runs aground, I will be responsible. If the stores mold, I will be responsible. If she sinks in a storm or is taken by pirates, I will accept my full share of the blame. But if the men quarrel, or happen to drink too much rum or ale, I will not lash them to the mast, nor will I lash them with a whip until—"

Interrupting him, Lord Blackwell asked, "What would you do for punishment?"

"Lock the whiskey up, or if that fails, dump it overboard."

"And if they quarrel?"

"If your Lordship expects a seaman to keep his tongue in check at all times, it is only because you have never spent six months at sea, confined to a small, extremely limited space with nothing around but the ocean and the sea animals to amuse you."

"If the quarrel comes to blows?"

"Whomever is left standing afterward will need no punishment."

"What if one man dies from the fight?"

"Then it is a matter of self defense. Or, if it is considered a murder, the killer should go before the royal courts and be tried as any other criminal."

"If you were captain, would you still feel this way?" Lord Blackwell asked him with a twist of irony in his voice.

"If I were captain, I would be forced to comply with his majesty's written decree, of course. Which is why I have no desire to be captain, Lord Blackwell."

"I don't understand you, John. But I respect your feelings. However, if you are ever to progress, you must next step up and be captain."

"Captains earn ten shillings more than I do as master. That is simply not enough incentive for me."

"So, you do have a price?" questioned Lord Blackwell, finishing his porridge.

"I haven't found a price high enough, sire. But if I do, I will let you know."

Just then they felt the bark move upon the water, as though a sudden gust of air had run into it. "The wind's freshening," said John. "We'd best get you off so we can set sail."

Lord Blackwell stood. "Think about what I've said, John. I hope by the time you return, you'll be ready to take on a ship of your own."

"Thank you, sire, for your concern and for your confidence."

They shook hands and left the cabin, finding young Thomas just

outside the door, waiting for them. "I'll clean up for you, Father, while you see Lord Blackwell to his shallop."

"That's a good lad," said John. "Thank you, Son."

"Will we sail today, Father?"

"It does feel like it, doesn't it Thomas?"

"Yes, sir." Thomas gave him a wide grin.

John nodded, then followed Lord Blackwell out on the weather deck. It only took a few minutes to see his Lordship safely off the *Warwick* and into a small shallop with his personal seaman.

"Farewell, John!" waved Lord Blackwell. "I'll see you in six or seven months."

"That you will!" bellowed John above the wind.

After watching the shallop a few moments on its journey into port, John turned aft and saw that Captain Dawson had come aboard and was already at the helm. Orders were shouted and three dozen men scrambled up the ratlines to release the square sails on the first two masts, while a dozen others pushed the heavy winch arms, bringing the anchors up from the sea floor. Toward the sea, leading to the Thames outlet, John could see the *Little David*, a bark only slightly smaller than the *Warwick*. Captained by Henry Walket, the *Little David* would sail alongside the *Warwick*, acting as the companion boat. Normally, there would be three boats sailing together on each crossing, but the *Neptune* was in dire need of hull repairs when they'd returned this last trip and Lord Blackwell had already sent it to dry dock until repairs could be made. The *Neptune* would be sent out with the next trio of boats returning from the Massachusetts Bay Colony. Meanwhile, the settlers in the American colonies needed fresh stock from England in the form of pewter, kitchen wares, spices, tea and tools, while

England looked forward to the salt cod, corn and tobacco from the Americas.

Hearing a bellow aloft, John looked up to see one of the seamen, Michael Downe, fall from the yard spar. Fortunately, his leg coiled in a line and brought his descent to an abrupt halt, preventing him from breaking his neck had he landed upon the deck. The line held him upside down in a precarious position. John leaped to the ratlines, grabbed the ropes with his strong hands and climbed up as easily as he would a ladder.

"I've got you, Big Mike," he said when he reached Michael, a man in his early twenties with wild hair and glaring green eyes.

"I think my ankle's busted," said Michael, gritting his teeth in agony.

Throwing the man over his shoulder, John said, "We'll get it fixed up in no time." He released the line and lowered Michael down to the other seamen.

"Did someone wake the ship's doctor?" John asked.

Simon Harris came out of the forecastle before the men could answer, his bald head bobbing in step to his long gait. Thin patches of white hair clung just above his ears. Simon had been a doctor all his adult life, in fact had a healthy practice back at Stepney, near London. But the past three years, Simon had been treating sailors during John's voyages to America and back to England.

Almost eight years ago, John's wife, Mary, passed away giving birth to young Thomas. For a while after Mary's passing, John didn't return to the sea. He spent the first two years of Thomas' life with his son and Simon, and with Simon's twin sisters, Naomi and Ruth, living in the hamlet of Stepney, near London. But when John refused to live off

Simon's generosity any longer, he had returned to the sea, making a trip to the Americas each Spring, returning to Stepney by late Fall. John always spent the winter near Stepney Parish, London. This arrangement seemed to suit Simon and his spinster sisters. The three gave loving care to Thomas in John's absence. Mary had been Simon's only child and losing her was hard for the older gentleman. John couldn't take Simon's grandson away from him, so he made the next logical course of action: he took Simon with them aboard ship for six or seven months each year, as soon as Thomas was old enough to train as cabin boy.

Attending to Michael Downe's ankle, Simon ordered the men to carry him below to the main deck, also known as the gunnery.

With this small crises over, John joined Captain Dawson at the helm as the *Warwick* and the *Little David* headed out to sea.

John's thoughts returned to the questions the child had raised that morning. It almost seemed like Thomas wanted him to know about a stowaway, if the way he'd asked was any indication. Yet John knew that was impossible. He'd checked the boat personally before leaving it last evening to dine with Lord Blackwell and the other officers at Chatham Harbor. Since it was foggy and late when they were finished, they had stayed the night at an inn near the Chatham dockyards, rather than cross the bay to the *Warwick* or the *Little David*. He'd had no concerns for Thomas' safety while he was gone, knowing the boy's grandfather slept in the room across the hall from the master's cabin. Why had Thomas asked him about stowaways and failing to report one?

Captain Dawson turned John's attention to more pressing matters. John had little time to reflect on young Thomas for the rest of the day.

Chapter Four

The Master Meets
His Match

". . . in the morning we set sayle at ten of the clock
with little wind at Nore North-west . . ."
John Dunton, A True Journall. . . .

*T*he *Warwick* had only been at sea a few hours when Rebecca studied her complexion in a small looking-glass hung on the wall near the bed. She seemed to have turned a bit green since the ship started to sail. Having never been aboard a boat before last night, she'd had no idea what to expect. Her blonde hair hung in tendril curls down to her waist. Normally she wore her hair pulled up and fastened into a braided knot at the nape of her neck, but the way her stomach felt, her hair was the last thing she wanted to worry about. She noticed that her eyes were still the color of the sea on a clear day, though not a true blue, for they had a hint of green which made them almost turquoise. Tall and slender for a woman of the seventeenth century, she stood five-foot four inches, and seemed quite delicate in appearance.

However, Rebecca possessed a determination to her character that few could equal. She rarely allowed herself the convenience of

appearing wimpish, which would have encouraged those around her to smother her with their attention.

Strong-willed, Rebecca had always forced herself to endure hardships without complaint. But that was before she'd sailed in a ship while burning up with a wretched fever.

Now, only three hours under sail, she found it impossible to keep anything in the confines of her stomach. She grabbed the basin Thomas brought her and spewed into it once again. *Praise the Lord God for young Thomas,* she thought miserably. After wiping her face with a damp cloth, she curled up in a ball on the lower bed and closed her eyes.

"I should get my grandfather," Thomas said as he returned with a clean basin, apparently dismayed to find that she'd already filled the one he'd left for her just a few minutes before. "He's the ship's doctor. He'll know what to do for you."

"No," Rebecca whispered. "I'm just seasick. I'll get over it shortly."

"But grandfather can—"

"He's duty-bound to report my presence to the captain. You heard what your father said about stowaways."

Thomas sighed and sat down on the edge of the bed, a forlorn look on his young face. "But what if you die?"

"I'm strong, Thomas. I've heard that seasickness passes after two or three days. I'll be fine."

"Well, keep these curtains closed." Thomas reached up and brought the blanket down that he had tucked under the upper bed's mattress. Then he climbed into the compartment with her. "It's just like having a secret hideout," he said, crossing his feet beneath him.

Rebecca felt her forehead and found it hot to the touch. She

doubted that seasickness would cause her to run a fever and she feared for what would. Her back ached as though she had boils running down it in wavy lines, with the most excruciating pain centered across her left shoulder.

Still concerned over the news that Edward's first fiancée had died unexpectedly, Rebecca wondered if the woman betrothed to Edward eight months ago was killed by his very hand. The thought nauseated her and she made use of the basin once again.

While Thomas wiped her forehead and face with a cloth, and held her hand when she wasn't vomiting, Rebecca sank deeper into delirium. Beads of perspiration appeared on her skin and drenched her clothes and hair.

After another hour of agony, she finally conceded that calling in Thomas' grandfather might be a good idea. If he reported her to the captain, and Rebecca was thrown overboard, she would surely drown. She resigned herself to her fate.

"Thomas," she whispered, feeling faint more than nauseous. "I fear you must bring your grandfather to me. But do so quietly, without attracting anyone's attention. Will you do that?"

"Straight away, Rebecca," said young Thomas. He gave her a clean basin, and took the soiled one with him as he departed, after securing the curtain around the bed.

THOMAS HURRIED DOWN the corridor and out onto the weather deck where he threw the contents overboard, washed the basin, then rinsed it twice, just as his grandfather had once taught him.

The other seaman on deck were tending to their various jobs, at

the same time enjoying the fresh breeze and the bulging ocean swells.

His father was still assisting Captain Dawson at the helm and hadn't noticed him. Thomas hurried below in search of his grandfather, who had finished setting Michael Downe's broken ankle, and was sitting with the young seaman on a bench just outside the galley.

When Thomas arrived, Grandfather stood and walked toward him. "Good day, lad. What brings you down here this fine, blustery day?"

"I need your help with something," said Thomas.

"Oh? What is it?"

Thomas placed a finger over his lips. "It's a secret," he whispered.

Simon Harris nodded in understanding. "Well, then, show me what you've been doing."

Thomas took his grandfather's hand and led him up onto the weather deck. He noticed his father watching him from the aftercastle, where John was speaking with Captain Dawson. Quickly, Thomas stood on tiptoe and pointed out to sea, toward the *Little David*. "Look, Grandfather. Captain Walket doesn't have any trouble keeping up with us in this wind."

Simon put his hands on the gunwale and inhaled the fresh scent of the savory sea. "Good for your lungs, you know."

When Thomas saw his father look away, he grabbed Simon's hand and pulled him into the forecastle. "You have to promise to keep it a secret," he said, putting his hand on the door.

"A secret?" questioned Simon.

"Swear on my mother's grave," Thomas insisted. "If you don't promise, I can't show you. And if I can't show you, then she might die. She's very sick."

Simon pushed the door open and nudged Thomas inside.

Thomas shut the door behind them. "Grandfather, promise!"

"All right," Simon said. "All right. I will keep your secret, Thomas."

"Swear it on my mother's grave!"

"This has gone far enough," said Grandfather. "Show me. Right now, Thomas."

Gulping down a lump of fear in his throat, Thomas stepped to the bed and lifted the curtain. Simon gasped and hurried over, sat down beside Rebecca and said, "What's this?"

"She came on board last night," said Thomas. "But she wasn't sick then. Now she can't keep anything in her stomach and she's burning up with fever."

Simon placed his hand on Thomas' shoulder. "Go to my room and get my wooden medical case."

"The one I'm not supposed to touch?" asked Thomas.

"Yes. You may touch it long enough to bring it to me."

Thomas turned and left the cabin, closing the door behind him. When he returned, his grandfather had rolled Rebecca onto her side so that her back faced them. He had undone the fastenings of her dress, and her back lay bare. What Thomas saw made him drop his grandfather's case and cry out in terror.

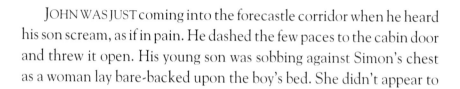

JOHN WAS JUST coming into the forecastle corridor when he heard his son scream, as if in pain. He dashed the few paces to the cabin door and threw it open. His young son was sobbing against Simon's chest as a woman lay bare-backed upon the boy's bed. She didn't appear to

be conscious, and her back was livid with whip wounds as deep and terrible as any John had ever witnessed. Angry welts, septic and oozing, stretched across her left shoulder blade.

Instantly, John realized who the woman was, and to whom she was betrothed. "Rebecca Webster?" he asked his son's grandfather.

Simon nodded. "She apparently came on board during the night."

"If this is why she ran away, someone should hang that barbarian!" John snapped, losing all sense of civility in front of his son and Simon. He closed the door and locked it, then joined his grandfather at the bedside. "What can I do to help?"

"Lift her up onto the table, where I can see her back more clearly. We will need some boiled saltwater. I'll have to clean the wounds, then pack them with yarrow and balsam. It will be terribly painful, and it would be in Thomas' best interest if he—"

"I'm staying!" Thomas declared. "She's my responsibility!"

"Very well," said John. "You're nearly a man now, Thomas. If you want to stay, you will have to help us."

Thomas nodded, his eyes daring his grandfather to intervene.

John lifted Rebecca up into his arms and carried her over to the table, where Simon slid a pillow beneath her head.

"Watch her while I get some boiling water," Simon instructed. "Come, Thomas, I'll need you to tear some clean strips of linen for me."

Thomas followed his grandfather out of the cabin and closed the door behind him.

After putting Rebecca on her right side, allowing the light from the window to illuminate her back a little better for the doctor, John filled a lantern and lit it with a flint and shavings, then hung it on a

hook in the ceiling directly over the table.

The woman moaned, and John went instantly to her, to the far side of the table so that he could see her face. Her eyes opened and he was surprised at the color of them, like the turquoise sea surrounding the Florida colonies.

"Are you John Dunton?" she whispered.

"I am. And you must be Rebecca Webster."

Rebecca nodded. "Will you find mercy in your heart, Master Dunton? Or, will you throw me overboard?"

"I will help the doctor treat your wounds and talk about mercy later on, when you're stronger."

"Without mercy," she moaned, "you may as well let me die."

"Let's get you well," he responded. "Here, drink this." John held out a small glass of amber fluid for her.

"What is it?"

"Whiskey."

"But—"

"Drink it!" John snapped. "Before the doctor arrives and scrapes the infection from your back." More kindly, he added, "It will help you bear the pain."

To his surprise, she said, "You drink it, but give me the bottle." She reached out and took the whiskey flask from him. Without even flinching, she put the opening to her mouth and poured it down her throat in great gulps. She had downed more than half of it before she passed out.

Chapter Five

Impossible Solutions

"And I will not be too tedious to set downe every
point what course we did steere . . . ."
John Dunton, A True Journall . . . .

John paced back and forth, waiting for Rebecca to awaken. He, Simon and Thomas had discussed her situation thoroughly, though there were no easy solutions to her dilemma. If he reported her as a stowaway, Captain Dawson would be compelled to pass sentence according to royal decree, and she would be cast overboard. If he reported her as the betrothed of Edward Blackwell, the good captain would take her back to England and turn her over to the barbarian, which was something John would never allow. Even if Rebecca was willing, which obviously was unlikely, John would never permit her to go back to his employer's son, Edward Blackwell, the Third.

Yet if John reported that he had brought her aboard ship as his guest, he would have to invent a good reason, something the captain could believe. Officers simply do not travel in the company of women unless they are betrothed or married. If John and Rebecca were

betrothed, she would be accompanied by chaperones to ensure her chastity.

John glanced out the port window and noted that the wind was picking up more with each passing moment. Before long, they could find themselves in near gale conditions.

This matter would have to be resolved soon. He had other duties needing his attention, and expected he would be up all night with the crew. The *Warwick* was headed into a storm in the English Channel, which could be treacherous in fair weather, and this would prove a real challenge for all of them. Without a plan of some kind, Rebecca was bound to be discovered by one of the other seamen before John had a chance to protect her.

When he heard her moan, he sank down onto the edge of the bed, where he looked at her curiously. She was exquisitely beautiful, like a life-size porcelain doll. He had no idea how she would accept what he was about to suggest.

"Hello," he said, giving her a faint smile. "How are you feeling?"

She rolled her eyes and closed them again. "Terrible headache," she managed to say.

"I expect so after all the whiskey you drank."

"My back," she said. "Is it—?"

"It will heal. Simon cleaned it thoroughly and packed it with yarrow and balsam."

Nodding, she asked, "Then what is to become of me, Master Dunton?"

"You do present a rather difficult dilemma, Mistress Webster. There are very few options where you're concerned."

"Be direct, sire. What will you do with me?"

Since she insisted on his being straight forward with her, John complied. "Do you have any desire to return to Blackwell Tower to marry your betrothed?" he asked, knowing she would have to be insane to want that.

She shook her head. "Never! I would rather die here, than go back there."

"I thought so," he admitted. "But I had to ask."

Rebecca nodded.

"The only way the captain will accept your unannounced presence on board will be if I claim that I brought you with me . . . as my betrothed."

"I have no entourage, Master Dunton. I brought no one with me."

"I then fear, Madam, that the only solution is to request that Captain Dawson perform our marriage vows at once."

"But surely, sire, he will see through such a ploy."

"He is not an unkind man, Mistress Webster. And he cares for Lord Blackwell's son as much as you do."

"And what of you, Master? Surely this proposal will not be in your best interest."

"Ours will be a marriage of convenience, for I have no natural affection for you, Madam. But I do have empathy for what has brought you here. We will make the marriage contract, then secure it in a safe place aboard the *Warwick*. When we arrive in the Americas, and you leave the ship, you may take the contract with you and burn it, if that is your desire. I will not pursue you, nor will I expect you to fulfill any portion of a woman's role in marriage on my behalf."

"Am I to understand that young Thomas has no mother?"

"She died in her travail with Thomas."

"Then I will agree to a marriage of convenience with you, sire, provided you allow me to befriend young Thomas while I am here. This will give me something to do that will make the crossing less burdensome for both of us."

Her request surprised John and he couldn't refrain from smiling. "I was going to suggest, Madam, that young Thomas become your charge while you are with us on this voyage, since he seems to feel that you are now his responsibility."

"I owe my life to young Thomas," Rebecca responded. "But I owe my future to you, Master Dunton. I cannot thank you enough—"

"You owe me nothing, madam. I am only doing what any man of good conscience would do in this situation. I have no desire to see you drowned or beaten to death."

A knock at the cabin door interrupted them. "Yes, come in," said John.

Captain Dawson, a decisive man, quickly entered and glanced momentarily at Rebecca, who was laying upon the bed, a basin in her hand, with a blanket pulled over her body in haphazard fashion. He gave her only a cursory nod, then said, "Thomas sent me."

"Permit me to introduce my fiancée, Rebecca Webster," said John evenly, watching for any sign of alarm on the captain's bearded face.

"The same Rebecca Webster as was betrothed to Edward Blackwell?" It came more as a wary question, than a reply.

"Was being the operative word, Captain. Their agreement, as I understand it, ended when her father passed away, freeing her to accept

my proposal." John nodded and smiled affectionately at his bride to be, hoping the captain would read the feigned expression correctly.

"She ran away from wealth and power to wed a mariner?"

"Indeed, sir. Such is the mind of a woman in love."

"I see." He stroked his beard thoughtfully. "It is my humble opinion, John, that the better man won her heart. I presume you wish me to perform the ceremony?"

"Yes, sir."

"And who are your witnesses?"

"Simon and young Thomas, sir. I'll get them." John stepped out of the cabin and motioned to his son and Simon, who immediately joined John in the port cabin.

"Convenient." Dawson smiled. "Very well. Let us begin. It's liable to get nasty before the night is over."

Captain Dawson looked down at Rebecca and for a moment John saw a hint of compassion in the captain's eyes. It pleased him.

"Are you able to stand, Madam?" the captain asked Rebecca.

"Not without fainting," insisted Simon. "She's been quite ill, having never been aboard a ship before."

"Very well. John, sit beside her and take her by the right hand."

John did as he was instructed, giving her small hand a gentle squeeze of encouragement. She looked up at him and her eyes brimmed with tears. For a moment he felt a twinge inside his chest that almost hurt, though he could not have explained it, even to himself.

Captain Dawson began the brief ceremony by saying, "John Dunton, mariner of London, do you take this woman, Rebecca Webster, as your

wife and earthly companion, from this moment forward until death separates you?"

"I do," John replied.

"Rebecca Webster, do you take John Dunton, mariner of London, as your husband and earthly companion, from this moment forward until death separates you?"

"I do," Rebecca whispered.

"Through the power vested in me as Captain of the *Warwick*, I hereby pronounce that you are husband and wife, sealed in holy matrimony, the same as though you were wed in the Church of England."

"Here! Here!" declared Simon, with Thomas echoing the expression.

"Very well. I will give you a few moments' leave, John. But I will expect you shortly. The storm's brewing and I will need all hands on deck."

"Yes, sir. Thank you," John said, standing and extending a hand to Captain Dawson.

The captain shook it and gave him a brief nod. "I suspect that what you have done this day will have far-reaching consequences, particularly when we return to England, John. I pray that you will not incur the wrath of Edward Blackwell."

"What Edward Blackwell does not know he cannot fight," suggested John. "For all that anyone on board this ship knows, Rebecca could have been my wife for several years."

"I understand. I will prepare your marriage contract on the morrow and present it to you privily, but I will not violate your secret."

"Thank you," said John.

When he'd left them, Thomas looked up at John eagerly. "Does this mean that Rebecca is now my mother?"

"She may act as your mother for as long as it suits her," said John stiffly, "though I would warn you, Thomas, that I have promised her freedom once we reach the Americas."

"Yes, sir," Thomas' voice faltered, as though he realized exactly how long he would have a mother before she sought her liberation.

John gave him a brief nod and tousled Thomas' ebony hair. "See that you take advantage while you have the opportunity." He turned to Rebecca. "You have the power within you to capture my son's affection. I pray that you will deal wisely with him."

Rebecca looked up at him, tears streaming down her cheeks. "I will do my best, sire."

"If you are to act as my wife, you must call me John, and I will call you Rebecca. But for now, you must rest. Come, Simon, I will sleep in your room for the duration of the journey. Rebecca will need her privacy."

He left the cabin, with Simon following him out onto the weather deck. The storm was intensifying. Before long, they would be drenched in white caps.

"It's a noble thing you have done, John. Mary would be proud of you."

"Mary is gone, Simon. It's time we both accept that."

While Simon went below deck to check on his other patient, John pulled on his oilskin cloak and went directly to the aftercastle deck, otherwise known as the poop deck.

"You've been at the helm for four hours, sir," he reminded his superior.

"Yes, I am a bit weary," said Captain Dawson. "I will retire to my cabin, John. Have Peter relieve you in four hours, unless you need me."

"Yes, sir."

John took the wheel in his hands, delighting in the feel of the vessel beneath him. Some of his favorite times were at the helm, with the spray drenching him, the ship climbing up fifteen foot swells and slipping down the other side of them. To his great relief, he had never been seasick.

For quite a while he thought about Rebecca and hoped that she was more comfortable than she'd been earlier. He couldn't help wondering how Rebecca felt spending her wedding night alone, which brought a smile to his face. *This is not the way I had hoped to spend my next wedding night, either,* he said to himself. *But such is my lot in life.*

REBECCA GROANED IN misery as the boat climbed up one steep wave and slid down another; the *Warwick* groaned with her. Thank the Lord God that she didn't have anything left in her stomach. The motion aboard ship was like trying to ride a galloping horse the size of Blackwell Tower. It had been like this for two days now and she had grown weary of it.

"Up the wave, down the wave. Up the wave, down the wave," she moaned. "Will it never stop?"

Thomas looked at her from the top bed and grinned. "I think it's fun!"

"You would," she muttered woefully. "I suspect you're just like your father."

"I'll make a fine mariner! That's what father says."

"He's been very kind to me," Rebecca mused aloud. "I'm sorry you never knew your mother, Thomas. But with a father like yours, I suspect he's tried to make up for her loss."

"He often tells me stories about her. They were only married a short time, but Father said that my mother loved him enough to last his whole life."

The sad tone in his voice worried Rebecca, and she changed the subject. "If this is your fourth year, you must have already sailed to America. Will you tell me about it?"

"Father always takes us first to the Laconia and Mason plantation. It's north of Plymouth Colony, but I don't think that's where we're going this time. At the plantation, we picked bushels of strawberries. I ate so many I thought I was going to be sick. They grow wild along the banks of the river there."

"Did you ever see any Indians?"

"No. But I heard about them. They've been helping the settlers learn how to grow corn and store it over the winter."

"Some say they are savages," said Rebecca.

"Father says he sailed the *Warwick* into Indian country five years ago, down near Jamestown. Henry Fleete captained, so Father wasn't worried."

"Why not?"

"A long time ago, while he was still in his teens, Captain Fleete was captured by Indians. He speaks the Indian language and Father says

that the Indians respect Captain Fleete now."

"If he was captain of the *Warwick* then, where is he now?"

"Father brought the *Warwick* back to England without him. Captain Fleete is going to be governor at a place on the Chesapeake called Baltimore."

"You've had some exciting experiences in the years you've been aboard, Thomas. Many boys your age are working in the fields and factories, with never an opportunity to see and do what you've done. You're very fortunate."

Thomas complained, "I still have to learn my reading and writing. Simon teaches me most of the time. I think he wants me to be a doctor."

"That would be a good profession, too."

"I want to be captain of my own ship," nodded Thomas, his dark brown eyes intense and focused. "That's all I want to be."

Rebecca sat up and noticed that the waves didn't seem quite as steep as they'd been earlier. The rolling and pitching of the bark had decreased, and now the *Warwick* slipped through the water with an easiness for which it was built. The more the waves settled, the better her stomach felt.

"I'm sure you'll make your way in the world very well, Thomas. You're resourceful and determined. These qualities will help you wherever you may go."

"The storm's dying, Rebecca. Would you like to get some fresh air now?"

Rebecca hesitated. Except for the captain and Simon, none of the men had met her yet. As for John, he had gone out of his way not to

visit her. She doubted he'd even inquired, though she was certain Simon and Thomas had kept John apprised of her condition. This suited her fine, for she felt a bit awkward about the situation, knowing that John was now her husband, though he had been true to his word. He had expected nothing from her, not even so much as a smile or a casual greeting, regardless of his right to do so. *Husband in name only.*

"Come on," insisted Thomas, not allowing her time to consider.

Rebecca stood and felt her head spin. "I think not, Thomas. First I must eat something and keep it down. Then I will be stronger."

A knock came at the cabin door. Thomas opened it to find Simon standing in the frame. "Grandfather, we should take Rebecca out on deck for some fresh air."

"If she's able to eat this evening and if the seas continue to abate, Thomas."

"But Grandfather—" he started to protest.

Simon held up his hand. "Other than ginger tea, she's not had nourishment for two days, lad. Let's give her food for strength before she has to face the world outside this room."

Thomas pouted, but Simon did not budge. Finally he said, "Then let's have dinner in here tonight, the four of us. Maybe it would cheer Rebecca and she'll feel more like eating."

Rebecca smiled at that remark. To Simon she said, "It would be nice to visit with you and Master Dunton. Perhaps you can prepare me for how long our voyage will be and where we will land when we reach America. I have no idea what to expect there."

"I will speak with him at once," said Simon. "It would be good for

John to break away from the crew and refresh himself." He turned and left them alone.

"Thomas, would you check with the cook to make certain it won't be a hardship for us to eat in here?" Rebecca asked.

"Straight away," nodded Thomas.

"And bring back the best dishes, a tablecloth and perhaps some flowers or candles, so I can set the table properly."

Thomas chuckled. "We usually don't grow flowers on board," he laughed. "But I'm sure I can find some candles."

After Thomas left, Rebecca glanced in the mirror and decided that she looked terrible. Her hair was tousled, her face was pale and she had dark circles under her eyes from lack of sleep. Removing her hair brush, she brushed her hair until she had all the tangles worked out of it. Then, she pulled her clothing from the two bags she'd brought with her. With little time to choose what clothing to bring, Rebecca had packed rather hastily. Now she longed for a few of the fine dresses she left behind, though she would never consider going back for them. She'd brought only three dresses, two chemises and petticoats, and a shawl, in addition to the thick velvet cloak that she'd worn when she escaped from Blackwell Tower.

Unfolding the dresses, she was dismayed to see how wrinkled they were, and she shook them out and laid them over the top bed, then used her hands to smooth out the wrinkles as best she could. Before she was finished, Thomas returned with a tray full of dishes and a table cover.

"Thomas, I really need to wash up," she told him. "Do you have fresh water for that?"

"No, Madam, we use seawater for our bath. I can bring you a bucket of it, if you'd like."

"Yes, please," she told him as he put the tray on the bed. "But Thomas, please don't call me Madam. If the other men hear it, they may think I'm not married to your father."

"May I call you Mother?" he asked, a quiver in his bottom lip.

"Oh, Thomas, I'm not sure that's such a good idea. Your father made it very clear that our marriage will terminate when we reach America. We plan to destroy our marriage contract, and he will no longer consider me his wife at that time. This is just a pretend marriage, you must know that."

"May I pretend that you're my mother until then?" Thomas' brown eyes widened. Rebecca could clearly see that he would be disappointed if she denied him this request.

"Why don't you ask your father at supper this evening?" she suggested. *Let Master Dunton explain it to his son.*

Thomas gave a sigh of resignation. It didn't take a mother to see how disheartened he felt. Then he turned to fetch her a pail of seawater.

While he was gone, Rebecca spread the linen cloth over the table, then neatly arranged the four place settings of pewter, and put the candles in a candelabra in the center of it. They were not the most attractive dishes she'd ever seen, but they were serviceable enough, considering the circumstance.

Returning with a large bucket of seawater, Thomas also gave Rebecca a linen towel and a bar of hard French-milled soap. "I had to borrow the soap from Grandfather," he told her. "It's the only kind on board that hasn't already been used by someone else."

Rebecca smiled. "See there, Thomas, you are resourceful."

Thomas grinned. "Of course I am, Mother." He stepped out of the room before she could correct him.

The little imp!

After she locked the door and put a blanket over the window opening, she lit the lantern, and gave herself a sponge bath, though it did nothing to make her feel clean. The saltwater made her skin sticky, which she abhorred. However, it really didn't matter how she felt, this would be her way of life for a long time to come. She would have to make the best of the situation and try to be cheerful about it. For four months, she had done the same while living at Blackwell Tower. She would do so once again.

When she was satisfied with the washing she'd given herself, she braided her long hair and fastened it into a knot at her nape, then slipped into an everyday dress and an apron. Afterward, she stepped to the cabin door and opened it. Removing the blanket from the window, she felt the wind rush by her on its way through the cabin door down the forecastle hall. She inhaled the salty fragrance of it and enjoyed the sensation for the first time since the *Warwick* set sail nearly sixty hours ago.

Unfortunately, she still felt a little dizzy and her stomach wasn't completely settled. Stretching out on the lower bed, she waited for the momentary nausea to abate. This time she did not retch, which was a great relief to her. Rebecca hoped this meant that she might finally be getting accustomed to the constant movement of the *Warwick*.

JOHN SHAVED AND cleaned up in the starboard cabin, dressed in

his best leather doublet and a ruffled silk shirt that hung loosely on him, regardless of the bulging muscles it hid, along with his newest breeches, leggings and high-top boots. Then he carefully tucked a pistol into a pocket inside his doublet, a habit that had become second nature. With piracy in full swing on the Atlantic Ocean, every good seaman carried something with which to defend himself. John's pistol was his weapon of choice, as was a small dagger concealed in a scabbard inside his right boot.

More than a little nervous regarding this dinner party that Thomas insisted he should attend, John didn't know what to think of the affair. Had Rebecca recovered enough from the sepsis in her back, as well as the nausea she'd been suffering, to sit at the dinner table without fainting? What was she thinking by letting the lad have his way in this evening's meal plan? Unable to answer these questions to his satisfaction, he joined Simon, Thomas and Rebecca in the port cabin.

To his secret delight, Rebecca had cleaned herself, coiled her hair and had some color in her cheeks tonight. She was already seated at the table and did not rise when he entered, as did Simon and young Thomas, nor would John have expected it. To his surprise, he found himself drawn to her in a way he'd not felt toward a woman in a long, long time. The emotions both startled and pleased him. It was good to know that he hadn't died with Mary after all, as he had supposed for almost nine years.

"Good evening," he said, bowing politely to her. "Thank you for inviting me to dine with you. I trust you're feeling better."

"Much," she responded, giving him a charming smile.

The three men sat down, John directly opposite Rebecca, with Simon on his right and Thomas on his left. No sooner were they seated,

when James appeared at the cabin door with a pot of Yorkshire stew and some fresh bread.

"You haven't met my wife, James. Forgive me for not introducing her sooner, but she's been quite ill with sea fever. Rebecca, this is James Taylor, our cook."

"Pleased to make your acquaintance, my Lady," said James, bowing formally.

"And yours," she said, giving him a polite smile.

"Will there be anything else, Master Dunton?" asked James before leaving.

"No. I'll have Thomas clear the dishes, James. Have a nice evening."

"Godspeed, sir."

After he left, closing the door behind him, Rebecca looked straight at John and asked, "Will you say grace, John?"

Her question caught him off guard. He hadn't expected it and he gave her a wary glance. "I'll defer that honor to Simon, if you don't mind."

"Not at all." If she was disappointed by this maneuver, she did not express it.

John bowed his head and listened as Simon offered an eloquent prayer for good weather, healthy food and a speedy recovery for Rebecca. When it was finished, John nodded, while Rebecca and Thomas said, "Amen."

Simon started the conversation, for which John was grateful, when he asked, "Are you feeling better, my dear?"

Rebecca smiled. "I'm weak, but I hope this meal will strengthen me."

John offered, "You're looking much better than your first day with us, Rebecca. You have more color in your cheeks this evening."

"Thank you, John. You've been very kind to me."

"Please," he insisted. "Enough said about kindness. I'm gratified just knowing that I have been of some assistance to you."

John served them all a portion of the stew, then broke the bread and passed it among them. As they ate in silence for a few moments, he managed to take a furtive look at Rebecca when she wasn't looking in his direction. She was a remarkably beautiful woman, a fact that hadn't fully registered in his mind when he first met her. Slim and delicate, he sensed that she was much stronger than she appeared, or that he was willing to admit upon their first acquaintance. She wore a simple blue dress with a white apron and a dainty necklace and locket unlike any he'd ever seen before. The locket was decorated with a gold filigree pattern that reminded John of French lace.

When he'd nearly emptied his plate of stew and eaten all his bread, John sipped on a goblet of red wine and hoped it would give him enough courage to ask Rebecca the questions that had been floating around in his mind for the past two days.

Simon finished his dinner first and asked Thomas, "May I challenge you to a game of chess after dinner, lad?"

"After I help Cook with the dishes, you mean," said Thomas half-heartedly.

"After I help you and Cook with the dishes," amended Simon.

Thomas' brown eyes gleamed. "Thank you, Grandfather."

Simon nodded and gave his grandson an engaging smile.

"Father, Rebecca says I must ask you for permission to call her Mother."

The question startled John and he thought on it carefully before he answered. He did not want Thomas to keep false hopes in his trusting heart.

When he didn't answer as quickly as Thomas apparently expected, the lad turned soulful eyes at him and begged, "Please, Father. If you can pretend you're married, why can't I pretend that Rebecca is my mother?"

"We are married, Thomas. Make no mistake about that. As proof, I have here our marriage contract, signed and sealed by Captain Dawson." He pulled the document from his doublet and handed it across the table to Rebecca. To his wife he added, "There is a false bottom in the small central drawer in the wardrobe. That will be the safest place to keep it for now. You may take it with you when you leave the ship."

"Thank you," she said.

"Then your contract means that Rebecca *is* my mother now," Thomas insisted. Clearly he would not back down.

Finally John nodded. "Rebecca is, by the laws of England, your mother."

"But John, when I leave the ship—" Rebecca began.

"We will deal with that when we have to," suggested John. "Would you care to leave these two to their chores and stroll with me on deck? The sea is nearly calm, and the wind has died considerably. You may enjoy the fresh air."

"Thank you," said Rebecca. "I'll get my shawl."

She stood up and walked over to the bed where she had laid out some of her clothing. Wrapping her shoulders in the shawl, she turned to John. "I'm ready."

Chapter Six

Surrender

". . . and they shall be one flesh."
Genesis 2 : 24

John opened the cabin door and escorted Rebecca outside, offering his arm when they were on the weather deck. As they walked up the steps to the deck over the forecastle, he introduced her to two of the men on board.

Michael Downe, who broke his ankle their first day at sea, was a jolly Welshman in his early twenties. He was currently responsible for keeping night watch from the forecastle. "Good evening to you, Goodwife Dunton. Glad to see you're feeling better."

"And to you, Goodman Downe."

"Call me Big Mike," he told her. "Everyone else does."

"I shall then," she responded. "I'm happy to meet you, Big Mike."

Elias Fox, who'd been talking with Big Mike, was an elderly man who looked as if he'd never spent a day on land. He was gaunt and weathered, his face had deep creases much like a walnut and nearly

as dark. "Call me Foxey, my Lady," said Elias. "They call me that because I'm crafty."

"As in devious or skillful?" Rebecca questioned.

Elias gave her a toothless smile. "A little of both, I suppose."

The clouds had cleared and the night sky held more brilliant stars than John could count. The moon, nearly full, illuminated the deck easily and they could see everything on board as though dawn had arrived. John led her down the forecastle stairs and across the ship's belly, over to the aftercastle.

Stepping up onto the aftercastle deck, where the helm station was located, John introduced Rebecca to Peter Bayland, the first mate, a short, stocky fellow with a penchant for rum and brawling. He had the helm at the moment and little time for conversing with anyone when he was officially on duty.

"Evening, Goodwife Dunton."

"And to you, Mr. Bayland," said Rebecca.

As they walked past Peter Bayland, John explained, "Peter might be rough around the edges, but he is an exacting helmsman, able to respond instantly if a situation arises that might put the ship or men at risk."

"You trust him completely?" Rebecca responded.

"I do."

"Have you ever seen so many stars in your entire life?" Rebecca asked John as she placed her hands upon the stern rail.

"Nearly every voyage," he answered. The wine he'd drunk at dinner was giving him a little courage now, and he decided he'd better ask his questions, for his mind would not know peace until he did.

"Where are the others?" she asked, unexpectedly.

"The other seamen are below. They make their beds on the middle deck, which some call the gunnery. Since the weather turned calm again, they have no purpose in being topside. Unlike you, who spent the past storm in bed, they were on the weather deck nearly forty-eight hours straight. They are probably taking a well-earned rest. When one is at sea, Rebecca, one sleeps in shifts or when the sea is calm. Otherwise, sleep deprivation sets in after a while. I've seen men who failed to lash themselves to the yard spars, fall asleep aloft, so starved for rest they don't even know it until they land with a thud on the weather deck."

"Being a sailor must be a risky occupation," she suggested. "Why do men even do it?"

"Certainly not for the money," John smiled at her question. "I suppose it's for the challenge and the freedom."

"Freedom?"

"Out here, man is master of his own destiny. Although we try to observe the laws the King imposes upon us, out here we're not entirely obligated. Life is less regulated, but more strictly defined. If we don't tend to the ship the way we should, we will all die. It tends to place life into perspective."

"Would that I could be master of my own destiny," she whispered, though John wasn't entirely sure that she meant for him to hear it.

"Forgive me, Rebecca, if I offend you, but I do have questions that I would ask of you," John said, hoping she wouldn't rebuke him entirely.

"What is it?"

"Young Thomas gave me what few details that you shared with him,

but the questions that remain are these: first, what did you do that drove Edward to whip you as he did?"

She did not hesitate, but stared straight into his eyes. For a moment he stood entranced by her beauty and charm. "I did nothing for which I am ashamed," she responded. "I told him no."

"No to what?" John questioned. "What did he expect from you that would make you tell him no?"

"We were not yet married. I didn't want him to—"

Needing no further explanation, John nodded and quickly said, "I see. Then, how did you come to be betrothed to Edward in the first place?"

"My father agreed to the betrothal last November, before he realized the evil in Edward's heart. When he discovered it, he tried to reason with Edward, to convince him to call off their agreement. In a fit of anger, Edward found a neighbor to bear false witness against my father and he was sent to prison. In December, Edward came to me and told me that my father had agreed to our marriage. Because I had no means of support, but to take in mending or tailoring, I struggled. Finally Edward invited me to Blackwell Tower as his betrothed. I agreed only on the condition that I be permitted to visit my father in prison. At that time I did not know that my father's imprisonment came as a direct result of Edward's devious nature."

Tears welled up in her eyes and John took out a handkerchief and dried them for her. "And then?" he asked curiously.

"When I first saw my father in that filthy hovel they call a prison, he had contracted some kind of fever. I was so shocked at Father's appearance that I can't even remember what the prison master called it. Father begged my forgiveness for agreeing to my betrothal and

explained that he'd been led astray."

"Then why did you continue the betrothal under these conditions?"

"Upon my return to Blackwell Tower, I told Edward that I would not marry him. He went into a terrible rage and I was lashed until I fainted completely. When I awakened, Edward told me that my father would die in prison if I did not agree to marry him. I felt trapped, I had no choice."

"And now?" John questioned.

"My father died the day I ran away. Edward had returned earlier that afternoon with news of my father's death. I was devastated. When Edward followed me to my bedroom, where I'd gone to cry for the loss of my father, he entered without knocking and tried to force his way with me. I told him *no* and I fought him with all my strength. But I am no match for Edward. He lashed me to the bedpost and whipped me until I. . . ." Tears pushed at her eyes, but she forced them back. "The earlier wounds had not completely healed. I knew I had only two choices left: Escape from Edward, even if it meant my death in the process, or stay and die when Edward punished me beyond the limits of my endurance."

"You have learned some painful lessons in your young life, Rebecca. I pray your experience does not harden you to other men who are less demanding than Edward Blackwell."

Rebecca turned to face him, tilting her head to look up into his eyes, and he was grateful she could not read the thoughts coursing through his mind.

Then, she opened her locket and showed him its interior. Two letters, "J. W." were etched into one side, while "R. W." was etched into the other. "My father gave this locket to my mother the day I was

born. The initials stand for my parents, Jeremiah Webster and Rebecca Webster. When Mother died, Father gave the locket to me. I have worn it ever since. Whenever I think of men, whether good or evil, my first thoughts always go to my father, who was a true gentleman in every sense of the word. I would rather put Edward Blackwell out of my mind entirely and never think of him again, for he is the saddest representation of a gentleman that I have ever had the displeasure to meet."

Relieved, John took the locket in his hand and closed it for her, studying the filigree pattern in the moonlight. "I've never seen one quite like this before."

"My father was a tinsmith, but he managed to repair gold pieces as well. He told me it took him nearly a year to make the locket because he had to do it secretly, whenever my mother wasn't watching. With his business downstairs and our living quarters upstairs, that wasn't very often."

John looked down at Rebecca and for a moment even her name escaped him, for all he could see in her eyes and her demeanor was that this woman was his bride. He had promised her he would not expect her to fulfill her responsibilities as his wife and he would have to honor that promise. Though looking at her now, with the moonlight illuminating her blonde curls and her eyes searching his own, he regretted that he'd ever made such a promise. Shaken to the core, he released the locket and stepped backward, away from her, yet not so far that they couldn't converse comfortably. Then he asked, "What do you plan to do when we arrive in America?"

"I hope to hire out as a seamstress or a school mistress. I can sew exquisitely fine seams, as my mother taught me, but I can also read,

write and perform basic arithmetic. Surely someone will be able to make use of my skills."

"You are a determined woman," he suggested. "I expect you will have no problem finding employment. I know a man in the middle colonies who may still be in need of a suitable tutor for his young children and for his wife, who never learned the skills that you have. I would be happy to introduce you when we arrive there."

"Do you speak of Captain Henry Fleete?" she asked.

"Why, yes. I suppose Thomas told you of Henry's experiences among the Indians?"

Rebecca nodded. "I've grown quite fond of Thomas. He has been most attentive to me during my illness. But I must apologize for putting you in such an awkward position, John. It was not my intention to obligate you as I have done."

He smiled, feeling touched by her apology. "With more than fifty men aboard, you would have been discovered sooner or later. For my part, I'm gratified knowing that it was Thomas who found you first. Otherwise, I fear what may have become of you."

"It was very foolish of me, I see that now. But I must confess that I had heard Lord Blackwell talking with Edward last month about your kind regard for the seamen aboard the *Warwick*. I prayed with all my heart that you would be a merciful man to whom I could turn in my hour of need." She steadied her hands upon the stern railing and looked aft as the ship slipped through the rolling sea at a gentle two or three knots.

"So that is how you came to choose the *Warwick*?" He was surprised at her confession and pleased to know that his character had been a prime consideration in her escape plan.

Rebecca nodded and turned to face him once again. "Yes, I thought how much like my own father you sounded, and I felt in my heart that I would find safety here."

"From what you say regarding him, your father was a man to emulate," said John.

She took a step forward and placed her head against John's chest, then wrapped her arms around him, so that he had no choice but to hold her. At first the position alarmed him, but when he felt the sobs she was trying to stifle, he realized she had never been comforted over the loss of her father.

Tenderly, John stroked the small of her back, being careful not to let his hands wander to the upper portions, where she was still mending from the lashing Edward had given her. Holding her with care and deep concern, he whispered hoarsely, "I understand your grief, Rebecca. I will stay beside you for as long as you have need of me."

Their embrace was like none other he had ever known, and feelings he'd denied himself for nearly nine long years surged through him. Rebecca, his bride, had suddenly become the only woman he wanted to—but he couldn't allow himself to think such thoughts. The very idea scared him and excited him beyond all reason. He had promised Rebecca her freedom at the end of their voyage. Their tender, lingering embrace threatened to undo his promise. Now, more than ever before, he actually wanted her to *be* a wife to him. However, he had no other choice, but to give her up. First and forever, John Dunton was a man of his word.

Somehow he had allowed Rebecca to find the feelings he'd buried deep inside himself, so deep he thought they were non-existent. To his great surprise, he found himself unwilling to release her. Gently,

he held her close until she had spent her tears and was comforted.

REBECCA FELT MUCH stronger when John returned her to the cabin. Simon and Thomas were playing a game of chess at the table.

"It's past your bedtime, Son," said John.

But Rebecca wasn't ready for Thomas to go to sleep yet. "May I tuck him in?" she asked. "My mother always sang to me at night."

"If you wish," John agreed. "Though if you're going to sing, I'd like to stay and listen. It's been many years since I heard a mother sing."

Thomas smiled. Rebecca, too. She realized it was John's way of making life easier between his son and his wife. "Only if you promise not to laugh." Rebecca gave him a warm smile.

"Neither of you will mind if I turn in?" said Simon, standing and walking toward the door. "I haven't your youth on my side anymore, and I'm tired."

"Goodnight, Simon," Rebecca said. "Thank you for everything."

"It's been my pleasure, my Lady," Simon bowed like a true gentleman. Then he left the room, pulling the door closed behind him.

Rebecca gathered up the chess pieces and the game board and put them away in a cupboard near the table. By the time she finished, Thomas was dressed in his nightshirt, and John was sitting at the table writing on a parchment, perhaps the ship's log.

She pulled the blanket down, then tucked Thomas cozily beneath it. When she was satisfied that he would be warm enough, she stretched out beside him and cradled his head against her shoulder, where she stroked his cheek and sang a melody her mother had often sung to her:

Close your eyes, my little one,
My little one, my little one.
Close your eyes, my little one do,
For Heaven watches closely over you.
Sleep to you, my little one,
My little one, my little one.
Restful sleep for me and you,
For Heaven's angels safely keep you.

When she finished, young Thomas had fallen asleep. To make certain that he would stay that way, Rebecca hummed another tune, but by the second chorus, her eyelids grew heavy and she slept.

JOHN STOOD UP and put his journal with ink and pen back into a drawer at the desk and removed Rebecca's clothing from the top bed. He draped the dresses over a chair, hoping they wouldn't rumple too much. From experience, he knew that women didn't like their day clothes wrinkled. Then, he climbed into the top bunk and looked down at the woman now cradled against his young son. They seemed so natural together. Moisture filled his eyes, and John hastily blinked it away.

How long he remained there, watching Rebecca sleep, John did not know. When he felt a hand on his shoulder, he opened his drowsy eyes and stared into the face of Peter Bayland, the first mate.

"It's your turn at the helm, John. I guess you didn't realize."

John rolled over and climbed down off the bed. "Sorry," he mumbled. "I'll be right there."

Peter left the cabin while John paused long enough to bend down

on one knee and kiss his son on the forehead before he left. Tempted to kiss his wife as well, John resisted, straightened abruptly and left the cabin.

Since it was his watch at the helm, John knew it was ten at night. He would have a four-hour shift, being relieved at two of the morning. Rotating every four hours, Captain Dawson, Peter Bayland and John shared the responsibility at the helm. This gave each man an eight-hour break twice in every twenty-four-hour period. John noticed that the heavy hourglass had already been turned over the moment he arrived. "Sorry, Peter," he said. "I won't let you down again."

"I won't hold it against you, sir."

"Now get some rest, Peter. I can manage from here."

Peter nodded and headed for the aftercastle corridor, where he disappeared from John's view.

The wind had died entirely and the seawater lay flat and smooth as a looking-glass all around him. Far to the north, John could see a few fires flickering from the Isle of Wight. The *Warwick* had nearly passed through the English Channel and would soon be headed into the Atlantic, provided they had enough wind to continue their voyage. Sometimes, the wind would be so strong it would push a sailing vessel through the channel and halfway across the ocean before fizzling out. Other times, like tonight, it would die just past the Isle of Wight and the ship would sit idle for several days before the wind picked up again. He had hoped for a fast voyage, but alas, it appeared that would not happen.

John would have to put men up into the crow's nest before they passed the Isle entirely, for they were entering treacherous waters where Moorish pirates were known to capture English ships. The prisoners

would often be taken to Morocco where they were sold as slaves, sometimes to the Algerians, a barbaric lot who were known to utilize their slaves up to their last living moment, sometimes as cannon fodder, the small ones while they were still alive.

Piracy on the high seas was something to dread and every ship headed for the Americas would do their best to be prepared. With these thoughts in mind, John lashed the wheel, then slipped below decks and awakened two of the seamen, assigning them to the crow's nest for the next four hours.

The crow's nest was not a job that excited the men. Four hours standing in a narrow, circular space, eyes peeled on the horizon for any sign of land or other ships, trying to prevent dizziness caused by walking around in circles, a more wearying job aboard could not be found. Even swabbing decks was preferable to being cramped into the crow's nest, especially for tall sailors.

If the wind had blown during his watch, John would have had no trouble staying alert. But he'd only slept an hour or so in the master's cabin earlier that night, and before that he'd had less than two hours sleep in sixty. Nights such as this challenged his ability to stay awake. By the time his fourth hour ended, with nothing-to-do other than stare at the glassy sea, he was nearly asleep on his feet. He stumbled down the stairs and across the deck to the forecastle corridor.

Out of habit, he absently went into the port cabin, where he removed his doublet, shirt and breeches, then climbed up into the top bed and fell quickly asleep.

AROUND THREE OF the morning, Rebecca awakened long enough

to realize that she had fallen asleep in Thomas' bed. She carefully crept off it, removed her dress and petticoats, leaving her chemise on as a nightdress, and climbed the ladder at the foot of the top bed, where she lifted the blanket and sleepily crawled beneath it. Sinking deeply against the comfortable mattress, she was grateful that John's mattress was softer than his son's. Leaning back, she expected to feel the wall behind her, but instead, she felt a man's well-muscled, warm body. His arm lifted, then rested across her waist, pulling her close against him.

Although Rebecca knew the man was her husband, she did not know how he had come to be sleeping in her bed, nor did she have any idea how to get out of the compromising position. What dismayed her all the more was that she didn't know if she really wanted to move away from him. The feel of his body next to hers thrilled her in ways she had only dreamed about, and she reminded herself that he was, after all, her husband.

Rebecca listened to his breathing for several minutes, and when she heard his gentle snoring, a sound she hadn't heard before now, she realized that John wasn't even aware that she was lying next to him. She didn't know whether to be disappointed or relieved.

For almost half an hour Rebecca remained awake, her back cradled against John's firm chest, his arm wrapped around her waist. Still exhausted from her illness, she could remain alert no longer. Her eyes grew heavy with sleep until she slipped into the world of dreams.

When Rebecca awakened, she could feel the sun, warm against her bare legs, as it shone through the port window. But she didn't open her eyes to see how the sun illuminated the cabin with its early morning rays. To her dismay, and great pleasure, she had rolled over in the night and her cheek now rested against John's bare chest, his arm cradling her head like a pillow. Their legs were entwined in an intimate position,

which made her even more afraid to open her eyes. *What must John be thinking of me?*

Searching her mind for some logical reason that would explain why she had climbed into bed with him, she could come up with nothing. The fact that she was here, snuggled up against him as though they'd been married for years, when it had only been three days, betrayed her feelings, something which no amount of excuses could explain adequately. Yet Rebecca failed to find enough strength within her to leave him, for she enjoyed feeling close to John, holding him and having him hold her. An unsettling hopefulness kindled deep inside her. Was it possible, in just three short days, that she had fallen in love? Would John ever feel the same way toward her?

Analyzing her emotions was something Rebecca had never done before. Impulsive and willful, she'd never contemplated what it might feel like to fall in love, to marry, to make love to her husband.

The thought of intimacy with Edward was something she abhorred. She had buried it every moment it surfaced in her fearful mind. With John, however, a warm sense of elation swept through her, and her skin tingled all the way to her toes.

When John kissed her forehead, Rebecca blushed. Knowing that she could not pretend to be asleep any longer, she opened her eyes and was pleasantly surprised to find John looking down at her with great tenderness.

"Good morning," he whispered, his voice husky from sleep.

Rebecca smiled at him, hoping he could see in her eyes what she was beginning to feel in her heart.

John's expression turned a little stern and he asked, "Are you sure this is what *you* want, Rebecca? I told you I would not expect it."

She closed her eyes again, searching her soul, asking herself if she really wanted to share the intimacies of marriage with John Dunton. Acknowledging that her husband had become the master of her heart, she whispered, "Yes." Then, she opened her eyes to gaze into his once more. "It is."

"If we do this, I will not be able to grant your freedom when we reach America. You do understand that?" A wrinkle creased his forehead as he questioned her.

The way he asked made Rebecca wonder if he was challenging her to deny him what was rightfully his, or trying to deny that he, too, wanted her.

Rebecca reached up and smoothed the crease away. "I do," she answered.

"You will be giving up your freedom, and you will remain my wife until death parts us," he continued.

"I accept that," she agreed.

"A sailor's wife is not an easy life, Rebecca. There will be times when I must heed the call of the sea. I may be gone for months at a stretch."

His questions worried her, but she refused to give the concerns place in her mind or her heart just now. Later, she would examine them, but not now. Not now. "Do you not want me to remain with you?" she asked, arching her body against him, kissing his chest and his neck.

"Merciful heaven," he groaned as he pulled her closer to him and kissed her hungrily.

LISTENING TO HIS parents whispering above him, Thomas slipped from his bed as silently as he could, grabbed his clothing and boots and left the cabin. He pulled on his breeches and fastened the buckles on his boots while he was still in the aftercastle hall, then he went out onto the deck where he climbed the ratlines to the top of the foremast and into the crow's nest.

Elias Fox, on duty there, greeted him cordially. "Ahoy, there, young Thomas. What brings you out this early in the morning?"

"Newlyweds," grinned Thomas. He burst out laughing when Elias gave him a knowing look.

Giddy with the excitement of it, Thomas could scarcely contain his happiness. For the first time, he had a real family, a father *and* a mother, the blessing for which he had been praying all of his life.

Ignoring Elias' protest, Thomas climbed the net above the crow's nest and swung back and forth from the topsail yard spar.

The sun sparkled on the water as though a thousand, weightless gold coins drifted upon it. Rain from the previous day had washed the air, scrubbing it with a windy freshness that filled the sails sparingly, giving them lift but little power. Inhaling deeply, Thomas felt the salt air scrubbing his lungs clean, as well.

It was the best day at sea the young boy had ever known.

Chapter Seven

Calm Before the Storm

*". . . a small ship of London, called the **Little David**, set*
out by a Mr. Armitage, a woolen draper at the sign of the
Beads in Cannon Street, for Virginia . . ."

Mariners Mirror vol. 9 no. 3

*J*ohn kissed his sleeping bride on the forehead, then left the port cabin as silently as possible, not wanting to disturb her. It was nearly ten of the morning and he was due at the helm in another few minutes. He would need to locate Thomas, who had apparently slipped out sometime earlier. John was not surprised that he had failed to hear Thomas leave. He'd been rather involved with Rebecca this morning, so it was little wonder that the lad had not stayed around long enough for John to get out of bed.

Inhaling the savory air, John realized immediately that today would be much like a day in the doldrums, when the wind refused to blow, and the seas remained as flat and lifeless as a puddle. However, he was determined not to let the uncooperative weather disappoint him. He had much to be grateful for and nothing was going to spoil it for him.

Looking up, John saw his son talking to Elias in the crow's nest. "Thomas!" he called.

Thomas slipped out of the nest and down the nets much like a monkey swings from branch to branch, with an ease of motion that only a child or a well-seasoned sailor could manage. "Good morning, Father," said Thomas. "Is Mother feeling better?"

John noticed the lad trying to suppress a grin. "I believe so," John told him. "But I'm letting her sleep a while." He wasn't quite ready to tell the boy why Rebecca needed extra rest this morning. The lad would figure things out soon enough.

"Father, will you catch some turtles for us? They're all over out there. Elias said Cook makes a great turtle soup."

"Perhaps." When Thomas pouted, he added, "After my watch." John tousled the boy's hair and headed toward the aftercastle steps.

Thomas followed along beside him. "Captain Walket is coming over in his shallop, Father."

John nodded in agreement as he looked to port and saw a shallop heading in their direction, rowing away from the *Little David*. "You enjoy going up to the crow's nest, don't you, Son?"

"Very much. I can see all the fish around us, though this morning there's mostly just turtles."

"Good morning, John," said Captain Dawson when John arrived at the helm.

"It is, indeed," John agreed with a smile as wide as his face.

Captain Dawson turned the big hour-glass over when the last trickle of sand had dropped into the bottom. "Peter will relieve you shortly,

John. I'm sure you'd like to hear what Captain Walket has to say when he arrives."

"May I take the helm in Father's absence, sir, as long as the sea is flat?" asked Thomas.

The captain considered. "Only if someone calls us the very instant you feel a breeze come in."

Thomas looked at the clear blue sky and said, "It doesn't look like we'll have much wind today, sir."

"You may be right, young Thomas. I believe you're turning into quite an able seaman, lad."

"Thank you, sir. I'm going to become a master, just like my father!"

John smiled proudly. "You'll pass me up by the time you're fifteen, Thomas. I didn't start out as a cabin boy, you know."

"No, you didn't go to sea until you were twelve, did you?" Thomas asked.

"Twelve, but large enough to pass for sixteen."

"Ahoy the *Warwick*," came a voice to port. "Permission to come aboard?"

"Take the helm, Son," instructed John. Then he hurried down the aftercastle steps and across the weather deck where he waited for Henry, a round, cherubic sort of man with puffy red cheeks and lively blue eyes, to climb the rope ladder Peter Bayland had lowered.

"John!" Henry exclaimed. "Quite a blow we had there for a few days, wasn't it!"

It was a declaration of fact, not a question, and John responded, "It didn't last though. I was hoping we could put another hundred

nautical miles between us and Land's End today, but apparently not."

"Henry, how good of you to come. I trust your men are all well." Captain Dawson added.

Soon, the three men were gathered in the Captain's quarters, eating a hearty breakfast of eggs, oyster fritters and fresh bread. As they conversed, John glanced out the starboard window and saw Rebecca walking across the weather deck toward the aftercastle steps, probably to join Thomas at the helm.

"Who is she?" Henry asked him.

Captain Dawson arched an eyebrow, as though asking John if he would share the information. John nodded.

"John brought his bride aboard with him, Henry."

"Your bride?" came the incredulous question. "Why, John! That's just grand. But I'm surprised at you, for you didn't invite me to the wedding."

"It was a hasty affair," John responded. "We would have done had we enough time, but it is a long story."

"By all means," said Henry, "tell me about her."

Since John and Henry had an ongoing relationship of trust, John explained the circumstances nearly exactly as he had done to Captain Dawson shortly before the ceremony. He already knew how Henry felt toward Edward Blackwell, so he was not surprised to hear his comments.

"Edward Blackwell is nothing less than a criminal, John. And his behavior toward Rebecca is reprehensible. When we return to England, I will demand that he confess before the courts regarding his behavior.

I will also speak with Lord Blackwell and give him a full account of the matter."

"Please," said John. "I would prefer that the matter be dropped. Besides, I won't be bringing Rebecca back with us when we return. The only way I can guarantee her safety is to keep her as far away from Edward as is humanly possible."

"But John," Captain Dawson protested. "I thought Lord Blackwell wanted to make you Captain when you return."

"That is the other reason why I have no desire to return," said John. "You both know my heart isn't in it. I could never harm one of my men, regardless of royal decree, nor could I cause my men to do something I cannot. Master is the highest rank to which I've aspired and I've been happy at it, but it's time to move on. I had in mind to build a merchant ship in the Americas and trade between the colonies. It's a new market over there, and many a man can make his own fortune if he's a wise steward."

Captain Dawson frowned his displeasure, but did not voice it.

Henry placed his hand on John's shoulder. "I've known you for twenty years, John. I've never had cause to complain against you. I learned to know your heart, and though it is tender, you still have the capacity within you to become a great captain. That will be my report when we return to England."

"Here! Here!" echoed Captain Dawson.

"Thank you," said John. "But my mind is made up, especially since Rebecca and I married."

"I've nothing to give you as a wedding gift," Henry sighed.

"I expect nothing," John answered.

Henry stroked his chin thoughtfully. "I have an idea."

"You don't need—" John began.

"Now hear me out," said Henry with the kind of persistence John knew could not be swayed. "I shall have you come aboard this evening for a wedding feast. I've a bottle of fine wine that I have been saving and this is the perfect occasion."

"I can't ask you to give up your last bottle of French wine, Henry. You've been treasuring that bottle for as long as I've known you."

"But I can," insisted Henry. "Besides, we have six women aboard the *Little David* this voyage. While you are performing your normal duties, your bride will be lonely. Female companionship may be just the thing to help her keep her sanity. I'm sure she must feel awkward being the only woman aboard the *Warwick*."

"She hasn't mentioned it," John allowed, though he felt uncomfortable accepting such a generous offer from Henry.

"Not another word about it," said Henry Walket. "Captain Dawson, do prevail against John for me. This would give me great pleasure. Besides, why should you have all the joy of Rebecca's presence? She would be a welcome addition aboard the *Little David*, if only for a few days."

"I see no harm in it," Adam Dawson said. "John, don't be so proud. Rebecca may enjoy the other women's company while you're on duty."

That was the only argument that finally held sway with John. He had no way to entertain his bride while he was working. And she might feel more comfortable around other women. "Very well," he said. "But the moment the wind shows signs of picking up, I will bring her straight back to the *Warwick*. Is that understood?"

Henry nodded. "Of course. She should not sail in the *Little David* while you sail in the *Warwick*. Now, when are you going to bring her to meet me?"

John stood. "I'll go get her right now."

WHEN REBECCA JOINED Thomas at the helm, the young boy grinned up at her, as though expecting a full report on what happened in the master's cabin that morning. If he expected her to tell him, he would be disappointed, for Rebecca could not share with anyone the depth of her feelings for his father.

Rebecca had no idea how John felt about her, however. Certainly, he'd made love to her with a passion that surprised her, but he never once confessed that he loved her. He'd also made a heroic effort to make her consider what their love-making would mean, to convince her that she did not want to share her bed with him. She hadn't been willing to consider anything but her own needs at the time. Now, in the stark reality of life aboard ship, she doubted that John's passion came from anything more than male desire.

Memories and doubts filled her mind and her heart. John had told her upon their first meeting that he had no natural affection for her, so she had no choice but to conclude that the consummation of their wedding vows was an act of physical need on his part. Their marriage was little more than a convenience to him.

For Rebecca, however, the entire course of her life had changed. She would remain John's wife until death separated them.

Bringing her focus back upon Thomas, Rebecca's heart overflowed with gratitude. Today she truly was the young boy's mother. She smiled

secretly as she put a hand on Thomas' shoulder. "Good morning, Son," she said, giving him a gentle squeeze.

Thomas' grin widened and his dark eyes fairly danced with excitement. "Mother!" he exclaimed. "I'm glad you came on this voyage with us!"

"I suppose you are." She smiled as the sun grew warm upon her face, and the heavy scent of savory fish in the air tickled her nostrils. Licking her lips, she could taste salt upon them and she wondered how long it would be before they reached dry land again. Everywhere she looked, the sea was flat and calm. The sun reflected off it as though it were a wavy mirror, but there was no land in sight anywhere.

"I love you, Mother," said Thomas, breaking into her thoughts. "Is it wrong for me to do so?"

Rebecca stared at him, puzzled how she could best answer him.

During her silence, he added, "I mean, I never knew my first mother, but I grew up thinking that I loved her, too. Is it wrong for me to love two mothers?"

"Thomas, you must never let go of the love you have for your first mother, for she gave her own life that you might live. Such an act is evidence of the greatest love one human can bestow upon another." Putting her arm around the young boy's shoulder, she cradled him against her side, hoping to help him through his dilemma of conscience. "Yet, the Lord God sent me to you and your father, I believe, for more reason than to escape from an abusive tyrant. We don't always understand God's ways, but we must trust that He knows what is best for us and what will help us become better people. You have endeared yourself in my heart also. We must both accept that our feelings are what the Lord, our God, intended."

"That's a very long way around saying that you love me, too," Thomas offered.

"Love is something I've only known toward my parents before I met you," she explained. "It seems somewhat different to feel toward you how my parents felt toward me. But, I will tell you truly, I have never loved another child as I love you now. I could not love you more if I had given birth to you myself."

"And my father," he wondered aloud. "How do you feel towards him?"

"My feelings for your father are private, young man. You would do well to refrain from asking him a similar question."

Thomas' lower lip quivered slightly. Rebecca knew her words sounded like a sharp reprimand, but sometimes a child must be taught proper manners. This was one of those times. She gave him a tender smile to soften the rebuke.

Returning her smile, Thomas kept his eyes on the horizon. "Father said he would not be able to keep his promise to give you your freedom once we arrive in the colonies. Does that mean that he loves you as much as I do?"

"You were listening a great long time," she responded, blushing warmly under the morning sun.

Thomas tilted his head up and squinted to look at her face. "Yes," he admitted. "But I am not sorry for listening. I never wanted Father to grant your freedom from us. Not ever."

"If you listened to everything, then you already know that your father and I will remain married for the rest of our lives. It is not something either of us wanted when we married. But now, there is no turning back. I'm afraid you're stuck with me, Son."

Thomas released his hands from the wheel and wrapped his arms around her waist. "I shall always be glad of that," he said, as he stood on tip-toe and pulled her down near his face, then planted a kiss upon her cheek. "I've prayed for a mother all of my life. I knew that someday God would give me one."

Tears formed in Rebecca's eyes, but she blinked them back and turned her attention to the wheel. "What would happen if we caught a big gust of wind just now?"

Remembering his duties, Thomas quickly stepped apart from her and placed his hands back upon the wheel. "I'm going to captain my own ship when I am grown," he told her with a matter-of-fact air.

"I believe you will." Stepping over to the stern rail, she looked down into the clear water and was amazed to see several large turtles swimming around the boat. "Have you seen all these turtles?" she asked her son.

"Of course, Mother. I was up in the crow's nest earlier. The ocean is full of them here. Father will probably dive for them later. They like to swim beneath the boat because it's shady there."

"You must know a great deal about sea life."

"A good seaman is alert to everything in the water around him."

"I see that," she offered, then turned her attention back to the turtles. Their gray-green shells were about two feet long and perhaps sixteen inches across. Their paddle-legs moved them through the water with surprising gracefulness.

Hearing footsteps upon the aftercastle deck, Rebecca turned and saw John approaching her. A mischievous smile curled the corners of his mouth and she recalled with vivid clarity how she had enjoyed that smile earlier in the morning. She blushed and hoped he hadn't noticed.

"I'd like you to meet someone," John told her the moment he arrived. "You, too, Thomas."

"But the helm, Father," Thomas protested at once.

"I'll take it for you." Peter, the first mate, came up the steps to the aftercastle deck. "I couldn't sleep anyway. The sea is too still for sleeping."

"Thank you, Peter. Perhaps I can return the favor sometime," John offered.

"Perhaps," said Peter, placing a hand on the wheel.

John led Rebecca and Thomas down the steps to the aftercastle corridor where they found the captain's door open. Taking her inside, he made brief introductions and invited her to sit at the table with them.

Thomas had developed quite a possessive nature that morning and he stood beside Rebecca as she sat down, then put his hand upon her shoulder.

"You're looking much better, Rebecca," said Adam Dawson. "When we first met, I was more than a little concerned that the voyage would not be good for you."

"Hopefully we won't have so many large swells to ride, Captain. For I don't want to go through that again." Rebecca made polite conversation and listened attentively when Captain Henry Walket invited them to spend a few nights aboard the *Little David*, at least until the wind came up again. The invitation pleased her, and she encouraged John to allow them to accept Henry's offer.

"Not without me," insisted Thomas.

"You may sleep in the forecastle with my family. That's where I will

sleep for a few nights," explained Henry. "Since we have no ship's doctor, we always have an empty set of beds in there."

After Henry returned to the *Little David*, John and Elias spent nearly two hours in the water catching turtles, guiding them to the *Warwick* where the crew hoisted them aboard, turning them on their backs, so they couldn't get away. The turtles were prized for their meat and shells. They would fetch a hefty price in America or England. In the meantime, they could be kept alive on their backs for several weeks with very little effort and they would add protein to the sailors' diets.

As the men cheered and placed bets on who would catch the most, the biggest and the first turtle, Rebecca watched in amazement as John climbed up to the gunwale several times and waited for a turtle to happen by. Then he would leap into the air and perform a perfect dive, deep into the sea. Latching onto a turtle, he would force the ungainly creature up to the surface, where the sailors would take it from him and wrestle it up to the deck. None of the men could swim, except John and Elias, and Rebecca found it fascinating to study how John managed it. She noticed Thomas watching with equal earnest.

"Father promised to teach me to swim when I turn nine," Thomas told her. "He says it's easy once you learn how."

"Do you suppose he would teach me as well?" Rebecca asked.

"Certainly," Thomas agreed. "He's offered to teach any of the men here, but most are afraid of the creatures in the sea. Father says you just need to give them a healthy respect and a wide berth."

"It must be wonderful to dive as John does. I can only imagine what he is able to see below the surface."

"In the Spanish colonies off Florida last year, I got to see the coral reefs under water. They are the most beautiful in all the world. At least,

that's what I thought when Father showed me."

"Your father is a remarkable man, Thomas. You have many reasons to be proud of him."

"So do you," suggested the young lad.

As the men caught turtles, Rebecca smiled and contemplated her marriage to John and the emotions that had blossomed inside her. Feeling much like a butterfly coming out of its cocoon, her heart soared with hope as easily as John soared from the gunwale to the sea. Would John someday share her devotion? Although John had said he had no natural affection for her, she prayed that in time his heart would change.

BEFORE THEY LEFT the ship late that afternoon in the shallop, John agreed to row back to the *Warwick* by four of the morning and take a six-hour watch at that time. Rebecca did not want John to go back without her, but she looked forward to spending one full evening together, until he began the next watch.

When they arrived aboard the *Little David*, John tied the shallop to a line handed to him by a seaman. They were greeted by five other couples. The women had spent part of the day preparing turtle soup, filet of flying fish, a rice dish made spicy with herbs and seasonings, and hot, raisin pudding for dessert.

After dinner in the captain's quarters, Captain Walket's two sons, Henry II and Christopher, ages nine and six, persuaded Thomas to join them in a game of piracy on the forecastle deck, and Thomas leapt at the chance to play with boys near his age.

The men went off toward the bow of the boat for a short time, while

Rebecca got acquainted with the women at the stern. Two of them, Helen Giles Danbury and Isabel Giles were sisters. Isabel was unmarried and traveling with Helen and her husband, Isaac. The other women were officers' wives: Jane Walket, wife to Captain Henry; Ruth Atherton, wife to first mate Daniel; Miriam, wife to Master Nathaniel Wilkinson; and Elizabeth, wife of the cook, Matthew Williams.

Miriam had been studying Rebecca quietly through most of the dinner and when the women were completely separated from the men, she asked Rebecca, "Are you not the same Rebecca Webster that was betrothed to Lord Blackwell's son, Edward?"

Rebecca felt the color drain from her face. The other women seemed to stand a little nearer, as though they were awaiting Rebecca's answer as eagerly as Miriam. "At one time, but our betrothal was broken."

"A pity," said Miriam. "I heard Edward was searching for you the night before we sailed. Did you run away from him?"

Rebecca answered evenly, hoping the women couldn't hear the quivering in her voice. "Our arrangement included specific promises made regarding my father. When those promises could no longer be fulfilled, the agreement was broken and the betrothal was no longer in force."

"How did you manage to marry John Dunton so quickly?" Miriam asked.

"Indeed?" questioned Jane Walket. "I once heard him tell Captain that he would never marry, for he could never love another woman like he loved his Mary."

"Unless, of course, you were in the family way before the wedding?" prodded Miriam.

"Your questions are most personal," Rebecca answered. "I would prefer to keep the answers private."

"We didn't mean to pry," Miriam apologized. "But you can hardly blame us for being curious, after the trampling Edward's men made amongst the boats the night before we sailed, searching for you."

"They even let one of the shallops loose," added Ruth.

Rebecca cringed, knowing full well that she had let the shallop loose herself.

"How long have you and Master Wilkinson been married?" Rebecca asked Miriam, hoping to change the topic of conversation.

"Thirteen years in September," came the response.

"Have you always sailed with him?"

"I dare not let him out of my sight," Miriam admitted. "It's not that I don't trust him, because I do. It's I, myself, that cannot endure the separation. My mind races when he's at sea. What if the ship sinks? What if he's captured by pirates? What if he falls overboard and no one notices? I cannot bear the agony."

Jane Walket added her voice, "When we heard that Miriam planned to go with her husband for each voyage, we conspired against our husbands, and insisted they allow us to join them."

"We don't always go together," insisted Elizabeth. "The voyage makes me sick the first few days, and I often wonder if it is worth the effort."

Rebecca smiled. "Yes, I know exactly what you mean."

The topic changed again, this time to concoctions and treatments for sea sickness, as well as palsy and cholera, then to child-bearing, a topic which held Rebecca's interest for quite some time, until she felt

John's hand upon her shoulder.

She looked up, grateful to see that he was ready to retire. "Good evening, ladies. I have enjoyed our visit." Rebecca took John's offered hand and bid them all goodnight, having enjoyed their company after the topic turned from herself, but also glad that her husband was ready to spend the rest of the evening with her.

As they walked across the weather deck, John told her, "I spoke with Thomas. He's agreed to stay in the young Walket boys' cabin with Henry and his wife. They told me not to worry about him."

"He's made friends that he hadn't expected to meet," Rebecca agreed. "I'm happy for him."

When they arrived at the aftercastle, John led her down the corridor to the captain's quarters. The table had been cleared of dishes, the floor swept and the bedding turned down on the large, four-poster bed.

To Rebecca's delight, there was also a basin, as well as a bucket, of fresh water, not sea water, with which to bathe. "Thank goodness," she sighed. "Now I won't feel of salt spray the rest of the night."

"Enjoy it," said John. "For you will only feel clean for a few hours. By morning, you will understand why fresh water is rarely used for bathing at sea." Then, respecting her privacy, John said, "I will join you in a few minutes. I've a concern to address privately with the captain."

After he left, Rebecca sponged her body with clean water, being careful to conserve a basin full of fresh water for her husband. Fortunately, the bucket was large enough for her to wash her long hair and rinse it, though she wasn't completely certain it had done any good. Her hair had a mind of its own, and encouraged by the damp sea air,

it wanted to curl in long ringlets. After brushing it until it fairly gleamed, Rebecca climbed into bed, where she turned her face to the wall.

Within a few minutes John returned, sponged himself clean, then slipped between the sheets and pulled her into his arms. "You are still awake, then," he said as she rolled over to face him.

"Of course. I was merely giving you privacy."

He nodded in understanding. "Have you enjoyed your day?"

"Immensely," she answered.

"Rebecca, I've something important to speak with you about and I hope that you will allow me."

"Naturally, John. You may tell me anything."

"When we arrive in America, I have decided to go into the shipping business on my own. There is plenty of timber there and I would like to build my own bark, one that I can use in the merchant trade for the colonies. I wonder if you are willing to sacrifice whatever we may need to in order to get my company up and running."

Rebecca was touched by his willingness to share his life with her. "I will do whatever you ask, John."

"That's just it, Rebecca. I'm not completely certain you would be happy at sea. And the business I am proposing will require that I captain my own ship from colony to colony. There will be times when we must, of necessity, be apart."

She studied his rugged face in the dim light of a single candle on the bedside table. "I am a strong woman, John. Separation, I've heard, can bring some couples closer together."

"And if we have children?" His dark eyes softened as he asked it.

"I will not be the only woman who ever bore a child, John. Good-wife Walket told me that she bore both her sons at sea."

"The reason for my concern," John explained, "is that Thomas' mother died during her travail with him. He was quite large for an infant and it may be that all the children I father will be equally large."

Rebecca snuggled closer to him and lifted her arm to stroke his sandy brown hair. "Please trust that I am stalwart, John. I may seem frail, but I have no intention of not being here to help you raise whatever children the Lord God sees fit to give us."

He leaned back into the pillow, staring at the ceiling above him. "Mary had no such intention either, but she died giving birth to Thomas."

Coming up on one elbow, Rebecca looked directly into his eyes and with as much conviction as she could muster, she said, "The Lord God would not bring us together only to separate us so quickly."

"I thought the same when I wed Mary, but now I have little confidence that God is remotely interested in me or my affairs. I certainly do not believe that He brought us together. You did that all on your own."

She heard the disappointment in his voice. How could she help him trust God again? "First," she insisted, "my name is not Mary. It's Rebecca. And as near as I can recall, none of the women in my family before me died in childbearing. As for how I came to search for the *Warwick*, it is my belief that the Lord God led me there. I am sorry that you do not share my convictions."

"Forgive me if I have upset you, Rebecca," he offered. "It was not my intent." Lifting his hand, he ran his fingers through her golden hair.

His apology did not assuage the sting she felt in her heart. Stub-

bornly, she said, "If we are to remain married, John Dunton, with no promise for my freedom, as you insisted this morning, you will do well to remember that I trust the Lord God to guide my footsteps every moment of my life. That you are unwilling to recognize His hand in your life is your own affair."

"In my opinion, your God was doing a poor job of looking out for you until you took matters into your own hands, Rebecca. Did your God even care when Edward Blackwell was beating you?"

"He often answers in ways that we do not understand."

"Or sometimes He does not respond to our beseeching at all."

"The Lord God always answers," she insisted. "Even when He must, of necessity, tell us no."

"I will try to remember that, Goodwife Dunton."

Chapter Eight

Bereft of Hope

> "... when 35 leagues beyond Land's End they
> were captured by a 'Turkish' pirate. ..."
>
> The Earl of Portland

*J*ohn thought long and hard on Rebecca's comments as he rowed the shallop toward the *Warwick* at quarter after three of the next morning. She filled him with hope and dread all at the same time. If God had sent her to him, as she believed, how would he know it? God had failed to answer his prayers nine years ago when he pleaded for his wife's life, even asking God to take John's life instead. *Where was God then?* Since that terrible night when Mary died, John had stopped communicating with Him. Indeed, he wasn't even certain that God was the least mindful of the common seaman.

Worse, his conversation with Rebecca earlier had driven a wedge between them that neither was willing to remove. Why had he persisted in arguing with her? It had accomplished nothing.

When the disagreement was long past, John had reached for her and she had responded willingly. Yet even in intimacy, he could feel

her hesitation. Afterward, he felt ashamed for what he had done to her. He had taken Rebecca as his wife in ways that he had not expected, and now he could not, in good conscience, grant her freedom from their marriage vows. Yet, John did not own Rebecca's heart, nor had he any hope of doing so.

Considering alternatives, he pondered if he should still keep his promise to her. If she did not conceive a child from their union, she could tell a prospective suitor that her first husband had left her. . . but this wouldn't be entirely true. He could not force her to lie simply because he had difficulty keeping his hands off of her. Never! Since no other solutions presented themselves, John had to acknowledge that Rebecca would be obligated to continue their marriage, regardless of her desire for freedom. Would such coercion eventually drive them apart?

As John rowed closer to the *Warwick*, the night sky began to darken with high cirrus clouds which blotted out the moon and the stars, indicating lower clouds within a day or two. The slurping of the oars as John made strong, determined strokes in the black water was the only sound penetrating the dark night.

Perhaps in time John and Rebecca would come to a meeting of the minds, as well as of bodies. Rebecca satisfied the physical aching he'd suffered through nine long years, might there also come love? When Mary died, John buried his love with her. For almost a decade, John doubted his heart could belong to another. *Could it?*

A faint light illuminated a small spot near the helm aboard the *Warwick* as John rowed toward it. *An oil lamp used for the night watch.* He hoped the man in the crow's nest had not fallen asleep. It was nearly impossible to tell unless one climbed up and looked. With the high cloud cover, this dark night would be the perfect opportunity for pirates

to sneak upon them unannounced.

Just as the thought crossed his mind, he heard something to his left and a little farther from the *Warwick* than John himself. A dozen oars sliced almost noiselessly through the water. The hair stood straight out on the back of his neck. Straining to see through the blackness around him, he finally found that for which he'd been searching. A low-slung long-boat, much like a wide canoe, was headed toward the *Warwick* with perhaps twenty pirates aboard. Since John's shallop floated between the pirates and the bark, he made a hasty decision.

Removing the pistol from inside his doublet, he cocked it and aimed carefully at the canoe itself. A flash of flame leapt from the pistol, and a loud bang almost deafened him. The lead ball hit the canoe hard, blasting a hole in the side, below the waterline. Immediately, it began to sink. Satisfied with his aim, John yelled for all he was worth, "Pirates! All hands on deck!"

Almost immediately the *Warwick* came alive with men swarming over it, running and yelling.

"Pirates!"

"Where?"

"There!"

"John sank their long-boat!"

"Pick them off in the water!"

Men took aim at the pirates floundering in the sea and fired a barrage of lead at them, hitting several. A few escaped, swimming strongly toward the *Little David*.

Turning back toward the *Little David*, John's heart raced in fear. He saw a cannon blast far from him and watched in horror as the ball

landed within a few feet of the *Little David*. "Man the cannons!" he yelled. "Set the oarsmen to task!"

Another cannon fired from an approaching pirate's ship. As it spewed flames, John noted the shape and size of the vessel from which it originated and looked for the telltale flag that pirates flew. To his dismay, this pirate displayed the markings and colors of a Turkish Man-of-War.

John had heard that the Turks capitalized on piracy, but they were so far from their own country, it astounded him. Hadn't their conquests been limited to the Barbary coast, Spain and Portugal? What else he'd heard about them made his blood run cold, and his hands sweat. They were no less barbaric than the Algerians.

"Attack!" he heard someone yell aboard the *Warwick*. The pirates had boarded the bark from the starboard side.

Swiftly, John took long, deep strokes with the oars, and headed towards the *Little David*. As he passed by the pirates who were swimming in the same direction, he beat at them with the oars and managed to slip past them. By the time he arrived, the men aboard the *Little David* had pulled up the rope ladder and were beating off pirates on all sides. John steered to the bow and heaved himself up onto the net. As he did so, someone grabbed him from behind and he was pulled back down into the shallop. Three pirates, their faces horribly contorted, pounded his head and shoulders with clubs. John fought them off, knocking two of them into the water. He grabbed the third by the head and twisted it until he heard the man's neck snap. Then, he dropped him into the water like a child's toy. It was the first time he'd ever taken a human life, and it sickened him, but not so much as thinking what lay in store for Rebecca and Thomas if he could not rescue them.

John made a second attempt to climb into the net at the bow of the *Little David*. Once again, someone pulled him back down. This time, a loud explosion next to his left ear deafened him. He put his hand to the side of his head, and to his horror, felt blood trickle through his fingers. Falling backward into the shallop, as if in slow motion, his feet struck the shallop sole, then his backside. His head wobbled to one side and his hand fell limp upon the gunwale.

John struggled to remain conscious. He could hear the muffled cries of women and children, the shouting of men, the clashing of swords, the volley of cannons firing overhead. To his amazement, he heard his own voice calling out, "Rebecca! Thomas! Rebecca!"

Then his world turned black and he remembered nothing more.

REBECCA HAD ALREADY dressed herself by the time the pirates attacked. She'd been unable to sleep when John left, and had just pulled on her green cloak, hoping to get some fresh air on the weather deck, when she heard a gunshot across the water.

After a terrible battle, the pirates herded the survivors like cattle and threw them down the companionway into the hold of the ship, the lowest level where the stores of food and trade goods were kept. The *Little David* had been leased to ship wool to the colonies, and to trade for tobacco, corn and salt cod. Now it seemed of little comfort to know they would be spending their days in a place where they would have wool for warmth, at least until the pirates sold it.

"Mother!" Thomas cried as Rebecca gathered him to her. "Where's Father?"

She stroked his dark hair and kissed his head as she clutched him

to her. Rebecca tried to remain brave for Thomas' sake. "He left for the *Warwick* an hour past, Thomas. He's probably safe by now."

"What if the pirates captured him, Mother?" Thomas' dark brown eyes beseeched her, and he clung to her as though his young life depended on it.

Forcing herself to remain calm and confident, she smiled at him. "If they did," she soothed, "they will have found more trouble than they can handle." She would only make matters worse if she lost her composure in front of Thomas now.

The young boy's eyes filled with tears and he wept bitterly as she held him close against her chest.

Now, most of the women were sobbing, while the men wore expressions of horror on their faces as they contemplated the fate awaiting them.

As Rebecca looked around, she saw that Captain Walket was unconscious and his wife, Jane, tended to a wound in his shoulder. Through her tears, Jane begged him. "Stay with me, Henry. Don't leave me now. I've already lost one Henry today."

Miriam had reported that she saw young Henry Walket II, face down in the water before they brought her down to the hold with the others.

Rebecca looked away, but she couldn't find a place where tragedy had not struck. Isabel consoled her sister, Helen Danbury, whose husband, Isaac, had been slain. Elizabeth was cleaning a flesh wound in Matthew Williams' leg, which had been slashed by a sword. Miriam Wilkinson, whose husband, Nathaniel, died in her arms moments after she'd seen young Henry II's body, was drenched with Nathaniel's blood. Miriam seemed to be in a state of shock so deep, Rebecca wondered

if the woman would ever come out of it.

One of the women shrieked and all eyes turned to her, following her pointing finger toward the bow of the hold. Rebecca saw a pool of blood and immediately turned her eyes from the scene. She slid her hand over Thomas' eyes, as well. Ruth and Daniel Atherton had committed suicide by slicing one another's wrists. They lay in each other's arms, apparently preferring death rather than face what their captors would do to them.

As for herself, Rebecca's grief would be the final agony, for she had no idea if her husband had made it to the *Warwick,* or if he had been cut down in attempting to turn back to the *Little David.* She had no doubt he would have tried to rescue them, if he'd been able.

They had quarreled shortly before the *Little David* was taken captive. John would always remember her last words to him: "The Lord God always answers," she had insisted. "Even when He must tell us no." *What must John be thinking about the Lord God now?* Surely this would be one more evidence to him that God paid Master John Dunton no mind. As Rebecca prayed for John and Thomas and for all those in the clutches of these dreadful pirates, she felt comforted, and knew that God was aware of their desperate situation. With a firm determination, she beseeched the Lord to spare John and Thomas, but for her own life, she pleaded not.

Would she spend the rest of her days wondering what happened to John? If he was dead, she would likely never know for certain. And if he was alive, where was he?

The total count of survivors aboard the *Little David* came to twenty-three men, six women and two children. They had lost twenty-seven men, one woman and one child. This was almost half of the crew, lost

to pirates thirty-five leagues beyond Land's End.

Shuddering, Rebecca forced her back to become rigid as she held her son, who was still weeping uncontrollably. She removed her green cloak and wrapped it around the boy's shoulders, then sank onto a barrel and pulled young Thomas onto her lap. "We'll find him, Thomas. Somehow, we'll find your father."

"Where, Mother? Where shall we look for him?"

"Aboard the *Warwick*, of course. That's where he was going, and that is where we must believe that he arrived. We must believe that the bark got away safely, and that John will now look for us, for a way to free us from our captors. And if, by the grace of the Lord God, we are spared, we must do everything within our own power to find him." She stroked Thomas' ebony hair, rocking him back and forth as she cradled him in her arms. "We will search for the bark, *Warwick*, my son, for that is what I did when I left Edward Blackwell. I prayed, and I trusted the Lord God to help me find the right ship and He did. We must be very brave and look for any opportunity to escape. And when we do, we will search until we find your father, just as he will search until he finds us."

Thomas continued to weep until the afternoon shadows filtered down through the companionway above them. By this time, the remaining crew had been forced to man the oars in shifts, for there was no wind with which to sail the *Little David*.

The men had distributed sea biscuits among their dwindling numbers and the women had hidden them in their pockets and petticoats, sewing small folds in their skirts to conceal them, knowing that as soon as the pirates discovered that they had food, it would be taken from them.

At dusk, Miriam stood up and walked toward the hold's companion-way steps. "I can give you great wealth," she called to her captors. "One of our members is worth a fortune back in Chatham. I can help you ransom her for more than you'll ever sell her for as a slave."

Rebecca gasped as all eyes looked toward her.

Jane bolted toward Miriam, leaving Henry for only a moment. She grabbed Miriam by the arm and tried to pull her back down the stairs that led up to the companionway. "Miriam, no! Don't do this! They'll ransom her, surely, but they'll kill you the moment they learn what they need from you. Don't you know not to bargain with the devil?"

Miriam's eyes were glazed, her dress brittle from her husband's dried blood. She pushed Jane away. Then, pounding on the door, she yelled again, "Do you hear me? I can help you make a fortune off Rebecca Webster."

The door opened and a tall, spindly-legged man stepped inside. "Tell me more," he suggested to Miriam.

"Promise my safe return to England and I will tell you."

"Miriam, please!" Jane persisted.

But the man merely pushed Jane away and took Miriam by the arm. "Tell me more," he said again, only this time there was no hint of compliance in his voice.

"Your word of honor, sir," insisted Miriam. "I will be released in England as a free woman."

The man nodded. "I will consider your offer, depending upon how well received this Rebecca is in Chatham."

Miriam pointed to Rebecca. "There, comforting the young boy.

Her name is Rebecca Webster, and she is betrothed to Edward Black-well."

"Son of the merchant, Lord Blackwell?" questioned the man, his dark eyes agleam with greed.

Miriam nodded. "Edward will pay handsomely for her safe return."

Rebecca turned away, refusing to look at the man, but Thomas jumped down from her lap and screamed at Miriam. "She's not either! She's my mother! She's married to my father!"

"The child lies," Miriam told him. "He is a delusional child."

Rebecca cried out, "No, Thomas! Come back!" She tried to grab him, but he was too fast for her.

Thomas ran headlong for Miriam and knocked her off her feet as his head collided with her abdomen. "You can't tell lies about my mother and get away with it!" he yelled. Bravely, he turned his attention to the tall pirate. "Rebecca *is* my mother, sir."

The man merely swatted Thomas away like he was a nasty little insect. Thomas went flying across the floor from the blow. But he wouldn't stop, and Rebecca retrieved him before he could be hit again. "Forgive him, sire. He is just a child," she pleaded.

"Are you the boy's mother?"

"Yes, I am." She held her head proudly, praying that this man would not see the fear she felt inside her.

"He is Edward Blackwell's child?"

"No. He is the son of John Dunton, my husband."

"She's *my* mother!" Thomas yelled, but the man took him from Rebecca's grasp and slapped him again, this time much harder. Thomas

landed in a heap against a barrel of rum, where he slumped into unconsciousness.

"Thomas!" Rebecca screamed, striving to reach him. The man grabbed her by the arm and yanked her away from him. She fought with all her strength, but he hit her across the cheekbone with the heel of his hand so hard she felt her teeth rattle.

"One more attempt to rescue the boy and you'll send him to a watery grave!" the pirate roared at her.

Two other pirates joined him. "Take both women up to the main deck. We will find a way to prove one of their stories."

"No!" Rebecca screamed. "Don't take me from my son! Thomas!"

Then something struck her against the back of her head, and she collapsed, unconscious.

Chapter Nine

Smoke from Blackwell Tower

*"A wise man feareth, and departeth from evil:
but the fool rageth, and is confident."*

Proverbs 14:16

*E*dward Blackwell paced back and forth across the woolen rug
in the library at Blackwell Tower. He had gray-blue eyes the
color of slate, a fine, straight nose and a dark demeanor. Having
been a greedy and spoiled child, he had never learned to harness his
temper. Viciously, he snarled, "A woman like Rebecca cannot vanish
into thin air!" Had he ever taken time to consider his treatment of
others, he would have realized why Rebecca despised him. It wasn't
his fault that her father had contracted prison fever and died before
their wedding vows could be exchanged.

Tall and wispy like his father, Edward considered himself an even
match to Lord Blackwell, though Rebecca had been bold enough to
tell him that he would never match his father's grace or kindness. *Yet
I am kind,* he thought to himself. *That Rebecca is still alive is certainly
proof of that!*

Four days had passed since Rebecca escaped and still no word of her had been found. "I warn you, Drurie, if you do not bribe it out of someone, I will beat it out of you!" he yelled. "Now find her! And don't come back here until you do!"

Walter Drurie, a goliath who looked as though he had been stuffed into a sixteenth century henchman's suit, complete with tight breeches, boots and a short, hooded cloak, pleaded with his master at the library doors. "But sire, we've looked everywhere. No one has seen her. She hasn't even been to her father's tinsmith shop."

"Then search again! Go back to the dockyards! Offer a higher reward! Someone has to know where she is!" Edward roared.

"Really, Edward," said Lord Blackwell, walking past Drurie into the library. "Is all this ranting necessary?"

Edward's demeanor mellowed immediately. "Father, you've no idea the depth of my feelings for Rebecca."

"Perhaps she's gone to stay with her extended family until after her father's funeral."

"Her father's already buried." When Lord Blackwell raised an eyebrow in surprise, Edward explained, "She didn't claim his body and the prison master had no choice."

"She might be in a state of shock, wandering around blindly somewhere. The death of a loved one makes the innocent daft at times. You, of all people, know this is true. Half the province is out looking for her. It can't be much longer before Rebecca is returned to us."

"I'm sure you're right, Father." Edward calmed himself. He had no wish to anger his father at this time. "It's just that I'm out of my mind with worry for her."

"I can see that, yes," agreed Lord Blackwell.

"Do your best, Drurie, to find her. Please," he added, knowing his father would consider that a better gesture.

Drurie nodded. "Yes, sire. I'll go to the docks personally and question everyone. If that fails, I'll take the men through the streets of town and on into London, if need be."

"Thank you," said Edward, controlling his desire to scream at the miserable man . "That's all I ask."

Drurie turned around and left them, his heavy footsteps sounding loudly against the slate floor. When he was gone, Edward sank wearily into a chair and hung his head in his hands.

Yes, he knew the anguish of losing a loved one—his beloved Sarah. For a while he had gone completely mad over her death. When he met Rebecca, it was almost as if the Lord had given Sarah back to him. The two women looked remarkably alike. Why couldn't Rebecca love him as Sarah had? Perhaps he'd pressed Rebecca a bit far the day her father died. But when she'd refused his advances, he had snapped. Something inside him came loose again, and to his horror, he'd found his hand on the whip, blood dripping from the end of it before he'd even realized he'd hurt her. He tried to focus on that day, but his mind wouldn't go there.

If she hadn't spurned him, none of this would have happened. This was all Rebecca's doing, every bit of it.

Why couldn't Rebecca act more like his lovely Sarah? Why?

THOMAS REMOVED A damp cloth from his face and looked up into Jane Walket's eyes.

"There, now," she said. "You're coming around, aren't you?"

He tried to sit up, but his head was still spinning, so he sank back down, hoping the ship's hold would be still. "What happened?" he asked. Then he remembered Rebecca. "Where's my mother?"

Jane shook her head. "They took your mother and Miriam away."

Thomas forced himself to sit upright. "Why did she tell him about Master Blackwell? Why?"

"We certainly hadn't expected that from her. Perhaps losing her husband the way she did drove her into a delirium."

"If I catch up with her," Thomas warned, "I'm going to cut her tongue out."

"Mercy, Thomas! You mustn't say such things!"

"Why not?" he grumbled. "Now my mother is gone. I have no one left."

Jane took his hand in hers. "You must try to remember whatever your mother taught you in the short time that you had her, Thomas, for this will bring her back to you in a way that will comfort you. Can you do that?"

Thomas inhaled deeply, then nodded his head. "She told me that I am resourceful and determined. Mother said these qualities will help me wherever I go."

"That's good, young man. And she said something about how to find your father, too. Didn't she?" Jane asked.

He quoted Rebecca's last few words to him. "I must find a way to escape and search for the bark, *Warwick*, for that is how I will find my father."

"In escaping, Thomas, you must make certain that you will come to no harm. Otherwise, you won't be strong enough to begin your search."

"Yes, madam, I believe what you have said is true." Then, seeing Rebecca's green cloak upon the planked floor, he wrapped himself inside it and inhaled the perfume that he had come to associate with the woman he now called Mother.

REBECCA AWAKENED TO find herself in a prone position upon the captain's bed, where hours earlier she had returned her husband's kisses with all the passion and depth of her soul. Her back was bare because the dress that she wore had been undone. The room was dark, telling her that night had fallen upon the *Little David*.

When she tried to sit up, she felt a stabbing pain in her cheek and she wondered if it was broken. Feeling carefully with her fingers, she was finally able to discern nothing seriously damaged, just some swelling and tenderness. This relieved her mind, but did nothing to assuage the pain.

"So," came a man's familiar voice from the darkness somewhere within the cabin. "Rebecca Webster has lashings on her back. You will tell me why."

"I have no obligation to tell you anything," she hissed. "Now go away."

She heard, rather than saw, his footsteps come quickly toward her. Suddenly her hair was yanked backward, forcing her onto her back. An angry, dark face glared into hers.

"You may have had options before I came aboard," he cautioned.

"But now, you belong to me."

Glaring back, Rebecca refused to give him any other response.

"You will soon learn to answer me when I ask a question." Then in a foreign tongue that she could not understand, he gave orders to two other men in the room.

Her eyes adjusted to the darkness, and she saw the men easily as they came forward and tied both her arms and her legs to each of the four bed posts. When they were satisfied that she could not escape, they left the room, closing the door behind them.

"Your traitor was most helpful, Rebecca Webster. She considered you a fool for running away from a man as wealthy as Edward Blackwell. Had it been her, she said, she would have killed to be in your shoes."

"I am a married woman," Rebecca insisted. "My son is Thomas Dunton. His father is John."

Ignoring her completely, the man said, "And I am your deliverer. If what I have heard is true, you will bring a healthy price, perhaps more than we will make off the rest of the crew and women put together."

"I am a married woman—" she began again.

He slapped her across her already sore cheek.

"And I am Aligolant, your captor. I am thinking that you ran away from Lord Blackwell because he whipped you. He wanted something from you that you would not give. Perhaps you are still a virgin and this has tempted him. He wants you, but he wants you willing. Yes, I see by the surprise in your eyes that I am close to the heart of your problem."

Rebecca closed her eyes, refusing to allow him to look upon them again.

"Ordinarily," he continued, his voice rasping with anger, "I have first choice over the women we capture. When I have satisfied myself with them, I sell them to the men at Salé. English women bring the highest price because they are amenable to a man's wishes. I have seen them go for a thousand ducats. But you, Rebecca Webster, will cost far more than that."

Rebecca bit her bottom lip to prevent it from quivering.

"Yes, you have reason to fear if it is Edward Blackwell who has whipped you before, because I will return you to your betrothed in exchange for a handsome reward. I will even forgo taking you to myself. Perhaps this will bring a better price from him."

He laughed, and Rebecca heard such evil in the hollow sound that she shuddered. When the brush of his footsteps led toward the door, she prayed that the Lord would bless her husband and her son and protect them from these pirates, and herself from Edward Blackwell.

After the door opened and closed, Rebecca waited a few moments before opening her eyes again. When she did, she was relieved to find that the horrible Aligolant had left her alone.

Trying to sit up a little bit and look around, Rebecca found that the most she could move at all was to roll onto her left or her right. The tight lashings at her wrists and ankles impeded any other progress. As her eyes adjusted more each moment to the darkness in the room, she began making out objects. The writing desk in one corner. A wardrobe in another. A rug on the floor to her right. On the left she saw a—

Merciful Father, who is that? she prayed as she stared in horror at a woman's body covered in blood and lying upon the cabin floor.

Miriam Wilkinson was dead in spite of what she had told the man called Aligolant.

Rebecca closed her eyes again . . . and wept.

EDWARD BLACKWELL SMILED to himself as he turned a gold and emerald broach over in his hand, amused by the way the bauble caught and reflected the light from the early morning sun as it filtered through the bed chamber window. "And you say this was found in the same shallop that was turned loose the night Rebecca left us?"

Drurie nodded. "I verified all the facts for myself, sire, trusting the matter to no one else. The same shallop was found floating out in the bay the next morning. The owner assumed that we had set it loose. But my men assured me they did no such thing. I searched the shallop myself, and under a loose floor board, I found the broach."

"Then she stowed away on either the *Warwick* or the *Little David*. She's four days ahead of us. If we leave today, which ship is capable of reaching her the fastest?" Edward's eyes narrowed as he contemplated what he was about to do.

"Only a caravel, sire. Perhaps the *Neptune*, but she's not quite ready to sail."

"Make her ready by sundown and put ten dozen men aboard, with four weeks' rations for them. We will travel light, under oar and sail, until we catch up with Rebecca and return her to Chatham."

"Yes, sire. I shall do my best," said Drurie glumly.

Edward wrapped his fingers around the henchman's throat. "Your best is not good enough! You will do as I say or you will suffer my wrath!"

Drurie gagged and sputtered until Edward released him. When he could finally breathe again, he said, "I won't fail you, sire." He turned and rushed from Edward's private chambers.

After he left, Edward removed his robes and put on his day clothes, then hurried to the breakfast table to greet his father. "We've found Rebecca," he announced. "I'm taking the *Neptune* to rescue her."

"Where is she?" Lord Blackwell asked.

"Her broach was found aboard a shallop that had been let loose the night she disappeared." Edward gave the broach to his father.

"Don't tell me she was abducted by pirates? They surely aren't so brazen as to come into our cities after our women?"

"Apparently so," Edward lied. "But we shall go after her at once."

"Is the *Neptune* ready to sail again?"

"Drurie is seeing to that as we speak."

Lord Blackwell stood and embraced his son. "I shall pray for a speedy rescue."

Chapter Ten

Awakenings

". . . I perceive that this voyage will be with hurt and much damage,
not only of the lading and ship, but also of our lives."
Acts 27:10

By the time John regained consciousness, the *Warwick* was headed south and had been under sail for several days.

"Don't sit up too quickly," warned Elias Fox, who seemed far more gaunt and weathered than before the pirates attacked them. His face had deep creases in it, reminding John of an unshelled walnut. "Your head's still mending."

"What happened?" John asked. "Where's my wife? Where's Thomas and Rebecca?"

"They were taken with the *Little David*. We followed them for one full day, then we headed south and they continued eastward. We haven't seen them since early yesterday morning." Elias explained.

"Whose at the helm, then?"

"They are."

"And what of Captain Dawson and the men?"

"They put up a valiant fight, John. You'd have been proud of them."

"Tell me the numbers, Elias."

"Captain was the third man to go. The first two were the men in the crow's nest. Someone came aboard early on and slit their throats. By the time the rest got here, we didn't stand a chance. If you hadn't made such a ruckus, we may have all been killed."

"The numbers, Elias," John insisted.

"Peter was injured, but I think he'll mend. We lost thirty-nine men, sir."

"Thirty nine!" John exploded. "That only leaves sixteen. We won't be able to retake the ship with sixteen men."

"Especially since Robert Boyer and myself are the only two who weren't injured. Most of the men are nursing sword and gunshot wounds and many have developed sepsis."

"What of Simon?" John turned his eyes away so that Elias would not see his reaction when he heard the news.

"A lacerated cheek that he stitched up by watching himself in the looking-glass. Otherwise, he's made his time useful tending to all the rest."

"Dastardly business, this," said John woefully. "I will take full responsibility."

"These men are from North Africa, Master Dunton. They apparently broke away from Turkish rule and are setting themselves up as an independent state, relying upon plunder for their income."

"Algeria?" questioned John.

"Morocco. I heard one of them mention going to Salé to sell us as slaves."

"We'd have all been better off dead," John moaned, thinking of his wife and son, "than to be sold into slavery."

"What of young Thomas?" came a gravelly voice behind him.

John turned to face his son's grandfather. "I didn't make it back to them in time," he said. "I was shot before I could rescue them."

Simon nodded. "I suspected as much. Fortunately, you've a head as hard as cobblestone. The bullet glanced off and only left a small slice above your left ear. I sewed it up while you were unconscious. How does it feel?"

"Better than my heart," John admitted, not caring who saw him in this state of melancholy. "My wife and son are captive, headed toward a place where only God can find them. Most of my men are dead. The captain. . . ."

Remembering the terrible struggle he faced at the shallop, John recalled with vivid clarity the man whose neck he had broken as easily as if it was made of fine porcelain. "And I have killed a man in self defense," he confessed bitterly, "though I do not feel ashamed of it. I have found my price and it matches the value of my wife and my son."

A WEEK LATER, Rebecca opened her eyes to find Jane Walket preparing a sponge bath for her.

"Jane?" Rebecca questioned. "How is it that you have been permitted to visit me?"

Rebecca was still confined to her lashings throughout the night,

but free to roam the confines of the captain's quarters by day. She had been let out of her forecastle prison once, when they forced her to help them throw Miriam's body overboard.

"They told me to bathe and dress you in clean clothing, for you will be presented to Edward Blackwell today."

"I knew we were at anchor," Rebecca sighed, "but I had no idea that we were in Chatham."

"We're not. We're at Portsmouth in Hampshire."

"Then they're flying the flag of England," Rebecca said, finally understanding why they had not been boarded or commandeered.

Jane nodded. "Master Blackwell is to meet the pirates two miles north of Portsmouth on the road to London by sunset. He was told to come alone with the ransom."

"The *Little David* must be far enough away from land on either side to make a hasty retreat, should Edward surprise Aligolant," Rebecca pondered aloud.

"That's correct," Jane agreed. "We are almost directly between Portsmouth and the Isle of Wight."

Jane placed a basin of water upon the bed and rinsed a cloth in it.

Rebecca said, "You don't have to do this, Jane."

"I must, Rebecca, or they will kill me the same as they did Miriam."

"They will likely kill us all no matter what we do."

"Then I will pray they will be more merciful with us than they were with Miriam. We heard her screams for several hours before she died."

"Why did she do it?" Rebecca asked. "Why did Miriam betray me?"

"Henry says she must have had a death wish," Jane admitted. "Just

as Ruth and Dan took their own lives, he thinks Miriam knew they would kill her once they had the information she could give them. Now, I agree with him. I think that's why she tried to bargain with them."

"At my expense?"

"You must forgive her, Rebecca. She wasn't responsible in her betrayal, for she was dazed at the loss of her husband, and she paid the ultimate price for her error."

"It gives little comfort. I would rather throw myself overboard than face Edward Blackwell again."

"Why?"

It was such a simple question, yet it had many complex answers. Finally, Rebecca chose the only response that would lend itself to understanding. "Let down my chemise and look at my back. Perhaps that will explain everything."

Jane gave her a curious look, but did as she was told. When she saw the ugly scars on Rebecca's back, she nearly gagged. "Edward did this to you?" she asked, as though she couldn't believe what her eyes clearly told her.

"He is not the man he pretends to be."

"This is why you ran away and refused to marry him?"

"No. I would have taken a whipping from him every day for the rest of my life in order to save my father from Edward's wrath, but when he killed my father, he no longer had a bargaining tool."

"He murdered your father?" Jane repeated.

Nodding, Rebecca said, "I suspect that he murdered his first fiancée, as well. I was not about to stay and find out if I was next on his list."

"Then you mustn't go back to him. What can I do to protect you?"

"You must do nothing, Jane. For if you defy them, they will do to you as they did to Miriam. Now bathe me and let me be."

It wasn't an easy task that Jane had been assigned. Some areas on Rebecca's back were still quite painful, but Rebecca did her best not to complain. When Jane tried to put Rebecca's clothing on her, it was impossible; Rebecca's hands and feet were still tied fast to the four bedposts. There was nothing either of them could do, so Jane finally asked Aligolant to release Rebecca.

Aligolant sauntered menacingly into the room, pulled a knife from its sheath, then cut the lashings from her wrists and ankles. "Make no attempt to escape, either of you, for you will be executed."

"You think death scares me?" Rebecca questioned him with a boldness that only she could muster.

"Obviously not, but there is another way to make you comply. It is called pain. I'm sure I can think of something that would be more painful to you than lashing your backside."

"I will throw myself from the tallest spire at Blackwell Tower the moment I find an opportune time."

"What is that to me? I will have the gold and you will no longer be a problem."

"How much will you take from Lord Blackwell?" Rebecca questioned.

"Enough that each farthing will be taken out of your hide. Edward will surely curse you for making him a poor man."

"Then you are a bigger fool than I previously thought." She laughed at him, but stopped short when he lifted his hand to strike her.

"Do you know something that I do not?" he glowered at her as though considering her a shark's appetizer.

"If you think Lord Blackwell will hand over any of his precious gold without a fight, you are sorely mistaken."

"Which is why I will not be going with you. Should Lord Blackwell have other plans to rescue you while retaining his wealth, I will have a counter attack waiting for him."

"That's what I thought," she laughed. "Then I shall never have to feel Edward's lash upon my back again, for I perceive that you plan to have us both killed."

Aligolant did not answer. He merely shrugged and walked out of the cabin.

"Rebecca!" scolded Jane. "Less defiance may have persuaded him to be lenient."

"I don't want him to soften," Rebecca explained. "I told you, I would rather die here than go back to Edward Blackwell."

"But what about your husband? And young Thomas? Are they not worth fighting for? Would you lay down your life now, only to learn that you might have been reunited had you lived?"

Her words brought a painful aching in Rebecca's heart. "You are right," she conceded. "I must try to endure, regardless of the hardship that awaits me, if only for the hope of holding my son or my husband, once again."

WHEN THE NEPTUNE passed through the English Channel, the *Little David* was already behind the Isle of Wight near Portsmouth, though

Edward Blackwell did not know it.

Driving the crew unmercifully, Edward kept the men at the oars day and night in four-hour rotations, and the sails full up when the wind was favorable. However, they were still lucky to make six nautical miles per hour. At the speed they were going, the *Warwick* and *Little David* would make it all the way to America before they caught up with Rebecca.

Edward had no one to blame but himself. The demands he'd placed upon his crew to prepare the *Neptune* had not given them ample time to complete the removal of the barnacles that encrusted the hull, which now impeded their progress by several knots.

Pacing back and forth across the aftercastle, Edward Blackwell continued to use the spyglass, but he could see nothing on the Atlantic horizon to encourage him. Weary of the trouble Rebecca Webster caused him, he wondered if he would still desire her once he saw her again, or if he would merely wring her lovely neck until she joined her father. No, killing her would be too easy. She would agree to become his beloved Sarah, or she would suffer a fate worse than death. Going down below the poop deck to the aftercastle, he stepped into the Captain's quarters and stretched out on the bed, where he slept peacefully for the first time in several restless nights.

HOW LONG THOMAS had been locked in the *Little David's* hold with the other passengers and crew, he didn't know. It was impossible to tell day from night and the prisoners were only afforded a single candle. They had been put on scant rations, one measure of dried peas and two pieces of hardtack per person per day.

Jane Walket had befriended him and treated him as though he were her own son, Henry II, who had been killed when the ship was captured. It was Jane who told him earlier in the morning that his mother, Rebecca, had been taken aboard the shallop to Portsmouth wharf, where she would be transported by carriage to a predetermined meeting place and ransomed for two hundred gold bricks, enough to exchange for a hundred-thousand ducats. The thought terrified him. Thomas knew that Edward Blackwell would beat his mother again, and he was powerless to stop him. If Rebecca didn't please Master Blackwell, would he then imprison her, as he did her father? Would she die before Thomas could ever see her again? Thomas shivered, and pulled his mother's green cloak tighter around him.

In addition to his concern for Rebecca, Thomas still did not know what had become of his father. No one knew whether or not he'd made it back to the *Warwick*. His heart felt heavy inside his chest and he wished his mother were here again, holding and comforting him, telling him that Father would be all right, that he would come looking for Thomas, and he would find him.

Thomas gleaned some information in whispered snippets when the adults thought he was asleep or not listening to them. There had been talk that they would be sold as slaves once they reached Salé in Morocco. Thomas had never been to Morocco. The name conjured up many images in his mind. He knew that it was south of Spain, which was south of France, which was south of England. He'd looked on his father's globe many times, and if he recalled correctly, Morocco was much nearer the equator, which meant it would be warm most of the time. As he remembered, his father had once told him that Morocco could be accessed from both the Atlantic Ocean and the Mediterranean Sea through the Strait of Gibraltar.

Since Thomas knew a little bit about where he was going, he pondered long and hard on why. The mere thought of being sold as a slave terrified him. What was a slave required to do? What could Thomas do to make certain that he would survive this ordeal,? Could he eventually escape and set out to find the *Warwick* and his father? He would have to prove to whoever bought him that he was resourceful and dedicated to serving them before he would ever be trusted out of his chains.

During the years that Thomas spent with his grandfather, Simon had read to him from the Bible. One of the stories Thomas loved was about Joseph and the coat of many colors. When Joseph was sold by his brothers as a slave, he was taken to Egypt where he worked for a man named Potiphar. Because Joseph was willing to serve his masters faithfully, he was eventually instrumental in saving his entire family, even those brothers who had sold him.

Considering carefully, Thomas made up his mind that he would be like Joseph, as helpful and resourceful as possible. He hoped to win the favor of his master, whoever he might be. If he did that, he might survive what lay in store for him long enough to find an opportunity to escape.

Chapter Eleven

Ransomed

> *"For those that bear their burdens well . . . are*
> *not out of hope . . . ."*
> Thomas More, 1516, from *Utopia*

Rebecca removed the blindfold and opened her eyes. She was standing on a road by herself somewhere north of Portsmouth and south of London. The carriage that brought her had been loaded with gold, and drove off, leaving her behind. To her utter amazement, she was still alive, and now she saw Lord Blackwell, Edward's father, walking quickly toward her.

Taking steps of her own, she hastened to greet him.

Lord Blackwell spoke before she could. "Quickly, my dear. We must get you away from here at the fastest possible speed."

His tone frightened her and she suspected that he knew they were very likely surrounded by pirates.

She took his offered hand and ran with a swiftness that surprised her. They reached Lord Blackwell's carriage and he helped her inside where she found two other men with pistols, as well as a hefty supply

of firearms and ammunition resting on the seat between them.

Lord Blackwell followed her, closing the door before he'd even turned to sit down. "Now, Mister O'Ryan!" he shouted.

The carriage lurched forward, throwing her benefactor onto the bench beside her faster than he'd anticipated. Within a few seconds, the four horses were racing down the darkening roadway at a faster pace than Rebecca had ever traveled in her life. The fact that there had been four horses attached to the carriage had been a certain sign that his Lordship had something other than acquiescence in mind. This thought both relieved and frightened her.

Suddenly, she heard men shouting and guns firing. The two men leaned out the side windows nearest them with their pistols raised. Returning fire this close to her caused pain and momentary, echoing explosions in Rebecca's ears. Lord Blackwell took her by the back of the neck and pressed her to the floor, putting her out of harm's way. Then he drew his own weapon and fired upon the encroachers with expert marksmanship, jolting one of the horsemen off his steed.

A few more minutes passed, and Rebecca could no longer hear anyone returning fire at them. She lifted her head from her position on the floor and looked up at Lord Blackwell.

He gave her a hopeless smile, then slumped over in a dead faint. Blood oozed from his right shoulder.

"Keep this carriage going and don't stop for anyone," Rebecca told the two men inside the carriage with her.

They nodded in agreement. One climbed out of the carriage and up onto the buckboard where he kept his pistol ready. The other man sat in the center of the bench facing her, a pistol in each hand, prepared to take anyone out from either side of the carriage.

Although the bucking and bumping impeded her ability to help, Rebecca still managed to remove the apron from her dress. She wound it up into a thick length of fabric. Unbuttoning Lord Blackwell's doublet and shirt, she took the apron and pressed it against his wound to stop his bleeding.

When they had traveled a good five miles or more, Rebecca told the driver that he could slow down to a more normal speed, which he managed to do without any problem. She doubted any of Ali's men had followed them this far.

Biting her lower lip, she looked over at the man in front of her, when he suddenly opened his eyes and looked at her curiously. "Where is Edward?" she asked. "Was he afraid to come after me?"

"No, my dear," whispered his Lordship, regaining consciousness.

Rebecca turned back to him. "You're going to be all right, Lord Blackwell. It's just a flesh wound."

His eyes rolled a moment, as though he struggled to remain conscious. "Edward went off in the *Neptune* to search for you," Lord Blackwell told her. "When he learned you'd been abducted by pirates, I dared not restrain him from trying to rescue you."

"How did he know about the pirates?" she asked.

"He found your broach in one of the shallops at Chatham Bay. It was a simple matter to deduce that you'd been abducted. And right in our own bay, no less. You must have been terrified."

"I was," she replied. "Thank you for paying the ransom for me, Lord Blackwell. I shall be forever in your debt."

"I didn't pay them so much as a farthing," he admitted, sitting up a little straighter now.

"But I saw the gold. And I heard the pirates exclaim that it was real gold bars that you gave them."

"Yes, it was. However, I arrived much earlier in the day with eighty of his Majesty's royal guards, at the insistence of Lord Vaine, of his Majesty's High Court of Admiralty. They surrounded the area for nearly a mile in all directions. When your paltry abductors approached, they were gated in as effectively as rounding up a few stray sheep. By morning, they will be hanging from the gallows at Portsmouth wharf."

"But some of them are English," she protested. "The pirates forced three of the captives to attend me. If we were stopped by anyone, they would know how to speak to them and put their concerns at rest."

"A man cannot be forced beyond his will, Rebecca. If they assisted in this dastardly affair, they will swing just as easily as the others."

"Lord Blackwell, I implore you. Do not do this thing. Those men have wives who are still held captive, who will be killed when they do not return."

His Lordship's pale blue eyes glistened. "I will send one of my men back with your message. The Englishmen will be spared, even if it is only to allow them to die at the hand of pirates, so that their wives will know what has become of them."

"Sire, they have the *Little David* at anchor at the mouth of Portsmouth, this side of the Isle of Wight. If his majesty would permit an armada to go after them, perhaps they could recover the ship and captives."

She could tell by his pallor that this news shocked him.

"The *Little David*? Are you certain?"

"Yes, your Lordship. They may have the bark *Warwick*, as well."

"This is far more serious than I had anticipated. We must stop in Winchester and warn the Earl of Portland."

"Thank you, Lord Blackwell," she sighed in relief. "May God bless you for your concern."

Satisfied that for now she was safe, Rebecca sank into weariness. She gazed out the window as night blotted out the vast forest through which the carriage traveled. With only a lantern to light their way, the carriage moved steadily toward Winchester. Her ability to remain alert waned, and she fell into a deep, exhausted sleep.

Rebecca awakened with a start. The carriage had stopped moving and it was daybreak. She was the only person left in the carriage. For a moment she wondered where Lord Blackwell had gone, but her two body guards were still on duty, standing outside the carriage doors, one on each side. Behind them, stood the four-hundred year old Winchester Castle, erected in the thirteenth century. While reported to have the finest and perhaps the longest receiving hall in the country, the exterior gave her the feeling of permanence and grandeur. The circular tower stood where the castle walls join those of Winchester city. The smooth facing stone was built in such a way as to make the tower impervious to assault. At the same time, the gardens caught Rebecca's attention. She had never seen so many beautiful roses and hedges as found upon the castle grounds. Inhaling their sweet fragrance, even from within the carriage, Rebecca longed to walk among them, though she thought the guards would not permit her to do so.

Winchester Castle was where the royals held court and passed judgement upon criminals. For a moment, she wondered if Edward Blackwell would ever be punished for his crimes against her father and herself. Then she shook her head. It was highly unlikely that Edward Blackwell would ever feel the sting of the lash.

Rebecca would be safe until Edward returned to Blackwell Tower, but she'd better have an escape plan formulated before he did, because she never wanted to see his face again.

WHEN LORD BLACKWELL returned, he gave Rebecca an uncertain smile. "Did you rest well?" he asked, as he opened the door to the carriage.

"Yes, thank you."

"Would you care to stretch your legs and freshen up a bit?" He offered her his hand.

"Please," she implored, taking it and stepping down from the carriage. "I haven't had a real bath in over two weeks."

"The Earl of Portland has instructed the chamber maids to attend to your every need, including dressing you in something more fitting. After you are refreshed, he has invited us to dine with him."

"I would be delighted. And how is your shoulder, Lord Blackwell?"

His Lordship moved it freely as he led her toward the castle's oversized doors. "The doctor took the liberty of dressing it while you were asleep. It is feeling much better." The doors to the massive castle opened as guards allowed them safe entry. Lord Blackwell escorted Rebecca indoors, his left arm held out to accompany her.

Rebecca found the interior of Winchester Castle quite stunning. Through the main doors they entered an enormous hall with slender, marble columns and an open-beam roof. Hanging on the west wall was a huge round table top with cream and green colored striping similar to the spokes of a wagon wheel. Rebecca had heard that the table was considered to be the Round Table of King Arthur's fame.

Doors leading to various other rooms were closed as they passed by, and Rebecca could hardly contain her curiosity at what she might find behind them.

After a short walk, about halfway down the great hall, she was met by an entourage of young women who had, apparently, been sent to wait upon Rebecca. While his Lordship went with two man-servants, Rebecca was escorted to a luxurious bedroom which had a wonderful wooden bathing tub, filled with hot soapy water in which she bathed. The chambermaids washed her long, golden hair thoroughly and rinsed it with plenty of fresh water until it was squeaky clean. When Rebecca bent forward for them to rinse the back of her hair more easily, one of the chambermaids gasped, then slipped out of the room, returning moments later with a woman dressed in golden silks and purple velvets.

"Good day, Mistress Webster. My name is Penelope Giles. I am the wife of Francis Giles, the Earl of Portland." Penelope's red hair was piled high upon her head to accommodate a jeweled tiara.

Rebecca sank back into the bubbles, feeling a bit awkward to meet a woman of royalty while naked and vulnerable. "Good day," she whispered, paling visibly.

"I don't mean to alarm you by my presence, but may I call you Rebecca?"

"You may."

"And you must call me Penelope, dear."

"Thank you, I would like that.

"One of my chambermaids reported that you have been whipped and some of your wounds are still oozing."

Rebecca cringed. "Yes."

"May I look? I will need to decide if the doctor should be summoned."

Pulling her long hair up to the top of her head, Rebecca leaned forward so that her back would be clearly visible.

Penelope gasped. "Good gracious, child. Those pirates are barbarians!"

"They are," Rebecca agreed, "but they did not whip me."

"Then who did? I shall have him arrested at once."

"He is out of the country at the moment."

"Then tell me his name, and I will post a bulletin to all the cities in England. The moment he returns, he shall be punished."

Rebecca lowered her head, wondering how she could ever accuse Edward without alerting Lord Blackwell to the problem.

"Tell me his name," demanded Penelope.

Realizing she would have to be forthcoming with the Earl's wife, she said, "May I whisper, madam?"

Penelope leaned forward and placed her ear next to Rebecca's mouth. "I fear, my Lady, that his father does not know. It is the son, Edward Blackwell, who has dealt with me in this manner."

Gasping, Penelope straightened. Her eyes widened in alarm and she said to the chamber maids, "Leave us."

When all the other women had left the room, Penelope wrapped a towel around Rebecca and helped her out of the tub. "My dear," she said, "the man should receive as many lashings as you have. I will bring my doctor in to treat you and to count them. That man shall have just punishment measured out to him, if I have anything to say about it."

"I don't know how to tell Lord Blackwell, my Lady. He worships Edward."

"That he does." Penelope inhaled sharply, as though trying to clear her mind from other clutter and concentrate on the task at hand. "I will take the matter up with the Earl. He will know how to proceed."

"Edward has committed a crime far worse than beating me, my Lady."

"What is it?"

"He took my father's life."

"Do you speak of murder?" asked Penelope, as though the very thought of *murder* frightened her. She paled visibly.

"Not in the strictest sense of the word, my Lady, but he is responsible for my father's death."

"Sit," instructed Penelope. "You must tell me everything, absolutely everything. Leave nothing unsaid."

Rebecca felt a comforting sense of retribution as she shared the past few months with Penelope, and she found a trustworthy confidante in the process. By the time she had finished telling her sad tale, the two women were both in tears and consoling one another as though they had always been the best of friends.

When Rebecca told Penelope about her marriage to John Dunton, the woman raised an eyebrow.

"Was your marriage consummated?" Penelope asked.

Nodding, Rebecca blushed.

"Have you any affection for this John Dunton?"

Again, Rebecca nodded. "Though John was plain to point out that

he had no natural affection for me." Admitting this fact aloud only added to the heaviness in her heart.

"As long as they are bedded often, husbands are usually content. I'm afraid that affection doesn't enter into many marriages these days. Most of our women are betrothed at an early age. Perhaps, in time, his feelings for you will grow."

"I carry that hope in my prayers every day," Rebecca confessed. "Even though I may never see my husband, or my son, ever again."

"My dear, you must not despair. Something must be done about these horrible pirates. I have heard the earl speak of an armada. Admiral Rainsborough has been pleading that a fleet be sent to Salé to rescue his Majesty's subjects, but no one seems able to come up with a battle plan. With the *Warwick* and the *Little David* both taken, perhaps there will be greater incentive for the King to do so."

"I shall ever pray for that, my Lady."

LATER, REBECCA JOINED Penelope, the Earl of Portland and Lord Blackwell for their noon meal. They were served a fruit compote made with apple slices and fresh strawberries, a bowl of rich carrot soup, fresh bread and basted chicken with vegetables. She had never seen so much food, nor tasted any so elegantly prepared.

When all had finished eating, they took their wine glasses and retired to a room the earl called the study. It seemed more like a massive library to Rebecca, with comfortable reading chairs near the windows and a round table with the most beautiful display of fresh flowers Rebecca had ever seen.

As they sat down, Penelope asked her husband, "What will be done regarding the *Little David?*"

The earl nodded his permission for her to have asked the question. "My men will report back to me as soon as they discern which of the Englishmen have been spared."

"I pray they will be able to recapture the ship," said Rebecca, hoping she wasn't speaking out of turn. "Thomas is aboard, as are women and other children."

"That is most unfortunate, my dear." The earl looked at her with soulful eyes. "I have two ships at Portsmouth capable of giving the *Little David* a fair chase, but there is no guarantee the *David* will still be at anchor by the time my ships' captains are alerted. If that is the case, I will take this matter to the king. He has mentioned his desire to send an entire fleet down to Salé, but without someone who knows the area to guide them, an attack would be useless and costly in terms of helping those unfortunate souls who have been taken captive."

"I see," said Rebecca, despairing that she had not been able to send help to her son still aboard the *Little David*. Her greatest heartache was in knowing that she had no speedy rescuer for Thomas. She prayed that he would be resourceful and find some way to stay alive until help could arrive.

Shortly before bidding them farewell, Penelope took Rebecca aside. "The earl will look into the matter of Edward Blackwell privately, so as not to embarrass Lord Blackwell. When he has enough evidence gathered against him, he will bring Lord Blackwell into the circle. His Lordship will have to stand aside and let justice prevail regarding his son. In the meantime, go with him back to Blackwell Tower so that his suspicion is not aroused. Tell no one that we have spoken. The earl

is a man of his word. He will deal fairly with you, Rebecca."

"What shall I do if Edward returns before your investigation is completed?" asked Rebecca fearfully.

"I will post a man and carriage at the docks in Chatham. The moment the *Neptune* is seen approaching, he will go straight to Blackwell Tower and bring you safely to me, before the ship can drop anchor, and the men disembark."

Putting her arms around Penelope, Rebecca gave her a generous hug. "I shall never forget you, Penelope. You have shown me true kindness. How can I ever repay you?"

"See that you write to me," Penelope told her with a smile. "Keep me apprised of any new developments."

"I will," Rebecca promised.

They went outdoors together and embraced one last time before Rebecca stepped up into the carriage. Within a few moments she was off again, bouncing her way along a journey that would take her back to Blackwell Tower, a splendid manor atop a hill near Chatham.

It was not home where Rebecca would live. Her real home was with John and Thomas, wherever they were.

Her father, while she lived with him, had a tinsmith's shop with a small apartment upstairs. This had all been taken away when her father was imprisoned.

Rebecca's husband and her son were gone, and where they were she did not know. With nowhere to go, and Edward's return imminent, Rebecca knew that she could not stay at Blackwell Tower for long.

Chapter Twelve

Retribution

". . . vengeance is mine; I will repay,
saith the Lord. . . ."
Romans 12:19

The gentle rocking of the *Neptune* under full sail, accompanied by the moist salt air cleansing his lungs and helping him breathe more deeply, lulled Edward into a dream-filled sleep.

Sarah. Always, Sarah Jenkins floated through his dreams. She was the most beautiful woman he'd ever met and the only woman who ever really loved him, other than his own mother. Edward could see her love radiating through her beautiful jade-green eyes as she looked on him. *Why, Edward?* she always asked. *Why must you torture yourself and others so? Know you not that I will always be yours? Death cannot separate us for long, dear Edward.* Then, the dream twisted into a freakish nightmare. He could see the carriage coming, but he couldn't stop it, regardless of his heroic efforts. And then the whip was in his hand and he was swinging it back and forth, back and forth, against the driver's back. But this time he also heard some sort of knocking, insistent knocking, disturbing him, forcing him to look down at his own hands

and see the whip one last time before he awakened.

"Yes!" he barked. "Who is it?" Glancing out the cabin window, he noticed the moon in the western night sky and judged the time around three of the morning.

"Captain Hammond," came the response.

"Enter," said Edward, sitting up and running a hand through his dark hair.

The captain pushed the door open and stepped inside. He was dressed in his military doublet and white breeches and leggings, with black knee-high boots polished vigorously. He carried a lantern in his hand.

"Is it my turn on watch already?" Edward complained at once.

"My man, Johnston, is taking this watch, sir. I came to tell you that we've passed the channel by twenty leagues. It's best if we turn back now."

"Why?" Edward moaned, standing up and wrapping a robe about him.

Captain Hammond fidgeted with a gold button on his doublet. "We didn't bring enough supplies to last a full crossing, sir. Four weeks' rations is all we had time to gather."

"We can make it in another three weeks, Captain. Have no fear."

"Sorry to disagree with you, sir, but we certainly cannot. If the wind holds steady the entire way, we will be lucky to make the Americas in six weeks time, but a normal crossing lasts eight or more."

"We should have three weeks' rations left. If we go another week and do not find her, we'll turn back then."

"There is one other problem," suggested the captain, his dark eyes daring Edward to contradict him on this point.

"What is it, man? Out with it!"

"There is the matter of pirates, sir. We are a lone ship, with no means to defend ourselves save four cannons per side, yet we brought little ordnance for them. If we are sighted by pirates, we might as well slit our own throats as let them take us captive."

"With motivation, the men can out-distance any vessel by rowing more vigorously, particularly if we hit flat weather at thirty to forty leagues, as sometimes occurs."

Obviously displeased with Edward's challenge, Captain Hammond frowned ominously. With great stubbornness he said, "Then let it go on record that I am firmly opposed to continuing this voyage any longer on the evidence of a single broach, sir. Mistress Rebecca could have been plundered and her broach stolen from her. She could have drowned for all we know. The men are beginning to complain that we are going to extraordinary effort for the love of one woman."

"So noted, Captain Hammond." Edward walked over to the window and put his hand upon the sill. He didn't want to beleaguer the captain, but he did want the man to know exactly who was in charge of this voyage. After a moment, he turned back and glared at his opponent. Tartly, he said, "Let the record also show that the captain not only opposed the master of the ship, he opposed the benefactor as well."

Captain Hammond nodded, then stepped quietly from the room in such a manner that Edward was reminded of a penitent dog with tail between his legs.

After the captain left, Edward picked up a goblet and poured a healthy portion of wine. When he had finished drinking it, he threw

the glass against the cabin door, where it shattered and fell to the floor.

TOWARD THE END of the *Neptune's* second week out from Chatham, a man shouted from the crow's nest. "Pirate ship off the port bow!"

Edward sprang to the nets and climbed up, then wrestled his spyglass from his doublet and peered through it. To his horror he saw the colors of the Algerian flag flying high atop the forward mast of a four-masted Man-of-War, nearly three times the size of the *Neptune*. She was sleek in the water and advancing on them at an alarming speed. The sails had been reconfigured so that they hung in four massive triangles, which would give the pirate's ship more speed and maneuverability than the *Neptune*.

"Come about!" Edward barked. "All hands on deck! Man the sails! Raise the topsails! Prepare to engage! Cannons at the ready!"

With each command he gave, it was passed along by the men until the ones who were assigned to that duty sprang into action. When he was satisfied that his orders were being followed in a fastidious manner, Edward again looked through the spyglass. The Man-of-War was advancing like a huge serpent about to devour its prey. There would be blood shed in the skirmish today, but he had the determination to see it through. After all, he was Edward Blackwell, the Third. More men than a few had cowered at hearing his name. Confidence bolstered his assessment of their situation.

As it came about, the *Neptune* slipped through the water with the grace of a sleek dolphin, but it was still much slower than its opponent. Edward could only fault himself for not waiting a few more days for the workers to finish cleaning the barnacles off the hull. His reasoning

in understocking the vessel was easily understood. He wanted to make as much speed as possible in order to reach Rebecca before she slipped out of his control altogether. By insisting they continue their course another week, a lone sailing vessel in a pirate's realm, he had delivered his crew, his ship and himself into the hands of the enemy. The only way he could spare their lives would be to surrender, for if they turned and fought against the pirates, they would all perish.

However, he knew his crewmen would fight for their liberty and their families before they would be taken by a pirate. The horror stories that circulated the dockyards made every sailor's heart prefer death to enslavement.

One more look through the spyglass told him that these pirates would overtake them in less than an hour. With heavy heart, Edward climbed down the net and walked back to the aftercastle deck.

"What say you?" asked Captain Hammond.

"One hour, maybe less. Shall we surrender to them, sir?"

"Over my dead body," roared the captain. "They will not take one of his Majesty's ships without a fight. You brought us to this, Master Blackwell. And the entire lot of it will be upon your head."

Edward leaned forward and spoke low so that only the captain would hear. "Surrender may be preferable to slaughter, sir. I, alone, am responsible for the lives of these men."

Captain Hammond ignored Edward's plea, and yelled loudly to get the attention of the crew. When all hands were still and all eyes were upon him, the captain said, "They will be upon us within the hour. Will you fight or will you surrender?"

A boisterous shout from the men gave the answer: "Fight to the death! The English will never surrender!"

When Edward realized he had no sway with the men in a battle such as this would be, he took the only course left open to him. With pompous bravery, he held up his sword to unite them together. No man would have cause to call Edward a coward. "We have sailed together and we shall fight together. If God is willing, we shall win. But if we die, we shall die together!"

"Here! Here!" the men shouted in unison.

Seeing them bolstered by his persuasion, Edward yelled, "As Master of the *Neptune*, I will fight as nobly as anyone on board this ship. It will never be said of Edward Blackwell that he regarded his own life above that of his crew."

"Now back to work!" shouted Captain Hammond. "If it's a fight they're after, we shall give it to them!"

Removing his doublet, Edward rolled up his sleeves, then jumped into service with the crew, rolling the cannons into position, stacking the cannon balls for easy access, hauling kegs of blasting powder, and preparing the torches. Then, he opened several chests of weapons and distributed them amongst his men. Some of the pistols were from his own personal stores, but that didn't matter now. They would need every piece of ordnance and ammunition they could find.

One of the cannons refused to roll forward, regardless of the men's efforts to budge it. When he realized the cannon was useless for defense, Edward packed it with powder, ball and fodder, preparing it for service. Then he had the men help him lift the rear end up and balance the blasted thing on its nose, supporting it with barrels of dried legumes. "If it comes to capture or death, I will light this cannon and blast a hole through the hull. At least the pirates will not get the *Neptune*."

"I will do it, sir," volunteered a young man named William Moore, a dapper lad with an easy disposition.

"You're not yet sixteen," Edward told him.

"No, sir. But I can't swim, either. I figure, this way I'll go down with the ship."

"Scuttling the ship is my responsibility, William." He didn't want the lad to think himself braver than Edward.

"But, sir—"

"If it makes you feel better, William, you may stand beside me. We will go down with the ship together."

"Aye, Master Blackwell. I would be proud to die in defense of the King's Royal Navy, sir."

Edward gave the younger man a wan smile. "Don't get your hopes up, William. We may still come through this thing in one piece."

They heard a sudden blast in the distance. Edward left young William and raced back up to the aftercastle deck. "Keep the stern in their line of vision, Captain. Don't let them see her petticoats until the last possible moment."

"Plan to lure her in, Edward," suggested the captain.

"Exactly," he replied.

"It's gratifying to see you accept your responsibility, Master Blackwell. I didn't know you had it in you."

Edward leaned over and spoke low, so that only the captain would hear him. "Actually, fear is shaking me to the core, Captain. But the men need someone to boost their confidence and since you're busy at the helm, who does that leave?"

"If I survive this battle, I shall write a glowing report for you, Edward."

"May I have your word on that, Captain?"

"You certainly may!"

Another blast was heard, but this one missed the starboard gunwale by two hundred yards. "Well, well," Edward grinned. "They may look big and mean, but they have no sense to aim their weapons before they fire."

Another volley sounded, this one striking the water in a huge spray that washed the deck, but didn't touch the hull. "They're getting good practice, anyway." said Edward. "Prepare to come about, Captain, on my signal."

A fourth cannon blasted toward them, this one traveling between the mainsail and the mizzen, narrowly missing the ship and landing to port. "Now!" Edward yelled.

Captain Hammond turned the wheel to starboard and the *Neptune* complied, gliding into position as though she had a mind of her own.

"Steady, oarsmen!" Edward shouted. His message was relayed to the men at the oars who were diligently keeping the ship from moving further forward.

"Prepare to fire!"

When the two vessels came into position, starboard to port, Edward gave the final command. "Fire!"

Within seconds of each other, four cannons spewed red flames and four lead balls the size of muskmelons arched into the air, the first one landed short, as well as the next. The third ball hit the top of the foresail, tearing the sails from the rigging, but landing to starboard of

the Algerian Man-of-War. The fourth ball, which Edward was almost certain would hit the stern, missed by only a few inches.

"Come about! Forward, oarsmen!"

They were on the chase once again, the Algerians blasting cannons almost repetitively. One of their cannon balls tore through the bowsprit like it was paper, breaking it off entirely. A second one landed on the aftercastle deck, dropping through two floors before it stopped cold, on the floor above the hold. It was too close, Edward realized. A few more like that one and they would be dead in the water.

"Port cannons at the ready! Prepare to fire on my signal!"

Captain Hammond steered to port, exposing the left side of the *Neptune*.

"Steady oarsman! Cannons ready! Fire!"

A volley of blasts rocked the deck as four more cannon balls tore through the sky toward the Algerian vessel. One hit the mizzen mast, toppling it onto the aftercastle. Another took out the starboard railing in the aft quarter. The third and fourth landed short. Disgusted, Edward braced for the next barrage from the Man-of-War.

Within seconds, several loud blasts and cannon balls came flying at them. Two landed on the forecastle, crushing it, but not going through to the hull. In its path, however, it left several men dead. The third and fourth cannon balls were long and landed on the opposite side, to starboard. The fifth knocked the rest of the railing off the aftercastle at the stern, without damaging the hull, but the sixth ball split the rudder from the hull, causing the *Neptune* to lurch, then shudder, before she listed slightly to port and failed to respond to any turn of the wheel.

The men looked to Edward to lead them. He shook his head. "Shall

we continue the fight?" he asked them.

"To the death!" they yelled in unison.

"Keep the cannons armed and in position. We may get another shot at her when she comes alongside."

The orders were relayed down the chain of command and the men stood ready at the gunwales, sabers and swords drawn, pistols steadily aimed.

Within a few minutes the Man-of-War came alongside them, and Edward called down below. "Ready to fire cannons, William!"

The message was relayed.

"Fire when ready!" Edward called out.

There was another round of cannon fire spewing from the starboard side. With the *Neptune* listing to port, this made the cannon balls leap a little higher, which ripped through the Algerian vessel's decking in four places, but all four holes would never sink her, for they entered high on the port gunwales and through the weather deck, then over the starboard gunwales and into the water. On their way, they took out seven Algerians, which buoyed the men's courage, giving them a slight edge over their opponents.

Soon men were jumping from the man-of war to the *Neptune*, their daggers drawn. Engaging the English in sword-to-dagger combat, some discharged pistols, but the English returned fire in the same manner, killing many Algerians with a ferociousness that took them by surprise.

Edward had run through a number of pirates with his sword, but they kept crawling up over the *Neptune* in droves. When he finally had to concede that they were losing the ship, he managed to slip away to the gunnery deck where William stood ready with a single torch. The

other men had loaded all the cannons for one more wild blast, then had gone on deck to help their comrades in arms.

"Ready?" William asked him, his voice almost squeaking in fear.

Edward nodded. "It's been a pleasure serving with you, William. I wish you Godspeed."

"Indeed," said William, handing Edward the torch.

With one swift movement, Edward lit each of the fuses on all eight cannons, the one facing the floor last of all. Then with their hands over their ears to withstand the shocking blasts, they waited only a moment for each cannon in turn to spew forth fire and hot lead, some balls taking out more Algerians and decking on the Man-of-War, some going straight down into the ocean, leaving in their quake a shuddering mass of hull, giving the pirates cause for alarm. The last ball exploded through the *Neptune's* gunnery deck, and then through the hull, taking a good portion of both with it.

The sound of gurgling came from deep below and Edward said, "Come along, William. I'll teach you how to swim." But even when he said it, he could hardly hear his own words. His voice sounded far away.

The young man's oval eyes grew wide as he realized what Edward was suggesting.

"Come along," Edward said once more. "Would you rather drown down here like a coward, or die with a sword point through your heart?"

"If you put it that way, sir," said William. "Let's go."

At least, that's what Edward thought the younger man said. His hearing had been damaged by all the cannon blasts and he wasn't certain of anything but the ringing in them.

The hull gaped open even wider, as water rushed into the hold, filling it up and making the ship list more and more to port. By the time Edward and young William reached the weather deck, a scene of carnage like nothing they had ever seen lay before them. Men who once were virile and healthy were dead or dying, and the decks were swathed in red as blood oozed everywhere.

Edward gasped as the enormity of the loss and his own role in bringing the men to this end, came upon him. These men were his crew and they were dying because Edward had refused to turn back five days ago. Shame swept over him in great waves of anguish. It would have been better had he died the death of a traitor.

Now, it was impossible to tell who was winning the fight. The crew of the *Neptune* fought for freedom, while the Algerians fought their battle for greed.

In any such combat conditions, it is often the case that those who fought for freedom and gave their lives in the effort, were the lucky few who really won the battle after all.

A deep groaning came forth and Edward could not tell whether it came from within himself, or from the belly of the *Neptune*. At the same moment, a terrible shuddering sickened Edward almost as much as the carnage smeared on the deck before him.

Fearing they would be dragged under by the sinking ship, Edward pushed William forward and yelled, "Jump!" but his words came out garbled, as though he was yelling from a hundred miles away.

Without knowing how to swim, the young man trusted Edward and followed his lead into the cold waters of the northern Atlantic. The temperature change shocked them both. Edward felt as though his lungs would not open to draw a breath, should he manage to reach the

sea's surface. But his thoughts were geared toward William, and he grabbed the young man by the collar of his shirt and pulled him up toward the surface. Taking that first gulp of air almost crippled them both. The cold gripped them with icy fingers of death. For a few moments Edward wondered if they would survive the freezing shock. Saltwater filled his mouth and he spit it out, gagging and coughing for several minutes, as did his companion.

When he finally caught his breath, Edward saw a large portion of the rudder floating on the surface and he struck out toward it with one hand, towing young William along with him. When they reached the rudder, William grabbed onto it quickly.

"Stay with it," he told the young man. "I'll see if I can help any of the others."

Shivering violently, William nodded as he pulled himself out of the sea and onto the massive slab of wood.

Edward wasn't gone for long. He located several of his men clinging to debris, but many more of them he found face down in the water. Hearing, *or was it feeling*, a splashing sound to his left, he noticed one of his men slip off a piece of gunwale railing. Edward dove for him, reaching him before he was sucked into the deep, then dragged him over to the rudder where William huddled half-conscious. After he helped the older man onto the rudder, Edward slid on with him. He recognized the man as Jonathan Plum, a seasoned sailor with a great knack for marlin spiking.

With horror floating all around him, and snatches of bubbles exploding on the surface, Edward was filled with new memories. He watched the *Neptune* give one last violent shake, stand on her nose and sink straight down into the sea, leaving the surface littered with

debris, the dead . . . and the dying.

Shuddering violently from the cold, Edward closed his eyes and prayed for deliverance, to no avail.

———

EDWARD LIVED IN an impenetrable fog for the next few days. The last real memory he could find inside his head was the attack by an Algerian Man-of-War, resulting in the subsequent sinking of the *Neptune*.

He looked around him, but he didn't recognize anyone other than William Moore, whose tongue was so swollen Edward wondered how the young man could even breathe.

Sitting in the hold of a sailing vessel, which he decided must be the Algerian's Man-of-War, he saw timbers that were busted overhead, and daylight filtered through from the gunnery deck above it. Arching to his right, an extremely painful position, he could see the round holes made in the weather deck above the guns and realized that was where cannon balls from the *Neptune* had penetrated.

Edward, William Moore and several others from the *Neptune* had been picked up by the Algerians some time ago, though Edward couldn't recall how long it had been, or even what day of the week.

Licking his lips, he realized his own tongue was just as swollen as William's and he wondered why. Sweat beaded off his forehead and dripped down his face, leaving his beard damp. Stroking his face, Edward was shocked at the amount of facial hair he'd grown. How long had it been since pirates attacked his vessel?

Having tried for several days to recall what the *Neptune*'s destination was before the attack, Edward now conceded that he may never

figure it out. A few times he'd asked William, "Why are we here? Where were we going?"

But William never really answered, or if he did, Edward could not hear it.

Trying to stretch his back a little, Edward gasped and shrank back into a hunching position, then moved his back slightly to the left and found a brief moment of comfort between spasms of pain.

What had happened to him since he was dragged on board? A memory of being dropped onto the deck on his face kept surfacing, but what the pirates had done to him since then he could not recall.

William's shirt was shredded across his back, as were several of the other men's, including Captain Hammond's. Dried blood stains were everywhere. When Edward finally realized what had caused it, another memory lashed to the surface of his mind. The agonizing blows from a whip had opened his back in great welts. The waves of pain were so terrible that he suddenly recalled having fainted.

Horror stories he'd heard about what happens to people when they are captured by pirates drifted through his mind. The thought of those terrible things haunted him and he remembered his father saying that it would be better to choose a watery grave than to be taken by pirates. In the Royal Navy, he'd been taught that a man would be better served by sinking the pirate's ship rather than to allow the pirates to continue raiding the Atlantic ocean, plundering on the innocent and defenseless. He knew that an imprisoned pirate would never hesitate to sink the ship in which he was held captive, even if it meant sealing his own doom, rather than be taken prisoner by the English. An English warship had been taken over by pirates a dozen or more years ago. Apparently the English had retaken the ship, put the pirates in the hold for safe

keeping, and headed toward England. Almost at their destination, they realized that the vessel was listing to one side. Upon investigation, they found that the pirates had pulled the hemp from between the hull boards and the ship was sinking. Bravely, the captain boarded his men onto the pinnace they'd brought along, bid them farewell, set the sails on his ship so that it would head out to sea until it eventually sank, drowning the captain and the pirates. When the pinnace reached safety, the men reported the event to the authorities. Since that time, most English ships traveled in twos or threes, with at least one large pinnace and a shallop tethered behind them.

Now, Edward scooted toward the hull a little more closely and looked around for a piece of hemp that he could pull free, but his hands and feet were shackled so tightly that he couldn't quite reach it. Then he realized why the pirates had shackled them down the center of the hold, in a single line, fastening all their shackles to eye-bolts. They knew the English would remove the hemp if they could, and they had prevented them from doing so, quite effectively.

Shuddering, Edward abandoned the idea of trying to sink the pirate ship and tried to remember what had happened to him after he'd been brought on board, but it was apparently so horrible that his mind could not recall it.

He asked himself, *What brought me to this point in life?*

For a long time, he had no memory of how he had existed before the Algerian's had attacked the *Neptune*. He struggled for hours contemplating where he used to live and who he was, but he found no memories to assist him in his search.

A brief flash came, then another . . . and another.

A woman floated into his mind, a beautiful woman with golden

hair that hung in ringlets down the middle of her back, and lips that trembled. Her eyes were the color of the turquoise sea. Yet, when she looked at him, all he could see was terror and hatred in those eyes.

When her name finally drifted into his mind, he whispered it over and over. "Rebecca. Rebecca. What have I done to make you loathe me so?"

When she did not answer, he searched his memory farther back, then gasped and shut his eyes quickly. Someone was whipping Rebecca as she leaned against a bed post, her hands tied high above her at the pinnacle. Fresh blood splattered against the creamy fabric of her dress, the back undone to make her punishment more painful. The whip seemed alive with a will of its own, with a fury that both shocked and sickened him. She screamed each time the whip struck her. Between each lash of the whip, she cried, begging him to stop.

Horrified, Edward looked down and saw that the whip was clutched tightly in his left hand. Searing flames of guilt engulfed him.

Another memory flooded into his mind, adding fuel to the fire within him. An older man in a prison cell, covered with little more than a flimsy doublet, sweat flowing from his skin in small rivulets. He was shaking uncontrollably, pleading for mercy. Through Edward's deceit, Rebecca's father, Jeremiah Webster, was arrested and incarcerated. His body, once strong, had wasted away from prison fever in the space of fifteen weeks. His death could have been prevented, but Edward had been blinded by his anger at Jeremiah's daughter, who had refused his private advances from the very beginning.

Quite suddenly, a thought kindled inside his mind that shook him to the very core. Now he realized why God had not helped him find Rebecca. Almost unwilling to admit it, Edward also knew why God

had permitted the Algerians to capture him, along with the remaining crew of the *Neptune*.

It was the price Edward must pay for his lies, treachery and violent abuse. How many lives had been lost because Edward had not controlled his temper? He'd been a man driven to the brink of insanity. Now, he looked around at the survivors from the *Neptune* and counted them. Twenty-three, excluding himself. From a crew of one hundred and twenty, only twenty-three remained alive. Ninety-seven men from the *Neptune* were dead.

Yes, retribution must be paid for their lives, but Edward, alone, would pay it.

Chapter Thirteen

Confessions

". . . except ye see signs and wonders,
ye will not believe."
John 4:48

rriving at Blackwell Tower late in the evening after two days' journey, Rebecca glanced around the bedchamber where she had lived for nine weeks before her escape to the *Warwick*. The room had been left untouched, as though Edward knew she would be coming home.

But this wasn't Rebecca's home, nor would it ever be. Rebecca prayed that her father's former holdings would be restored to her. With Penelope's help, Rebecca now had hope.

Sooner or later, Lord Blackwell would learn the truth regarding his son, but right now he was blind to Edward's character flaws. Without substantiating proof, Lord Blackwell might accuse Rebecca of lying. The scars upon her back would not be evidence enough, now that she'd been captured by pirates.

Rebecca prayed she could go back to her father's tinsmith shop.

When he was cast into prison, all his belongings were confiscated and given to Dudley Hogge, the man who had accused Jeremiah of stealing. Hogge's lie had been profitable, not only in terms of what Edward Blackwell must have given him, for he now had possession of her father's holdings, as well.

After the servants at Blackwell Tower prepared her bath, Rebecca washed herself and changed into a clean chemise, petticoats and a gown made of silk brocade in a rich, dark burgundy. Tending to her hair, she braided it while it was still damp and knotted it in a pretty coif at her nape.

She was just finishing when there came a knock at the bedroom door. "Yes, enter," she instructed.

Wilson, the head butler at Blackwell Tower, entered, his head bowed as he came toward her. Following him were two servants and the chamberlain, who was in charge of managing the private chambers of the house, Rebecca's included.

Rebecca stepped right up to Wilson and hugged him. "Thank you so much for helping me that night," she said, blinking back her tears.

After she released him, Wilson took her hand gently in his. "It was the worst moment of our lives when we heard you were kidnaped by pirates. After you left here, the household staff spent every spare moment praying for your safety. We are gratified that God heard our prayers."

Wilhelmina, Wilson's sister, nudged him aside and drew Rebecca close, embracing her with tender regard. "Praise be to God that you survived, Mistress."

"Thank you." Rebecca pulled back. "And to both of you, Margaret and Helena, for keeping my chamber things as I left them. Next time

I flee from this place, I will take all of my personal belongings with me."

"How will you ever escape a second time?" Wilson asked. "Lord Blackwell has put guards at all the doors both night and day."

"When I leave here, I will be justified," she told them. "I am not permitted to say how. Not yet. But I have gained other friends who will see that justice is rendered in my behalf."

Tears welled up in Wilhelmina's eyes. "It is a miracle, Mistress."

"Indeed!" Rebecca smiled, holding back tears of her own. "When that day comes, you will be grateful that you assisted me the day my father died. I will remember your kindness."

"To see you escape from that monster's clutches is the only kindness we wish, Mistress," said Wilson.

Hugging them both one more time, Rebecca said, "Thanks be to the Lord God who gave me such friends as you."

When they had left her, Rebecca knelt beside a chair near the fireplace and prayed. For nearly an hour, she stayed there, pleading that God would be merciful to those she loved and bring them back safely to her.

After ending her prayer, she sank down in a chair and watched the fire licking flames toward the chimney. Rebecca had not felt so alone in all her life as she did at that moment. Taking her mind back to the night she arrived at the *Warwick*, she remembered how desperately she had longed for some kind human to comfort her in the loss of her father. She had found that comfort in the arms of the ship's master, John Dunton.

Her every thought since the *Little David* was captured had been of John and Thomas. They were both a part of her now, the only family

she had left on the earth. Now they were gone. Where they were, she had no way of knowing. Thoughts of what the pirates might do to them plagued her so much that she rarely slept. Even when she did, it was always a fitful sleep, disturbed by nightmares of the two she had come to love with all her heart. When darkness finally penetrated through the window into her bedchamber, Rebecca rose from her chair and stretched out on top of the bed, hoping to fall asleep.

When Edward returns— she thought to herself, then refused to dwell upon the man she loathed. Instead, she turned her thoughts heavenward. *Please God, allow the earl to conclude his investigation before Edward returns.*

It was nearly midnight when she slipped out of her clothes and in between the bed covers to sleep. As the hours ticked by, all she could do was pray and wait sleeplessly for the dawn.

THREE WEEKS LATER, Rebecca was embroidering upon a rich brocade fabric in the parlor at Blackwell Tower. She had earlier made a drawing of the bark, *Warwick,* under sail and had transferred it onto the fabric to make a wall hanging. However, today she was unable to concentrate on her work.

She knew that Lord Blackwell was beginning to worry that something terrible had happened to his son, because Edward had not come home yet. He'd been gone almost five weeks, though the workmen had reported that the *Neptune* had only taken enough provisions for four weeks.

Rebecca felt a strange sort of tenderness for his Lordship. She knew what it was like to panic when someone you love is lost to you. Staying

sane day after day; pacing floors; being unable to eat or sleep; worrying where they are, if they are well, or barely alive. All these emotions she knew only too well. Little wonder Lord Blackwell was growing more irritable day by day.

Something miraculous had happened to her. She had discovered something quite extraordinary that she dared not share with anyone at Blackwell Tower. Not yet. Her monthly cycle had not come at all in March and now it was the middle of April. Tenderly, Rebecca placed a hand on her flat abdomen and wondered to herself if the child growing within her would be a boy or a girl. Would he look like John? Or Thomas? Would he resemble his mother more?

Having no one at Blackwell Tower with whom she could share her news, she retired to her bedchamber. Remembering Penelope, she took a piece of parchment from the table drawer, along with inkwell and feather pen, and wrote:

> *The seventeenth day of April, in*
> *the year of our Lord, 1635.*

> *Dearest Penelope;*
> *My fondest greetings to you and your husband,*
> *the Earl of Portland. The most pleasing information*
> *that I have received in a long while has come to me*
> *this morning: I have learned that young Thomas*
> *is going to have a sibling added to his family some-*
> *time in December or January. I am certain that you*
> *will understand why I chose to share this glad tiding*

with you. I trust you are well and I look forward
to hearing from you.

Affectionately yours,
Rebecca Webster

She deliberately used her maiden name, in case the parchment should be intercepted by anyone. After she had sealed the parchment with a few drops of wax, she placed the Blackwell Tower imprint upon it, then took her letter downstairs to the servant's kitchen where she found Wilson eating lunch with his sister.

Since Lord Blackwell had gone down to Chatham dockyard earlier that morning, she asked Wilson to send her letter as quickly as possible.

"Yes, Mistress. Godspeed to you."

She stood on tiptoe and kissed Wilson on the cheek. "Thank you, dear Wilson."

She watched him leave, then went upstairs and stretched out on her back on the big bed. She had completely healed from Edward's whipping by now and felt remarkably comfortable.

"Oh, John," she whispered. "How I long to tell you of the child within me! This child is more than a miracle to me. It is a sign that the Lord is still watching over us. I pray every morning, noon and night, that you are safe, that you will come back to me, and that young Thomas will be spared, as well." When she was finished, she dabbed at her eyes, closed them and fell fast asleep.

She awakened to a terrible cry of pain and anguish that startled her. Quickly she moved from the bed to the door and down the stairs to the parlor where she found his Lordship kneeling next to a chair, his head in his hands, weeping inconsolably. Several of the household

staff gathered near them as Rebecca knelt beside him, patting his back tenderly.

"Lord Blackwell," she whispered. "What is it? What is wrong?"

A paper slipped from his hands, but he was too distraught to hand it to her or to explain. Rebecca picked it up and read it aloud for all to hear:

The sixth day of April, 1635.

To the right honorable Lord Blackwell,
I regret to inform your Lordship that on Monday last, Captain Harrison, of the **Hercules,** *along with three other vessels, found a path of debris about twenty leagues from Land's End, on their journey back from the Americas, among which was a portion of a stern rail with the name* **Neptune** *clearly legible. Some of the debris was brought into Portsmouth, where it was examined by myself and several others. It was determined that the* **Neptune** *was deliberately sunk, presumably by pirates. Whether or not the crew survived is unknown. It is with heavy heart that I relay this information, for I ever rest at your command.*
Amos Miner
of his Majesty's Port Authorities.

The moment she read that the *Neptune* was sunk, several of the servants began crying. Moisture welled up in Rebecca's eyes, as well, but they were not tears for Edward, rather for Lord Blackwell, who had always treated her as a daughter.

Taking his arm, she lifted him up onto the chair and tried to comfort him, to no avail. Fearing for his health, she told Wilhelmina, "Send for the doctor, straight away."

With assistance, Rebecca was able to move Lord Blackwell up to his chamber, where she put him to bed. The doctor arrived twenty minutes later, breathless and huffing with difficulty. He examined Lord Blackwell thoroughly, mixed some herbs together to make a soothing tea for him and gave Rebecca instructions that his Lordship should drink a cup of it every few hours until he was feeling better.

After the doctor left, Rebecca gave swift orders to the staff, then sat by his Lordship until dawn, leaving only to refresh herself and return to him.

It took nearly a week before Lord Blackwell began to recover. And most of that time Rebecca had spent with him, reading or embroidering while he slept. Ever watchful, she felt a deep tenderness for the man who had fathered Edward Blackwell.

THE FOLLOWING WEEK, Rebecca received a letter from Penelope, saying that the earl had completed his investigation. Her father's property, including his household belongings, would be restored to her immediately. As for Dudley Hogge, the man who had accused Jeremiah of stealing, he had been sent to prison and his property confiscated. There was no mention of Edward, but there was a request for Rebecca to come visit Penelope.

When she showed the letter to Lord Blackwell, he read it thoughtfully. His health had improved and he was back to doing most of the

things to which he was accustomed, though he hadn't spoken about Edward to Rebecca yet.

They were sitting in the parlor, his Lordship reading while Rebecca sewed the last few stitches in the hem of a dress she'd been making.

"You must be pleased to know that your father's good name has been restored to him. I only wish it could have been before he passed on," said Lord Blackwell after he'd read her letter.

"Yes," she murmured. "I miss him so."

"Would you like to go to Winchester Castle?" he asked.

"Very much."

"Do you not like it here?"

Rebecca looked up from her sewing. "You have been most kind and gracious to me, your Lordship. I shall be forever in your debt."

"But you are prepared to leave me?" His voice softened, and she could tell that he didn't want her to leave Blackwell Tower.

"No," she admitted. "I will never be prepared to leave you, your Lordship, for you have always made me feel most welcome here. But I must get on with my life. Not that I have any desire to offend you, sire."

"But since Edward is not coming back, you have no more reason to stay?" he guessed. It was the first time Edward's name had been mentioned in two weeks.

"Sire, I pray for your sake that Edward is alive, that he is safe."

"Do you also pray these things for your own sake?"

Rebecca lowered her head, considering how best to respond. Finally she lifted her eyes to meet his and said, "I do not wish to disrespect

your son's name, your Lordship, but the truth is that I've no desire to marry Edward."

He nodded, as though he already knew she felt this way. "I understand."

"Do you?" she asked. "For I feared to tell you what is in my heart."

"Rebecca, there are many questions in my mind regarding your relationship with Edward. I have not asked because I respect your privacy. And I, too, fear what your answers might be."

Considering this, Rebecca hoped that she could talk truthfully about Edward now. "You may ask me anything you want, Lord Blackwell and I will answer truthfully. My father taught me that fear of the unknown is much worse than the unknown could ever be."

"Your father was a wise man." He ran thin, strong fingers through his silver hair, his pale blue eyes almost devoid of emotion. "Very well. I will ask some of the questions I've pondered ever since we heard about the fate of the *Neptune*."

Rebecca folded the dress and put it in a basket by her side, giving him her full attention, while praying that he would receive her answers well.

"Someone in the household, I won't mention who, brought me some distressing information regarding the condition of your back." His pale eyes studied her, watching as though he wanted to discern her answer before he asked the question, "Did the pirates whip you?"

She shook her head and felt her eyes well up with moisture. "No, sire. The leader slapped my face several times and they tied me to a bed for most of my journey, but they did not whip me."

He exhaled as though he had deflated all plausible theories for the

scars upon her back. Finally, he lifted his head and asked fearfully, "Did Edward whip you?"

Tears spilled down her cheeks as she nodded her head in the affirmative.

Lord Blackwell gasped, apparently shaken by this information. "Will you ever be able to forgive him for it?"

Turning her head from side to side, she whispered, "No, I cannot. Not now." Then, to give his Lordship some comfort, she added hastily. "Maybe someday. But the memories are still too painful."

"Is that why you ran away?"

Rebecca bit her bottom lip. "One of the reasons," she admitted.

He seemed to consider her guarded answer, but he did not press her for additional information. Folding his hands in his lap, he said, "When Sarah Jenkins died—"

She gave him a puzzled expression.

"Sarah Jenkins was betrothed to Edward before you met him," explained Lord Blackwell.

"He never mentioned her."

"No, he wouldn't have. He loved her so deeply that when she passed away, I thought I would lose him, as well. He locked himself in his chambers and wouldn't come out for days. We often heard things being thrown around and breaking. When he did come out, his room was a shambles. Paintings had been sliced open, the draperies shredded. It was horrible. Gradually he returned to normal, or at least as normal as he could be after Sarah died."

"What caused her death?" Rebecca asked, fearing the answer, yet wanting to know for certain if Edward had killed her.

"She had gone into London with Edward and her parents for a few days to attend the theater and shop for her wedding clothes. From what her parents told me, a carriage went out of control and ran over her, breaking her neck. They say she lived only a few moments afterward, then died in Edward's arms. When he realized she was gone, he took the whip from the carriage driver and nearly beat him to death with it before they could stop him."

"That explains a great deal," she admitted, grateful to know that Edward hadn't murdered Sarah Jenkins, which made him no less guilty for her father's death, but she wouldn't share this feeling with Lord Blackwell. Not now, not with Edward gone. There was no reason to sully his name any further.

"You look much like Sarah. Your eyes and the color of your hair. I had hoped Edward was past the insane raging over her death, but apparently I was wrong. Can you ever forgive me for not protecting you?"

"It was not your fault, Lord Blackwell."

He hesitated a moment, as though considering her comment. Then he said, "I will miss you, dear Rebecca. You've been a ray of sunshine around here, though you have not had much to shine about the past few weeks."

"There is something else I must tell you, Lord Blackwell. It will be common knowledge soon and I think it would be best that you hear it from me."

"I'm listening," he said with a gentle nod.

"When I ran away from Edward that night, I stowed away on the *Warwick*. I had heard you telling Edward that Master Dunton was a

kind man and I prayed that he would have mercy on me and not have me drowned."

"Yes?"

"Master Dunton did have mercy, but the only way he could protect me was to announce to the captain that I had come on board as his guest because I was his fiancée. The captain married us that very day."

"You're married to John Dunton?" questioned Lord Blackwell. His eyes widened and she noticed his astonishment at this information.

Rebecca nodded, then braced herself, thinking that he would yell at her, or perhaps throw her out immediately.

"Why didn't you say something sooner?" he asked.

"I wanted to tell you before now, but I didn't want to hurt you."

"I am so sorry, my dear, that you felt that way. There is nothing you could do that would hurt me. I'm grateful to learn the truth. What will you do now, with your husband missing?"

"I don't know," she responded. "Father's tinsmith shop in London and his upstairs apartment have been restored to me. I will live there. I'm quite a good seamstress, which will help me support myself."

Lord Blackwell arched his eyebrows in surprise. Then he offered, "If there is anything I can do to help you, Rebecca, please feel free to ask me. You have carried many burdens in your heart since your return."

"I will remember your offer, Lord Blackwell."

"If John has not returned in a year, Rebecca, he will be declared dead, you know that?"

"Yes, of course."

"I know I am an old man, child, and you are young and resilient. At the end of the year, if John has not returned to you, will you consider coming back to Blackwell Tower to live?"

"What?" Her eyes widened in surprise.

"Not for the reasons you may think," he insisted. "I would be a father to you, since yours is gone. You would have a comfortable home. I would take care of you."

"Lord Blackwell! I do not know what to say!"

"Just say that you will consider your options, should your husband be dead to you." His pale blue eyes softened. "I would not expect anything more than that you provide conversation and companionship for me into my old age. With Edward swallowed up by the sea, having a daughter around could be very entertaining."

"You are too kind, sire. But I shall always hope that John will come home to me. Thomas, too. I will pray for their deliverance all the rest of my life." She looked directly into his sad, blue eyes. "I will pray for Edward's return also. His return to you."

"Then I will add my prayer to yours, for your happiness is all that matters to me now. Perhaps with both of us praying for Edward, John and Thomas to return, the Lord will hear us."

"I hope so," she agreed. "I certainly hope so."

Chapter Fourteen

A Home for Rebecca

*". . . for whither thou goest, I will go; and where
thou lodgest, I will lodge;"*

Ruth 1:16

"Isn't it splendid?" said Penelope dropping a slip of parchment onto the table. "We have sent these out all over England, and to many parts of France and Spain. If anyone receives any news at all about John Dunton, or his son, Thomas, they will contact us."

"The only problem, dear Penelope, is that Thomas was to be sold as a slave in Salé, Morocco. And we have no idea where John is." Rebecca didn't want to offend Penelope for she was doing all within her power to find John and Thomas. But Rebecca was beginning to face the truth, and her hope waned.

The endearing woman rubbed Rebecca's shoulders. "It's a start," she encouraged. "And my husband has ordered that these documents be hung in every one of his Majesty's ships. Perhaps a mariner will spot him and let him know that we are looking for him."

"I shall pray so," said Rebecca, though she wasn't optimistic.

Rebecca had been staying at Winchester Castle for a week now. Tomorrow she would be leaving to live by herself in the apartment above her father's tinsmith shop. To her delight, she had rented the shop to a tinsmith who was looking to start his own business. Married and with two young daughters, he wanted to rent the upstairs apartment, too, but Rebecca would have nowhere to go if he did.

The rent money would give her enough to purchase food for her and her unborn child. If she could take orders for dresses, chemises, petticoats and children's wear, she would have a little extra for the other necessities of life. It would have to do, though she had to admit, if only to herself, that she would be lonely until her child was born. The Lord God had always provided someone to care about her, she acknowledged. He would just have to send someone new. Perhaps the wife of the tinsmith would befriend her.

Early the next morning, Rebecca waved goodbye to Penelope, then rode in silence from Winchester to the outskirts of London. When the carriage finally halted, she looked out the window. Seeing her father's name gone from the shingle above the door of the tinsmith shop brought tears to her eyes. She had not been in this house for almost six months.

Going up the stairs to the apartment where she grew up, Rebecca almost cried. Both her parents were gone, as were her husband and son. She would be all alone, something she'd never really been in her entire life. The thought frightened her.

Then she remembered the child within, and her vow to remain cheerful so that she would be well-practiced by the time he arrived.

Rebecca was certain she was carrying a boy, and she had already named him John. *Little John.*

Opening the door to her living quarters, she stepped inside and looked around. The main room held a fireplace constructed of river rock, with a big black pot and a tripod swing to hang it on. A shelf with a dozen assorted books including the family Bible. A table and three chairs. A shelf with an odd assortment of dishes and cookery. A built-in basin with a drain that ran outside, down a grooved tile on the sloping roof and onto the garden, a parcel about twenty feet square where her mother used to raise beans, cabbages and tomatoes. Outdoors there was a well, dug by her father many years ago, with a bucket for hauling water back to the apartment.

The main room separated two modest bedrooms. The smaller had been Rebecca's for as long as she could remember. Inside the larger room was a comfortable bed big enough for two people, a dressing table with a mirror, a chest of drawers, several hooks on the back of the door, and a row of shelves. On the bed, Rebecca put a carpet bag and some of her belongings that she'd carried in with her. The carriage driver brought up the rest of her things and put them into the smaller room until Rebecca could decide what to do with them.

After the driver left, Rebecca sat down at the table and cried until there were no more tears left in her. She hadn't expected that coming home would mean being reminded by everything she saw around her that her father was gone. The depth of her loneliness surprised her. Her arms ached for John and Thomas. Hadn't she felt just this way the night she ran away from Blackwell Tower? Wasn't it this same, lonely feeling that had driven her into John's arms that night on the ship where he'd comforted her as she'd wept for the loss of her beloved father, and that had driven her into his bed the following morning?

She had an insatiable need to be with her family, with human contact. The seven or eight months until her child would be born were going to be the most lonely of her entire life.

She looked sadly around the apartment. Was this to be her home for the rest of her life? Would she never see her husband or son again? Right now, Lord Blackwell's offer to take care of her if John didn't return in a year seemed a likely possibility, and the thought made Rebecca shudder.

"Enough!" she demanded. "John's baby will not want a mother who has nothing inside but self-pity." And with that remark she stood and began the task of putting her belongings away. It didn't take long, for all she had was her clothing, sewing notions and her books.

Unexpectedly, she heard a knock at the door. Stepping over to it, she looked through the glass and saw two elderly women standing at the top of the stairs landing. One held a copy of the notification that Penelope had sent out to be posted around the entire country.

Rebecca opened the door. "Yes," she said. "May I help you?"

"Are you Goodwife Dunton, as mentioned in this notice?" the rounder woman asked.

"I am. But how did you know to find me here?"

"We went straight to Winchester Castle the moment we saw this notice," she said, holding up the parchment. "The earl's wife kindly insisted we take one of her carriages straight to you. It seems we only missed you by a few hours."

"And you are?"

"Ruth Harris," said the thinner woman. "We're sisters of Simon Harris."

Tears filled her eyes as Rebecca realized who they were. She didn't even know Simon had sisters. "Please, come in," she said, wiping at her eyes with her finger tips.

"I'm Naomi," said the rounder woman. "We're twins."

"Please, sit down," Rebecca insisted, pulling the chairs away from the table for them. "I—I'd offer you something to eat but I haven't anything today. I just arrived myself and found the cupboards bare."

"How did you come to marry John?" Naomi asked. "When we saw the notice at Stepney Parish, we couldn't believe it."

Ruth added, "We didn't know John's ship had been taken by pirates, either." She dabbed at her eyes with a handkerchief.

"John and I married in mid-March aboard the *Warwick*. Oh, there's so much to tell, I hardly know where to begin."

"Just start at the beginning," insisted Naomi. "If John is your husband, that makes you our family, you know."

"Of course," said Rebecca.

She spent the next few hours sharing her story with Naomi and Ruth. They laughed and they cried and they sighed when they learned about the child that would be born come winter. When she was finished, she concluded by saying, "Here I thought I had no one left, and I find Thomas' grandaunts on my doorstep."

"My dear," said Naomi, "did John not tell you that he had a house near London?"

"No. We didn't have much time together. He spoke of going to America to start a merchant's vessel trade. There are many things about John that I wish I knew."

Ruth said, "Well, there is one thing about John you should know.

He won't want you living here, wallowing in memories of your dead father. When John and Mary married, they lived with us in Simon's house until Thomas was born. Afterward, Simon sold him a piece of property right next to our house, where John built a lovely cottage. It's much larger than your apartment, and it has a little fruit orchard and a nice garden spot."

"You must come with us, Rebecca," Naomi insisted. "You're our family now. You can rent your apartment out to someone, can't you?"

Rebecca laughed. "The tinsmith wanted to rent it, but I told him no."

Ruth gave her a determined look that indicated she would not take, "No," for an answer. "Well, you just tell him that he may move in here. Come along, Naomi, let's help Rebecca gather her things. She's coming with us!"

Rebecca was so overwhelmed she started to cry again, only this time it was for joy.

"Now, now," comforted Naomi. "If we'd known, dear, we'd have come long ago. I wish now that John had said something about us."

"It's just like in the Bible, isn't it Naomi?" Ruth asked. "You remember?"

"Remember what?" Rebecca asked.

"Why, our names were taken from the Bible for a reason, dear."

"Yes," Naomi agreed. "When Ruth was bereft of her husband, she went to his mother and told her, *'for whither thou goest, I will go; and where thou lodgest, I will lodge.'* "

Chapter Fifteen

Salé, Morocco

"Dunton was sold to a Moor named Aligolant, among whose prisoners were several Dutch and English sailors."

The Earl of Portland from Winchester Castle

May 1635

*T*he market place in Old Salé was filled with the aroma of warm and wonderful foods: sweetbreads, flat breads, a strange, round fish the size of a man's torso roasting on a skewer over an open fire, tomatoes and corn, sweetly spiced meats, and herb-steamed vegetables. The aromas mingled and wafted into John's nostrils, as though begging him to reach out and take some. John had never known such hunger. He now understood how one could be driven into thievery by such stomach pangs as he suffered.

For the past month and a half, he had existed on dried peas made into a pasty soup, one cup per day, and two pieces of hardtack. Trying to be optimistic, he thought, *at least we had ample drinking water, mixed occasionally with a little rum.*

Forcing his mind away from the food, John saw bright bolts of fabric,

some sheer, others sturdy, in various shades of blue, yellow, orange, red, purple and green. There were wind chimes and pottery of all shapes and sizes. The market was a pirate's wife's dream. Women wore baubles on their arms and ankles that tinkled when they walked.

One sight that caught his attention right away was the built-up gardens everywhere. Down the middle of the streets, waist-high walls made of a red-brown stucco had been built into rectangular garden boxes, which made bending over to weed them a simpler and less stressful chore. The gardens contained every kind of plant that John had ever seen, and many he couldn't identify. There were pepper plants in countless varieties, as well as tomatoes, cucumbers, squashes, melons, peas, beans and radishes. In other boxes, berry plants, grapevines, olive trees, mustard trees, pomegranates and citrus trees grew. Bees hummed everywhere and tall beehives made of hemp stood in many of the gardens. Flowers of every imaginable variety grew in the raised beds, from begonias to petunias. Herbs were planted in companion pots next to the walkways leading to the Moroccan homes.

Most of the houses were one story tall, constructed of the same stucco type material as the garden boxes. They were square, rectangular and U-shaped, some with elaborate courtyards. The floors were often left natural, and had become hard as slate from years of walking on them, wetting and packing them, when necessary, to smooth out a bumpy spot. Many of the windows had shutters that closed, but no glass or iron. The Moroccans had taken their environment and molded it into whatever they could devise using natural materials indigent to the region, mostly clay.

John found the city of Salé fascinating and he could hear his companions commenting now and again on something that had caught their interest. Like the other men with him, John's ankles were chained

together, as well as to the man in front and behind him. Sixteen men all stumbling together in a line, they looked much like a human centipede trying to learn how to move all its legs in unison.

A Roman tower stood at the highest point south of the Bou Regreg River, but on the north, a large castle, with a massive brick wall that completely encircled Old Salé, protected a cathedral and many shops. Due east of the city stood a church with a tall spire that overlooked the castle.

The pirates' haven made a startling contrast to the beautiful gardens. A row of brick and clay buildings had been built right next to the Bou Regreg River. The Port of Morocco joined Port Shelly by a wall that bordered all of New Salé. Battle-scarred men with whips and daggers tucked under their belts were everywhere. People were huddled into groups, waiting to be sold, much like a cattle auction. All of them were shackled, like John and his men, at the ankles and some at the wrists. Tattoo artists made a hefty income off pirate customers, while scantily clothed women lured men from the doorways of their evil dens. The exchange of gold, jewelry, ducats and anything else of value empowered the common bartering system.

When they reached the auction block, a garrisoned and heavily guarded area where people were herded into corrals like so much cattle, the company was ordered to stop and wait. A huge tent, with perhaps a hundred slaves ready to be sold to the highest bidder, was swollen with customers.

"Wait!" the captives grumbled. "That's all we've been doing for eight weeks. Waiting."

They arrived in Salé the first week in May, but that was two weeks ago. From what they could glean in the way of information from their

captors, by eavesdropping on conversations while aboard the *Warwick*, they learned that they were waiting for two other ships to join them. After the first of May passed, they were apparently joined by another ship, with one more to come in later in the month.

Still, they'd waited in the hold of the *Warwick* for fifty-seven days, from the time they were captured thirty-five leagues from Land's End, until they found themselves at the auction block.

As they were pushed into one of the corrals, John heard a muffled cry. He turned around and looked down. To his great astonishment and joy, he saw the bedraggled form of his little son, Thomas. The lad was lively, though much thinner than when he'd last seen him. Wearing his brown breeches, hose and shoes, his dark hair was matted and filthy, his lips parched and his eyes filled with horror and wonder, all at the same time. To his surprise, John saw that the lad wore Rebecca's green velvet cloak, now crumpled and dirty, around his frail shoulders. It was much too long for him, and he had rolled the end of it up and fastened it with a piece of twine so that it didn't drag on the ground.

"Father?" asked the boy. "Is it really you, Father?"

Recognizing John's anxiety, and his desire to hug his son, the two men on either side of him knelt down on the ground with the ankle that was attached closest to John, so that he could kneel and speak with his son face to face.

When John knelt in front of Thomas, his eyes filled with tears as he said, "Yes, Thomas. It is I."

The young boy threw his arms around John's neck and hugged him, crying against him for a great, long time. When at last Thomas composed himself, he pulled back and gazed lovingly into his father's

dark brown eyes. "You've grown a beard and your hair needs a trim," suggested Thomas.

"I could almost say the same for you. The pirates took away our shaving utensils and shears. Do I look that bad?"

Thomas nodded. "You're thinner and you don't smell so good."

John laughed. "They don't provide us with bath water or soap, either."

"I thought you were dead," whimpered Thomas. "Mother and I both prayed for you before they took her away."

"Where did they take your mother, Son? Do you know where?"

"They ransomed her for two hundred gold bars to Edward Blackwell."

"No!" John gasped, grateful that he was on his knees now, for he would have collapsed at this news. "When?"

"Within a week of our capture, but they took her away from me the very same day. They kept her shackled to the bed in the captain's quarters until the day she left."

"Shackled to the bed?" John gasped.

"I overheard Jane telling Captain Walket. I don't think they wanted me to know."

John shuddered as he realized the implications.

"Did Edward pay the two hundred gold bars?" John asked in dismay.

"Yes, but they didn't get to keep it," Thomas told him. "Some of Lord Vaine's guards surrounded them, and they were all hanged the next morning at the wharf. That's what Captain Walket told us when he returned to the ship."

"Henry went with them to collect the ransom?" The news was coming at him so quickly John could hardly keep up.

"Yes, but they were angry. They shot Captain Walket dead, right in front of us, and warned us that we'd better not disappoint him again."

"You've had some terrible experiences, Son" John lamented. "I should have left Simon to raise you back in London."

"I'll be all right, Father. Truly I will. I've been pretending that I'm Joseph, with the coat of many colors. You know him from the Bible, don't you?"

"If memory serves, Son."

"I'm going to be the best slave, resourceful and dedicated, like Mother said. And as soon as I can make a safe escape, I will come to find you again. Mother told me to search for the bark *Warwick*, for if I found that ship, I would find you on it. That's right, isn't it?"

"Of course it's right. And if these pirates happen to sink her, why, I'll build another one just like her so you'll be able to recognize her when you come."

"Will you be sold as a slave today, too?"

"Yes, Thomas. I'm afraid my lot isn't any better than yours."

"I'll be all right, Father. You'll see. I'm a man now."

The young boy gulped and restrained his tears, no doubt thinking John hadn't noticed.

Bravely, Thomas said, "We'll be together again. I know we will because I pray every morning and every night that God will somehow find a way for us."

John turned his head, unwilling to let Thomas see his own futile attempt at holding back tears. He nodded up the line a bit and smiled at Simon. Apparently, Thomas hadn't recognized his own grandfather, though Simon had passed by him before John had.

"Grandfather?" Thomas questioned. "It's really you, Grandfather. You're still alive, too."

Simon tried to reach his grandson but the people around him didn't seem to care that this was perhaps the only reunion they would ever have.

Simon nodded at John, indicating that he wanted him to look ahead. They were taking his group next. Quickly, John helped his two companions stand up with him.

They moved toward the auction tent, yet all John could do was look back at his son, and hope for a miracle. "I love you, Thomas. Never forget your father loves you." He saw Thomas nod, but was now too far away to hear his reply.

John felt desperation come over him. He wanted to break the shackles from his feet, grab the boy and run with him. If he could do that, even if they were both killed in the attempt, at least they would die together.

This way . . . this way was barbaric and monstrous. A lump formed in John's throat, gagging him. He wondered, as he and his men were shoved to the front of the display line, if he would choke on it and die.

Inside the tent, a tall, gaunt man with dark skin and high forehead stepped forward and looked the prisoners up and down with his sinister black eyes. "So, this is what's left of the *Warwick's* crew?" he asked.

"Yes, sir," said Peter Bayland, who was the first man up in the line.

"Speak only when you are spoken to!" the man snarled.

They were a sorry lot, all sixteen of them, with clothes that hung in threads, bodies filthy, faces unshaven. The man assessed each one of them, then asked, "Is there one named John Dunton among you?"

John gasped when he heard his name mentioned. The expression did not go unnoticed by the man questioning them. He strode authoritatively over to John and glared at him as though he wanted to carve John's heart out of his chest.

Swallowing his fear, John held his head proudly and said, "I am John Dunton."

The man remained in the same position, as though daring John to blink, or even to move. "My name is Aligolant," he hissed. "Your woman cost me two hundred bars of gold, Dunton, and I'm going to take it out of your hide!"

Refusing to be baited by the man, John glared back at him with all the fury an emaciated human can possess.

When Aligolant saw that John would not cower toward him, he barked, "Two hundred ducats for John Dunton. Then kill the rest of them. They won't last a day on a pirate's ship."

"You will take all my crew or I will not serve you," said John.

"I give the orders around here, Dunton," Aligolant warned.

"To me, yes you do. But I give the orders to them. Without them, I will not obey your orders. You will take all of us, or none of us."

"You dare threaten me?" Aligolant yelled.

"We are all dead men anyway," John told him. "Why does it matter to you whether they die now or in a few weeks? If you would have me serve you, you will bring my crew with me."

"What would I get in return for such a favor?"

"I am an obedient servant and can navigate anywhere in the oceans you care to sail. I will even fight to the death for you, if necessary. But if you take me without my men, I will look for any way I can to destroy you when you least expect it. Then I will cut your body into tiny pieces and feed you to the sharks."

"I believe you would try," admitted Aligolant. "I might as well kill all of you now."

"That is your choice," said John, calling the man's bluff. "But then, whose hide will you use to extract your two hundred bars of gold?"

Aligolant seemed to consider John's remarks thoughtfully. "If I let your men live, what may I expect?"

"You may expect that my men will never disobey me. You may have my word of honor that I will not kill you while I remain your slave. And you may expect that I will serve you faithfully."

"For how long?" Aligolant tormented him.

"For as long as it takes."

Finally, the crafty pirate sighed in defeat. "Very well. I will take your entire crew with me. But every time one of them displeases me, John Dunton, I will punish you."

"It is a fair bargain," said John, "but there is one more thing."

"You cannot have your son as part of your crew, Dunton. He's a strong boy. He will fetch a healthy price. I must have something to offset my losses."

Surprised that Aligolant knew about young Thomas, John begged, "But he is only a boy. What possible value could he have to anyone but his father?"

"We have made our bargain, Dunton. Besides, I have agreed to sell him today, and a pirate doesn't go back on his word to other pirates."

John sighed wearily. He had no more bargaining tools at his disposal. "Then will you buy him back for me? I will reimburse you well. There is great wealth at my disposal in London. I would repay everything he costs, and more." John pleaded, grasping for anything that would sway Ali.

"This conversation is over," said Aligolant as he walked away. Just as he reached the entrance he turned back and said, "I consider it my right and privilege to deprive you of your son, Dunton. Perhaps it will remind you that your woman deprived me of my gold." Ali's last words gave John the real reason why the conniving man would never consider Thomas for part of the crew.

John felt an agonizing heaviness in his chest over leaving the auction block without his son, not knowing who would buy him, nor how they would treat him. The life of a slave was not the life he had hoped to provide for Thomas, nor was a life filled with whippings and persecution the kind of home in which he wanted his wife to live.

After the worst beating of his life when he returned to the *Warwick* with Aligolant and his crew, given in the heat of his new master's anger towards him, John felt that he deserved every single lash, for he had failed his family entirely. The excruciating pain from whip-welts all over his back did not keep him awake that night. Rather, it was the remorse he felt, knowing he had been unable to protect his wife and his son.

Aboard the *Warwick* the next morning, Aligolant brought aboard a skeleton crew of the mangiest-looking Moorish pirates John had ever seen. Shackles were removed from the slaves' ankles and they were

given instructions to clean the ship from bow to stern, prepare the hold for supplies, and when those supplies arrived, to store them orderly. The men were so relieved to be out of their shackles, they didn't concern themselves with making an escape plan, yet.

Some of the men were put on sail duty, cutting, sewing and reshaping the sails for the *Warwick,* so that there would be three enormous triangular sails, instead of the four square sails and one triangular the bark had previously carried. John had heard this new triangular design made a vessel sail faster, closer to the wind and with greater maneuverability. This would be an interesting experience, regardless of the circumstances, he reasoned.

As he dove off the bow that same morning to fulfill one of his duties, to catch fish for his crew, a large round fish, a variety he had seen in the market yesterday, swam lazily below him. He had volunteered for the assignment because he was only one of two men who knew how to swim. Fortunately for him, the fish was so surprised to find John suddenly atop of it, that John was able to subdue it easily by putting his hands through the large fish's gills and ripping them out. Mortally wounded, the forty-pound fish gave very little fight.

After John handed the fish up to Elias Fox, who had been given the position as Cook since James Taylor had not survived the pirate's attack, John did what he could to rub the salty water over the open welt-wounds on his back, chest and legs. The salt would act as an antiseptic, hopefully preventing him from developing infection.

Taking in several deep breaths to expand his lungs, John dove straight for the bottom of the crystal clear water, beneath the *Warwick,* and gathered several scallops, clams and mussels.

Swimming up toward the bow, he reached an area just above the

waterline known as the "head" of the vessel. The "head" was where the crew and passengers relieved themselves by stepping through an aperture built into the front of the ship accessible by use of a rather large port and lock assembly, with a small platform and two iron rings from which to hang on.

John handed the shellfishes up to Peter Bayland, who was waiting for them at the head. Peter broke them open, immediately, and ate the raw flesh with an eagerness born of starvation.

John made at least fifteen trips to gather additional rations. Each time he came up for air, another of his crewmen would be waiting for him at the head, ready for his morning protein. When all fifteen Englishmen had eaten the supplementary food John had provided for them, he made one last dive to gather several more scallops. After he surfaced near the head, he popped them open with a sharp dagger and ate the raw insides. It was not the most appetizing food he'd ever eaten, but it was keeping him and his men alive, and had become the mainstay of the seamen's meager diets.

John then gathered seaweed and brought a large bundle up to Elias, who made a seaweed soup for the men, which wasn't bad tasting. It was one kind of food that the pirate, Aligolant, didn't mind the men eating. However, if he'd seen all the shellfish they ate, Aligolant would have confiscated it for himself and the Moors and let the Englishmen starve. Their master turned his nose up at seaweed soup, however. No self-respecting pirate would stoop to such deprivation, which suited John and his men perfectly. Aligolant, who rarely got up before breakfast, was unaware of the Englishmen's additional protein breakfasts and late night snacks.

Although John's open lash-wounds stung terribly in the saltwater, he refused to give Aligolant the satisfaction of hearing about it.

Every day, John worked three times harder than any of the other men and every night for the first two weeks, he was whipped mercilessly. Once it was because Peter Bayland had taken a swing at one of the Moors who had taunted him. Another time, Elias had stolen an extra sea biscuit. But soon the men learned to keep their emotions and actions in check and their hunger bridled, because for everything they did wrong, or not exactly to Aligolant's liking, he would fly into a rage and lash John severely.

Every morning John raided the sea for whatever he could find that would serve as meat for his men. Meanwhile, his muscles grew stronger from the burdens placed upon him as a slave to Master Aligolant.

Since John refused to let even so much as a gasp escape his lips during his daily beatings, the pirate soon found no satisfaction in whipping him, nor in torturing him in diverse ways. This came as a relief to John. His lash-wounds began to heal, and he soon found favor in the eyes of his captor.

While they were in Morocco, the English slaves could see no plausible way to escape, and John pointed out to them that escape was not an option. The only way they could return to England was if they returned in the *Warwick*, which would be a show of good faith to King Charles that they were still his loyal subjects. Whatever they did would have to be carefully planned out and stealthily executed. Otherwise, they would die aboard ship as worn out slave-sailors, whipped into submission at the whim of a barbarian.

Though he encouraged his men toward patience and perseverance, John kept his true feelings to himself. He had learned to hate while working in Salé as a slave to Aligolant. Every time he looked at his captor, he thought of Rebecca tied to the captain's bed aboard the *Little David*. He'd promised Aligolant that he would not kill him if Aligolant

spared the lives of John's fifteen crewmen. But he hadn't promised that he would prevent one of his men from doing so. The dark thoughts John kept secret against Aligolant were no less potent than those he harbored toward Edward Blackwell. Every night when he went to bed, he found sleep almost impossible. Visions of Rebecca being forced to succumb to Edward Blackwell nearly drove John insane, and he realized more every day that the feelings he had for Rebecca had little to do with physical longing.

When he wasn't worrying about Rebecca, he fought off fears about Thomas. The things John imagined men could do to his son were unbearable, and he didn't know how to shut the images from his mind.

With the passing of time, John learned that hate only cankered his soul and made him bitter. After a while, he put his hatred away, realizing that he would not be able to rescue the ones he loved if anger, hatred and hostility drove him to commit crimes far worse than his enslavement. In order to be of value to his family, he would have to deny such feelings and disallow them to ever surface again.

Contemplating the fate of his wife and his son did not serve any worthwhile purpose, so John began to concentrate on making himself useful. But should the opportunity ever arise for him to rescue his son, he would be ready.

On the twenty-sixth of June, more than three months since their capture, the moon shone fully upon Salé harbor and the surrounding hillsides. Silently, John left the hold, where he and the men were forced to sleep. He walked upon the deck, thinking about young Thomas, who should celebrate his ninth birthday this day. As he walked, he looked out over the Atlantic Ocean and pondered how he could best serve his son. What could he do that would serve a useful purpose toward rescuing Thomas?

And then it came to him. With planning and cunning, John could present King Charles with in-depth information regarding the layout of Old Salé and New Salé . The pirates' lair could be captured with the right information in the right hands. John would have to provide that information.

John knew the English would never help him strike back at New or Old Salé if they did not know the layout of the cities, or the number of strongholds within the cities' walls. They would need a battle plan. Without detailed maps, they could make no plan. If John was ever to be a useful tool to King Charles and the Royal Navy, he would have to commit to memory every strategic point of value regarding both sides of the Bou Regreg River.

Climbing up to the crow's nest, John found the Moorish man on duty there sound asleep. Without disturbing him, John sank down onto the topmost spar yard. From this advantageous viewing point, he studied the lay of the land in the moonlight, and noted the position of the Roman Tower on the South, the chapel on the North. He visually stepped off how many feet of stronghold bordered New Salé where the pirates' haven lay. He counted the number of buildings and committed to memory every detail that he thought might possibly be useful. The information he brought back could assist the king in mounting an attack and rescue effort. After a few hours of quiet, meticulous study, John left the Moroccan lookout asleep in his perch, unaware that John had ever been up there.

For weeks afterward, whenever John went into town with one of the Moors to get supplies, or climbed aloft to work on the rigging, he committed to memory everything that he saw, so that he could recall the entire area with exacting detail. His keen mind created and

concealed the map the English needed to rescue their countrymen . . . to rescue Thomas.

With time, Aligolant relaxed his hold upon his captors, perhaps thinking that John and his men had learned to enjoy the pirate's life. Finally, he allowed them a little more freedom, and a little more food. Still, it was never enough, for they worked from the moment the sun rose in the east until the dark night descended upon them. Yet, in the grayness of dawn, they would wait at the head for John to serve them whatever raw shellfish he could scavenge from the ocean bottom. Each Englishman knew that their lives were spared, their strength bolstered, because the master mariner from London had befriended them. The bond between them grew ever stronger, and they looked to John for leadership, and for life-sustaining food.

THOMAS WAS NOT sold at the auction block the day he saw his father, but within the week he was traded to a man named Ali Zuny, who was a hard task master, expecting sixteen hours of service every day. Thomas was required to haul water, carry supplies, swab decks, kill chickens, help the cook, and fetch anything which Ali Zuny requested. Still, Master Zuny fed his slaves better than those who had taken the *Little David*, so Thomas had no cause to complain. What worried Thomas the most was that he had heard Ali Zuny would be taking his slaves to Algeria come December. The stories they told about that place made his hair stand on end.

In time, Thomas had proven to Master Zuny that he was honest and diligent in his duties. Within a few months, Thomas was given the trusty position as an errand boy.

BY THE END of July, Aligolant had learned to trust John with duties other than loading supplies on and off various ships as they came into port. Tuesdays was the local market day when the farmers and vendors brought wares into the city to sell or barter. John was given full charge of provisioning. The Englishmen, who still considered themselves as John's crew, were never allowed to leave the dock, but did the loading and unloading in his absence. John was bound by his loyalty to his crewmen, and could not risk any harm coming to them by John's stepping out of bounds when he was away from the *Warwick*. However, every time he left the ship, his eyes and ears were open to any sight or sound regarding his beloved son.

John was amazed at the number of English subjects who were now slaves in Salé and the outlying areas of Morocco. At the rate they were coming in, it was entirely conceivable that close to twenty thousand English men, women and children would be sold at the city's auction block. The numbers sickened him, more because they were in such poor condition when they arrived. The more he saw of the slave trading, the more he wanted to get back to England and organize a massive rescue effort, not only for Thomas, but for his countrymen and women, as well.

During his second time at the market, John came upon a man he knew from London, who was once wealthy and of a kind demeanor. "Master Robert Woodruff! It's good to see you, sir!"

"John? John Dunton! What brings you to Salé?"

"I was captured. And you?"

"Same here. But they soon learned that I had money in London,

so they freed me for a nice bounty. It cost me every cent I owned, but they left me with my ship and now they allow me to trade freely with them. I even have a government permit and all that rubbish."

"Robert, why have you not gone to the king for redress?"

"I intended to, but unfortunately I was forced to help them on a couple of their raids, as no doubt you have. When my countrymen heard of it, they labeled me a pirate. Now I have no country, just my ship, a small shack by the river and my wares."

This information saddened John. "I'm sorry to hear it, Robert. But at least you're alive and well, from the look of you."

"I manage well enough, John. Though I miss our homeland."

Changing the subject, John asked, "Have you heard where the children go, who are sold here?"

"Everywhere. Turkey, Portugal, Spain. Why do you ask?"

"You haven't seen my son, Thomas, have you? In your travels about?"

"They got Thomas, too! This is a sad state of affairs, a sad state, indeed."

"Then you haven't seen him?"

"No, John, I'm sorry. But now that I know he's missing, I'll keep my eyes and ears open. If I can be of any service to you, John, any service at all, just ask me."

"If you do find him, would you buy him away from his master for me. You know I'm good for the money, Robert."

"Yes, I know that, John. I will watch for him."

"Thank you."

"Godspeed, then."

John nodded, but he did not respond. When Robert Woodruff left him, John doubted that he would ever see him again. If Robert was trading with pirates, he was leading a dangerous life. Not many pirates lived to see forty.

Having heard that the *Warwick* would be sailing to England in August to capture English women because they brought a healthy price at auction, John knew he might not live long enough to come back and search for his son. He hadn't seen Thomas since that day at the marketplace. John was determined to thwart Aligolant's plans, for he would never commit the degrading acts of his captor, even if it meant his own death.

Still, John held out hope for news of Thomas every time he went to the marketplace. John asked every person he met if they knew anything about a young boy, nine years of age, with black hair and brown eyes. To his great disappointment, no one could — or would— help him.

On August 8th, a week before the *Warwick* was rumored to leave Salé, a local merchantman known as Christopher Willoughby stood behind John as he waited at Master Liberger's front door for a basket of eggs, a favorite of Aligolant.

Without seeming to speak to John, the man whispered low enough so that only John could hear, "Your son is with Ali Zuny's ship, which trades between Algeria, Turkey and Morocco."

"How do you know this?" John whispered back.

"I have seen him run errands for Zuny between my street vendors and his master's."

"Please, sir, I beg you, buy the boy from Master Zuny if it is possible. I will pay you double whatever it costs you." When Willoughby arched an eyebrow, John said, "Triple. Whatever it takes. I have money in England and can reimburse you well for your trouble."

"How do I know you will pay me?"

"Robert Woodruff knows me, sir. From when he lived in London. He will vouch for me, I assure you."

"I will see what I can do, my friend." Then Christopher Willoughby walked away, as though he'd never spoken to John at all.

John grit his teeth so hard his jaw ached. Dare he hope? Dare he even dream that his son would be redeemed and given back to him? He dared not, for he knew how easily hope could be dashed, but he couldn't help it. For the first time since his captivity, John felt a nugget of hope growing within him.

Walking back along the quay with a large basket of eggs in one hand and a barrel of olive oil in the other, John thought long and hard about his young son. Dare he risk kidnaping him, now that he knew where he might be found? Could he smuggle young Thomas aboard the *Warwick* without anyone knowing? The answer to his question glared back at him in stark reality. If Thomas turned up missing, the people in charge of the auction block would find him. Everyone knew John had been asking about him. Reluctantly, John had to admit that this was something he could not risk, not until the very last night before they sailed.

Then John gulped. Aligolant would throw Thomas overboard the moment they set out to sea. He searched the ship on a daily basis for

anything amiss. And he'd already found plenty of reasons to punish John, as John's scarred chest, back and legs attested.

Any rash decision could be a deadly one. If Christopher Willoughby could buy Thomas from Ali Zuny, John could certainly persuade King Charles to send a fleet to Salé to rescue the oppressed and bring them home, including Thomas and all the other English subjects forced into slavery by these barbarians.

Though it was a difficult decision to make, John hoped he would not live to regret it. Under cover of darkness, on their last day at anchor, John would kidnap young Thomas away from Master Zuny, and take the lad with him when they set sail next week.

As it turned out, John didn't have an opportunity to smuggle his son anywhere. As was his custom, he awakened just before dawn the following day, ready to do some diving and foraging for seafood for his men, when he felt the movement of the bark beneath him, he raced outside to see what had happened. The wind had come up favorably in the night. The sails were filled with air and the *Warwick* was already headed northerly toward England.

Chapter Sixteen

Retaliation

"*A bark belonging to Aligolant was fitted out for a raid into the English Channel, principally to try and capture English women, being of more worth than others.*"

The Earl of Portland from Winchester
Castle, 26 Sep 1636

Rebecca wiped the perspiration from her forehead with the sleeve of her shift and decided she had done enough in the garden for one day. It was mid-August already and she had been working since daybreak, hoeing the rows of cabbages, carrots, beans and turnips, some of which she planned to cook tonight with supper.

The countryside around John's cottage came alive at dawn and she often came out early so she wouldn't miss it. Birds sang a cheery welcome, reminding Rebecca of the first time John said good morning to her. Flowers opened their sleepy petals as the sun kissed them awake, reminding her of Thomas' smile the evening she asked for flowers for the dinner table when they were aboard the *Warwick*.

Although Naomi, who tended the flower gardens, told her the

names of the different blooms, Rebecca couldn't keep them all straight. Roses and hollyhocks, dahlias and lilies, periwinkle and pansies, poppies and so many others. Finally, she'd decided to just call them flowers.

Ruth, on the other hand, was a more domesticated woman, preferring to spend her time baking in the kitchen or sewing in the parlor.

John's Cottage, as Rebecca had named it, sat at the edge of a hamlet near Stepney Parish on the outskirts of London. The rural area of Stepney Parish was quite beautiful. From *John's Cottage* Rebecca had a marvelous view. She could see far over a verdant field, a lush-flowered meadow, and a narrow strip of salt marsh to the many ships of sail that passed up and down the river, Thames, which wound through the valley like a wide silver ribbon between Stepney and the vibrant green hills of Kent and Surrey.

The cottage had two very large rooms at ground level, a parlor and a working kitchen, and stairs that led up to three more rooms. The first bedroom was quite roomy, nearly double the size of the other two, with a four-poster bed, a brick fireplace with tripod swing and a large kettle for heating water, a dresser with seven drawers, a dressing table, several dandy hooks and a chest at the foot of the bed that held memorabilia which John had saved from his voyages, as well as some of his journals. She hadn't read John's journals yet, fearing that if she did, it would mean that she thought he was never coming back.

The second room was most curious. It held a large tin tub, big enough for a person to sit in. It rested in an alcove above a brick hearth and directly over the chimney of the downstairs fireplace. Apparently, it was used for warming water to a suitable temperature for bathing. There was also a draining tube, attached to the iron tub, that led through a small hole in the wall to the outside of the cottage. A dressing table with basin and pitcher stood along one wall, as well as

a free-standing shelf with soft cotton drying and washing cloths stacked neatly on them.

It took her quite a while to figure out what the last object was, and when she did, she could not suppress a giggle. At first sight, it appeared to be nothing more than a hardwood box with arm rests, until she located a hinge in the front that enabled the box to open, like a cupboard. Inside, she found a bronze bucket that fit snugly, with no space between the top of the bucket and the bottom of the seat. Finally, Rebecca found another hinge and discovered that the seat of the chair lifted up, forming a backrest. In its place was another seat made of hardwood with a hole in the middle of it that had been sanded until it was smooth as satin. It was the first time she'd seen an indoor privy, which even the Earl of Portland and his lovely wife, Penelope, did not have. Blackwell Tower had no indoor privy, either, only the chamber pots that were emptied quite frequently by the chamber maids.

Thomas' bedroom was smaller and held a single bed, a small dressing table, a child-size bag with steel marbles in it, two slates with chalk, a globe of the world, a small wagon with wooden building blocks, plus an assortment of rocks, pieces of flint and sticks that boys have a tendency to collect.

Rebecca was completely satisfied with *John's Cottage,* with one exception. Her family did not, at the moment, live there with her.

Even if her husband and son were still alive, they might never return to Stepney. Thoughts of what had become of them were almost more than she could endure.

If John never returned, she would never know if John loved her when their child was conceived, or if he just needed her in ways that

men need women. Did love have anything to do with the consummation of their marriage?

Shaking her head, she scolded herself. *Just because he didn't say he loves me, it doesn't mean that he does not care.* Then she recalled something Thomas had shared with her aboard the *Warwick* when first he talked about his parents. John had told Thomas that he and Mary loved enough to last a lifetime. Considering this memory, Rebecca realized that John had no need for another love. Did he?

She sighed, then stubbornly stretched her back, refusing to let sad thoughts ruin her day. Determined, she carried the hoe to the tool shed.

Naomi waved to her from the back porch of Simon's house. "Are you feeling well?" she asked.

Grateful for her grandaunts' gracious attention, Rebecca nodded. "Just finishing up."

"Do you have time for tea? Ruth's been baking biscuits."

"Let me wash up and I'll be right over."

Naomi smiled. "We'll wait for you."

As she went to the well and drew a bucket of water for the house, she thanked the good Lord one more time for the two women who had rescued her from a lifetime of loneliness that chilly May day when she'd arrived at her father's tinsmith shop and apartment.

After refreshing herself, Rebecca walked over to the Harris' home and found Naomi and Ruth waiting for her on the back porch with sweet biscuits and chamomile tea.

Sitting down in the rocking chair that Simon once used, she felt something move deep within her slightly rounded abdomen. It surprised

her at first and she gasped.

"What is it?" Ruth asked her, a look of concern on her face.

"It's little John," she answered. "I just felt him move for the very first time."

JOHN DUNTON AND Captain John Rickles, a Dutchman who had been captured by the Moors in 1630, shared the responsibility of sailing the *Warwick* to England. To avoid confusion, John Rickles, who was formerly a boatswain's mate, was called Captain, even though John, technically, outranked him. John Dunton, master as well as navigator, was called by his given name. From Morocco to the English Channel, they flew the Moroccan flag with the pirate's flag just below it. But when they neared the channel, the flags were replaced with the flag of England to avoid detection.

John stayed at the helm most of the voyage from Salé, Morocco, to the English coast, alternating with the captain every four hours. Normally, they would have had three men at the helm, but Aligolant trusted none of the other men to do the job. In addition to John's fifteen men, there were three other Dutchmen, thirty-one Moors and five Flemish renegades.

Darkly, John thought of the pirate's life he would now be forced to lead and realized he could not be a pirate, regardless what Aligolant thought. If they were to capture English subjects and take them prisoner to Salé, he could not participate. In the Royal Navy he'd been taught, as had thousands of royal seamen, that piracy was not to be tolerated and that it would be better to lay his life down willingly, rather than to be forced into piracy. If he continued with Aligolant, or by his

willingness to participate, forced his men into piracy, he would deserve a pirate's death.

Somehow he would have to make his stand against the pirates, though when he discussed it with Captain Rickles, they could not agree on a plan because the odds were almost two to one against them.

John was amazed at the quick response the bark now had under triangular sails, and this voyage was a constant source of learning and wonder. The configuration seemed to make a great deal of difference in how the vessel handled. The *Warwick* could sail within fifteen degrees of the wind and still make headway. Now, John understood how the pirates overtook the square-rigged English vessels with such ease. He studied every point of sail that Captain Rickles put upon the bark and how to run the lines and yard spars to best advantage. This would be something he would design into his own vessel, should his dream of owning his own merchant shipping company ever come to fruition.

As they sailed into the English channel, the first boat they came upon was a small fishing vessel with nine men aboard. Pulling alongside them was no problem at all. With the English flag flying aloft, they no doubt assumed that the *Warwick* was on the King's errand and they dropped their sail and made ready to be boarded.

To their great surprise, the Moors went over the gunwales and took possession with little more than a whimper of protest from the fishermen. After the Moors brought the nine men aboard, they tethered the fishing vessel to the *Warwick*, much disappointed they had captured no women.

With the welcome addition of nine able-bodied men, John passed the word privately that they would meet later that night to plan a

mutiny after the Moors had celebrated themselves into inebriation.

It was nearing one in the morning when Aligolant fell asleep, and half of the Moors with him. The other half stood duty topside, with Captain Rickles at the helm.

John, still pretending to be asleep, prayed they would not be detected as he lifted his head from the floor. A silent gasp escaped him as he realized he had soundlessly voiced his first prayer since Mary died. *Great timing, John!* he scolded himself. *Do you really expect God to help you after you've ignored Him for nine years?*

Shamed, John nodded toward the bow, the farthest distance from Aligolant and the sleeping Moors, and slipped silently to that position, the seamen following closely behind him.

When they had gathered together the three Dutchmen, nine English fishermen and fifteen mariners, John whispered just loud enough to be heard, "Captain Rickles and I have been planning a mutiny, men. It's risky, but with nine more to fight with us, we believe we can overpower the Moors and drive them into the hold."

"We're with you, John," said Elias.

The mariners nodded eagerly.

"And you?" John asked the eldest fisherman, a big man called Derek.

"Of course," he responded eagerly, nodding his head.

"I don't know how well your men can fight," John added as a precaution. "But we'll need every ounce of courage you can give us."

"You're thinking of how easily we surrendered," said Derek. "But the past three months, them that resisted the pirates were massacred."

"This may be our lot as well," John warned. "But if we don't fight

now, we'll end up like Captain Rickles, whose been forced into slavery for the past five years."

The Dutchmen nodded. The one named Isaac asked, "What do you want us to do?"

"First," John explained, "we'll divide into two groups. One group will take the sleeping Moors, the other will take the ones awake. If we can avoid killing them, we should. Especially Aligolant. I'd rather see them all swinging from the gallows as a warning to future pirates. But if you get in a tough spot, remember that they will kill you if they get a chance."

"How will we decide what group to go in?" Derek asked.

"Captain Rickles and I are in agreement on this." The men expressed their understanding, so John continued. "Captain wants the three Dutchmen and twelve mariners to deal with the Moors on deck. I want Simon, Elias, Peter and you fishermen to help me with the sleeping Moors.

"Obviously, the only way this will work is if we have one captain. When the next watch ends, Captain Rickles will come down and pretend to sleep. When the Moors, who are up on deck now, come down about the same time, you'll wait until they fall asleep. As soon as they're asleep, the captain's group will meet back here. He will instruct you who to take out and where. The moment he comes out on the deck, he'll go to the water barrel and take a drink. That's my signal to tell the guard that I'm going to the head. The Moor will take the helm. As soon as you see me come below, the captain's group will position themselves on deck, in preparation to take the Moors, while my group takes the sleeping ones. Hopefully, by the time you get up there, the

new watchmen will still have hangovers. It's probably the best opportunity we'll have."

John looked around at the men with him. He could see both fear and courage surfacing on their faces in the dim light. "Are we all agreed?" he finally asked.

Some men gulped, some smiled, but all of them nodded.

"Good. Now get some rest if you can. We have about two or three more hours to refresh ourselves."

"Someone's coming," Elias whispered.

The group froze in unison, none of them daring to breathe. Suddenly John saw a movement out of the corner of his eye and turned just in time to see Peter Bayland grab the Moor, who was coming toward the head. He covered the Moor's mouth with one hand and slit his throat with the other. For several seconds, the Moor struggled as blood leaked from his neck. He soon became limp as a rag doll.

Peter then dragged the body over to one side and covered him with some old canvas sails. When he returned he smiled and whispered, "That's one more we don't have to worry about."

John had asked the men to avoid killing if they could and Peter had set a poor example on how to accomplish it. He wasn't aware that Peter had a knife, but on closer inquiry he found that the only men without weapons were the fishermen. He sent the captain's group back to bed and prayed they would get some sleep, but they probably would be unable to do so.

With only his own group to work with now, John assessed the situation more closely. "The good thing going for us is that most of them will be asleep. Peter, I don't think we'll need to slit everyone's throat. Do you understand?"

Peter nodded, but John wasn't certain now that he could trust him. Disregarding this concern, he thought, *So what? A dead Moor is a good Moor.* Then he silently chided himself for such thinking, distancing his heart as far away from a pirate's as possible.

John looked gravely at the fishermen. "Believe me, there is an easier, less bloody method of subduing them. We will have thirteen men and Aligolant to contend with. Before you go back to bed, every three minutes one of you will go into the galley and take a brick from the hearth. Hopefully they will have cooled enough by now. When it comes time to subdue your men, hit them right here," John pointed to his temple. "Fairly hard, but not so hard that you'd kill them. Do you understand?" From their expressions, John could see that they were glad it would be no worse than that.

"If you have questions or concerns, you must talk with Simon. He is a doctor and he can show you precisely where to hit, and exactly how hard."

Simon gave him a weak smile and John knew that he did not like his assignment, but he would do it and be grateful that was all he had to do.

"As soon as you've put a man out, take his weapon in your free hand so that someone doesn't use it against you. Make sure all the Moors are subdued, then some of you will help the others on deck, while some of you will drag the Moors to the hold and drop them down to Peter Bayland."

"Why me?" Peter asked.

John sighed. "Because if any of them come to and begin to resist, you will know how to handle them."

Peter smiled, understanding now.

"These men are used to clubbing fish, not killing people," John added. "But Peter, I will know if you had a choice, once this is over, and it will not go well for you if you did not use your best judgement."

John saw him squirm ever so slightly and knew he'd made his point.

"How will we know who is to go and who is to stay?" asked Derek.

"How many of you are over thirty?"

Five of the fishermen raised their hands.

"You five will go on deck, Simon and the younger men will stay below."

Perhaps they didn't understand John's logic in choosing the older men, but John hoped that, in a similar situation, some kind Master would want to protect Thomas' young eyes from witnessing the carnage of combat.

While Simon and the others began rotations in going to the galley, John pulled Elias aside.

"As for Aligolant," he said. "He sleeps with a pistol and a sword, but he was so drunk when he finally went to bed an hour ago that he may not be any problem at all. Between the two of us, I think we can subdue him. He must be left alive, even if no one else is, for I gave him my word I would not kill him."

Elias smiled. "I can be quiet as an ocean breeze. He won't know what hit him."

"You have a weapon, I suppose."

Elias pulled out a small knife that was sharp enough for shaving, and said, "Of course."

John nodded. "His pistol is my main concern. I have access to a

sword, so that is one area in which I will be of some use. Timing will be everything. We need to take Aligolant before he hears what is going on out here, but not so early that he will wake up the Moors before our fishermen friends get a chance to overpower them."

FOR THE NEXT hour, John remained awake and alert. It took over half an hour for the men to get their bricks from the galley and he noticed that some carried two of them.

He tried to focus on something else, to let his mind rest, but he found it impossible. Everything in his future hinged on what would happen next.

If they were successful, would his men be imprisoned as pirates along with the Moors?

Would Simon survive the mutiny? He'd been complaining of chest pains lately, and with his medical supplies used up on the Moors the past five months, he had nothing left with which to help himself.

It was entirely possible that John could be killed in the attack, as well as his men. If they were not successful, Aligolant would have no choice but to execute all of them.

But if, by the grace of God— then John reconsidered. Did he even have faith that God would assist him? After all, God hadn't been too helpful up to that point. In nine years time, John had lost one wife to the grave, one wife to pirates and a woman beater, and his only son. Had God forgotten John? Or had He ignored John's plight because John had forgotten Him? Did he have enough faith to trust God to help him now?

Searching his heart, he remembered Thomas saying, "I'll be all right,

Father. Truly I will. I've been pretending that I'm really Joseph, with the coat of many colors. You know him from the Bible, don't you?" Indeed, Thomas' last words to John had penetrated his thoughts nearly every day since he had last seen him. "I pray every morning and every night that God will somehow find a way for us."

Tears came to John's eyes. The faith of young Thomas had shown him more courage than John thought a child could possess. He had no one else to trust now, no one except God. For the first time in over nine years, John searched the deep recesses of his soul and allowed himself to rely on God once again. Bringing himself up to his knees, he pleaded for a pardon, begged for mercy, and pledged his heart.

When his face was wet and his chin dripped great tears upon his doublet, John ended his prayer and looked around him, wondering if the men had seen, hoping they had slept. What he saw amazed him. All those who would fight for freedom were kneeling, following his example.

AT TWO OF the morning, John tucked a pair of shackles quietly into his doublet and went on deck to relieve Captain Rickles. When he took the helm from him, he placed his left hand on the wheel first and gave the captain a nod. It was their private signal that the men had been briefed and were ready for action.

"Good morning, John. I trust you slept well."

"Yes, sir."

"I'll record my watch, then go to bed. Send someone down to wake me at six of the morning, will you?"

"Yes, of course."

Captain nodded and walked wearily down the steps as John turned the hourglass. When the Moors saw Rickles calling the watch, they followed to wake their comrades and trade places with them.

Within a few minutes twelve Moors came up from the gunnery deck to take their places. For a moment, John recounted, then he remembered that the thirteenth had been taken out of commission earlier in the night.

For the first hour of his watch, nothing exciting happened. He could tell the men had hangovers because they were grumbling with one another. Some were even stretching out on the deck to sleep a little more, unconcerned that there would be trouble for doing so. The *Warwick* was not governed as one of his Majesty's ships and they had no quarrel with the task master, who was sleeping the night away in the aftercastle.

John had just turned the hourglass for the second time when he saw the captain come up on deck and lean over the railing, spewing violently. Immediately John sensed that something had gone wrong. That wasn't the signal. The captain was supposed to get a drink of water.

Captain Rickles wiped his mouth with a handkerchief and walked toward the water barrel. He took the cup from the hook and opened the lid, then dipped the cup in and brought it back again. Looking up at John for only a moment, he put the cup to his lips and drank. Greatly relieved, John whispered, "Thank you, God. *That* is the signal."

John looked at the guard leaning against the stern rail. In broken Arabic, he indicated his need to make use of the head. The guard grunted and came to stand at the wheel. Using his hand to indicate, John told him, "Straight ahead. No turns."

Then he walked down the steps from the deck of the aftercastle and went below. To his horror, two Moors were lying in a crumpled heap near the walkway. "What happened?" he whispered to Peter, who was standing nearby with a bloody knife in his hand.

Elias stepped forward out of the shadows. "We had no choice," he whispered. "They noticed the bricks missing from the galley and were on their way to notify Ali."

John sighed, both relieved and distressed. At least he understood now why Captain had come out of the gunnery deck, spewing overboard. "Let's just get this over with," he told them. He stepped inside and pulled one of the dead Moors out of the way, while Peter did the same with the other.

"Is everyone else ready?" John asked.

"They are," said Elias. "And in position. They're just waiting for us to get into Ali's cabin."

"Then let's go." John didn't wait to see if Elias was with him, he turned and headed back out to the deck, keeping close to the aftercastle wall.

The Dutchmen and Englishmen crept out of the companionway in twos, stealthily getting into position.

John sank into the forecastle corridor. He could hear Elias breathing right behind him. Another few steps and he reached the cabin. Knowing that Aligolant was right handed, it would be John's job to disable him so that he could not pick up the pistol. Satisfied that Elias was ready, he nudged the door open just far enough for both of them to fit through.

He could hear Aligolant snoring, which would muffle their approach somewhat. Taking a big gulp of air, John slipped into the

room and stealthily made his way to the far side of the bed while Elias took the opposite side.

"Wait for the signal," he mouthed to Elias, who nodded his assent.

In under fifteen seconds, but what seemed an eternity to John, he heard Captain Rickles yell, "To life and liberty!" John lunged at Ali, grabbing his right arm before Aligolant was even awake. In his struggle to get away, Aligolant fought like a madman. When John heard the pirate's arm snap, he knew the man could not continue fighting.

Elias grabbed his left arm as Aligolant roared like a cornered beast. "To arms! To arms!" Ali yelled, but it was entirely too late.

John knocked the pistol from the bed to the floor, removed the shackles from beneath his doublet and snapped one onto Ali's right wrist. Then, he wrapped the chain around the bed frame and snapped the other end to Ali's left wrist.

"I'll kill you for this!" Aligolant raged.

"I don't think so," John said calmly, which surprised him because he was shaking violently inside. "You did bring the other shackle, did you not?" he asked Elias.

"Yes, but I've been waiting to see what trick he may have up his sleeve."

"Use it now," John instructed, grabbing Ali's right ankle.

Aligolant kicked and screamed and swore to no avail as Elias and John managed to shackle both ankles to the opposite bedpost. "Watch him," he instructed. "Don't let him out of your sight for a second! And find all the weapons he has hidden in this room."

"Yes, sir."

John slipped out the door and down the forecastle corridor. A great

commotion was taking place on the deck as the seamen and Moors fought and yelled. Ignoring them, John went down the companionway to the gunnery deck stealthily, in case there was trouble. All of the Moors, save one, were subdued, and this one had his sword drawn, his back to John. He was facing off with the four young fishermen who'd stayed behind to lower bodies into the hold. John motioned for the men to remain silent as the Moor threatened them menacingly.

Swiftly, almost in one fluid movement, John grabbed the Moor's sword hand with one fist and struck the Moor's face with the other. The man went limp and the sword fell from his hand.

One of the young men picked it up immediately, and John dragged the Moor over to the hold. He was just starting to awaken when John put the shackles on his wrists, behind his back, and another set on his ankles.

"Stand back," he told Peter, who was down below in the hold. "Here comes a live one."

He lifted the Moor by both arms, causing one of his shoulders to pop out of joint. The man screamed in agony.

"Please," John said. "You'll thank me later. If I'd sent you down there feisty like you were, Peter would have slit your throat." He dropped the Moor into the hold and looked back at his four companions. "Carry on, gentlemen." Then, he went back to the weather deck to see what he could do to help up there.

To his relief, the English and the Dutch conquered, and the Moors were being put into shackles. Satisfied that they had the situation well under control, John grabbed two sets of shackles and returned to Ali's cabin, where Elias had amassed a small arsenal of weaponry, five pistols, at least a half dozen swords and daggers, a hatchet, plus all the clothing

and bedding in the room.

Staying on task, John reconfigured the shackles so that Aligolant had one set on each wrist and ankle; then each shackle was attached to one of the four posts, so that Aligolant had no choice but to lie spread-eagled on the captain's bed.

When John was finished, he studied the array of "weapons" Elias had discovered, then laughed aloud. "What's all this?" he asked, indicating the bedding.

"We wouldn't want him to be hanging himself before his Majesty gets a chance, now would we?" Elias asked.

"Certainly not. And we certainly cannot kill him, ourselves, while he's in our custody, can we?"

"No, sir. You gave him an Englishman's word of honor."

By six in the morning, the Moors were locked safely in the hold, with exception of Ali, who remained shackled to the bed on all four posts, a guard sitting in the cabin with him full time now.

After making sure his men had eaten all the breakfast their bellies could hold, John suggested they take the *Warwick* straight for the nearest port, which would be near Hurst Castle. A cheer went up as all of the men agreed eagerly.

Then John called for the men's attention. They stopped their boisterous approval and gathered around him on the weather deck.

John began his plea with them. "I'd like permission to borrow Derek's boat and set my men aboard her, to sail for Chatham immediately. I have friends there who will vouch for me and for those whom

I request. It's entirely likely that we'll all be taken prisoners by the English until a court date can be held. I would like to spare my men any further suffering and anguish than they have already endured at the hands of these barbarians. As for myself, I will remain aboard. If they put me in prison, I will suffer for them, until such time as my innocense can be established."

"Will they put us in jail, sire?" asked Derek, the elder of the fishermen.

"No. You have just been captured, and you still have your papers in order. My men have nothing but the clothing on their backs and you must admit that they look like pirates."

"I will go with them," said Derek, "and vouch for them if we should be stopped."

"That would be most gracious of you, sir."

"As for you, Captain Rickles, and your three men . . . ." He left the sentence open.

The captain glanced at each of his men, then made his decision. "We, sir, will stay with the bark. We have no quarrel with your men taking their leave at this time."

"Very well." His eyes grew misty but he forced his emotions aside. To his fifteen valiant seamen, he said, "Provision yourself well, for you've at least six days to Chatham."

Simon spoke up immediately. "But John, I can't leave you here."

"You've been a dear friend, Simon, as much a father to me as the one that raised me. But I have to think of Rebecca and you are the only one she will trust after all this treachery."

Simon nodded. "I understand, John. But I do not like it."

"Neither do I. But you are my only hope. You must let her know what has happened and take my marriage contract with you, to prove that she is my wife. If Edward will not release her, you must have him arrested."

"John, there must be something we can do to vouch for you, if you're arrested," argued Simon.

The other men nodded in assent.

"Do you remember Lord Henry Vaine, who lives eight miles from Blackwell Tower on Old London Road?"

"Yes." Then Simon smiled. "Yes, of course. He will vouch for you."

"Exactly." John had served under Lord Henry Vaine for five years before taking his position with Lord Blackwell at Chatham. Lord Henry Vaine acted as overseer of his Majesty's ships in the southern region of England. He also kept records for King Charles, in regards to several other men's vessels, as well.

Simon nodded. "I will go to him at once."

"First make certain the rest of my men are looked after. When they are refreshed and rested, then go to Lord Vaine."

They embraced for only a moment as the men hastily prepared the fishing vessel for their voyage. When his fifteen men were safe aboard the fishing vessel, John knelt upon the deck and prayed with all the gratitude in his humbled heart, unashamed that anyone should see him.

BY FOUR IN the afternoon, they had taken the pirate and Algerian flags and hung them over the gunwale, which symbolized the Moors' utter defeat. But the English flag flew proudly aloft, buoying the men's

spirits like nothing else could. They were pulling into port at Hurst Castle, escorted by smaller boats, caravels and cogs. But the bark started listing to port, a complication John had not anticipated. The Moors and Flemish renegades in the hold were pulling out the *Warwick's* hemp, and trying to sink the ship. Somehow, they had managed to damage a bulkhead. Water began leaking into the hold, and John could not let the pirates drown inside it. He spoke with the captain, who concurred with his assessment, then he instructed the Dutchmen to hoist all the sails and make them ready, which they did with good speed.

Then, John turned the *Warwick* to starboard, toward land, while filling the sails with wind. He noticed that the tide was full, and he knew that he was consigning the bark to an early grave, but he had no choice. He could not release the prisoners, and neither could he let them drown.

The *Warwick* picked up speed and rushed toward the muddy bank of the harbor, slipping through the water for its final dance with the wind, until it came to a halt with a sickening jolt and a groan. High and dry, the *Warwick* would never be pulled out to sea again, for it was too far up on the bank to ever be floated off.

With a nauseating lump in his stomach, John and the crew waited for King Charles' royal guards to come aboard. When they did, they placed John, the captain and the three Dutchmen in irons, as well as Aligolant and all the drenched Moors in the hold.

Now, bereft of his wife, son and the sturdy *Warwick* that had carried him faithfully to America and back again, many times, John was taken to Hurst Castle where he was charged as a pirate. The entire lot of them were imprisoned until their story could be sorted out in court.

Chapter Seventeen

Trial by Fire

*"Subsequently the whole crew were tried at Winchester,
the Moors condemned to death . . ."*

The Earl of Portland, in a letter
from Winchester Castle.

September 1635

While John languished in jail, fearing that he would be convicted with the Moors and sentenced to hang from the gallows at the Portsmouth dockyards, he thought solely of being reunited with his family. His nights and days became confused because of the lack of adequate lighting in the prison cells. The conditions were horrendous and rats infested the place. Food rations were slim, a few crusts of bread and filthy water. Even the pirates had fed them better when they were in shackles while aboard ship.

Boils broke out on his skin and he had no way to drain or clean them. Several times he felt as though he was burning up with fever, but he shared none of this information with his cell mates, the three Dutchmen and Rickles, who had bravely sailed the *Warwick* with him

on its final voyage. For their own part, they fared no better than John did.

In an effort to be optimistic, he told his comrades that prison life could have been much worse. They were fortunate because they were separated from the Moors. He doubted this consoled them, for they, too, feared for their lives.

They were interviewed nearly every day, usually by three men. Every time John was asked into the inquisition room, he begged the high officials to send for Lord Vaine, who would vouch for him.

On one such occasion, a pompous, bulgy little fellow rebuked him with the comment, "If I should send for Lord Vaine every time someone claimed to be Master John Dunton, his Lordship would never be able to leave this place, what with his having to be called in to testify so many times."

"What do you mean?" John asked.

"Good fellow, the Earl of Portland has put up notices regarding you all over the country. I dare say three of every five men we arrest these days claims to be John Dunton. Why should I believe any of the lot of you?"

Shocked by this news, John said, "Then the fact that I knew nothing of these notices should convince you of who I am!"

"Three of every five say that, as well."

When John was returned to his cell, his Dutch comrades and Captain Rickles were unable to console him, for he realized Lord Vaine might not be located in time to testify in his behalf. The only hope John had of being acquitted was if Simon could reach Lord Vaine in time to prevent five innocent men from hanging, and now it seemed as if that hope had vanished.

UNDER COVER OF darkness, a crowded fishing boat slipped into Chatham Bay, the oarsmen exhausted and hungry. It had taken them nine days to reach their home port. Their supplies had been rationed the past four days to half what they'd eaten before.

As Simon looked upon the swarthy crew, he felt inspired to say, "From Isaiah 48:17, the Lord gave utterance that may encourage us now that we have made safe passage to England. He said, *I am the Lord thy God . . . which leadeth thee by the way that thou shouldest go.* Gentlemen, my first duty now is to Captain Dunton, who still calls himself Master. You may go the eight miles to Lord Blackwell's, whose tower is closer, if that is your wish. But as for me, I will first report to Lord Vaine, a journey of sixteen miles. If I hasten—"

"We're going with you," said Peter Bayland.

"Here, here!" the others echoed in agreement.

Simon revised his words. "If we hasten, gentlemen, we will reach Lord Vaine's before dawn and remain undiscovered until he gives us leave to go home."

Nodding and grunting in agreement, the fifteen men disembarked at the wharf, bid Derek, the fisherman who'd accompanied them, farewell, and took the main road out of Chatham as quietly as they had arrived.

A cock crowed in the distance and a dusky dawn lightened the sky as they made their way through the courtyard and up to the massive doors of Lord Vaine's mansion. None of the men had never been inside his Lordship's private domain, with exception of Simon, who had spent many pleasant evenings in the parlor with the man known as one of

King Charles' private councilmen of his High Court of Admiralty.

Squaring his shoulders, Simon reached forward and lifted the door knocker, then pounded it loudly against the door. It took several minutes of such knocking for anyone to answer. Finally, a small, withered-looking man named Barnaby Mills came to the door and set it ajar.

"What brings you beggars to his Lordship's house at this hour?" he demanded.

"Barnaby, it is I, Simon Harris, doctor from the *Warwick*."

Mill's eyes widened and he studied Simon cautiously in the early light. When he finally recognized him, he gasped. "It can't be!"

"It is I, Mills, I assure you. We have escaped from the pirates who held us bound and are come to beg his Lordship's consideration for Master Dunton, who at this moment is likely thrown into prison."

Mills peered closer, then stepped back, aghast. "Come in at once. I will wake the household and prepare refreshment for you. Come in. Come in."

The men were brought inside and assigned bed chambers, where the servants hastened to bring them hot water for bathing, shaving utensils, and clean clothing from Lord Vaine's personal supply. Nothing was spared them. When they were properly attired, most in clothing of far greater quality than they had ever worn, they were escorted into the dining hall, where the cooks had prepared them a feast such as they had never tasted. Bacon and ham, sausages and eggs, fried turnips and fresh garden beets, with cookies and coffee, tea and milk.

When they had eaten so much they could scarcely waddle away from the table, Lord Vaine called them into the parlor, where they were each given a comfortable chair and a glass of the finest wine available.

Two secretaries came in to record the proceedings so that nothing would be left out.

With Simon acting as spokesman, he began by telling the full story of Rebecca's stowaway experience and of her subsequent marriage to John Dunton. As he explained the circumstances, he presented the marriage contract to his Lordship as evidence that the two had married. This news did not seem to surprise Lord Vaine, nor to concern him in the least, which Simon thought was very curious.

Simon soon got down to the business of detailing all that had transpired since the *Warwick* left Chatham Bay over six months ago. It took no small amount of time, but when they were finished, all fifteen men had attested to the truthfulness of their story.

Apparently satisfied with their conduct, Lord Vaine stood and paced across the floor as though contemplating what he must say. When he had collected his thoughts, he turned to them and said, "I can only say that God has shown you great mercy in preserving your lives during your ordeal, for which I give my humble gratitude. Were it not for John Dunton, I expect the lot of you would have been killed at Salé. Therefore, I give all, save Simon, leave to return to your families. First you will be taken to the Chatham port offices, where you will each be compensated for your time and troubles. From there, you will be dismissed until March of next year. You are to be commended for your integrity and your loyalty to the King." He dismissed them with a vigorous handshake and named an amount that they would be paid that surprised even Simon.

When they were gone, he turned to Simon and said, "Are you prepared to travel, doctor, or shall I let you rest for a while?"

"I cannot rest, your Lordship, until I know that John is acquitted

and free to resume his life."

"That's what I expected of you," said Lord Vaine. "We will leave at once."

Within the hour, his Lordship's fastest carriage was racing toward London, then south toward Winchester. For the first six hours, Simon slept as though he was an infant in the lap of his mother. When he awakened at last, Lord Vaine said, "I thought you told me that you cannot rest, Sir Simon." He gave him a brief smile.

"Ah, but I did not say that I could not sleep," Simon reminded. "There is a difference, your Lordship."

Lord Vaine smiled. "Yes, I suppose you are right."

"Begging your pardon," said Simon, "but you have me quite puzzled. You showed no surprise when I informed you of John Dunton's marriage to Rebecca Webster. Do you know if she is still at Blackwell Tower?"

For a moment, his Lordship's face paled and a wan smile appeared. "It has been reported to me that Edward Blackwell was aboard the ship *Neptune* in search of Rebecca when it was attacked. Edward Blackwell and the crew are presumed drowned, or if not, then they have been taken captive. Perhaps you or one of your men saw him while you were in Salé?"

Simon remained silent, too shocked to say anything for a moment. When he'd recovered his wits, he said, "I'm sorry to hear it. But I am certain the men would have mentioned it to me, had they seen Edward Blackwell in Salé."

"Yes, I'm quite sure of it," said Lord Vaine. "In fact, Lord Blackwell has posted a reward for his son's safe return."

"I pray that he will find him. We heard that Rebecca was ransomed

to Edward for two hundred gold bars, your Lordship. Was she safely returned?"

Lord Vaine nodded. "Yes, shortly after Edward left Chatham in the *Neptune,* Lord Blackwell came to me regarding Rebecca. We made a plan to capture her kidnappers. Lord Blackwell paid her ransom, then allowed my men to recover it once he had her safety assured. Lord Blackwell told me of her marriage, and of his son's treatment of her. I was most distressed."

"Is she still at Blackwell Tower?" Simon inquired, relieved to know that Rebecca had been spared.

Lord Vaine smiled brightly this time and his eyes fairly danced as he told Simon the news. "Why, she's living at *John's Cottage* where she belongs. Your two sisters have embraced her as though she was their daughter. Their generosity came at Rebecca's greatest time of need, now that she is in the birthing way with her first infant."

Simon's mouth dropped open. "Begging your pardon, sire, but did you say *infant?*"

"You didn't know, I'm sorry." Then he added, "No one knew until last May."

Fears worked their way into Simon's heart. Young Thomas had told his father that Rebecca had been shackled to the captain's bed while aboard the *Little David* and now Simon worried. Was the baby John's?

Apparently perceiving his concern, Lord Vaine comforted, "It *is* John's child, Simon. Rebecca told Lord Blackwell that the pirates were able to restrain themselves for two hundred bars of gold."

WHEN THE PRISONERS were sent to Winchester Castle that chilly

September day, the weather had turned surprisingly cold. The night had left frost sprinkled about on the flower stems and grass blades. Puddles had a thin sheet of ice upon them and the leaves were turning yellow, orange and red, portending a cold winter ahead.

They rode in a caged wagon, with their hands and feet shackled to eye-bolts secured to the floor and benches. The entire ride, Aligolant glared at John with malicious intent. The man's lower right arm was swollen and festered, and John felt a pang of remorse at having been forced to break it three weeks ago.

After a twenty-mile ride, they ached for relief. As the castle came into view, John prayed more fervently that his life would be spared, that Lord Vaine would arrive in time to redeem him. To John's great disappointment, they were put into cells for the night, for they had arrived too late to hold any trial that same day.

It was nearly midnight, John guessed, when he saw a torch coming toward his cell down a long, dark corridor. A woman with flaming red hair, wearing a deep, green brocade gown, followed behind two guards, with two additional guards following her.

When she arrived at John's cell she looked at the four Dutchmen and John with a hint of compassion in her green eyes. Squaring her shoulders proudly, she asked, "Which of you claim to be John Dunton, Master of the *Warwick?*"

Her question surprised him and John stood to face her, knowing that he must look like a derelict in her eyes, for his face was unshaven, his beard and hair crawling with lice, his body so filthy as to cause even himself to retch. His clothing was threadbare and tattered and very much like the clothing a pirate would wear. "I am John Dunton," he responded, though he could not muster the same pride that this woman

seemed to carry with her.

"You will answer my questions exactly," she stated. "If I am not satisfied with your answers, you will be forbidden a trial, and will be taken this very night and hung in the courtyard for all to see what happens to any liar who would betray the King."

"I understand," said John, nodding to her to indicate that she should proceed.

"Where were you born?"

"In London."

"Where is your current residence?"

"Near Stepney Parish, on the outskirts of London."

"What is your son's name?"

"Thomas."

"How old is he?"

"Nine."

"Are you married?"

"Yes."

"What is your wife's given and maiden name?"

"Rebecca Webster."

"What date were you married?"

"The seventeenth day of March this year, being 1635."

"Where did you marry?"

"Aboard the *Warwick*."

"Who performed the ceremony?"

"Captain Adam Dawson, who is deceased."

She looked at him closely, as though trying to tell whether or not he had lied to her, but John did not fear her.

Finally she said to the guards, "Bring him with me."

As they unlocked the cell gate, John shuddered. She could not have found him in a lie, for he told none. Yet she had instructed that he would be taken and hanged that very hour if he lied to her. For several long moments as he was escorted in front of the first two guards, John agonized. The woman apparently didn't know that he had married, and had likely concluded that in confessing his marriage, he had lied to her. Would the trials never end? Would God never show him mercy? Would he never see his bride again, nor find their son, Thomas?

Tears filled his eyes, but he blinked them back. He had said nothing for which he could be ashamed. If he was to die, he would die with his head held high. He was innocent regardless of what this woman believed.

When they finally left the great, long corridor, she turned into a foyer area, where she faced him and said, "You have Lord Vaine to thank for your life, John Dunton. We have had so many come forward claiming to be you that I have wished we had never posted anything whatsoever about you."

"You believe me?" he questioned, surprised and relieved.

"Of course," she answered. "No one could have known about Rebecca, or your marriage date and who married you. That information we have kept private from everyone."

"Forgive me, my Lady, but did you say I had Lord Vaine to thank?"

"He arrived here less than an hour ago with Simon Harris and

demanded that I question you. Had he not pleaded with us so diligently, I would have never done so, and you likely would have been hung as a pirate tomorrow."

"Then you know that Rebecca is truly my wife?"

Penelope smiled. "Kind sir, your wife has become one of my dearest and most treasured friends. She has been aching for your return."

"Then I'm being released?"

"Oh, no. We must satisfy the orders of the court. There must still be a trial. But at least now you will have proper verification and people who will speak for you."

"Thank you, my Lady, but you could have told me this while I was with my comrades."

A mischievous look formed on her face and she placed a hand upon his arm. "Kind sir, it is my duty as the mistress of this household to see to the comfort of my guests. You will not face trial in the morning dressed as you are. Nor will you sleep on a stone cold floor. Lord Vaine and Simon Harris are waiting to attend to your every need, sir."

Having given him this information, she said, "Goodnight, sir. It has been a most gratifying evening."

"Goodnight," said John. "And . . . thank you, my Lady."

He was then escorted up two flights of stairs and into a large bed chamber where two servants had drawn him a hot bath and laid out bedclothes for him. John couldn't remember a time when he'd been pampered so lavishly.

It didn't take him long to make use of the bath, though it shocked him to see how filthy the water was afterward. Several boils had opened on the insides of his legs and arms, and he could see from the looking

glass that he'd lost a considerable amount of weight. When he was finished, a manservant entered with shears in hand and gave John a haircut and a shave.

Exhausted, yet hungry, he put on a bed robe and asked for some food, which was brought to him quickly on a silver tray. As he sat down to eat the healthiest dinner he had ever eaten, a knock came at the bedchamber door.

"Come in," said John. "Though I can't imagine anything else I could need, you've given me every comfort."

The door was pushed open and standing in the frame were Simon Harris and Lord Vaine. John stood and went to them both, embracing them with tears flowing unashamedly down his face. "Lord Vaine! Simon! I cannot thank you enough for all that you have done for me."

"Please, John. Sit. Eat," implored his Lordship. "We will visit while you do, if you don't mind. When Penelope told us you were here, it was all we could do to wait until you'd had time to clean up."

John resumed his position at the table and his two friends joined him. Soon the servants brought them food as well. But it was a silent meal for a few minutes, while John ate more food in one sitting than he had in many months. When he was finally refreshed, he wiped his mouth with a linen napkin and asked. "I suppose sometime one of you will tell me about Rebecca. Simon showed you the marriage contract, didn't he? Edward did let her go, didn't he?"

When neither man answered immediately John said, "What are you hiding from me?"

"Rebecca is fine!" Lord Vaine answered. "She's been at your cottage since May!"

"Naomi and Ruth took her in the moment they heard about her,"

said Simon. "I haven't seen her yet, since we were concerned about reaching you in a timely manner."

"It appears you made it just in time," said John. "For which I will ever be in your debt, both of you. But tell me about Rebecca, your Lordship. Please!"

Lord Vaine folded his hands. "First, let me apologize to you, John, for Edward's treatment of Rebecca. Lord Blackwell had no idea his son was beating her. If he had, he would have punished him."

"I didn't believe for a moment that he knew about it," John told him. "But what of Edward? Did he confess?"

"He died," said Lord Vaine wearily. "He went after Rebecca in the *Neptune*, but his ship was sunk, apparently by pirates. He was either taken captive, or was drowned in the depths of the sea. Lord Blackwell considers him dead, John. He cannot bear to think of him as a slave."

"I'm sorry to learn of it," said John truthfully. "I would have lashed him myself at one time, but now that I know what that is like, it is something I hope never to experience or witness again."

Lord Vaine's pale eyes widened, but he had no need to express his regrets.

John could see the pain this information caused him and chose to make light of the matter. "Well, at least Rebecca's scars and mine match now." His Lordship almost smiled, but not quite, so John switched the subject back to his wife. "When did you last hear anything regarding Rebecca?"

"I have a letter from her that I brought with me. Perhaps you'd like to read it." Lord Vaine pulled a piece of parchment from his doublet and handed it to John.

Unfolding it, John stood up and went over to the dressing table where a candelabra illuminated the writing better for him.

> *My dear Lord Vaine;*
>
> *Thank you for all that you did in providing your guards to capture those barbarians that held me captive. My husband, John Dunton, will be pleased when he learns of your kindness. May God bless you for the goodness in your heart. By now you have learned that I am in the family way. Therefore, I beseech you to include John and young Thomas in your prayers, as they will have family here, waiting for them to return.*
>
>

Respectfully yours,
Mrs. Rebecca Dunton
>

"My wife is with child?" he asked, struck with fear and hope all at the same time.

"Yes," said Simon, stepping over to rub John's shoulder. "Rebecca assured his Lordship that her virtue was not compromised."

A feeling of relief swept over John like nothing he had ever felt before and he sank onto a chair beside the dressing table before his knees buckled beneath him. Gratitude came over him in great waves which made it difficult to breathe. Then came the regret that Thomas may never know this good news. Suddenly, he could hold his tears back no longer. "We are to have a child," he whispered in both wonder and disappointment. "Oh, Thomas! I must bring you home to your family."

Chapter Eighteen

Where Two Hearts Meet

"It was Gods great mercy that wee did come. . . ."

John Dunton's Journal

T
he following morning John's boils showed remarkable improvement. The good doctor, Simon, had lanced them before John retired the night previous, then packed them with salve and dressings. Much relieved, John then insisted that his Dutch companions be cleaned and their boils attended to, as well as a decent breakfast served to them. His wishes were obeyed immediately, to his great relief. Then he put on the uniform of the Royal Admiralty, complete with hat and sword.

At breakfast, John was introduced to the Earl of Portland at Winchester Castle, and his wife, Penelope, whom he'd met the night before. Simon and Lord Vaine joined them in the dining room. The earl asked John specifically to mention nothing of the pending trial, so that the earl could judge the matter only as he would hear it in court. John was more than willing to comply. He had tired of all the interrogations, and he prayed that today's inquisition would be his last. Longing

235

for nothing more than to go home, where Rebecca awaited him, John felt impatient and restless.

By nine of the morning, John was escorted to the court by four royal guards. When he arrived, the Moorish and Flemish pirates were seated in one section, the aristocracy in another. John was escorted to a middle table where Captain Rickles and the other three Dutchmen were sitting, already cleaned and dressed in immaculate Dutch uniforms. He nodded to them briefly, but he knew by the smiles they returned to him that they now had hope, as did he.

As trials go, this one was short and succinct. The charges of piracy, murder and unlawful possession of his Majesty's ship were read against them all, including John, the Dutchmen, Moors and Flemish. It was then asked if anyone would come forward to speak for any of the accused.

His Lordship stood up, regally clad in the uniform of the High Court of Admiralty, and was introduced by the court crier as, "The right, honorable Lord Vaine, one of his Majesty's private councilmen of his High Court of Admiralty."

Lord Vaine stepped forward and bowed before the assembly of earls, dukes and judges. With his voice resounding to every ear, he said, "Right honorable officers of the court, I stand before you as your equal, an officer and representative of the high and mighty Prince Charles, by the grace of God, King of England, my intention being to speak for Master John Dunton of London, a master mariner in his Majesty's Royal Navy. I have known Master Dunton for the past seven years, he having worked his way up from able seaman to master mariner under my watch. He is a man of integrity and honor, who would willingly lay his life down in defense of the Crown, the King and the Kingdom of England. Master Dunton has an impeccable, unblemished record of

service and one that has never been questioned before this day. It is his testimony which you hold before you and to which he has signed his name. I am here to verify that he is, indeed, the same man who served under my command. He has given his full account of his proceedings from the 17th day of March, 1635, to the present day, that being the 26th day of September, of the same year. If you ask me, 'Do I believe his account?' I will tell you that I would believe John Dunton's testimony before I would believe my own."

There was a brief chuckle from the crowd, but the Earl of Portland pounded with his gavel and the court came to order once again.

Lord Vaine continued. "As for myself, many of you know that I would rather lay my life down than bear false witness to any man."

"Here, here," came the response from a number of the court officers.

"So saying," his Lordship added, "I ask that you acquit John Dunton from all the charges against him, restore him to his rank as Master in his Majesty's Royal Navy, and consider his request to acquit the four Dutchmen sitting with him, who were instrumental in bringing these pirates to justice."

Afterward, the court reviewed all the testimonies and depositions, questioning each man in turn regarding their course of action in the matter of the raid upon the *Warwick* and the *Little David*.

When the pronouncement was made, John and the four Dutchmen were acquitted, while the Moors and Flemish pirates were sentenced to be hanged by the neck until dead, at the gallows at Portsmouth dock, at twelve o'clock noon tomorrow.

Immediately Aligolant threw himself down on his knees and yelled,

"Spare me, John Dunton! You gave me your word that you would not kill me!"

A hush came over the crowd as John turned to face him. "I have kept my word, sir." John said loud enough so that everyone could hear his response. "I will not kill you, Aligolant, but by your own treachery and barbarism, you have killed yourself."

AFTER BIDDING FAREWELL to Captain Rickles and his men, John went with Lord Vaine and Simon to the carriages, anxious to begin the last leg of his journey home. To his dismay, one of the butlers prevented his departure by imploring him, "The Earl of Portland would have a word with you, Master Dunton."

John nodded and followed the man back into the castle, with Simon and Lord Vaine joining him. He was led to a large chamber he recognized as a war room. The walls were covered with maps and charts, while still more charts lay across a massive table.

The Earl of Portland awaited him at the end of the table. "I am sorry to detain you, Master Dunton, but I wonder if you might be of some use to his majesty, King Charles, in regards to the situation at Salé in Morocco."

"While I was in Salé, I asked myself that same question, sire," John responded. "The answer came to me that I should commit to memory every little detail of the city and its strongholds and weak points. The Moroccans are eager to be done with the pirates, but they lack the manpower and weapons of war to stage an all-out battle. They have begun to separate the city into two sections, with Old Salé here," he

pointed to the map spread out on the Earl's table. "And the New Salé here."

"Would you be willing to meet with our generals to give them the details they would need to launch a massive attack?"

"Are you suggesting that an attack plan is already in progress?" John asked, more hopeful than ever before that he might still rescue his son.

"Admiral William Rainsborough has suggested so and has already rallied several captains to his ranks. Would you be willing—"

"Yes, sire!" John interrupted, feeling the blood begin to sizzle within his veins. "I would be willing to meet with them and tell them everything that I have memorized. I would also be willing to go with them to Salé to redeem his Majesty's loyal subjects. Sire, there are thousands of English men, women and children in slavery in that country. They must be rescued, sire. If not by their own countrymen, then by whom?"

"You are correct, Dunton. We are responsible for his Majesty's subjects. But do you think that a rescue effort would be effective?"

"I would be willing to stake my life on it, sire."

The earl smiled thoughtfully, his eyes aglow with compassion and a hint of daring. "Yes," he said. "I believe you, John. We have a summit meeting planned for October. Would you be willing to accompany me and express your interests to Captain Rainsborough?"

"Naturally."

"I will send my best cartographer to visit you, John. His name is Ralph Hall. Perhaps between the two of you, a more accurate map of Salé can be drawn up, along with some strategic attack diagrams."

"Thank you, sire. I am most eager to assist in this endeavor in any way that you, or Captain Rainsborough, would ask."

"I know that your son was left behind in Salé when Aligolant brought you back to England, John. I will pray that you may find him when you return."

"Thank you, sire. Perhaps we will have enough prayers registered that God will take heed and answer them."

"He most certainly answers our prayers, John. The unfortunate thing is that sometimes He must tell us, 'No.' "

REBECCA PUT DOWN her sewing, having finished a dress for Lady Greenfield's daughter who wanted to be a midwife and would be apprenticed in the spring. Weary, she stood up and stretched, surprised at how much the infant within her had grown the past six weeks. It was now the 28th of September, and she was six months into the birth cycle, with only three months or so until little John would be born. He was kicking her nearly all the time, and she had become accustomed to his movements within her. An active baby. She had heard that when an infant stopped moving, then a mother should worry. Fortunately, little John rarely had a quiet moment. Sometimes he even woke her up at night with all his bouncing around inside her.

She smiled. If she didn't have little John within her, she didn't think she could get through another day. To her dismay, she'd turned into a wimpy woman who cried at the silliest things, a broken fingernail, a lock of hair that came loose, a pumpkin that was still too small to harvest, a carrot that broke in half while she was weeding around it. Little things. Stupid little things that caught her unaware at the wrong moment sent her up to her bedroom where she would cry for an hour before she felt better again. Rebecca wasn't certain that John would like her this way.

Naomi and Ruth both told her that moodiness was a normal part of a woman's birthing cycle, but she'd never really told them how terribly moody she could be sometimes.

Thinking back to the day she ran away from Blackwell Tower, she realized that *that* woman was someone special. Daring! Determined!

What would she have done if she'd actually made it to America, where she would have had no one to care for her? How would she have survived when she finally discovered that she didn't really want to be alone? Would she have met someone else to love? Could she ever love anyone as much as she loved John? It seemed as though they'd been separated forever. Perhaps he was never captured. Perhaps he went on to America without her. Perhaps he *was* captured. Perhaps he was a slave in Salé. Perhaps he was dead—

No! He's not dead! He's not! He's coming home! He just has to come home. . . .

Frustrated with herself, she pushed her anxieties away, back into the deepest recesses of her mind, unwilling to allow them to come forward again, at least not tonight. Then, she climbed upstairs, removed her pinafore and gown and slipped into bed, pulling the quilt up over her.

Nights were growing chillier. She should have made a fire to keep herself warm, but not now. She was simply too tired to worry about a fire.

Within minutes she was fast asleep.

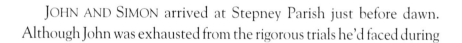

JOHN AND SIMON arrived at Stepney Parish just before dawn. Although John was exhausted from the rigorous trials he'd faced during

the past six months, he was gratified to know that Rebecca had apparently fared well in his absence. Their marriage seemed such a brief encounter that he could scarcely believe she had actually moved into his home to await his return. He had finally admitted, if only to himself, that he loved her. Could he tell her about his feelings for her? His life had taken such a downward spiral that he still feared he would enter the house and find her gone.

The carriage driver left him and Simon at Stepney Hill Road, where they walked the short distance together. Then, saying goodnight to his son's grandfather, John looked at the cottage he'd built, never dreaming before he'd left here last March that he would marry a woman with whom to share it. Running across Simon's front yard, John jumped the hedge with one swift movement, surprised that he could still do so. Then he raced up to the door and stopped cold.

Should he walk right in and call to her? Would it frighten her to wake up in such a manner? Should he slip in quietly and await in a chair by the bed until she awakened naturally? He would love to watch Rebecca awaken, something he'd only seen one time before. He smiled, remembering the moment all too well.

Making his decision, John opened the front door and walked soundlessly to the stairs. The third one would creak, he remembered, so he skipped that step altogether. The door to the bedroom was open and he looked inside, praying she would still be sleeping there. He was not disappointed.

Sleeping peacefully, Rebecca looked like an angel to him, with her golden hair flowing around her face, tendril curls escaping from her nightcap, her long lashes caressing her cheeks. She was a vision of everything he had conjured up in his mind the past six months, hoping

without ever really having hope that they would be together, once again.

He knelt beside the bed and took her hand in his, noticing how small it seemed in comparison. She tugged her hand away and rolled over, away from him, unaware that he was even there. John smiled, his soul filling up with the smell of her, his eyes delighting in her delicate beauty, a memory that he hadn't been able to get out of his mind for six long months.

Coming around to the other side of the bed, he sat down upon it and gazed on Rebecca until the sun peeked over the distant hills, sending shafts of sunlight through the window. The room grew brighter as the sun arose, revealing movement beneath the chemise she wore. He sank to his knees off the side of the bed and watched in delight as a little hand or foot, or perhaps an elbow, played inside Rebecca's swollen abdomen. Reaching his hand out, he placed it upon her and felt the little fellow try to kick it away. John laughed, caring no longer if he awakened her, for the child within her fascinated him.

Rebecca opened her eyes. "Oh," she sighed. "It *is* you." Then, her eyelids closed again.

He waited a moment, wondering how to proceed. "Rebecca," he whispered. "I'm home."

"Go away," she mumbled, still sound asleep. "I'm having the most delicious dream."

"Am I in your dream?" he whispered.

"No, John is. He's feeling the baby move and I don't want to disturb him."

This time he laughed aloud, throwing his head back in pure joy.

"It's not funny, John, it's—" Then she sat straight up and looked at him, blinking as though she couldn't believe it was really him.

"It's— It's— " she sputtered.

"Go ahead," he coaxed, grinning from ear to ear. "You can say it!"

"It's— It's really you!" She threw her arms around his neck and laughed and cried and sputtered, "It's really you! John, you're really here! John! I can't believe it!"

"Merciful heavens, woman!" he groaned, teasing as he climbed into bed with her. "I can see I won't get a moment's peace with you this morning."

Suddenly, she pulled back and looked at him, her face streaked with tears, her hair unkempt, her beautiful turquoise eyes searching his soul. "Oh, John," she whispered, "I've missed you so!"

That was all the encouragement John needed. He kissed her fiercely, quickly, repetitively, aching for her beyond his ability to control. Afterward, he kissed her sensuously, with calculated precision, making her ache for him beyond all reason. When she was satiated, he kissed her leisurely, longingly, realizing that he could never live again without her touch, her lips, and her heart.

IN OCTOBER, JOHN met with King Charles and Admiral Rainsborough, who had been named General of the Salé Fleet of his Majesty's Royal Navy at Westminster. The captain was a starched, stiff-upper-lip sort of man, forty-eight years old. His father, Thomas Rainsborough, was a merchant and shipowner. William Rainsborough had followed in his father's footsteps and had sailed on several trips to the Mediterranean. In the 1620's, William had commanded the

merchant trading ship *Sampson* and had established himself as an authority on maritime matters. He was often consulted by the Lords of the Admiralty.

John, along with Ralph Hall, a timid cartographer with exactness and precision in map drawing, had been working together for two weeks. Through their diligence, they were able to display the charts and maps of Old and New Salé that they had drawn from John's memory.

King Charles and the Lords of the Admiralty were impressed with John's reports. Because of this, plans were finalized to mount a major offensive strike in the Spring, with eight major warships, several barks, caravels and pinnaces. In addition, they would bring a thousand seamen, with seven captains, one general, a vice admiral, rear admiral, eight masters and one commander. John would retain his role as master and was very pleased when General Rainsborough asked John to serve with him aboard the *Leopard*, from which he would command the armada as General of the South Squadron of his Majesty's Salé Fleet. They scheduled a number of meetings at Westminster, but the final assignments would take place at Chatham, beginning the twentieth of January. There, they would complete all the preparations regarding provisions and food supplies, with the hope that they could set sail by the tenth of February, 1636.

RETURNING HOME BY mid-November, John found Rebecca anxiously awaiting him. "The most wonderful gift arrived," she exclaimed happily before John had even taken off his wool doublet. "Come upstairs and look."

Her laughter was contagious, and John soon followed her up to the

bedroom. Beside the bed was a beautiful, hand-hewn cradle made of olive wood, with three little angels carved into the head. "Lord Blackwell dropped it off on his way to London while you were gone. The wood is from Jerusalem. And I found this beautiful fabric to make a quilt for little John. What do you think?" She held the fabric up to the window so he could see it by a better light.

"It's blue," he complained at once.

"But I thought you liked blue."

"I do, but what if she's a girl?"

"I hadn't considered that," she sniffed, blinking back a few tears.

He pulled her into his arms. "Simon warned me the last few weeks would be the worst on your emotions. Come downstairs and I'll make you some tea."

Following him down, Rebecca sat on a chair in the kitchen and waited while he brought in the water, stoked the fire and hung the kettle over the flames. "It seems a lot of trouble to go to for a spot of tea, doesn't it?" she asked.

John smiled patiently, but did not comment. He put the tea leaves into the kettle and pulled a chair up beside her to wait for the water to boil.

She hadn't asked him about how his trip to Westminster had gone and he wondered why. It was as though she'd put up some barrier to the subject, preferring to talk about cradles and quilts instead.

"Are you feeling well?" he asked. "You didn't really say when I arrived."

"Tired," she admitted. "I seem to sleep all day and stay awake all night."

"That's perfectly natural the last few weeks, you know. It's the body's way of preparing you for sleepless nights ahead."

"Yes, Simon told me last week that I could expect it, but I didn't believe him until Monday. I tossed and turned all night long, unable to get comfortable. Then, the moment the sun rose in the morning, I fell asleep and didn't wake up until late in the afternoon. Ever since then I've been off schedule. I don't know how you'll sleep with me while I'm like this."

"Fortunately, we only have six or seven more weeks to worry about it."

The water in the kettle started to boil. John moved over to it and dipped out a cup of hot tea. Then, he put a small wedge of honey in the cup and gave it to her. "When did Simon say that the baby is due?"

"I conceived the twentieth or twenty-first of March," she said, blushing. "He said to count nine months from then and add two weeks."

"By January fifth," John added it up as he dipped a cup of tea for himself. "I hope it comes a little earlier than that."

"It?" she asked. "Since when is a baby an it?"

"Since we don't know whether the baby is a she or a he."

"Oh, I've got an idea," she suggested. "I'll keep calling the baby a boy. You should start calling the baby a girl. Then when he comes, one of us will be pleasantly surprised."

"Since you picked a boy's name, it's only fair that I should pick a girl's."

"I think he might look pretty silly with a girl's name, but I will humor you."

"You're already used to calling him, little John. It's a good name and it seems to suit us. What if we name her little Jane, if it—" he corrected himself. "If *she* is a girl?"

"That will work," she agreed. "But John, why the fifth of January?"

The moment he'd been dreading had arrived. Rebecca was obviously absorbed with the birth of their child, but John thought often about Thomas. Surely Rebecca wouldn't ask him not to go after his son? She'd hardly said anything about Thomas since John arrived home six weeks ago.

"Well?" she asked again.

"I must be in Chatham on the twentieth of January to prepare one of his Majesty's ships for the armada. King Charles has given the order to conquer Salé and rescue our countrymen."

Her cup rattled on its saucer as she placed it onto the table. She was visibly shaken by this information, and John wished he had found a way to break it to her more gently. But how does a man meekly tell his wife that he is going to war?

Rebecca's hands dropped into her lap and she lowered her head. Watching her carefully, he saw her shudder as she tried to suppress her emotions.

John lifted her into his arms, then carried her into the parlor where he sat down in his favorite chair, keeping Rebecca on his lap. "I know you don't want another separation, but I have to go after our son. Day after day, night after night, I ask myself: What am I doing in England when my son is a slave in Salé? I have no choice but to go after him. Now that I've got the King's backing, I will go."

Great wracking sobs came out of Rebecca as she buried her face against his neck and wept. Unable to console her, John rubbed her back

and waited. After a long time, she gave a sigh and held her head up to look at him. Her eyes seemed haunted with fear, her face was flushed. Just to look at her made his heart ache. "Rebecca, I have to go. He's my son."

He felt her stiffen. "He's my son, too!" she exclaimed hotly.

"I'm sorry," he apologized. "I didn't know how you felt about Thomas. You never speak of him."

Rebecca softened. "John, I'm only crying because I miss Thomas terribly. I've tried not to speak of him, for it pains me to do so. Of course, I'm frightened of war, but I fear pirates more, for I have seen what they do to innocent people. When you said that King Charles had approved the armada, my heart leapt for joy. The day of our son's deliverance is almost here."

"And I thought you were going to beg me to stay," he teased.

She shook her head. "No, John, you must go. He's our son. He's *my* son. I love him as much as . . . ." She hesitated, as though she'd started to say something else, then changed her mind. Finally she continued. "As much as I love little John. If I didn't have him to care for, I would go with you. I would fight to the death to bring Thomas home to us!"

The fervor he saw in her eyes astounded him and he knew he'd married a determined woman who loved his young son tenaciously. This pleased him more than anything else about Rebecca.

Chapter Nineteen

Thomas Clings to Hope

*"Therefore be not grieved . . . for God did send me
before you to preserve life."*
Genesis 45:5

T homas huddled into a ball and pulled the green velvet cloak over him to keep out the cold, the same cloak his mother had brought on board the night she stowed away. After he arrived in Salé, a pirate had tried to take it away, but Thomas had screamed and clawed the man, like a child possessed of an evil spirt. No one bothered him about it, afterward. It was perhaps the only time he'd ever asserted himself through his entire ordeal.

At first the cloak had Rebecca's fragrance on it and reminded him so much of her that he felt comforted, as though he could smell her essence in the perfume that she had worn. Now, it was filthy and torn in two places, it smelled of dust and human sweat and soil. It had little emotional comfort in it, but it did keep him warm, especially after the rain the last two days, when the damp air made him feel even colder.

He hadn't seen his father since May. Six months ago. Recently,

he'd learned that the *Warwick* had sailed from Salé in August. Had his father sailed with the bark . . . and without Thomas?

Thoughts and fears plagued Thomas. Did his father know where he was? Were his parents still alive? Did they still think about him? Pray for him? Love him?

To make matters worse, Thomas learned that Ali Zuny was planning to leave Salé in less than a month, to take his slaves into Algeria and sell them. From everything he'd heard of Algeria, it was the worst place a slave could be sold, for the Algerians hated Christians and persecuted them severely.

For a long time, Thomas didn't know what a Christian was, but one day he'd heard Ali Zuny say that the men who believed in Jesus Christ should be castrated, something he had also said about Christians. It was at that moment that Thomas knew. Believing in Jesus Christ and being a Christian were one and the same thing. Thomas believed in the Savior with all his heart. He would rather die than deny Him.

If Algerians hated Christians so, why did they buy them for slaves? Perhaps to torture them, Thomas decided. Vengeful, Algerians sometimes came to the marketplace to laugh over their conquests. Many slaves starved to death or died from exposure and disease. When slaves wore down and became useless to the Algerians, they could still serve one final purpose . . . as cannon fodder.

Hadn't Joseph with the coat of many colors won the confidence of his masters by being obedient and industrious? He could not recall a single moment from the story he loved, where Joseph wallowed in self-pity. Joseph accepted his lot in life, learned to be trustworthy, and that was what Thomas decided he must do.

He prayed that God would be patient with him when he faltered.

If he was to be sold to another master, Thomas would look on the bright side. It couldn't be much worse than his servitude under Ali Zuny. He prayed he would be purchased by a kind master who fed him better and didn't drive him so hard.

Thomas feared that his resilience and spirit were wearing down, and he was just small enough to fit inside a cannon. The thought terrified him.

However, Thomas vowed, he would not cry. Slaves don't cry. He had learned this lesson in a very painful way. Never again would Thomas cry . . . not until he found himself safe with his father or his mother. Only then, would he allow himself to cry.

Chapter Twenty

Winter Dreams

> "A *virtuous woman is a crown*
> to her husband . . ."
> Proverbs 12:4

January 1636

Rebecca closed the Bible and placed it back on the mantle in the parlor. Reading it gave her great comfort when John was away from her. She had hoped John would return earlier than this from his trip into Westminster. He'd already been gone ten days. Final arrangements for the raid on Salé were being made and his presence had been requested unexpectedly, to clear up a couple of problems with the strategic diagrams.

Simon told her that little John would be born at any time now, though she had not felt any pains worthy of mention. Rubbing her bulging abdomen tenderly she said, "Son, you mustn't stay in there too long. My skin is beginning to itch from being stretched so tightly. Will you please not delay your coming?"

A vigorous kick told her that little John was listening. "Yes, I know

I told you to wait until your father arrives, but I am beginning to feel quite miserable."

Stepping to the kitchen, she lifted the cloth from the bread bowl and saw that the dough she had previously kneaded had risen enough to shape into loaves. She punched it down eagerly, spread a thin layer of lard in the pans, then kneaded the dough into two tight ovals. Placing the dough seam side down in the pans, she put the cloth over them, then set them near the fireplace for the final raising. Afterward, she washed the bread bowl, dried it and put it away.

Because her father had been a tinsmith, Rebecca's kitchen was well supplied with baking pans, kettles, buckets and cooking utensils, but the most useful tools she'd found were the various size barrels her father had made, with slats of pine and tin straps tightened around the girth in five places to keep them together. These, she'd filled with flour, wheat, oats, dried beans, rye and barley, as well as honey, sorghum syrup and lard.

Simon's property, next to *John's Cottage*, had a small group of sheds at the back that housed a few livestock including hogs, milk cows and chickens. Rebecca shared the chores of keeping the animals fed and watered, and she benefitted from her labor in terms of milk, lard, eggs and meat.

However, it wasn't necessary for her to help, as Naomi, Ruth and Simon had pointed out on a number of occasions. She was their family, and families take care of one another. Always, she responded, "That's exactly what I'm doing." Her assistance came less often now, as she could only waddle to get from one spot to the other.

Her greatest effort outdoors these days was gathering the eggs, which she now decided to do. It was near noon and the hens would

have finished laying by now. Putting on her cloak and bringing a tin basket with her, Rebecca went outside. The air was cold and so moist that the dampness soaked through the fabric of her dress. She went directly to the hen house and opened the door. Inside the nests she found six large eggs. Even the chickens were feeling the brunt of an English winter. They were laying ten to fifteen eggs last summer, but now they were down to half that amount. Rebecca put the brown eggs into the basket and went back outside, locking the hen house door behind her.

She stepped across the Harris' spacious back yard through the orchard, where branches, barren this time of year, stretched out like arthritic hands and fingers. Within a few minutes, she was knocking at the back door to Simon's home.

"You don't have to knock," Naomi scolded as she opened the door. "I've told you time and again, dear. You are family."

"And you forget that I grew up in the city. It was considered improper to enter a home without knocking." She smiled and gave Naomi a hug. "Good morning, Auntie. How are you feeling today?" she asked, hoping to throw Naomi off guard.

The smile that stole across Naomi's face told her she had succeeded.

"Much better, dear. The storm that came through last week certainly threw my rheumatism into turmoil, but now that it's past, I can move my shoulder much more freely." She took the basket from Rebecca and preceded her into the house.

The Simon Harris home was much larger than *John's Cottage*. Four bedrooms upstairs. A library, parlor, kitchen and healing room on the main floor. Simon was already in the healing room taking care of a woman complaining of apoplexy. One of his twin sisters often assisted

him, and today, it was apparently Ruth's turn.

"Ruth made a batch of your favorite biscuits," said Naomi, giving Rebecca a plate with a dozen honey-cookies.

"She's always baking something for me," Rebecca admitted. "But since she's working with Simon today, I thought she might not bake bread. I'm making two loaves this morning, so I'll bring one over later."

"Lord Vaine stopped by last night, dear. He didn't go over to see you because he saw no light, and he didn't want to disturb you. He said to tell you that John should be coming home sometime today."

Rebecca smiled eagerly. "Wonderful! Oh, my! I'd better hurry back and tidy up a little."

A quick kiss on the cheek, and Rebecca hurried from the Harris' home and over to *John's Cottage*. She had such a surprise in store for him when he arrived, she could hardly contain her excitement.

Now she swept, mopped and dusted the furniture, then put on a big pot of chicken and bean soup. Stoking the fire, she opened the brick-lined baking oven to find the temperature just about right, and slid the two loaves of bread into the oven.

Upstairs in the smallest room that John liked to call the chamber, she cleaned the furnishings thoroughly, then carried fresh water from the well to the bathing tub and built a nice fire in the fireplace, so John would have warm water in which to bathe, when he returned. Someday, if she should ever live so long, she would like to have water brought into the house directly, but short of hiring a servant to do it, she supposed that this was a winter's dream that would fade with the first sign of spring.

After putting fresh linens on the bed, Rebecca washed the soiled clothing in the kitchen sink and hung them to dry on a line in the

kitchen, where it was warmest.

By then, the bread had baked and cooled and Rebecca felt satisfied that she had done her best to make John comfortable on his arrival.

She delivered a loaf of bread to the twins and Simon late that afternoon, then returned to see if she'd left anything amiss. *John's Cottage* was in perfect order, with John's surprise resting on the parlor mantle so that he couldn't possibly miss it.

Thinking a nap might help her relax, she went upstairs to the bedroom and curled up on her side on the bed. It was impossible to sleep on her back anymore, since little John had grown so large. Exhausted, she realized she had worked harder that day than she had in a long, long time. It felt good to be so tired.

As she drifted off to sleep, she dreamed of pirates and of being held hostage on a bed in the captain's quarters of a sailing vessel. One of the pirates entered the cabin and began stabbing her in the abdomen. The pain of the wounds were excruciating and she awakened with a start, relieved to find it had all been a dream. But the pain did not ease, now that she was awake, and she realized her birthing time had arrived.

She slipped off the bed in between the pains and staggered downstairs, and out the back door. Holding her abdomen when the pains came and waiting until they subsided before continuing, she stepped across the yard until she finally reached the Harris' back door. This time she didn't bother to knock, she just opened it and gasped as another pain hit her.

"Why, Rebecca!" Naomi declared. "Ruth! Simon!"

Immediately Simon emerged from the healing room and glanced into the kitchen. "It's time, is it?" he asked.

Rebecca could only nod in the affirmative.

"Let's get her back to the cottage and up to her bed. She'll feel more comfortable there."

Rebecca gasped as the pain seemed to rip through her with such intensity she wondered why she didn't split in two. When it subsided, she stood quickly and said, "They're awfully close. Every few minutes."

"I can deliver the baby here if you'd like."

The back door opened, and John poked his head inside, saying "Is Rebecca over here?"

She looked up at him and smiled, ignoring for a moment how much pain she had. "You made it just in time."

"I'll carry you home," he said, apparently realizing her condition. "Will that be all right?" he asked Simon.

"Yes, but you might want to wait between contractions, they're very difficult for her. I'll bring the birthing stool, it will make this easier for her."

Rebecca held her breath as another wave of pain grew in intensity, but she would not cry out. John's first wife had died in birthing and she had heard from the twins that Mary's cries of anguish were most grievous for John to bear. When she'd heard this, it made her determined not to worry him unduly.

When the pain passed, she whispered. "Now, John."

He scooped her up into his arms and carried her quickly out the back doorway, across the porch and down the stairs. Moving quickly across the yard, they almost reached the cottage when she had to make him wait. "Stop, please. Don't move for a few minutes." Closing her eyes, she whispered inside her mind, *You can do this, Rebecca. You can do this without screaming.* She waited until the pain started to ease, then

opened her eyes and nodded. "Now."

Again John hurried, cradling her tightly against him. She tried to breathe slowly and deeply, which seemed to help her remain calm. Into the cottage and up the stairs, John had just placed her upon the bed when another wave of pain seared through her.

Naomi and Ruth had followed him, and now they entered the bedroom. "You wait downstairs," said Ruth to John. "We'll tell you when the baby is here."

"No!" Rebecca begged. "John, you must stay with me."

"A gentleman simply does not attend a woman in her travail, Rebecca, unless he is her doctor." This from Naomi, who frowned disapprovingly.

"Then, don't consider John a gentleman, not today. He lost his first wife and did not get to say goodbye to her. His last memories are of her screaming. I will not put him through that."

"But dear," Ruth agreed with her sister. "This is most unusual."

Another pain swept her thoughts inside herself. *Remain calm. Be brave. You can do this. You can do this for John.*

When it had passed, she was still clinging to John's hand. "He will stay with me!" she growled and the sisters knew there would be no denying her.

"Then, we will make a privacy curtain," Simon said, bringing the birthing chair into the bedroom. "John will be able to comfort her and we will be able to help her deliver."

"Are you sure, Rebecca?" John asked, and she noticed for the first time that the color had drained from his face.

Nodding, she said, "I need you with me, John. Just holding your hand gives me strength."

He kissed her forehead tenderly. "Very well," he said. Then to Simon, "What do you want me to do?"

"Get some rope and a cloth. Make a curtain that will protect her privacy from the waist down. Then you stay on the other side. Keep her comfortable and focused. Everything will be all right."

John quickly made a privacy curtain for her, then sat beside her.

Rebecca held his hand and talked to him between the waves of pain. But when her body stiffened in agony, she always closed her eyes and talked herself silently through her pain. Soon, she was bearing down, squeezing John's hand, feeling his other hand stroke her forehead with great tenderness. Then, she heard a most wonderful sound, her child's first cry.

Suddenly, tears came to her eyes and spilled down her cheeks. Rebecca laughed aloud, "We did it, John. We did it together."

Naomi came around the curtain, holding a precious bundle wrapped in a soft blanket. "She's beautiful, don't you think so?"

"She's a girl?" Rebecca asked in amazement.

"Yes, dear."

Placing the tiny infant in Rebecca's arms, she left them behind the curtain.

"A girl," she murmured, as she looked up at John lovingly.

His eyes were swimming in tears as he gazed at his wife and infant daughter. He was speechless.

Finally he found his voice and whispered, "Little Jane."

Rebecca laughed. "And all this time I thought she was a boy! No wonder she kicked me so often."

Then she remembered, "Oh, John. Did you see the surprise that I put on the mantle?"

"You mean the plaque you made that reads, *John's Cottage?*"

"Yes. Did you like it?"

"It's very nice. Where do you want me to hang it?"

"Outside, over the front door. I wanted to surprise you when you arrived home."

"You did, Rebecca. You did!"

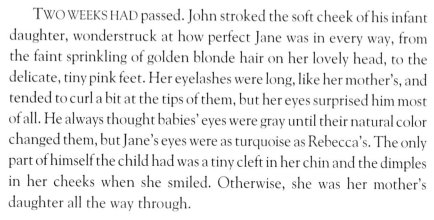

TWO WEEKS HAD passed. John stroked the soft cheek of his infant daughter, wonderstruck at how perfect Jane was in every way, from the faint sprinkling of golden blonde hair on her lovely head, to the delicate, tiny pink feet. Her eyelashes were long, like her mother's, and tended to curl a bit at the tips of them, but her eyes surprised him most of all. He always thought babies' eyes were gray until their natural color changed them, but Jane's eyes were as turquoise as Rebecca's. The only part of himself the child had was a tiny cleft in her chin and the dimples in her cheeks when she smiled. Otherwise, she was her mother's daughter all the way through.

Recalling nine and a half years back, he could picture himself sitting in the parlor at the Harris' home, holding another infant. Thomas had thick, black hair, a turned-up nose with a little rounded spot at the tip, and long, slender fingers and toes, just like his mother's.

Although little Jane comforted him, made him laugh aloud when

she pulled a crooked smile, or studied his face unceasingly, as she was doing just now, she hadn't taken away the ache in his heart for Thomas. No one could do that. No one but Thomas.

His heart ached for other reasons: knowing he would have to leave his wife and daughter tomorrow, knowing he may never return. The Salé Fleet was not being sent as a peaceful armada. Their entire purpose was an act of war, to restore the Moroccans to their former independence, to destroy the pirates infesting their nation and to rescue the English subjects who were enslaved in that land. Many lives would be lost in the endeavor. England would have to pay a heavy price to ransom the oppressed, and John was just as willing as any other loyal Englishman to lay down his life, if necessary, in carrying out King Charles' orders.

When he returned from Salé, if by the grace of God he wasn't killed in that place, it would have to be with Thomas, otherwise, how could he face Rebecca a second time and tell her he had failed in his quest to bring their son home?

Memories washed over him in waves. During Thomas' first voyage to America, three years ago, he'd been so excited. "What's this, Father?" "How does that work?" "What's a boatswain?" "Where do the dolphins sleep?" "Why do they call it the head?" So many questions. Though he'd tried to be patient and answer them, the child wearied him with his pondering. Now John would give anything, even his own life, to hear his son ask him any question.

Not knowing where the lad was, how he was being kept, if he was hungry, or hurt, or happy . . . death would have been kinder, perhaps, for then he would know that Thomas was at rest. Not knowing was a parent's worst nightmare. Without Rebecca and Jane to console him, he doubted he could have maintained his sanity. And yet, tomorrow

he would leave them both.

Rebecca had such devotion for Thomas, it astounded him. Apparently, she felt no such affection for John, for in all their times together, she had not once told John that she loved him, nor had he confessed to similar emotions. She missed him when he was away from her and seemed delighted whenever he returned. And in lovemaking, she was as eager as he. But did she love him? He hoped that she would say so before he left. If she did, it would give him the courage he needed to reciprocate.

Suddenly, Jane opened her mouth and gave a wide yawn, then sucked a little bit on her lower lip. "You won't get any nourishment out of thin air, young one," John laughed. Jane's lower lip quivered and she started to squall. "Rebecca, I think she wants her mother," he called, knowing his wife was still up in the bedroom.

"Just coming," she said as she hurried down the stairs. "Hungry, is she?"

"If not, then she's just not satisfied with the way I hold her."

"You don't snuggle her close, John." She took Jane from him and sat in a chair opposite to nurse her.

"My chest isn't soft enough, that's the problem," he grinned.

"I've packed what you asked," said Rebecca, changing the subject. "As well as some carrot bread. I think you'll like it for the carriage ride tomorrow."

"Thank you. You haven't made a bread that I haven't liked yet. Unless it's hardtack."

"Will the armada leave right away, then?"

"No, we've the provisioning to see to first. I've ordered everything

that we'll need, plus a double portion for those who will be coming back with us. The supplies will be arriving beginning this week, some time. I only hope they got the decks painted red by now. Last week, they hadn't even started.

"Why are the decks being painted at all, John? That's a lot of bother, isn't it? And why red, of all colors?"

"It's for a dual purpose, Rebecca. I don't suppose a woman would understand the color scheme, but we paint the decks red because when blood is spilled on it, it's less noticeable and doesn't seem to make the men quite so ill at the sight of it."

"And the other reason?"

"It has a tendency to frighten and inhibit pirates. They see us coming from a hill off in the distance. Through their spy glass they see the deck is red, and they say to themselves, 'That ship has killed so many men its decks are stained with blood.' It's quite an intimidating scene, actually. We'll have eight warships, three caravels, two cogs, an assortment of pinnaces and over a thousand men. The pirates who've overtaken the hillsides surrounding New Salé will see quite a sight. Imagine how we'll look with so many of King Charles' ships, his Majesty's colors flying aloft, and our decks dipped, as it were, in the blood of our conquests. Can you imagine such a sight?"

"No," she sighed. "I have no desire to see it, either. But I do want you to know how proud of you I am. To think you'll be aboard the general's ship as Master of the *Admiral* is comforting, somehow."

"Although the ship is named the *Admiral*, for purposes of the expedition, we are calling it, the *Leopard*. Sounds more ferocious, doesn't it?"

"If I were a pirate, I would be shaking out of my skin," she laughed.

"It does my heart good to see you this excited, John. To know you're going back for Thomas has fired you with enthusiasm, hasn't it?"

He hung his head, feeling ashamed of so many things. "Rebecca, I cannot tell you how it pains me to have left Thomas there. I only saw him once. We were both in shackles, and I could do nothing but hug him to me and beg God to spare him. Had I to do it over again, now I think I should have defied them all, grabbed him and taken him with me."

"They would have killed him, and you, as well. You know that children are the true victims in the slave trade. They're not worth much until they're older."

"That is the only thought that held me back that day. Since I left Salé, I have prayed night and day that Robert Woodruff or Christopher Willoughby will have bought Thomas by now, and that all our son is doing is to waiting for me to come get him."

"We both have," she admitted, as tears trickled down her cheeks. "John, I know you'll do all in your power to find him, and . . . ." Her voice trailed off.

"And what?" he asked softly

Rebecca gulped, as though fearing to say the rest. "If you must give up your life to guarantee his freedom, I will forgive you." The tears spilled over again and she continued, "As I've held little Jane and wondered how I could ever be without her, it has broken my heart all the more that Thomas is not with us. I don't want to lose either one of you. But if, once you are in Salé, you believe that you can ransom Thomas' life with your own and you choose to do it, I will understand. I would do the same in your position."

He sank to his knees and placed his head against her lap, as she

sat nursing their daughter. "I will do my best not to let you down, Rebecca."

With her free hand she stroked his hair and whispered, "I trust you so, John. Please never forget."

He lifted his head and gazed into her eyes. With absolute conviction, he said, "And I will strive with all my strength to deserve your trust. If I have a chance, even though it be desperately slim, I will take it for Thomas' sake. Knowing that your heart and mine are one in this regard will give me courage."

He placed his head upon her lap again. Rebecca still had not said she loved him, only that she trusted him. It would have to be enough.

Chapter Twenty-One

The Salé Fleet

> *"John Dunton went aboord his Majesties Ship the Leopard*
> *at Chatham the 26 of January, to see his victualls and*
> *provision taken in for the Voyages . . ."*
> John Dunton's Journal, January 1636

*A*rriving at Chatham dockyards at six of the morning, John found the *Leopard* tied to the dock. He still couldn't get over the size of her, even though he'd seen her several times over the last few weeks. The *Leopard*, a Man-of-War sailing vessel, had been built at Woolwich in 1635. It was ninety-five feet long, thirty-three feet at the maximum beam, and carried six hundred tons burthen, with thirty-six large cannons, eighteen to starboard and eighteen to port. One hundred-eighty seamen were assigned to her. John was relieved to see that her decks were finally painted blood red.

General William Rainsborough, also an Admiral, was a large, rather gregarious man in his late forties. Although he enjoyed comradery, he could be exacting and demanding. He held the position of the highest ranking officer of the South Squadron of the Salé Fleet. John felt most fortunate to be sailing with the General, and even more so to act as Master beneath him.

Next to the *Leopard* was the *Antelope*. Built in 1618, it measured ninety-two feet in length, thirty-one feet nine inches at its maximum beam and had a burthen of six hundred tons. It was almost identical to the General's ship, except that it had less ornamentation. The *Antelope* also carried one hundred-eighty seamen. Sir George Carteret, a member of one of the influential Carteret families from Jersey in the Channel islands, would serve as Captain of the *Antelope* and Vice Admiral of the Salé Fleet.

Simon, one of the *Leopard's* doctors, was expected to arrive on the fifth of February. Although John had tried to persuade Simon to stay home with the women, Simon had insisted on joining the armada. Thomas was still his grandson, and John couldn't argue with that.

On the day John arrived, the wind blew from the northeast, the opposite way they needed to sail, and until it shifted, they would be delayed. The scheduled departure date was the tenth of February, but every sailor knew that God didn't always read the Admiralty's schedules when He ordered the weather each day.

As John walked along the wharf, the acrid scent of fresh tar assailed his nostrils and made his eyes burn. The Chatham dockyards had been built nearly ninety years ago and had grown to become the chief arsenal of the Royal Navy of England, and considered the premiere dockyard in all of England.

Numerous buildings with massive dimensions had been built along the quay, and in them were huge warehouses, dry docks, a ropery more than a thousand feet long, and shipping and receiving offices for all the major importers and exporters, as well as military offices and barracks.

In addition to the *Leopard* and the *Antelope*, there were six large

warships anchored in Chatham Bay, waiting to go to sea. The *Mary* and the *Hercules* were both merchantmen's ships hired for the fleet; the *Mary Rose* carried twenty-eight great cannons; the *Providence Pinnace* and the *Expedition Pinnace*, sister ships, had just been built; the *Row Bucke*, a bark much like the *Warwick*, carried fifty seamen. In addition, several caravels, cogs and pinnaces would sail with the armada, giving it strength in numbers.

Thinking of his son, Thomas, John could almost hear what Thomas would say if he were walking alongside his father now: "How many battles has the *Leopard* seen, Father? Do you think General Rains-borough will let me take the helm sometime? We'll show them not to mess with England, won't we, Father?"

Now John asked himself for the thousandth time, *What kind of father leaves his son in Salé while he sails for England without him?* Even though he knew he hadn't any choice in the matter, this did not console him.

When John was in Morocco, he hadn't heard anything regarding his son until the day before the *Warwick* sailed, and hadn't sufficient time to verify it. For all John knew, Christopher Willoughby could have been playing him for a fool. Until he arrived in Salé, he had to trust that Robert Woodruff would guarantee John's ability to pay whatever Ali Zuny wanted for the lad. Although John had brought plenty of gold with him, Lord Blackwell had also sent a treasure chest full of ducats to buy the boy back. If that failed, John planned to go into New Salé and Old Salé himself, and steal Thomas away at knife-point, one way or another.

The supplies John had ordered for the *Leopard* arrived early in the afternoon and John checked containers and boxes as some of the crew loaded them into the hold. The *Leopard* had plenty of room to carry the provisions he'd ordered, but it would take every inch of space in

the hold, as well as some in the gunnery deck and on the weather deck. Provisions for those rescued from the clutches of the barbarians had to be stocked, also.

By the tenth of February, all the provisions and supplies had arrived and were stowed away. On the fourteenth the wind shifted in their favor, and they were able to get as far as Gillingham, where they anchored for the night. In the morning the wind came up against them once again and they were forced to stay two more days before continuing onto "Telbery Hope," where the rest of the seamen met them. Not until the fourth of March did a fine gale pick up, then they were able to sail past the southernmost piece of land in England called the Lizard. Rounding the northwest corner of France, they set their course for the coast of Spain.

In his journal, John recorded: "*And I will not be too tedious to set down every point what course we did steere, and every day how the wind was, because I will make it as short as I can, and sayling alongst the Coast of Spaine with a faire wind, and sometimes a contrary wind, wee did not see a sayle nor a ship all the way. . . .*"

On the twelfth of March, John reported for duty at midnight. Conditions were blustery, and the waves nearly fourteen feet tall. Occasionally the lingering mist from a wave striking the bow would waft back to him, tickling his nostrils with savory. It was a fresh breeze, the kind that sailors dream about, and he thoroughly enjoyed his watch at the helm.

Suddenly, he heard a man in the crow's nest yell, "There's trouble brewing. The rear admiral's ship is waving the lamp!"

"All seamen on deck!" John called to Fuller, his first mate, a gentleman with ruddy cheeks and dancing brown eyes, who relayed

the message along to the men. Crewmen in various stages of dress scrambled up onto the deck from the lower levels and stood at the ready.

"Prepare to come about!" John gave the call.

Before Fuller had a chance to relay the command, the men scrambled up the nets and prepared to hoist the heavy sails up to the top most yard spar, where they secured them with line. Then, they waited aloft while John turned the wheel sharply to the right, putting the nose of the *Leopard* through the wind. The ship slipped through the sea easily, and soon lay abreast of the *Hercules*. The other ships in the armada stood down until they could see what the *Leopard* intended to do.

"Ask if the *Hercules* is in immediate danger. If not, tell them we will stand by until dawn, when an assessment can be made," John instructed.

"Aye, Master Dunton," said Fuller. At the starboard gunwale, he relayed the message, then brought the news to John. "They lost their main mast, sir. They have recovered the square sails and yard spars, and will try to hold their position with the mizzen and foresails."

"Very well. We'll have a long watch ahead, Fuller. Tell the men."

It would be a difficult watch. The *Leopard* would have to circle the *Hercules* until morning. For the next three and a half hours, the men flying aloft had to hoist and then lower the sails every ten to fifteen minutes, depending on what point of sail they were on. And John called repeatedly, "Starboard tack."

The *Leopard* had six helmsmen, and each took their watch at the helm in four hour shifts. General Rainsborough, the kind of man who would work hard as another, and often did, always took the sunrise

shift. Although it wasn't required of him, the general often spent time at the helm. He said it reminded him of his younger days, and he enjoyed it immensely.

At four of the morning, General Rainsborough joined John at the helm. John gave his report, and the condition of the *Hercules*, then began the relay for the changing of the crew, calling his own men to relief, as well.

After the general's crewmen were in position, John left the situation in Rainsborough's capable hands and went to the forecastle to sleep.

When he awakened, he learned that the *Hercules* had departed for "Lishorne" to set a new mast and would catch up with them later, most likely at Salé. John had breakfast with the general and was relieved to hear that no one had been seriously injured when the broken mast came down.

On the twenty-fourth day of March, one year and three days from the day the *Warwick* and the *Little David* had been captured, the armada arrived at Salé, Morocco. General Rainsborough ordered the ships into position, with the *Mary Rose* and the *Expedition* southward, and a spot reserved by the *Roebuck* for the *Hercules*, which was to join them when it was re-masted. The *Mary*, the *Antelope* and the *Providence* dropped anchor north of the Salé harbor, below the castle at Old Salé that overlooked it from the north, blocking escape from the Bou Regreg River. The *Leopard* took the middle position, right in the harbor's mouth. The pinnaces, caravels and cogs positioned themselves between the larger ships. Anchors were dropped, and the cities of Old and New Salé, Morocco, found themselves surrounded on all their coastal boundaries.

This strategic arrangement made it impossible for ships to enter

or leave Salé harbor without encountering a ship from his Majesty's Royal Navy.

The armada carried an impressive display of firepower and John prayed it would be enough. Pride in his fellow countrymen surged through him and he glared at New Salé, as if daring them to try and keep him from his son. But John knew the pirates would never give up without a fight.

The artillery crew stuffed their cannons and prepared to fire at a moment's notice. Every man rested in rotation, four hours on duty and four hours off, though they did not leave their battle stations. The infantry, dressed in full military uniform, lined the decks at the ready, as General Rainsborough had commanded.

The Royal Navy made a grand showing, and John could imagine the pirates' astonishment and fear. If young Thomas was watching somewhere, he prayed the vision would bolster the lad's confidence and give him the hope he needed to survive until John could go into Salé, personally, to get him.

By midnight, no one could sleep. The waiting kept everyone edgy, John included. He paced the aftercastle deck, convinced that if he remained on duty throughout the night, this would encourage his young son and give him hope.

Suddenly, John heard something in the water, like a porpoise jumping, or a large fish breaking the surface. The infantry murmured, almost in unison. Then someone yelled, "Put down the ratlines! Quickly!"

John dashed over to the gunwale to look for himself. Several men in the water swam toward them. A flurry of soaked white flags, miniature in size, were fastened to small sticks and held between the

men's teeth. Frail and thin as twigs, they came, using what little strength they had left to climb up the heavy nets. The men on board reached out to them, pulled them aboard, comforted them, shocked at the condition of the withered, tortured men. As they started to come aboard, John could see that the 'flags' were little more than torn pieces of clothing, most of it bleached by the sun for months.

Almost all of them were Frenchmen, with a few Spaniards. They were so emaciated John wondered how they had the strength to swim out to the ship. Seven of the men were still in shackles, connected to one another, but they had buoyed each other up, making certain that no one drowned. Their clothing was tattered, and some of them wore little more than undergarments tied through the legs and around the waist. All of them bore scars upon their backs and tattoo insignia across their left wrists.

General Rainsborough instructed his first mate, Henry Maddock, whose brother, Robert had been captured four years past, "Feed these men, refresh them, have the doctors attend to their needs, then bring them, one at a time, to my cabin. If any of them speak English, bring those straight away."

To John, the general said, "Find someone who speaks French and Spanish and bring them with you to my cabin."

"Yes, sir!" John exclaimed. Would young Thomas find a way to swim out to him? Remembering that he hadn't yet taught Thomas how to swim tore at his conscience in a painful manner.

John located a cook who spoke Spanish and the general's cartographer who spoke French. He brought them to the general's cabin where they were briefed on their duties. Within a few minutes, a knock came at the general's door. "Enter," came his command.

The man entered, then said, "Greetings, General Rainsborough. I am Antonio Dermando, son of a peasant from southern Spain."

"You speak the language well, Antonio." The general's eyes sharpened.

"My grandmother, she was English."

"Please, sit," John encouraged. "You must be exhausted."

Antonio nodded and sank into a chair opposite the general. John sat to the general's right at the square table, making a record of the refugee's name, nationality, city of origin and any other comments he deemed important.

Formalities were taken care of first, then General William Rainsborough said, "How long have you been in captivity?"

Antonio shook his head. "Perhaps two years. I don't know. It is difficult to tell the months when one is enslaved."

"Tell me of conditions in Salé at the present time."

"Deplorable! You have come just at the right time. The governor of New Salé sent for all the captains and renegades and commanded them to sail for the coast of England. They were to hoist all their boats and go ashore there, and fetch the women and children out of their beds. The price for English females is very high here in Salé. Some are sold for five thousand ducats, but they suffer terrible, these women. God has shown mercy, for He guided you to Salé at our darkest hour."

"What are the pirates saying, now that we've arrived? Do they show signs of wanting to surrender?"

"No, sir. The king asks me if I know your ships, and I tell him you are sent from the King of England. He says, 'What care I for the King of England or his ships? What care I for all the Christian kings in the

world? Am I not King of Salé?' Some say to him, he will be sorry if he heeds not the King of England, but these few are run through with the sword."

The general considered this information for a moment. Then, "How many ships do they have?"

"Many ships, but they cannot come out of the harbor now. They were supposed to sail to England, but your armada is blocking their way. Their captains are very angry."

"What say you regarding the strength of their navy?"

"I trust that God will weaken them, for their strength is the strength of evil."

General Rainsborough nodded his head in understanding. "Very well. Since you speak English so well, I will send you back to Salé on the morrow, along with some of my men. You will take them to this King of New Salé and to the old king as well. We will have letters prepared for them. You will deliver the letters and return to me with my men. Is that agreeable?"

His eyes became thoughtful as Antonio considered his options. "If I do this, you will allow me to stay with you until you sail back to your country?"

"Yes."

"Will I be a prisoner of England?"

"No, my good man. You will be free."

Antonio's face lit up with joy and he said, "God bless you, General. And God bless your king, who is wise beyond my understanding."

General Rainsborough did not acknowledge the man's praise. He merely turned the conversation over to John. "I believe Master Dunton

has something to ask you."

Antonio turned to John, who said, "Have you seen a little boy, nine years of age, with black hair and brown eyes and a few freckles on his nose? He goes by the name Thomas Dunton."

Considering, Antonio shook his head. "I am sorry, sir. He is your son?"

John nodded.

When they concluded, Antonio left them to rejoin the other refugees and another one took his place. Few of the French spoke English, and the Spaniards not at all. It took until nearly morning to interview all of them, but their answers verified what Antonio had told them.

The information gleaned was both discouraging and uplifting for John. To bring in so many slaves before a shot was ever fired was heartening for them all. The thought that these barbarians had planned to come onto English soil, into their private houses, and take their women and children from their beds horrified him. He found great relief in knowing that his cottage was at Stepney Parish, near London, and more difficult to get to than one of the coastal cities.

<hr />

ON THE TWENTY-SIXTH of March, three letters were sent with Antonio and four armed artillerymen. The first two were addressed to the Kings of Old and New Salé. They were short and to the point.

*The 26ᵗʰ day of March in the year of
our Lord 1636.*

Greetings.

In behalf of King Charles, King of all England,

I demand the return of his Majesty's Subjects, as
well as all Christians in your possession. In addition, we demand satisfaction for shippes and goods,
and for all those Christians that you sold away to
Algeria and other countries before we came here,
which did trouble them very much, and move their
patience. If we do not receive satisfaction in two
days time, we will commence firing our cannons
and artillery until you and your city are destroyed
entirely.

> In duty to his majesty, King Charles . . .
> General William Rainsborough,
> General of the Salé fleet.

The third letter was from John:

> The 26th day of March in the year of
> our Lord 1636
> Master Robert Woodruff;
>   Greetings. In August last one Christopher
> Willoughby did inform mee that my sonne was then
> with one Ally Zuny. This man Willoughby agreed
> to purchase my son, after that you vouched for mee.
> Since I know not where Willoughby sits down, I
> must turn to you to advise mee.
> > Awaiting your response,
> > Master John Dunton of his Majesties
> > Royal Navy

When Antonio and the guards left, they carried John's heart with
them. Watching them slip through the calm sea toward land, it was

all John could do to restrain himself from diving overboard, swimming to them and joining them. But he knew that negotiations were better left to the general. If John had his way, the city would already be in ashes, and Thomas safely by his father's side.

Chapter Twenty-two

Battles of the Brave

*". . . wee and the **Antilop** did shoot above 100*
pieces of ordnance at that ship. . .
John Dunton's journal

When Antonio returned on the evening of the 26th, he told General Rainsborough that the King of New Salé had laughed at the letter he received. The King of Old Salé was unavailable, but the acting governor said he would contact him and send his instructions as soon as possible.

Somewhat discouraged, John stood his watch from midnight to four of the morning, then slept until around ten. After breakfast, he went aloft to the crow's nest with his spyglass. A young man nearing sixteen was on watch and John relieved him, though this was not John's responsibility, but he felt that he had to do something to locate his son. For several hours, he watched the marketplace and the auction block, his eyes searching up and down the narrow streets, but little trading was going on and he saw no sign of Ali Zuny's ship, nor of young Thomas.

Around three o'clock that afternoon, he turned the spyglass toward the northeast and saw a Salé Man-of-War trying to make its way into the harbor by staying as close to the shore as she could without drawing fire from the ships guarding it. "Man-of-War approaching the harbor!" he yelled to the general.

William Rainsborough lifted his spyglass to look for himself, then turned to his first mate. "Battle stations! Cannons at the ready!"

As the first mate relayed the orders to the crew, they could hear similar commands being shouted aboard the neighboring ships as captains and masters learned of the encroacher.

John, knowing there was nothing he could do at the moment, stayed aloft, relaying positions and actions of the Man-of-War and the *Antelope*, an English war ship and part of King Charles' Salé fleet. To his delight, the *Antelope* shot over the enemy ship, and at her, with many cannon balls.

The Man-of-War belched flame from its mid-section and several cannon balls hit the water three hundred feet short of the *Antelope*, which responded with a blast of cannons firing almost in unison. It, too, was short of its target, and the seas were so choppy that little could be done to stop the Algerian Man-of-War.

"Advance!" John yelled down to the general.

"Hoist the top sheets! Haul anchor!" Rainsborough barked the orders quickly, the men complied, and the *Leopard* approached the opening, prepared to block the Man-of-War from entering.

As the Man-of-War approached toward the mouth of the harbor, it continued to fire at the *Antilope* and then at the *Providence*, which had held back, awaiting a signal from the general.

John could almost feel the anger boiling in his veins. An Algerian

vessel dared to try slipping between them during broad daylight.

"The master is to give the general the final call," came a relayed voice up to John.

Nodding, John said, "Stay at the ready!"

The command was passed back to William, and the *Leopard* advanced deeper into the harbor. When the Man-of-War's bow barely passed theirs, John calculated that the Algerian ship wouldn't have time to reload their cannons after wasting their shots at the *Antilope* and the *Providence*. Fiercely, John yelled, "Fire away!" and plugged his ears in anticipation.

The great guns of the *Leopard* spewed forth cannon balls time and time again, striking the Man-of-War with little resistance. By the time the English were finished with it, the Man-of-War was taking on water and pirates were diving into the sea to swim to safety.

As they did, the *Antelope* lifted anchor and joined in the barrage. Soon cannon balls were coming at the Man-of-War from behind, as well as from the side. The ship gave a staggering shudder, rolled over on its starboard side and sank within a few minutes.

The *Leopard* was near the castle now. Suddenly, cannon balls flew above them from the castle, as well as from New Salé. However, the *Leopard* was so close to the cliff the shots cleared the masts and landed a good five hundred yards beyond them.

Cheers went up from the men. At the general's command they maneuvered the ship back far enough to hit the castle, but not so far that they could be hit by cannon blasts from the castle. Dropping anchor, they maintained this advantageous position and spewed cannon after cannon at the castle and into New Salé. They continued this

barrage for two days, killing many Moors. Within his Majesty's Salé Fleet, not one life was lost.

On the 29th of March, 1636, they saw a large white flag draped along the walls, indicating that the people of Old Salé were willing to talk.

General Rainsborough ordered a cease-fire, and the ships returned to their former positions, hoping this would persuade the pirates to satisfy their demands, as spelled out in the letters sent to them three days earlier.

However, the general and John agreed that the white flag might be a ploy. They expected some kind of retaliation. Rainsborough ordered that all men should stay at their posts, sleeping in four-hour shifts.

John relinquished his place in the crow's nest early on the 29th, to clean up after a long siege. He planned to dine with General Rains-borough in his cabin, and with the other officers of the Salé Fleet, including John's first mate, Timothy Fuller, and Captain George Carteret, vice-admiral from the *Antelope*.

General Rainsborough's first mate, Davis Thompson, a tall, heavy-set man with glaring eyes was the kind of man one wouldn't want to meet in a dark alley. Thompson remained on deck, in command of the *Leopard* in the other officers' absence.

"Gentlemen," William said, getting straight to the point when their meal was consumed, the dishes cleared, and the wine flowing freely. "Today we received a letter from the governor of old Salé, in which he states that they desire peace, for they are done with the pirates of the new town and I believe we are near an agreement. However, the new town is still not ready to comply with our demands and we stand

ready to fight them, if necessary. In the meantime, the governor of Old Salé asks that we send a doctor to them, for they are without one, and many are injured or sick. What say you?"

Sir George spoke first: "If they will send over three of their best men as a gesture of good faith, then we should be lenient and send three of ours."

"Any opposed?" questioned Rainsborough.

"Who will you send?" asked George Hatch, captain of the *Mary*. "We have only one doctor, one surgeon and one surgeon's assistant. Do you propose that we risk sending all three?"

"Naturally not," Sir George spoke up.

"No," William agreed. "We would send our surgeon's assistant and two men to accompany him, along with a few medical supplies."

"Very wise," said Edward Symons, captain of the *Providence*.

"I ask permission to go with them," said John.

General William gave him a knowing look. "I know you are most anxious to find your son, John. But it would be safer for all concerned if you would wait long enough for us to determine how the pirates at New Salé react to our helping the old city."

John nodded. "Yes, you're right, of course." He was bitterly disappointed. His son could have been killed by all the cannon fired at the city the past two days.

When the meeting adjourned, John sought the quiet of his cabin.

Simon would be helping refugees for hours. Every night since they arrived, several people had eluded their captors and swam to the *Leopard* for safety. Simon tended to their medical needs, which ranged from septic lash wounds to starvation.

John stretched out on the top bunk and stared at the ceiling, but saw nothing. He was consumed with anguish, to be this close to Thomas, yet unable to leave the ship. To be so near, yet so far away, was almost more than John could stand.

During the next several days, the inhabitants of Old Salé and New Salé battled one another, commanding the full attention of all the men aboard the *Leopard*. Cannon fire from the English was exchanged again, and again, mostly into New Salé, for the older part of the city wanted nothing to do with the battle.

From his perch in the crow's nest, John noticed that the men of New Salé were attempting to build a bridge over the river upon boats with deal-boards. A pirate army was preparing to march across the bridge into Old Salé with their horses, many thousands of them. Alerting Rainsborough immediately, ships in the Salé Fleet fired a steady barrage of cannon balls until the bridge was destroyed, and the pirates had their hands full trying to care for the wounded and dying. The slaughter of pirates was profuse and terrible.

Fighting between the two cities escalated, but cannon fire from the ships could not reach the hub of the battle, so the seamen were obliged to watch from their vessels and wish they had some way to help the citizen-warriors of Old Salé.

Meanwhile, the pirates took their ships up the river a few hundred yards, so that the cannon balls from the Salé Fleet could not reach them.

On the eighteenth of April, the re-masted *Hercules* came into Salé from Lishorne. Captain Brian Harrison came aboard to learn the status of the war to that point. By the thirtieth day of April, the tide of the battle turned in favor of the English. The inhabitants of Old Salé again

put white flags over the wall, inviting the men from the Salé Fleet to come ashore.

Several of the general's men went ashore, and learned that the King of Old Salé was willing to turn the town over to the King of England and give the seamen anything and everything in the city they so desired, if they would rid them of the pirates. Several squads were formed, some to decide where best to build trenches from which to fire cannons and sink the ships taken up the river; some to see how the old town was fortified; some to see how many cannons and great guns they had, and to assess what other weaponry was available.

The seamen went to work fortifying the city, while John located the perfect spot from which to destroy the ships upriver, and dug trenches with his crew for the cannons.

All through the rest of April and into May, John and his crew worked in the trenches. By night, as his men slept, John made a house by house search for his son in all the parts of Old Salé, but found no sign of Thomas. He often ventured into New Salé at night, hiding in alleys, searching for his son through open windows, but it was dangerous work, and unfruitful without a torch to light his way. Twice he was almost captured, but managed to escape both times.

By the time the trenches were finished, John had searched all of the old town and a few parts of the new town, but had not found his son, nor anyone who knew of Thomas' whereabouts. Nor could anyone tell him where to find Master Woodruff, to whom John had written that first day after they arrived at Salé, nor Christopher Willoughby, who had agreed to purchase Thomas from Ali Zuny, if Master Woodruff vouched for John's ability to repay him.

Much discouraged, John feared that Thomas was already dead, or

had been sold to someone from another country, or that he would be killed once they started the cannon blasting again. He had serious doubts that Thomas could survive after that day arrived.

Trusting that God knew where his son was and would watch over him, John carried a prayer in his heart every waking moment that Thomas would be protected, that guardian angels would keep him from harm. It was the only thing he could do now. *Please, God,* he begged. *He's my only son. Keep him out of the way of cannon blasts and safe from what we must now do to our enemies for the release of our countrymen and other Christians.*

Turning the gunnery trench over to the captain of the gunmen, John returned to the *Leopard* broken-hearted, exhausted from working hard all day and searching all night for weeks, rarely getting more than an hour or two of sleep in any twenty-four hour period. After cleaning himself properly, he collapsed on the top bunk and slept for thirty-six hours.

He awakened to the blast of cannons firing from the *Leopard* and he hurried out on deck to see what was happening. The town of New Salé was under attack from sea and land, and pirate ships up river were on fire. Screaming and yelling, both ashore and aboard, men exchanged cannon balls, fire balls and other weaponry intent on total destruction.

The battle raged on for weeks. When they weren't firing into the new town from ships and from the old town, they chased and attacked newcomer pirate ships that were headed for Salé. The *Leopard* and all the other ships in the armada worked together to sink or capture as many of the pirates' ships as they could, and were successful much of the time. They chased several ships into the rocks by the cliffs, running them aground. The pirates ships then broke apart, killing nearly all the pirates aboard. None of the pirates were spared, for the English knew

they would plunder and enslave again. The red decks of the armada failed to run even redder with blood, for most of the blood spilled during these battles was the blood of the pirates, who had plundered and tortured and enslaved thousands of English subjects and other Christians.

King Charles' Salé Fleet captured several men-of-war ships with fifty great guns each, killing all the pirates aboard, taking no prisoners. When a ship was captured, they put their own Englishmen aboard, and draped the pirate flags over the side of the gunwale, then flew the flag of England aloft, to encourage the inhabitants of Old Salé and further intimidate the pirates.

Some of the fleet's gunmen were wounded or maimed, most in Old Salé. But when each day's tally had been taken, far fewer Englishmen were killed than the pirates of New Salé.

Still the battle continued. On the twenty-third of June, 1636, John wrote in his journal, "... *our Generall did goe aboard the* **Expedition** *in the morning, to see how they would row, and they did row after three leages a watch, and did row under the Castle, and the Castle did shoote at her, and shee did shoote at the Castle, and into the Castle, and over the Castle, and into the towne, and over the towne, and the Castle at her, and shee at them, and so they did lye shooting one at another, untill foure a clocke in the afternoon; and then shee did come off again, and did come unto an Anchor hard by the* **Leopard**, *and came off very well, and had never a man hurt we give God thankes.*"

The inhabitants of Old Salé were no less prosperous in their attempts to drive the pirates out of New Salé. They crossed the river at night and set all the cornfields, wheat fields and orchards on fire, so the pirates of New Salé suffered great starvation.

On June first, the Governor of Old Salé was captured, after it was discovered that he was actually the King of Old Salé. It was this king who had invited the pirates to take control of the city, in exchange for his own slaves and a percentage of the plunder. Learning of this treachery, they had no choice but to take him by boat to the King of Morocco at Safi, under cover of darkness. A message was passed along from the *Leopard* to his Majesty's ships, warning them ahead of time not to pursue them. They hoped that once the King of Morocco dealt with him, he would be severely punished. The old king was loved by his people and hated by his servants. John could only hope that the Moors' devotion would eventually be their downfall. On the thirteenth day of June, the new town sent a small boat with crew and a letter, addressed to General Rainsborough, who requested the *Leopard's* officers, as well as the captains from the other ships, to join him. John hoped this would be New Salé's surrender, but he was disappointed.

Pacing back and forth across the aftercastle deck, the general said, "They ask that we make peace with them and fight no more, and if we stop now, they will not fight us anymore, but they will not return any of our subjects, nor any Christians. I will not make peace with them until they return to us all those people whom they have taken."

Much discouraged, John said, "Perhaps they cannot give us our countrymen and other Christians because they no longer exist. My son has not been found among them in almost three months, though we have searched everywhere, and offered rewards left and right."

"Then, they'd better show us where they are buried!" General Rainsborough raged. "For I will not return to England with the paltry few that have escaped from them. How many have you counted now, John?"

"Seventy-two men, women and boys."

"How many did we estimate were taken captive before we came, sir?" questioned Fuller, John's first mate.

"More than thirty thousand," said John. "Perhaps unrealistically, we hoped that at least a third of these would still be alive."

"I say we hang the lot of them," Sir George suggested. "Let's go ashore and hang the bloody lot of them!"

"They may still outnumber us," General Rainsborough commented. "But I will say this much, I am dedicated to this cause, and I will not return to England unless we take with us every single Christian and English subject still alive in New Salé.

"Here! Here!" came the hearty response of every officer.

William nodded, squared his shoulders and glared at the two Moors who had brought him the letter of peace. He walked down the stairs to the weather deck and stood in front of them. "Tell your leaders that there will be no peace until our demands are met. We want our countrymen and all Christians released, as well as reimbursement for all that has been stolen from our subjects. If you do not meet our demands, we will continue this war until you are all dead!"

The two Moors were outraged. "Then we shall all die!"

General Rainsborough was not impressed. "You bring me the Christians and my countrymen or there will be no peace!" Before they could resist him any further, he ordered the guards, "Get these vermin off my ship!"

The two men were taken by the legs and arms and cast into the water. When they tried to re-board the shallop they'd used to cross the harbor, the guards within it used the tips of their swords to persuade them to learn how to swim.

Early the next morning, they received word that over a hundred men fled from New Salé into Old Salé the night before, begging for food and offering their services to the old town, willing to lay down their weapons and seeking peace.

Later in the day, a large Man-of-War came against the fleet from the south and the *Providence* chased it onto the rocks, where it split into pieces. The ship and its crew were crushed against the granite cliffs by the angry surf.

Four other ships, all Men-of-War, came to trade at Salé, but the General of the *Leopard* forbade it and ordered his men to take possession of the ships, forcing the would-be traders to swim for the shore.

Still, the fighting continued in pockets throughout New Salé, for the pirates were determined to fight to the death. On the twenty-seventh of June, two ships came into the harbor and the *Providence* shot a hundred pieces of ordnance and killed all the men aboard them. A thousand Moors, all pirates, shot at the *Providence* with small shot, but at noon they gave up shooting. The *Providence* came away well, not a man hurt, but her ropes, sails and sides were riddled with small shot. They did not know how many Moors the *Providence* killed, perhaps more than five hundred, before the Moors gave up.

July came without any change in the fighting, except that there were fewer and fewer Moors to kill. Where there had been ten thousand at the onset, now perhaps two or three thousand remained in New Salé.

On the twenty-sixth of July, John took his first mate, Fuller, the master gunner, and several other men with him, and relocated the great guns and cannons from the trenches to the head of the river, where

they began to boat them across to the north bank of the river for the last big siege of New Salé.

When many of the remaining Moors in New Salé saw that they were about to be struck again with cannon fire, this time from their side of the river, they fled from the city to the south and to the east. Unaware that the citizens of Old Salé had burned all the countryside south and east of the city for more than thirty leagues, many perished of starvation in the charred wheatfields and cornfields.

When slaves saw their masters fleeing from New Salé, many of them escaped to the *Leopard* and the other ships in the armada, some in shallops, and some by swimming.

On the twenty-seventh of July, the *Providence* was approached by a pinnace that came along side, with letters from the King of Morocco. They had the King of Old Salé in chains. He was a pitiful man, with deep creases in his sun-wrinkled face and cold, black eyes. Captain Edward Symons ordered the king removed, placed aboard the *Providence*, then brought to the *Leopard*.

John had just arrived from New Salé after another day of getting the great guns and cannons across the river, when the *Providence* slipped along side the *Leopard*.

The general read the letter from the King of Morocco aloud to everyone aboard:

> To General William Rainsborough of the Salé Fleet, now engaged in taking the city of Salé from those pirates.
>
> Greetings. I present you with the King of Salé. He has made his peace with me and I have sent him

to resume his duty as King with the following provision: that he make his peace with you in regards to the Christians. For the town of New Salé was very nearly none of my affair, without your assisting me in restoring Salé to my people. Therefore I am in your debt. Do with Salé's king what you will . . . .

Rainsborough stopped reading and glared at the king with eyes that clearly wanted to burn the man's heart from his chest.

The king smiled wanly.

William flew into a rage when he saw the old king's expression. With the swiftness of an eagle, he swooped down and dragged him, gagging and completely flustered, to the net where he tied a noose in a long rope and tossed it over the yard spar. "Thompson, get me a tall barrel!"

Davis Thompson, the first mate, immediately set a wooden barrel about three feet tall just below the hangman's noose.

Slipping the loop over the king's head and around his neck, and placing the king upon the barrel, Rainsborough tightened the noose so that the man had to stand on his tip-toes and stretch or be rope-burned.

With the prisoner's hands shackled behind his back and his ankles shackled together, the old king sputtered and gasped, "Please, General. Do not do this thing! I plead for your mercy!"

"How much mercy did you have for all the English subjects and Christians brought into your city by the pirates? Did you spare any of them?" General William fairly roared at the cowering man.

"You may have *all* my Christians. All of them, I beg you. Please. My people will perish with no one to govern them."

"Or they may govern themselves well in your absence." Tormenting the king, Rainsborough put his foot upon the barrel as though he intended to knock it out from under him.

"Please!" the king squealed. "I will give you all the Christians in the whole city! All of them!"

"And the English subjects?" questioned the general, his foot still in position.

"I will give you all of them! I swear!"

"Until every single one of them is aboard one of King Charles' ships, you will remain where you are. Thompson, put five men on guard around this man until all the Christians and English subjects have been brought aboard."

"Aye, sir!" Thompson grinned. Then he barked orders at five crewmen who immediately gathered around the old king.

"John, go into New Salé and tell everyone that we have the king in shackles and that he has ordered the release of all the slaves. Tell them that if they do not comply with this order by noon tomorrow, the king will be hung where he stands. We want all who remain in that city to see how the King of England deals with traitors and pirates. Tell them if they are not quick about bringing us the slaves, we will begin blasting New Salé until they do!"

"Yes, sir."

"And John, turn over every stone until you find your son."

"Yes, sir!"

John did not have to be told twice. "Fuller," he said to his first mate,

"From every ship, gather two dozen men and an officer, and have them meet me at the cannons in New Salé immediately."

"Aye, sir," said Fuller, a look of relief crossing over his face.

At last, thought John, *I can search for my son without hindrance. I pray, merciful God, that you have spared him.*

Chapter Twenty-Three

A Cloak of Discovery

*". . . and it was agreed upon that they should bring all our
Christians aboard in their boats. . . and they did make
as much haste as they could. . . ."*

John Dunton's Journal

ohn kicked at a pebble on the quay as he waited for all the men
from the eight main ships of the Salé fleet to arrive. He had one
hundred seventy-two men at his command and he would make
swift use of them.

Upon arriving at New Salé, John and twenty-four men from the
Leopard delivered the governor's message, which was verified as the
Leopard sailed through the mouth of the harbor and lead-lined into
port until it rested in six fathoms of water. The *Leopard* was positioned
so that everyone in Salé, new or old, could see their king in shackles,
his neck in a noose. No sooner had the inhabitants witnessed the king's
predicament, than they went to their tents and houses and started to
bring forth their slaves.

When all the pinnaces had disembarked, John looked his men over

thoughtfully. Their uniforms were well worn, but not threadbare, and their swords and knives were sheathed at their waists, ready for any resistance. On their faces he saw relief and determination. Hostilities were coming to an end, and their countrymen would be rescued.

Satisfied with their appearance, John gave his instructions. "We will remain in groups of twenty-five, with an officer in charge of each. Disburse according to the maps you have received, into the seven sections of the city."

The officers nodded in unison, prepared to carry out John's orders.

First mate Arbigard, from the *Antelope,* spoke up. "We didn't receive a map, Master Dunton."

John answered swiftly. "Your men will remain at the quay to process incoming slaves. So far, the inhabitants have been agreeable, and they are bringing the enslaved to us, but remember, they cannot be trusted."

Arbigard smiled. "We will see that everyone who is brought to us is accounted for, sir."

"The rest of you," John spoke loudly. "See that you search every closet, under every bed, in every dark corner, under everything large enough to hide a woman's shoe. Take every slave that you find, be he Christian or English, woman or child. And if slaves from other nationalities desire to throw their lot in with us, bring them as well. In particular, keep alert for my son, a young boy ten years of age. He has black hair and brown eyes, dimples in his cheeks and a few freckles on his nose, and he answers to Thomas. When I saw him last, he was quite thin and pale, and he wore a woman's green velvet cloak to warm himself. My crew will search the rubble of houses and shops left standing along the quay. If you find my son, bring him to me at once. Doctor Harris, along with his surgeon and assistant, are available to

treat anyone who will need medical aid prior to boarding. We now have one hundred twenty-three refugees gathered out of a city that should have had more than thirty thousand. If you find graves, bones or bodies bring them to us, that we may bury them properly and try to establish some form of identification for them, so that their families can be notified of their demise. Speak with those still living, for they may know the deceased by name. By all means, keep a tally of the dead that you find, along with their names, that we may account, in some measure, to his Majesty, King Charles, that we have done our best to find his loyal subjects."

"Here! Here!" cried the men, in one thunderous roar.

"Officers! Advance!" John yelled above them.

As each group went off, John prayed, *Please, God. Please!* Then he turned to his twenty-four men, among whom Fuller stood proudly. "Men, we will cover more territory if we break into four groups of six. Watch your backs. If anyone resists, slay them. We will rescue all of our countrymen, or whoever opposes us will die!"

They advanced on the city, passing Moors who were bringing slaves to the quay of their own free will, eager to comply with the general's order. To his dismay, John saw that the Moors were not much better off than their emaciated servants, women and children among them, but he saw no child that resembled Thomas. Or, if he did, when he turned the child around to get a better look at him, the face was always different. They traversed the city all night and into the late hours of morning, turning the city upside down, and still they found no sign of young Thomas.

They found many slaves lying on sod floors, damp with excrement, in such emaciated condition that their masters had abandoned them.

Knowing they had rescued some of these from certain death brought some comfort to John.

In searching for his son, however, John found only a lesson in futility.

Near noon the following day, John reluctantly admitted defeat and hoped that one of the other groups had more success than he. Returning to the quay, he and his men searched the faces of the refugees, looking into the eyes of every child for the dark brown ones belonging to Thomas, to no avail.

When the final reality struck John, it had the force of a cannon ball. He sank to his knees and called aloud, using all his strength, "Thomas!" The sound reverberated over the water, landing upon each of his Majesty's ships, now inside the harbor.

"Thomas!" John yelled, over and over again. Then he bent his head to the ground and wept, uncaring who witnessed it. He felt no disgrace that he, a grown man, should cry aloud in front of all the slaves, Moors and Englishmen. He could only feel the terrible shame of losing his son, his only son, to pirates who had drained the young boy's life from him.

Images of Thomas' suffering swept into his mind, filling it with revulsion. How had his son died here in Salé? Had he been tortured? Beaten? Starved? Had his little body been abused and driven beyond what he could endure? What had his last thoughts been? Had he wondered why his father hadn't rescued him? Had he cursed his father for ever having brought him into this world?

How would John ever tell Rebecca that their son was lost to them? How would he face her, knowing that he failed in his quest? How could he bear to see the look on her face when she learned of his defeat? And what of his daughter, Jane? How would he explain, once she was old

enough, that he'd put her brother's life at risk and lost it in the bargain?

Thousands of thoughts tumbled into John's mind as he wept upon the quay at Salé, Morocco, for the little boy he could not find.

QUITE SUDDENLY, JOHN found himself lying atop the bed in his cabin. He was aboard the *Leopard*, but he knew not how he got there. He sat up quickly and bumped his head on the ceiling of the forecastle.

"Stay still, John," coaxed Simon. "You're liable to hurt yourself."

"How did I get here?" John asked, trying to remember.

"Your men carried you," Simon explained. "You were on your knees for over an hour when I finally got to you. The crew didn't know how to care for you. When we lifted you up from the ground, you could neither speak nor hear. They brought you back to the *Leopard*, where I forced you, with Fuller's help, to drink nearly a quart of wine. Finally you passed out." He rubbed the bald crown of his silver head thoughtfully. "Perhaps I gave you a little too much wine because you've been asleep for two days."

"That's why I have a headache as big as this blasted ship!" John groaned. "And what of Thomas?" he asked. Then he remembered. "We didn't find him, did we?"

Simon shook his head. "No, we didn't, John."

Looking into Simon's shocking blue eyes, John studied Thomas' grandfather for a few moments. He noted how much balder his head seemed and the thin patches of white just above his ears and nape seemed more white somehow. He'd forgotten that Simon loved Thomas every ounce as much as John, but he saw it now in the cloud across the older man's eyes and the slump of his shoulders.

Rolling off the bed, John put his hand upon Simon's shoulder. "I'm sorry," he whispered. "Thomas' death will be on my head, not yours. I, alone, will have to answer for it."

The tears welled up in Simon's eyes and John pulled him close. Together they wept, this time in private, away from the staring eyes of the crew.

On the eighth of August, General Rainsborough ordered four ships, the *Antelope*, the *Providence*, the *Expedition* and the *Hercules*, along with two pinnaces, to range the coast of Spain, and to look for Turkish Man-of-War ships, pirates and others that might hinder their return to England.

All the countrymen and Christians who had been freed from Salé had been accounted for, and John scoured the list of names recorded in his two-day absence.

His eyes read down the list, a faint hope in his heart that he would find Thomas' name upon it, that somewhere along the line, someone had not notified him of Thomas' safe rescue. *Philip Lucey, William Hardaye, Richard Daye, William Frost, Edward Blackwell III, William Moore, John Fighter, David—*

John stopped and stared at the name, *Edward Blackwell III.* Lord Blackwell's son was on the list of slaves released. Could it really be his Lordship's son, this Edward Blackwell III? When the *Neptune* sank, was Edward captured alive and taken to Salé as a prisoner? Taking the list with him, he went up on the aftercastle deck to consult the general.

"Good afternoon, John. Feeling better, are you?" asked General Rainsborough, as soon as he'd finished giving some instructions to his first mate.

"Quite, thank you, William. There's a name on this list, sir, that

I'm familiar with, and I wondered if you'd seen it," John began.

"Who is it?"

"Edward Blackwell, son of Lord Blackwell at Chatham."

"Yes, he is on the list, isn't he?"

"I haven't seen him aboard, sir."

"No, I sent Master Edward and his companion, William Moore, over to the *Hercules* the first day they arrived."

"Why wasn't I informed of this, sir? It is my responsibility to make sure all the rescued are cared for adequately."

"Yes, I know what your duties are, John. But you did marry Edward's betrothed the day after she disappeared from Blackwell Tower. . . ." He left the sentence open, perhaps hoping for John's elaboration.

"He doesn't know that, sir. The *Neptune* went down before he could be informed of our marriage." When General Rainsborough did not respond, John persisted. "Sir, were you concerned that I would not respect Edward's care if he was aboard the *Leopard?*"

"No, John" admitted William. "But I did think to myself that if I were in your shoes, and the man who'd whipped my wife was brought on board, regardless of his condition, I would not have the empathy to give him any better treatment than what he gave to her." He gave John a wan smile.

"I wasn't aware that you were privy to that information, William."

"Lord Blackwell and I have been like brothers for years, John. He's also considering whether or not his son is responsible for Jeremy Webster's death. Knowing all this, I'm surprised that you're not in a rage against him."

"You know very little about me, sir. The reason why I have repeatedly refused a captain's position is because I could never apply the accepted standard of punishment to any of my crew, regardless how grievous their sin," John admitted.

Apparently surprised, William said, "I've seen no sign of remorse in you, over killing Moors and pirates."

"A pirate's death is justifiable, sir, for they are savages who will continue to kill and plunder as long as there is breath within them, but I believe there are better ways to discipline one's own crew."

"I'm disappointed to learn of this," the general admitted. "I had intended to recommend you for captain grade when we return to Chatham."

"I would not accept it," said John. "Not unless it was aboard my own ship."

General Rainsborough nodded. Then he said, "If you would have Edward and his companion back aboard the *Leopard*, I will order it as soon as we join up with them. You do know that the *Hercules* was sent to patrol the coast of Spain until we return from Safi and our visit with King Laisbi, of Morocco.

"I would, sir. Very much. But, I assure you that I bear Edward no ill will. If he has been imprisoned at Salé the past sixteen months and lived to report it, he has suffered enough punishment for his sins. I will not add any measure of pain to him."

ON AUGUST TWENTY-FIRST, the *Leopard* sailed out of Salé harbor and headed toward Safi, where the King of Morocco had his palace.

Later that night, John took his place at the helm, glad for something

to do besides sit in his cabin and torture his mind with questions. It was a brisk wind, near twenty knots, and the waves burst around the *Leopard* at a forty-five degree angle, the bow slicing through them with ease. The *Leopard* was built for wind and seas as they were tonight, and John guessed they were sailing eight knots, maybe ten.

A salty mist lingered around his face and he sucked it in, enjoying the feeling of the moisture in his nostrils and lungs. Licking his lips, John tasted the savory. It reminded him of just such a night five years ago when Thomas had gone on his first voyage aboard the *Warwick* to America.

"How does the sea float in the air like this, Father?" six-year-old Thomas had asked when the mist was so thick it almost dripped from the lad's nose.

"I don't know, son. I suppose God has His hand in it somehow."

"Oh!" the young boy had sighed almost reverently. "This must be how God kisses us."

John had smiled. "I suppose," he'd said. "Although I never considered it as such before tonight."

"'God is all around us,' Grandfather says. Whenever we want Him, all we have to do is talk to Him, and He'll be right beside us, listening."

"What would you say, if you could talk to God right now?" John had asked, curious to learn what his son was thinking.

"I'd say, thank you for the kisses. They're a little wet, though."

"Is that right?"

"And then I'd say, make sure you take some of my kisses back, and give them to my mother in Heaven, because she didn't get any yet."

John sighed within himself, pleased to find the memory as fresh and

stirring as though it had happened only moments ago. "Well, young Thomas," he whispered in the misty night air, "I suppose Mary will get plenty of attention from you now, won't she?"

When no one answered, John looked out over the deck and across the forecastle. A few men were drinking warm rum and talking amicably on their watch at the bow.

John would have to get on with living now. It would be difficult, but he would learn to manage. He had two special reasons to keep on going.

Jane would be seven months old by now. Very likely she would be sitting up on her own, perhaps learning how to crawl. Maybe she had some teeth already.

And then he thought of Rebecca. How he missed her. On nights like this, he wished she was in the master's cabin, waiting for his watch to end, with her golden hair aglow on the pillow and a smile on her lips, a hint of teasing in her turquoise eyes. John vowed that the moment he returned to his wife, he would tell her of his love for her, regardless whether she loved him back, and he would never leave her again without telling her so. Indeed, he considered himself a foolish man for having kept his feelings from her as he'd done. If she did not love him in return, he would have to show her, somehow, why she should. But she must know his heart.

Trying unsuccessfully to put his grief for his son aside, he prayed that Thomas would forgive him, though he dared not ask God to forgive himself. There was no forgiveness for a man who failed to protect his family and keep them safe from harm. Knowing he would be unable to sleep after his watch, John went out to the bow and enjoyed the salt spray as it soaked his face in a matter of minutes. It

would be a long night, he decided. A long night, indeed.

On the twenty-third day of August, 1636, the *Leopard* arrived in Safi where they anchored in twenty fathoms of water. The general and John, along with several of the other officers, accompanied Robert Blacke, who was an interpreter for the King of Morocco, in a shallop over to the quay. They were met by dignitaries and treated kindly. When the articles of peace were drawn up, signed and witnessed, the Ambassador appointed by the king made plans to accompany the *Leopard* to England, where they would present King Charles with all the documents pertaining to their peace agreement. While the Ambassador prepared his entourage, John and the other officers spent some time in Safi as guests of King Laisbi. The generous king sent extra supplies and provisions to the *Leopard* for their voyage home.

On the twenty-first of September, they took their leave of Safi and headed the *Leopard* north toward England. It wasn't until they reached the coast of France that they caught up with the *Hercules* and the ships accompanying it on their patrol of the Spanish coast.

On their third day with the *Hercules*, the wind died and the seas turned flat and glassy. With the general's permission, John sent for Edward Blackwell and his companion, William Moore.

John wanted to speak with Edward alone, but when they arrived he was still on watch at the helm, so he sent Fuller to attend to them. Fuller later reported that upon their being brought to the *Leopard*, Edward had collapsed. Since John was detained at the helm, he instructed that Edward be carried to the doctor's cabin for treatment.

When John finished his watch, he turned it over to the first mate and went directly to the forecastle to see how Edward was feeling.

Edward Blackwell, pale and withdrawn, had dark circles around

his gray-blue eyes. His fine, straight nose and dark hair still seemed to give him an air of superiority, regardless of his current condition. Having been aboard the *Hercules* for the past several weeks, he was not as emaciated as he must have been at the time of his rescue, but his body was still quite thin, his ribs markedly visible beneath the yellowed skin. He sat in a chair being examined by Simon, but he was so weak, he could scarcely hold his head up.

Seeing John enter, Edward whispered, "It's John, isn't it? John Dunton?" Then he coughed, and as he did so, he bent over just enough that John could see the top of his back, which was covered with lash marks, scars and bruises.

"Yes, Edward. Have you been treated well since your rescue?" John asked, a sudden pang of empathy sweeping through him.

"Well enough, thank you. I am still having trouble keeping solid food down, not having had any in so many months. We were fortunate to get a little gruel once in a while."

When Edward coughed again, William Moore picked up an old cloak from the bed to cover Edward's shoulders with it. Tattered and worn, it was barely recognizable, but John noticed the green color immediately and took it from William, pulling it to his face and smelling it, as though it might have any hint of Thomas' scent left in it. "Where did you get this?" he demanded.

"A young lad named Thomas, sir," said William quickly, as though worried that he would be punished if he did not speak at once. Then the name registered. "Thomas Dunton. Is he your relation, sir?"

John nodded, "My son. When did you see him last?"

William shrugged. "I cannot say, sir. I was delirious with fever back then."

Edward lifted his eyes up to John's and said, "It was before the last pirate boat sailed into Salé during the siege, Master Dunton. Long before that, the pirates had left us for dead. William and I were both so sick we fainted in the middle of the road and waited to die, thinking our lives were over."

"How did you come to have Thomas' cloak?"

Coughing violently, Edward couldn't answer right away. When he had finally calmed, he whispered, "The boy saved our lives, John. We were starving and near frozen from the cold. Thomas found us and hid us in a haystack. He brought us food and water. To keep us warm, he gave us the cloak."

"Do you know what became of him?"

Edward shook his head. "No," he gasped, and gulped several sips of tea before he could continue. "Thomas was to be sold on the auction block soon, and he had nourished us well enough by then that we wanted to try and escape. We asked him to come with us, sir, but he refused. He said that it would be far easier for his captors to find three runaways than it would for them to find one little boy. He told us to keep the cloak, sir, and to tell you, if we reached you safely, that he will soon escape himself. He said he would search for the bark *Warwick* and find you."

"When did you last see him, Edward?" John asked, his eyes filling with tears as he pictured his little son, pretending to be Joseph with the coat of many colors, going out of his way to comfort and care for the man who had whipped Rebecca.

"April last." Edward answered, then he went into a terrible spasm of coughing, and Simon gave him some more tea.

"Enough questions for now," Simon told John. "He's still very weak."

"May I stay with him?" asked William. "He saved my life that day on the *Neptune* when we were sunk by an Algerian Man-of-War. It is the least I can do to stay with him until he is safely returned to his father."

"Of course," said John. He lifted the cloak to float it over Edward to keep him warm, when a slip of paper fell from the pocket. "What's this?" he asked William, picking it up.

"Captain Hammond wrote that letter of recommendation for Edward, shortly before he died. It details our capture by pirates and Edward's exemplary manner in dealing with them like a true Englishman. Edward has read it perhaps a dozen times every day, sir."

John gave the paper to William. "See that this letter is preserved for Edward, for I fear he has not the strength to do so himself."

"Yes, sir." William folded the paper and placed it inside his doublet. "I shall guard it with my life, Master Dunton."

"You're a good man, William. You may have my bed to sleep upon while Edward is recovering."

"Oh, no sir! I am just as comfortable on the floor. Over the past sixteen months of captivity, I have learned to sleep anywhere."

"Very well," said John, "but you must stay in here, where there's less chance you'll bring something infectious back to Edward. It is his health that we must concern ourselves with now."

Suddenly, Edward sat bolt upright and screamed, "We have to go back! We must take Thomas with us! Please, sire, I beg of you. We have to go back!"

John whirled around to face him, but when he saw Edward's eyes, glazed over as though he wore a mask of death, he shuddered. The man was completely delirious.

"Is he always like this?" John asked.

William nodded. "He credits young Thomas for saving our lives and has been fixated upon returning the favor ever since we last saw him."

Nodding, John said to Simon, "Come to me when you have Edward comfortable."

After Simon agreed, John went out on deck to speak with General Rainsborough.

"How is he?" William Rainsborough asked.

"He's very sick. Simon will be able to tell us more later."

"He doesn't appear well enough to stand the rest of the voyage, John."

Nodding, John said, "I agree. But he was able to give me some information about my son as early as April last."

"Oh?"

"The cloak he wore, did you see it?"

"A shabby thing, wasn't it?"

"My wife wore that same cloak the night she ran away from Edward."

They talked for a while about Edward's condition and the last time Thomas had helped the poor man. Finally, Simon came from the forecastle and walked toward them. When he arrived atop the aftercastle deck, he said, "I believe it's a good case of pneumonia, along with

313

scurvy and starvation. He's only been able to eat liquids. While aboard the *Hercules*, the cook had been soaking hardtack in water, grinding it into a thin gruel. Edward's been drinking that several times a day."

"That's all?" John asked, surprised to learn it. "We brought more food than hardtack aboard his Majesty's ships."

"They had no doctor aboard, and the men thought the hardtack would be least likely to upset his stomach. The first few times he tried to eat solid food, he vomited."

"Surely, he can have some split pea soup, perhaps eggs or dried fruit. We brought plenty of that with us from Safi."

"I am having the cook prepare some for after his tea is settled."

"Did you say anything to him about Rebecca?" John asked.

"No. It is not my place to tell him."

"We must let him recover as much as possible first. Hopefully, before the end of the voyage he will be strong enough, but if not, I'm certain Lord Blackwell will tell him eventually."

"Your empathy astounds me," said the general. "Surely you want retribution for all that he has done to your family."

He shook his head. "I want nothing more than peace between us."

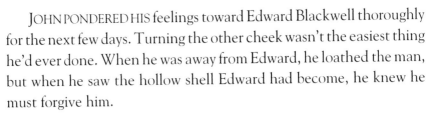

JOHN PONDERED HIS feelings toward Edward Blackwell thoroughly for the next few days. Turning the other cheek wasn't the easiest thing he'd ever done. When he was away from Edward, he loathed the man, but when he saw the hollow shell Edward had become, he knew he must forgive him.

Edward had been beaten brutally during the sixteen months he was

enslaved. Though he didn't mention it, John knew that it must have been horrible if the quantity of nightmares Edward awoke from was any indication. Many times Edward awakened, screaming Thomas' name, insisting they had to go back. Then he would fall, trance-like, back upon the bed and sleep fitfully again.

They didn't discuss Edward's enslavement after that first day. Sometimes these things are better left unsaid, some memories need to be buried... and if they are asked to resurface, they would only cause more anxiety and melancholy.

By the fifth day of October, 1636, the armada reached the southernmost piece of land in England called the Lizard, and were nearly home. Within four days, they reached Chatham and waited for the right tide and conditions to enter the bay.

Excited and anxious to be on English soil, John and the entire crew made short work of securing the *Leopard*, and putting her stores in order. Then, bidding farewell to General Rainsborough, he took Edward Blackwell, William Moore and Simon with him across the bay in a shallop.

Lord Blackwell hadn't come into Chatham to welcome the fleet home. John thought this rather curious, but he did not mention it to Edward. A carriage and driver from his Lordship's warehouse took them eight miles along the road toward England, and they arrived at Blackwell Tower near dusk.

John stepped out of the carriage and up to the front door to knock. Wilson answered with a wide grin. "We heard you had arrived, Master Dunton," he said as he shook John's hand.

"Is his Lordship at home?"

"He's resting, sir. Took a cold in September and cannot seem to shake it."

"We have Edward with us, Wilson."

The elderly gentleman's chin dropped as his mouth fell open. "Sir Edward?" he asked in amazement.

"Yes, we've brought him back from the pirates."

"Bring him in, Master Dunton. I will awaken his Lordship straight away."

By the time John and William Moore got Edward out of the carriage, John could hear Lord Blackwell's exclamation, "Merciful God in Heaven! Where? Where?"

Edward smiled weakly at John and whispered, "It's comforting to know that someone missed me."

Within moments, John had helped Edward, still a very sick man, into the foyer, where he watched Lord Blackwell dash down the stairs and grab his son, hugging him with all his strength. "My son! Dear, dear Edward!"

The two men wept, heads on each other's shoulders. Leaving Simon with them to aid in Edward's recovery, John returned to the carriage.

"Drive on," he told the driver. "To *John's Cottage* as quickly as you can."

Chapter Twenty-Four

Bitter-sweet November

*"The number of all the Captives that came out of Salley and
Saphia is in all, three hundred thirty nine men, woemen,
and boyes, as doth appear by a true Cope."*

John Dunton's journal

ebecca stepped out to the garden where she picked the ripest and most robust pumpkin and brought it back inside. After checking on Jane, who was still asleep in her cradle, she took a knife and cut the pumpkin in half, then scooped out the seeds. She washed the seeds carefully, patted them dry, then put them upon a small cotton towel to dry for next year's planting. Naomi and Ruth had taught her much since she'd come to *John's Cottage*.

She had learned to raise and butcher chickens and pigs, plant and tend a vegetable garden, bake and cook many breads, cakes and pies, and prepare a variety of different meals. John would be proud, on his return, to know that she had been able to provide food in abundance for herself and Jane. She also learned to dry many fruits and vegetables on cotton fabric stretched over the roof during the driest time of day. When these foodstuffs had dried adequately, she stored them in

wooden barrels that she'd inherited from her father's tinsmith shop. Self-sufficiency had become a motto for her in John's absence.

The Lord God knew how much she missed John and Thomas! Few hours passed without little prayers in behalf of her husband and son. Inhaling deeply, she forced the melancholy from her thoughts, and returned to her duties. Rebecca cut the pumpkin into small pieces, then put it in a heavy iron pot, covered it with an inch of water, put the lid on tightly, then hung the pot from the fireplace tripod to steam until it was soft. In the meantime, she made a pie crust with flour, lard and salt, then formed it into two pewter baking dishes.

She was just washing her hands when Jane awakened. Picking the precious nine-month-old up into her arms, she carried her to the rocking chair where she played peek-a-boo for a time, delighting in Jane's squeals of laughter. When Jane wanted to be put down, Rebecca spread a cradle blanket upon the wood floor and sat her daughter upon it. Then, she gave Jane a small rag-doll that she had made for her, shortly after John left. It was a male doll, with breeches, a ruffled shirt and a doublet that looked very much like the ones John wore.

"Shall we pretend Father is coming home today, darling?" she asked. "See, he walks right up to the door and calls to us, 'I'm home!' and we jump up—" She held the doll up in the air, then as she made the doll dive toward Jane's neck, she said, "And snuggle, snuggle, snuggle against Father's neck." This sent Jane into peals of laughter.

Rebecca next worked on Jane's vocabulary. "Say mama!" she coaxed.

Jane struggled for only a minute before she cooed, "Mum."

"Close enough. How about Auntie Naomi?"

Jane smiled. "No-mee!" she squealed.

"Auntie Ruth?"

A moment's hesitation, as though Jane was thinking very hard. "Oof!"

"Yes, that's very good. Ruth!"

"Oof!"

"All right, darling. Now for the hard one . . . can you say papa, darling?" She enunciated *papa* distinctly, hoping Jane would finally say the word she had been working on for the past several weeks. But Jane turned away and began reaching for the blocks atop the mantle. Discouraged, Rebecca gave her the doll. As Jane busied herself, Rebecca resumed her preparations for their dinner, which they usually ate in mid-afternoon.

Rebecca, Naomi and Ruth had worked out a perfect arrangement for their evening meal. They alternated days to prepare it. Rebecca had Tuesday and Friday. Naomi had Monday and Thursday, while Ruth had Wednesday and Saturday. Then on Sundays, they made a simple meal together and shared it. This arrangement meant that Rebecca didn't have to cook a big meal, or do dishes four days a week. It was convenient for all of them and they saw no reason why they couldn't continue sharing their evening meals, even after John, Thomas and Simon returned from Salé.

Before long, she had a nice chicken in a roasting pan baking with the pumpkin pie in the hearth oven, and the rest of the pumpkin mixed with some cooked rice, honey and cream, and put into a kettle to keep warm. Then, taking Jane with her, Rebecca went back to the garden and picked some kale and two ripe tomatoes. Returning to the house, she washed and sliced the tomatoes, cleaned the kale and placed it around the outside of the chicken that was about halfway cooked, then

put the lid back on the chicken to continue the baking process.

By the time it was ready, *John's Cottage* smelled like warm cinnamon and steaming chicken with herbs and greens. Ruth and Naomi arrived with a loaf of bread leftover from yesterday.

They were just sitting down to eat, when a knock came at the door. "Now, who can that be?" Rebecca asked, more to herself than to her aunts.

She stood, walked over to the door and put her hand on the knob. As she pulled it open, she got the surprise of her life. John stood on the stoop with a bouquet of fall flowers, fresh from Rebecca's own garden. He had a finger over his lips, indicating he wanted her to be quiet. Smiling deliciously, Rebecca held her exclamation of delight.

"Pardon me, Madam," he said with a short curtsy, "but I found a few of these flowers in your front yard and I wondered if you knew that they belong to the most beautiful woman in all of his Majesty's Kingdom?"

"You are too kind, sir."

"A man would be a fool to walk past a cottage such as yours and not pay homage to the woman living there." He bowed gallantly.

Rebecca curtsied. Then she gave him a mischievous grin and threw herself into his arms, nearly crushing the flowers in the process. Fortunately, John had good reflexes and she only managed to break a few stems.

"John!" Rebecca laughed and cried at the same time. "I'm so glad you're home!"

He kissed her soundly, then noticed Ruth and Naomi behind Rebecca, grinning broadly and holding his little girl, who had more than

doubled her newborn size since he last saw her.

Pulling him inside, Rebecca took Jane from Naomi and said, "John Dunton, it's time you get reacquainted with your daughter. Jane darling, this is your father. This is the time that I really want you to say it, darling. Say papa."

Jane wrinkled her nose and looked up at John curiously.

"He's your papa, Jane. Please say papa, darling."

Jane held out a chubby hand and touched John's face. Her eyes filled with wonder and she cooed, "Dawr – wing."

"Close enough!" John laughed aloud and clapped his hands for Jane to come to him. For only an instant, Rebecca saw recognition in Jane's eyes, as though remembering John from long, long ago.

Jane stretched out her hands and let him take her in his arms and hold her to him as he whispered, "Jane, little Jane, how much I've needed to see you again."

He sank wearily with her onto the nearest chair. Suddenly, he was crying, something Rebecca had never seen him do. And then she sensed what had happened. She glanced outside, and saw that the carriage had already gone, and there was no little boy standing in the yard, waiting to see her again. Thomas had not come home with John, and that could only mean one thing.

Choking on a sob that caught in her chest, she closed the door and turned to John, knowing the truth before he had a chance to tell her.

When he looked up at her, the pain in his eyes made her tremble. "He's gone," she whispered. "Isn't he?"

John nodded, then tore his eyes from hers, as though he couldn't bear seeing the disappointment and anguish she would feel.

Ruth asked, "And Simon? Is he—?"

"He's still in Chatham," John said quickly. "There are so many who are ill. It may be weeks before they are well enough to travel on land."

Relief for Simon, grief for Thomas, settled upon the elderly women and they both started crying in unison, which frightened Jane until she, too, let out an angry squall.

Rebecca took Jane from her father, then she sat on his lap to comfort both her husband and her daughter. Trying to be brave, she wondered what had ever happened to her son. What had she ever done that would make God want to take him away from her?

"I'm so sorry, Rebecca," John whispered, his voice filled with agony. "He apparently died sometime between April and July, when we finally took the city."

"Did you find his body?" she asked, hoping that they could at least bury him.

John shook his head. "We had knowledge of over thirty thousand of his Majesty's subjects who had been taken by the pirates of Salé. Certainly when I was held captive there, I counted at least two thousand go through the auction block, but by the time we got them out, we were only able to save three hundred and thirty-nine people."

"We will ask for a memorial service," Rebecca said bravely. "For Thomas, and for all those who died at Salé."

"Yes, of course," John agreed. "And we will light a candle every night in remembrance of our son who lives with God."

Placing Jane upon her father's lap, Rebecca went into the kitchen and pulled a candle from the dripping rack, one that she'd made from beeswax and tallow, and brought it into the parlor. Methodically, she

put it into a candlestick, lit the candle from the fireplace and placed it upon the mantle. "I light this candle in memory of our little son, our Thomas. . . ."

Rebecca stopped. She couldn't go on. She started to tremble, regardless of her attempts at being strong and brave for John's sake.

John quickly gave Jane to Ruth, then rushed over to Rebecca and pulled her close against him.

Rebecca turned and looked up into John's eyes, the same eyes their son had inherited. Shaking her head from side to side, she screamed, "No! He can't be gone! I would feel it in my heart! John! He can't be gone!" Then she collapsed in his arms, weeping inconsolably.

AFTER JANE WAS tucked into her cradle and was sound asleep, John took Rebecca to bed, and held her as she snuggled up to him beneath the heavy quilt. It seemed she couldn't stop thinking about Thomas, and John didn't know how to comfort her.

Rebecca would sob for a while, then ask a question of him. When he answered, she would sob a little while longer. Several times she did this, and he was beginning to wonder how she would ever get over losing Thomas.

"Rebecca," he began when he thought her tears were finally spent. "Have you minded living here at the cottage, having Jane, or . . . being married to me?"

She came up on one elbow and stared down at him. He could barely see her surprised expression in the darkness of their bedroom. "What kind of question is that?" she asked. "Of course I haven't minded."

"I didn't ask in order to offend you," he offered. "But I've worried

about you while I've been gone. It wasn't fair of me to break my promise to you, nor to create a child with you, basically forcing you into a long-term relationship when your only hope in coming to the *Warwick* was to escape Edward's clutches. You got more than you bargained for, and if you feel that I've ruined your life by—"

Placing a finger upon his lips, Rebecca interrupted him. "John," she whispered. "Dear, sweet John. If I hadn't fallen in love with you so quickly, I might have minded. But all that changed the moment it happened."

Her confession stirred him as nothing else could have. "Then you do love me, too?" he asked quickly, before his courage failed him.

She sat up a little straighter. "Too?" she questioned, her voice a blend of timidity and hope.

John pulled her back into his arms. "Yes, Rebecca, I love you, too."

For the next several minutes, he wondered if he shouldn't have told her in quite the manner that he did, for all she could do in response was weep against his shoulder again. He waited patiently for her to finish, and when she did, she lifted her head and placed her lips longingly against his. When she finally released him, he smiled and asked, "When did you know that you loved me?"

"The night on the *Warwick*, when you held me on the aftercastle deck. My father had died, and I had yet to be comforted. I knew that you were merciful because you married me to save my life. I learned that you were also kind and compassionate when you consoled me that night. John, if I didn't love you, I would never have agreed to—" She paused.

John read between the lines and nodded, grateful to know she had loved him first. It made his own actions in their romance seem less

liable, somehow. He kissed her eagerly, and she responded with as much fire and passion as she had that morning on the *Warwick*. Her response reminded John that he had fallen in love with her about the same time.

JOHN PACED THE floor with his ten-month-old daughter, hoping to put her to sleep, while her mother finished with the kitchen dishes. Jane took away some of the pain in his heart over losing Thomas, but she could never replace him. No one could.

Fortunately, Rebecca was learning to accept the fact of Thomas' death, though there were times when she would get a far off look in her eyes and he would know she was doubting the truth of it, once again.

Jane gave a soft little sigh, and John was relieved that she was finally falling asleep. She seemed to sense something was wrong. Often she would crawl over to Rebecca, pull herself up onto her wobbly feet, hang onto her mother's skirt, then pat Rebecca's leg, saying, "Mum. Mum?"

November seemed colder this year than he remembered at any other time. Perhaps it was the emptiness in his heart that made him feel that way. John worried constantly about Rebecca, for he knew she was still aching and disbelieving. Yet, how could he help her when there were times he felt the same way?

Sometimes he'd sit in the parlor in the afternoon and watch the front gate hang in place, closed and silent. He could remember seeing Thomas push the gate open and walk up the flower-lined path to the front door.

Refusing to torture himself any longer, John carried Jane upstairs

and put her in her trundle bed, tucked the cradle blankets around her and returned downstairs to the kitchen.

"She's out, is she?" Rebecca whispered, as she dried the last pan and put it away on a shelf.

He nodded. "She's got her mother's beauty," he observed casually.

"And her father's determination," she admitted. "She's—"

Someone pounded on the front door, interrupting her.

John slipped into the parlor and opened the door. To his surprise, Lord Blackwell's servant was standing on the stoop. "Wilson?" he asked. "What on earth are you doing out at this hour?"

"Lord Blackwell told me to bring this straight to you," Wilson gasped, apparently out of breath.

"Come in," John insisted, remembering his manners. He held the door open for Wilson to enter, then closed it behind him and showed Wilson into the kitchen where the candles burned a little brighter.

Rebecca turned and smiled at Wilson. Giving him a quick kiss on the cheek she said, "Wilson, you look like you're out of breath."

"Too excited to wait, my Lady." Turning to John, Wilson said, "His Lordship received this post for you, just today. It came with a notice that Christopher Willoughby of Salé, Morocco, had passed on, and this letter was found among his personal effects. It is addressed to you, Master Dunton." He handed the letter to John, then sank wearily into a chair. "The carriage is waiting to take me back, sir. But I promised I would wait to see if there was anything important in the post. His Lordship has been most distressed over Thomas, especially since the lad was responsible for saving Sir Edward's life. Do you mind if I wait?"

John took the letter and slit the seal with a knife. "No, of course

not. Sit down," he said. "You, too, Rebecca. I'll read it aloud." Opening the seal, he unfolded the parchment and smoothed it out, then held it close to the lantern so he could read it more clearly:

*From **Salle** the 21 of July 1636.*

Sir,

> *Yours, all the rest being absent was given to my hand, in which you enquire for your sonne, who was sent for Argere 7 moneths past: I offered Ally Zuny 200 ducats for him, if that he would let him remaine in my house, before hee sent him for Argere: to have seene what Master Woodroofe would have done for him, as you intreated mee, at Master Libergers house when you went to Sea, being then sicke, as I am now: as for the Case of those men, they are all in chaines, and are almost dead with the mashmore and stocks, but most for want of bread: but resolving to continue a siege will not give it them; and except God give some speedy remedy I am afraid shall be all starved: for these people will have peace with no Saint, but with the Generall if hee shall please. So being sorry that I could not prevaile to keepe your sonne here,*
> *I rest in haste from my bed,*
> *Yours at command,*
> *Christopher Willoughby, Merchant*

A lump formed in his throat as John considered Willoughby's letter. "If he intended to send it to me in July, then seven months before that

would be December. Thomas was sold to someone in Algeria last December! He wouldn't have been in Salé when the armada arrived."

Wilson shook his head. "He'd have been better off dead than sent to Algeria," he warned them.

John could only nod his head. Then, "But Edward said he saw him in Salé in April."

"You must be mistaken, sir. Edward was in Algeria until the end of April. When the *Neptune* was taken by an Algerian pirate, Edward was sold in Algeria upon his arrival there in late April of 1635. He escaped from Algeria a year later, in 1636, but the ship on which he stowed away, out of Algeria, was sunk by one of his Majesty's ships at Salé. He and William barely made it to land. William couldn't swim and Edward had to drag him ashore. When they reached Salé, they were captured once again by the Moors."

"You're certain of this?" John asked Wilson, feeling a surge of excitement welling up within him.

"I am," Wilson nodded.

"I must speak with Edward at once," John decided, grabbing his doublet from a hook by the front door.

"John, what does all this mean?"

He turned and gave Rebecca a determined smile. "It means that our son may still be alive. If he wasn't in Salé when the armada was there, he may very well be in Algeria."

JOHN AND WILSON arrived at Blackwell Tower shortly after dawn. Wilson insisted John eat breakfast with him, until his Lordship was

ready to receive him.

Apparently, Lord Blackwell had other plans. He strode into the kitchen quickly, his demeanor most anxious. "Was it something important, then?" he asked.

John let him read the letter and waited until he was finished. Then, he confessed. "I had suspected that the lad was still alive after hearing one of Edward's nightmares. He was hysterical and kept saying, 'We have to go back for Thomas.' I should have mentioned it to you, earlier."

"When was this nightmare?" John asked.

"About two weeks ago."

"He had the same dreams aboard the *Leopard*. Sometimes it was all we could do to restrain him. But at the time, I thought he meant that Thomas was in Salé, not in Algeria."

"He does have some lucid days," said his Lordship. "And he claims that he was in Algeria until after Thomas cared for him in the haystack. William Moore verified the information just last week and I considered sending a man out to tell you then, but I didn't think much could be done about it, now that it's nearly winter. The ships have been pulled out and put in dry dock until March."

"But the armada left in February this year."

"Under the king's command. We cannot order another armada without financial and political backing, especially against Algeria. Taking Salé was like putting one drop in a bucket. To take Algeria would require us to fill the whole bucket, John. Surely you know that?"

John sighed. "I'm not giving up," he insisted. "My son may be in Algeria waiting for me to find him."

"I will help you as much as I possibly can, John. You know that. But first you will need to petition the king for support of another armada. Speak with Lord Vaine, he tends to favor you, and tell him that I will give you my full support, as well. At least there will be two Lords of the Admiralty on your side. When you've rallied enough support, come back. I will have at least one ship you can use."

Although John went away heavy-hearted, his hope had returned in full measure. Thomas might still be alive. *In Algeria!* That thought scared John more than any other.

With long, deliberate strokes, John penned the letter:

> *To the Right, Honorable Lord Vaine*
> *One of his MAJESTIES privie*
> *Councell of his High Court of*
> *Admiraltie.*
>   *Right Honourable, in September last was*
> *twelve month, I redeemed my selfe prisoner from*
> *Sally, being sent out Master and Pilote . . . with*
> *twenty-one Moores and five Flemish rennagadoes,*
> *unto the coast of England to take Christians. I*
> *brought them into the Isle of Wight under the*
> *command of Husk Castle, where I was detained*
> *as a Pirate, and sent to Winchester with the rest,*
> *till we were tryed by the Law . . . I found much*
> *favour at your Honours hands; For which I must*
> *ever rest ingaged . . . and have no way to testifie*
> *my thankfulnesse more, than by presenting this my*

poor indevour to your Honour: which if you please to accept and consider of, may be a means to relieve more as you have done mee; for my onely sonne is now slave in Argeire, and but ten yeares of age, and like to be lost forever, without God's great mercy and the Kings clemcie, which I hope may be in some measure obtained by your Honours meanes, and then your poore suppliant shall be ever bound to pray for you and yours all his dayes, and ever rest at your command,

JOHN DUNTON,
Mariner.

When John was satisfied that he'd written the letter with enough information and pleading, he folded it over, splattered a few drops of wax from a candle off the mantle, then placed his Master Mariner's seal against it. Satisfied that he had the matter of finding his son well underway in terms of what he would need to do to get another armada ready, John allowed hope to drip steadily into his soul.

Finding Thomas was nearly all John could think about, and he felt like a man possessed, as though his one and only reason for living was to find his son. Worried that he would drive Rebecca away by his obsession, he tried as best he could to include her in all his decisions and plans regarding Thomas' rescue.

When a post came back to him two weeks later, it took his hope away.

Greetings, Master Dunton;
I was distressed to read your letter, regarding

*your son. You must rest assured, knowing that I
have given the matter my full attention. However,
the king is unbendable. It is his opinion that to
strike against Algiers at any time in the near future
would be tantamount to suicide. Their strength in
numbers alone would outstrip us. A fleet such as
The Salé would never be enough for Algiers. Ten
times as many ships would be required. I am sorry
that I could not prevail for you in this regard.*

> *With all respect and kindness,*
> *Lord Henry Vaine, of his Majesty's*
> *Royal Navy.*

The letter slipped from John's hand and Rebecca picked it up to read it. Afterward, she wept against his shoulder for a long time. When her tears were spent, Rebecca asked, "What are you going to do now, John?"

He tilted her head up and wondered how she would react to his response. In her eyes he saw two emotions he hadn't expected: hope and trust. Knowing she felt this way gave him courage.

It would be up to John to rescue his son. He had no ship, no crew, no fleet, no armada. But determination filled his soul. "I'm not giving up!" he said with a fervor that surprised even himself. "Thomas is out there somewhere!"

###

About the bark Warwick

John Dunton's mastering of the bark, Warwick, which sailed between England and America as early as 1620, is factual. Sometime between 1631 and 1636 John and his son were taken captive by pirates and enslaved at Salé Morocco. Later, John and his crew retook the captured bark and presented his former captors at Hurst Castle. Because of his keen mind, John successfully memorized details regarding Salé that enabled him to come up with a working map and a war plan for England. John Dunton mastered the Admiral and detailed the account of the Salé Fleet that successfully defeated the pirates during the battles that ensued, and rescued the English subjects and Christians from their captors. These are all facts of historical record. Fictionalizing such an exciting story brings it to life in a way that historical accounts cannot.

Author Notes

A. *Search for the Bark Warwick* includes the following real characters from seventeenth century history:
    1. John Dunton and his son, who were taken captive by pirates sometime between 1631 and 1635
    2. The eight captains of the Salé Fleet (as well as the ships of the Salé Fleet)
    3. Lord Henry Vaine
    4. The Earl of Winchester
    5. Christopher Willoughby
    6. Aligolant
    7. Ali Zuny
    8. Masters Liberger and Woodruff.

B. The number of surviving seamen and the fishermen Aligolant captured before John Dunton's mutiny are correct. Their names are unknown.

C. The number of captives left aboard the *Little David* is true, but their names are unknown. It is unknown what year the *Little David* was captured. It may have been earlier than 1635, but probably no earlier than 1633. It is unknown if the *Warwick* was captured at the same time as the *Little David*.

D.   How John's son came to be missing is true, as is John's retaking of the "pirate's bark" and his being imprisoned at Hurst Castle. The trial at Winchester Castle is accurate, though not verbatim.

E.   Fictional characters include Rebecca Webster, Lord Blackwell II, Edward Blackwell III, William Moore, Simon, Naomi and Ruth Harris, Penelope Giles and most of the people aboard the *Little David*, the *Warwick* and the *Neptune*.

F.   A twelve-year search by the author has proven fruitless, and the name of Thomas' birth mother has not been located. It is assumed that she died sometime prior to the attack made by Aligolant against the *Little David*.

G.   The original bark *Warwick* may have been taken by pirates at a time other than when the *Little David* was taken. The first *Warwick* in the novel was a three masted sailing vessel sixty feet long, eighteen feet wide at the maximum beam, with a seven foot hold, that sailed several times between America and England during the 1620's and 1630's. In 1636, the *Warwick* was run aground "in a Dorchester inlet." For purposes of the novel, the author has run it aground near Hurst Castle in September 1635.

H.   John Winthrop's journal states that the *Warwick* was attacked by pirates in 1630 and never heard from since. However, Captain Henry Fleete's journal aboard the *Warwick* from 1630–1631 with John Dunton as Master contradicts Winthrop's statement.

I.   There are many discrepancies as to when the Salé Fleet left Chatham. Some accounts say it was in 1637, others say 1636. The author has chosen to use *John Dunton's True Journall of the Sally Fleet*, published in 1637, as the authority on when the armada left Chatham (1636).

J.   Thomas Dunton's given name is unknown.

The sequel to **Search for the Bark Warwick**, a completely fictional work, is in progress.

Miscellany

1. The burthen tonnage was an official figure, used not only for commercial purposes but also, for example, to calculate port dues. It was originally a measure of the number of tons of wine that could be carried. Centuries ago, a burthen was calculated by this formula:

    (Length x Max Beam x Depth of Hold) in feet
    divided by 100 = tons of burthen

2. William Bentinck (1649–1709) is known as the *First Earl of Portland*. However, in the ninth issue of the Mariner's Mirror, 1923, a letter from the "Earl of Portland from Winchester Castle," dated 16 Sep 1636 to the Lords of the Admiralty, is quoted, wherein the *Little David* story is detailed. The true name of this "Earl of Portland" remains unknown.

3. One source gives the burthen for the *Leopard* at five hundred sixteen tons.

4. One source says the *Antelope* carried a burthen of five hundred twelve tons.

5. One source says the *Mary Rose* carried three-hundred-twelve tons burthen. The *Mary Rose* was built at Deptford, England in 1623. She was eighty-three feet long, twenty-six feet nine inches wide at the maximum beam, and carried four hundred tons burthen, with twenty-eight great cannons and one hundred-forty seamen (JDJ).

6. John Dunton's Journal (JDJ) says the *Mary* was a merchantmen's ship approximately eighty-five feet long, with a burthen of four hundred tons, twenty-eight great guns and one hundred-forty seamen.

7. The *Hercules,* another merchantmen's ship, was approximately eighty-five feet long, with a burthen of four hundred tons, twenty-eight great guns and one hundred-forty seamen each. JDJ

8. One source says the *Expedition* carried three hundred-one tons burthen and the *Providence* carried three-hundred-four tons burthen. JDJ says the *Providence Pinnace* and the *Expedition Pinnace*, were sister ships. Both were built at Bermondsey, England, just prior to the Salé Fleet expedi-

tion. They were ninety feet long, twenty-six feet at the maximum beam and carried three hundred tons burthen, with fourteen great guns and one hundred seamen each.

9.   One source says the bark *Warwick* was run aground in 1635 and was disassembled. Another says the "ordnance was removed."

10.   One source says the *Row Bucke* carried ninety tons burthen. JDJ says the *Row Bucke*, a bark very similar to the *Warwick*, was built and launched at Woolwich, England in 1635. She was fifty-seven feet long by eighteen feet one inch wide at the maximum beam. The *Row Bucke* carried eighty tons burthen, ten great guns and fifty seamen.

11.   An exact copy of Willoughby's letter to John Dunton appears in the novel. Only the numerous "s" letters have been changed from the original document, which had been formed using an "*f*" shape in the seventeenth century.

12.   An exact copy of the original letter to Lord Vaine, with the only changes being the many "s" letters have been standardized from the "*f*" shape as on the original document. Parts of the letter have been omitted for clarity.

13.   Husk Castle is actually Hurst Castle, the error of spelling came in the *John Dunton's True Journall of the Sally Fleet*, published in London, 1637, by John Dunton, master.

14.   The location of Lishorne, the port where the *Hercules* went to get remasted, has not been determined. Like John Dunton's spelling for Salé (Sally and Sallee), Lishorne is likely a misspelled name.

15.   The *Warwick*, with Captain Henry Fleete and Master John Dunton, was chased by pirate ships coming out of Dunkirk in 1630. They were finally able to shake them, but only by sailing an alternating course fourteen days. If the wind hadn't held in their favor, they would have been captured then. Captain John Winthrop reported in his journal that the bark was taken captive by the Dunkirkers and never heard from since. He was likely quite surprised when the *Warwick* sailed into Salem, Massachusetts, about two weeks after Winthrop's fleet arrived.

16. There were several caravels, cogs and pinnaces that sailed with the Salé Fleet, giving the armada the appearance of strength in numbers, but these vessels were not identified by name.

17. What happened to the captured pirate ships during the siege against Salé has not been determined.

18. It is estimated that less than two percent of the English and Christians captured by the pirates between 1620–1636 survived their captivity by more than a few years, and that the actual number of captives was well over 30,000.

Other Books by Sherry Ann Miller

One Last Gift

First in the five-book Gift Series, *One Last Gift* revolves around Kayla, who gave up religion ten years earlier to pursue a lifestyle completely foreign to her upbringing. When she receives a disturbing telephone call from her father, Mont, she reluctantly leaves her fiancé, her sailboat, and her challenging career in San Diego, and hastens to her childhood home high in the Uinta Mountains. Her return stirs up questions from her past she thought she'd buried years before: Why does Mont tenaciously cling to his faith, regardless of his daughter's rejection of it? Isn't God just a crutch people use when they don't understand science? Does her mother really live in the Spirit World, as Mont insists?  Kayla conquers one issue after another until she faces the greatest obstacle of her life in a desperate race for survival. Will tragedy turn Kayla's analytical heart back to God, or will it take a miracle? *One Last Gift* placed third in the national "Beacon Awards" (2000) for published authors. Now available from your favorite bookstore. If they don't have it, please ask them to order directly from Granite Publishing & Distribution (800) 574-5779. ISBN# 1-930980-01-9

Gardenia Sunrise

Frightened by the drastic measures it will take to provide even the remotest hope for a cure to her cancer, Brandje flees to her villa on the west coast of France where she hopes to prepare herself emotionally and spiritually to meet God. Her plans are interrupted when Nathan, an American with a hot temper, arrives for his annual holiday at the villa, unaware that his reservation has been canceled. Brandje's remarkable journey of spiritual and romantic discovery touches the soul with enlightenment, hope and inspiration. *Gardenia Sunrise* is a powerful conversion story that will linger in your  heart forever. Now available from your favorite bookstore. If they don't have

it, please ask them to order directly from Granite Publishing & Distribution (800) 574-5779). ISBN# 1-930980-33-7

An Angel's Gift

While *One Last Gift* dwelt on Kayla's conversion, *An Angel's Gift* answers the question she left behind: What about Ed? When Alyssa drops in at the Bar M Ranch (literally!), she disrupts the life of the ranch foreman, Ed Sparkleman, and keeps him jumping hoops almost beyond what he can endure . . . *what a hero!* Along the way, Alyssa's confidence is shaken, and she must learn to trust God once again, but not until after a desperate sacrifice and the miraculous trial of her faith. *An Angel's Gift* placed fourth in the Utah "Heart of the West" competition (2002). *An Angel's Gift* is installment two in the five-book Gift Series. Now available from your favorite bookstore. If they don't have it, please ask them to order directly from Granite Publishing & Distribution (800) 574-5779). ISBN# 1-930980-98-1.

The Tyee's Gift

What about Abbot? Where did he go and what happened to him after Alyssa broke their engagement in *An Angel's Gift?* You will find all the answers to these questions when Abbot becomes Tyee (pronounced *tie-yee*, it means Chief or Great Leader) to a little boy and his trusting Aunt. Escape to the Northwest with Abbot, meet beautiful Bekah, go on an archaeological expedition, sail the Pacific Ocean in a terrific gale, and watch the miracle of *The Tyee's Gift* unfold. *The Tyee's Gift* is installment three in the five-book Gift Series. Coming in the fall of 2004. Ask your bookseller to inform you when it arrives.

Charity's Gift

Hans' story, the fourth book in the Gift series, is in progress.

Search for the Warwick II
The sequel to *Search for the Bark Warwick* is in progress.

Readers' Comments

Sherry Ann Miller loves to hear from her readers. Please write to her at Sherry@sherryannmiller.com, or visit her online at www.Sherryannmiller.com.

Read what others are saying about her novels:

An Angel's Gift

I have read all of your books at least twice. I just finished reading **An Angel's Gift** for the second time. Thank you! Thank you! We forget how thin the veil really is. When I read **One Last Gift**, I had a really hard time with it, emotionally. When I read **Gardenia Sunrise**, it was the same. But when I read **An Angel's Gift**, it really, really got to me. I have struggled for several years with this very thing, and you made me realize that it is all possible. I can't wait for the sequel to **An Angel's Gift**. You have a wonderful talent and a way of letting us see how things can really be if we have FAITH!
~Diane Robertson, Orem, Utah
P.S. Do you have any idea when the sequel will be out?

Yes, Diane. *The Tyee's Gift* will debut sometime in the fall of 2004 .
~ *Sherry Ann*

I read **An Angel's Gift**, and I loved it very much. You are a great writer, I love all of your books. I can relate to all the characters and feel their hurts and joys. I would like now to hear how Abbott has handled the rejection and if he finds someone whom he can love. Keep up the good work.
~ Ida Nelson

Hang in there, Ida. Abbot's story will be found in **The Tyee's Gift**.
~ *Sherry Ann*

Gee, thanks a bunch Sherry Ann. Thanks to your *An Angel's Gift* I got a total of maybe four hours sleep last night. For those who've read it, you know

what I mean. I started reading it late yesterday afternoon, and got so engrossed in it I couldn't put it down . . . thus, so much for my wife's "To-Do" list. I want you to know, I accomplished nothing last night except reading your book. . I hope I'm making you feel downright guilty, Sherry! Just Kidding. :-) What a great novel! ~ Kyle Smith, Taylorsville, UT

Warning to all my readers: Begin my novels in the morning. Please. Sorry, Kyle, that you didn't get that warning before you started. ~ Sherry Ann

I recently lost my father, and have felt his presence many times since his passing. I have always felt that love and guidance comes from those beyond the veil, and was thrilled to have that same message portrayed in your book, **An Angel's Gift**. Although this is the first book I have read of yours, it will certainly not be the last. I look forward to reading more of your wonderful works. Thank you! ~ Johanna Thorson, Ogden, UT

It is my humble testimony, Johanna, that our departed family is always nearby, though it is never easy to lose a loved one. Rejoice in the blessing that you know where they are, and probably what they are doing. Then throw yourself into serving the Lord, and you will find the sad times brighten, as will your hope for a happy reunion. ~ Sherry Ann

I just finished **An Angel's Gift** and thoroughly enjoyed it. To have "angels" (deceased loved ones) appear to one, how wonderful! Thank you for writing such wonderful stories. ~ Lois L. Larsen, Emmett, Idaho

I have just finished reading your books **One Last Gift** and **An Angel's Gift**. I was so touched by both stories. I have felt the blessing of angel's in my life and just felt so complete when I finished **One Last Gift**, as if it gave me a tangible power for believing in angels. Thanks for the good stories and I look forward to reading **Gardenia Sunrise**. I was also wondering if your stories are built around real life situations with the angel's appearance after death, or is it totally written from your imagination. Thanks again for the good books. ~ Debra Packer

One Last Gift is entirely fiction, but the miracle in it stemmed from a story I heard from a deer hunter in my youth. **An Angel's Gift** *is fiction, but I've always believed that with God, nothing is impossible.* **Gardenia Sunrise** *is a really good example of what the Lord can do when He performs His mighty miracles. Personally, I have lived from miracle to miracle throughout my life, from the moment of my birth to the present day. The Lord has spared me too many times to count, and often in such miraculous ways as to stagger even my imagination. My mission, as a writer, is to teach the validity of miracles, for too many dismiss them as fantasy, when they are real and powerful. As for angel visitations, my grandparents, and now my parents, watch over me from beyond the veil. I have felt their presence many times, and I'm always excited when they come to visit.*

~ Sherry Ann

I just read **An Angels Gift**. I read it over the weekend in the mountains while my husband and sons were fishing. That is my idea of a vacation! I loved the book, and when I was done my husband read it, and now that we are home our daughter will take it home to read while her baby sleeps. It was a great read. My only question now is where can I find the first book in the series? My local bookstore no longer carries it and I can't get it at the public library. Any suggestions? Thanks for a very uplifting book.

~ Patti Clement, Mesa AZ

Your book store should be able to get **One Last Gift** *. Have them order ISBN: 1-930980-01-9 from Granite Publishing & Distribution, L.L.C. (800) 574-5779.* **One Last Gift** *recently went through a new printing, so your bookseller should have no problem getting it now.* ~ Sherry Ann

Gardenia Sunrise

I have devoured your books cover to cover. I loved the first two, but especially **Gardenia Sunrise**. I find myself thinking of the settings of the book as very real places that I am now anxious to go visit. The characters are written so well as to make me cry and even laugh right out loud with their joy. My testimony has been strengthened, and my personal goals renewed, to be of more comfort and cheer to my family. I am hoping there will be a sequel for Gardenia Sunrise. ~ Penny Butler, Roy, Utah

Another sequel? What a great idea, Penny! I can't promise anything until I finish the Gift series and the sequel to **Search for the Bark Warwick***, but it's got my vote. I'll pray about it and see what the Lord wants me to do.*

I recently read **Gardenia Sunrise** and absolutely loved it! I noticed somewhere in the book about a previous title, **One Last Gift**, and the upcoming sequel. I was thrilled! Thank you very much!

~ Marcy Frey

Thank you so much for **An Angel's Gift,** and **Gardenia Sunrise** and **One Last Gift**. I read each one as it was new. In August I read all three, and last night I finished reading them again. I can't thank you enough for sharing your gift with all of us readers. I can't wait until you publish another book. Your testimony comes through so wonderfully in all of your books. I'm 72 and many days not able to do much, but I have these great books to take my mind off myself and live the great stories of your characters.

~ Barbara Anderson

Participate in Sherry Ann's *Readers' Comments* and receive a free, autographed copy of the book in which your comment appears. All ten people whose comments appear in **Search for the Bark Warwick** will, and you can, too. Simply e-mail Sherry at Sherry@sherryannmiller.com, putting the title of the book in the subject line, and your comments in the body. If your comments are selected for inclusion in one of Sherry's books, you'll get your own copy of that book, and a personal note from her. Permission to use your comments must be included, as well as your full name, and current e-mail and postal addresses. Thanks!

About the Author

Mother of seven, grandmother of twenty-four, Sherry Ann Miller loves her family, the Lord and His Gospel. She also enjoys sailing, fishing, clamming, crabbing, long walks on the beach, writing, crocheting, baking, marine biology and family history. Sherry's greatest challenge: health issues that forced her to retire in 1994. Her greatest blessing: health issues that keep her at home, writing and gathering family histories!

Sherry has an unusual philosophy about her life: "I like to compare my life to bananas. When they're green, they're unyielding, it takes a knife to pry the fruit from the peel, and they leave a bitter taste in your mouth. When they're almost yellow, they become more amenable to peeling and begin to delight the taste buds, but they're still not quite perfect. However, when you put them on a shelf and leave them to ripen, they become sweet and delicious, especially for making banana bread. At this point in my life, I'm fairly sweet, and making good use of every moment I sit on the shelf. When I am mixed in with my ancestors on the other side and brought to the Lord's oven, I hope to bake up beautifully."

Visit Sherry Ann online at
www.sherryannmiller.com or
email her at
Sherry@sherryannmiller.com